'Exceptional . . . particularly for . . . Fiona's narrative sears the pa[ges]'

'A copper who rivals Lisbeth Sala[nder . . . fic]tion'

'With Detective Constable Fiona "Fi" Griffiths, Harry Bingham finds a sweet spot in crime fiction – a female protagonist with stunted emotions, a passion for protecting women . . . think Stieg Larsson's Lisbeth Salander . . . Denise Mina's Paddy Meehan or Lee Child's Jack Reacher'   *Boston Globe*

'What really matters in this novel is the sweet, strange complexities of Fiona's mind . . . A dark delight' *Washington Post*

'A most intriguing detective'   *New York Times*

'In Bingham's hands she [Fiona Griffiths] comes exuberantly to life . . . Richly enjoyable'   *Daily Telegraph*

'A quite brilliant novel and Griffiths is a superb protagonist'
          Crime Fiction Lover

'This compelling crime novel amply proves the freshness and flair that Bingham has brought to the police procedural'
          Daily Mail

'Fiona Griffiths will haunt you long after you finish this book, and send you scurrying to find what else Bingham has written'
          York Press

Harry Bingham is a successful crime thriller author and the creator of one of the most critically acclaimed and engaging female protagonists in crime fiction in DC Fiona Griffiths. He also runs The Writers' Workshop, an editorial consultancy for first-time writers, and Agent Hunter, a service which helps connect writers with literary agents. When he isn't working, he's probably looking after not one but two sets of twins, but can still just about remember a time when he found time for rock-climbing and wild-swimming. He is married and lives in Oxfordshire.

Also by Harry Bingham

THE DEEPEST GRAVE

Fiona Griffiths Book 6

HARRY BINGHAM

An Orion paperback

First published in Great Britain in 2017
by Orion Books
This paperback edition published in 2017
by Orion Books
an imprint of The Orion Publishing Group Ltd
Carmelite House, 50 Victoria Embankment
London EC4Y 0DZ

An Hachette UK company

1 3 5 7 9 10 8 6 4 2

A CIP catalogue record for this book
is available from the British Library.

ISBN 978 1 4091 5280 4

Typeset by Input Data Services Ltd, Somerset

Printed and bound by CPI Group (UK) Ltd, Croydon, CR0 4YY

www.orionbooks.co.uk

To N, as ever.

'And each woman stands with her face in the light
Of her own drawn sword,
Ready to do what a heroine can.'

(*Elizabeth Barrett Browning* – almost!)

1

Cardiff, March 2016.
Jon Breakell has just completed his *chef d'oeuvre*, his masterpiece. The *Mona Lisa* of office art.

The masterpiece in question is a dinosaur made of bulldog clips, twisted biro innards and a line of erasers that Jon has carved into spikes.

'There,' he says.

Stands back. Inspects.

'Do you think it needs claws?' he asks. 'Paperclips maybe?'

He starts to break paperclips into spikes. Tries to figure out the claw conundrum.

Foolish boy. Complacent child.

As Jon – head down, attention buried – works with his paperclips, I get out the Great Crossbow of Doom, as Jon himself christened it. The Great Crossbow involves no fewer than six rubber bands, the really thick, strong sort, and it uses, for its shaft and crosspiece, an entire boxful of pencils taped together. The thing is a bit bendier than it ought to be, but it can still fire the little metal edge-piece stolen from the office whiteboard more than thirty feet across the room, and Jon's desk stands a lot closer than that.

He fixes his paperclip spikes into a bulldog clip and gently attaches them to his only slightly tottering dinosaur. There's a moment of serious wobble where it looks like the whole

1

thing might collapse, but Jon adjusts a grip somewhere and the edifice stabilises.

'There!' he says, genuinely proud.

And, fair dos, that pride is justified. This hasn't been the first dinosaur he's constructed, but it's easily the biggest and certainly the best. It's taken him all morning to get this far.

But I am a hunter and my heart has no mercy.

I load the Great Crossbow of Doom and pull it back till the pencils groan against the walls of their sticky tape prison. Jon half-turns to me, wanting, I think, to harvest the praise that is his due.

Turns enough that he sees what happens next.

The Crossbow straining to its uttermost. A quick release. The whiteboard edge-piece flying through the air and striking Jon's tyrannosaur in its unprotected belly. An explosion of metal stationery and spiked erasers. The edge-piece falling to the floor, its deadly mission complete.

'Fi!' says Jon. 'Fuck's sake.'

'It's the Great Crossbow of Doom,' I explain. 'It's doomy.'

'Fuck's sake,' Jon says again, down on his knees now, finding bits of lost tyrannosaur under his desk.

And that's how we are – me, Jon, the bones of the fallen – when Dennis Jackson comes in.

Dennis Jackson, my boss. The detective chief inspector who presides over our happy breed, this little world. A world that is, theoretically, devoted to the investigation and prosecution of major crime, except that the good citizens of Cardiff are too tame, too meek, too unimaginatively law-abiding to generate much crime worthy of the 'major' dignity.

'What the bloody hell is going on?'

I twang my crossbow. 'Maintaining order, sir. My duty and my pleasure.'

Jackson bites his thumb. He has the look of a man meditating some tedious comment about how the construction and

2

demolition of dinosaurs is not what Jon and I are paid to do.

He doesn't say that, though even thinking it is tedious.

Instead, he fingers the wodge of paper on my desk. On the topmost sheet, there's a figure scrawled in blue biro, big fat digits thickened out by a lot of cross-hatching and multiple outlines. The figure is '453'. On the sheet beneath, there's a similar figure, but in black biro, that says, '452'. And so on, all the way back to one that reads '19 December 2014, Rhydwyn Lloyd, RIP.' Four hundred and fifty-three days since my last proper corpse.

Jackson says, 'You're still doing this? You had an attempted murder in Llanrumney just four weeks ago. Gary Whateverhisnameis.'

I shake my head at that. How does anyone think that 'attempted murder' counts the same as actual murder? They shouldn't even call it 'attempted': that's just a way to flatter failure. The crime is as close as you can get to the opposite of murder. And not just that, but bloody Gary Whateverhisnameis was stupid enough and drunk enough to pull a knife on someone in a pub where there were about twenty-five witnesses, and the entire investigation comprised little more than sitting Gary the Moron down in an interview room, telling him to make a full statement and then listening to his tedious, self-justifying repetitions as he confessed to the whole damn thing. I mean, I'm happy to accept that destroying bulldog clip dinosaurs is not strictly speaking within my job description, but then again my job description does actually involve major crime and as far as I'm concerned, DCI Dennis Jackson, fine man that he is, has signally failed to deliver his end of the bargain.

I don't say that and, in any case, Jackson has already moved on.

He takes a bit of paper from the stack by the printer and fiddles around in my pen-holder mug, one that I was given by

3

the office secret Santa in December. On one side the mug says 'grammar police' and on the other, 'warning. I am silently correcting your grammar.' When I was given the mug, it came with black insulating tape over the word 'silently'.

Jackson finds a biro and scribbles till the ink flows.

Then he takes my 453 page and throws it away. On a fresh sheet, he writes:

16 March 2016
Gaynor Charteris
RIP

Places that where my 453 one previously lay.

I say, 'Gaynor Charteris. What, a coroner's inquest thing?'

That's not good English – my own internal grammar copper is already stripping down and refitting that sentence – but Jackson knows what I mean. I mean that any unexplained death needs to be examined by a coroner and plenty of those deaths require some form of police involvement, however sketchy. I don't count those things, however, and Jackson knows it.

Jackson says, 'Yes, there will need to be a coroner's inquest, of course.'

'OK, let me guess. Some granny slipped on the stairs and we need to confirm there were no suspicious circumstances.'

'Well, I don't yet know much about the incident, but I understand that, yes, there were some circumstances that do possibly seem suspicious.'

My face moves. An involuntary thing. I don't know what it says, what it signifies.

I just about manage to speak, though, and what I find myself saying is, 'Suspicious circumstances, sir? I mean, what? An open window, something missing, that kind of thing?'

'Well, I don't know about the windows. That part hasn't been reported to me. But the uniformed officer currently attending the scene did say that this woman appears to have been beheaded. I daresay there'll need to be some further forensic work needed before we can be certain, but it appears that the weapon of choice was an antique broadsword. It's obviously early days, but I'm going to stick my neck out and say that no, Gaynor Charteris probably did not slip on any stairs. And I'd appreciate it, please, if – Jon, Fiona – the pair of you could act like a pair of grown-up, professional detectives and get your arses over to the scene without fucking anything up or making me want to strangle you.'

He hasn't even finished his speech, before I have my jacket on, bag over my shoulder, keys in my hand.

2

Dinas Powys.

A biggish village just outside Cardiff. A wooded valley. A low hill.

The road we want is a cul-de-sac. Two lines of smiling semis. Concrete ramps and little carports. Ornamental willows and a scatter of catkins. On a low wall, in the sunshine, a ginger tom licks its parts.

Around one house, crime tape.

A pair of coppers. A mutter of radio.

Police vehicles too, of course. Two patrol cars. A scientific support services van, door open, half-blocking the road. Also, a silver Vauxhall Astra carelessly parked, front wheel on the pavement, the car itself at a loose diagonal to the kerb. That artfully poor parking signals the presence of some plain-clothes police presence, possibly the divisional surgeon or more likely whatever DI has been given this case.

'That's Jones, that is,' says Jon. 'Bleddyn bloody Jones.'

Bleddyn Jones: a DI recently shuffled down from Bridgend. A close friend of the Chief Constable, according to unreliable Cathays rumour. I've seen the guy kicking around the office, of course, and we've had a few glancing encounters, but I can't say I really know him. I do note, however, that Jon, who knows him better, does not wear an expression garlanded with joy, merriment and delight.

We park, properly, and walk to the house.

The CSIs want us to put on paper suits, paper overshoes, and masks before we go further. Someone provides us with the necessaries. As usual, no one has bothered to bring a suit that is even remotely in my size, so I go flapping around like someone struggling free of a discarded parachute.

We enter the house.

A beige carpet ascending calmly. Coats sitting comfortably on pegs. Women's coats only. Some boots beneath, including one pair of muddy walking boots. On the wall, a pre-Raphaelite print. A bored-looking woman at a loom, a big circular window behind.

There's someone tramping around upstairs, but most of the noise is coming from the living room. Jon sticks his head round the corner. Says, 'Jon Breakell and Fiona Griffiths. Just arrived.'

A voice tells us to come in, and we do.

The room was probably once quite carefully put together. Comfortable, tidy. A mixture of John Lewis good taste and little flashes of personality: old pottery, a display of Roman coins, prints of some medieval pageant or tournament.

But the way it is now, we don't spend so much time admiring the tapestry-style chesterfield or the hand-knotted Persian carpet. In part, we're distracted by the obvious disturbance in the furnishings. A coffee table thrown aside. A fallen lamp stand. But mostly, it's hard to take in anything much except a woman's corpse outstretched on the floor, in the spot where the coffee table once stood. I say 'corpse', but what lies on the floor is only the body. The woman's head sits on a little bureau in the corner, drizzling the last of its blood and ooze into a mess of computer wires.

The head boasts short grey hair, splitched and spotted with blood. Hazel eyes, with the lamps gone out. The mouth sharply down-turned. Her natural look, maybe. Or some post-mortem muscular contraction. Or something else. But she looks shocked or grumpy, as though meditating a scathing comment on the state of her carpet.

Beside the body, a sword – an antique broadsword, Jackson called it. And in the body, planted deep in the chest, three spears.

The spearheads themselves look genuinely old. They have the dug-up, cleaned-up, age-pitted look of real museum pieces. Their shafts, on the other hand, are short and obviously modern. New wood. Broom handles, repurposed.

At first glance, it doesn't look to me as though the spears played any part in the killing. There's a large volume of blood in the room, of course. Much of it draining from the hacked-off stump, plus a generous backsplatter from the process of hacking. But the spear-wounds themselves haven't bled all that much, indicating that the body was largely free of blood by the time the spears were planted.

I could happily – *would* happily – spend hours alone in this room, if given half a chance, but Jones's little terrier face, with its angry little stub-end of beard, comes vibrating up to us.

He speaks like an office memo, all pre-packed executive summary. You can almost watch the bullet points firing from his mouth. The headings, the sub-headings, the checklists.

'Deceased is Gaynor Charteris,' he says. 'Doctor Charteris, that is. Not a medical doctor, but a part-time lecturer in archaeology for the Open University. Perhaps some local teaching commitments too, we're trying to track those now. Sole resident at this address. Divorcée, two adult kids, thought to be living abroad. Age of the deceased: fifty-three. No known money problems. No known disputes. No sound of disturbance reported.

'Rectal temperature is the same as ambient, so that's saying twelve hours plus since time of death. Rigor mortis still present in the larger muscles, so we're thinking a maximum of twenty-four, thirty hours, something like that, but with blood loss on this scale, who knows? Anyway, we'll get better estimates soon.

'Cause of death and murder weapon both obvious enough. Murder weapon seems to have been on site—' he nods behind us at a stretch of wall, where empty fixings seem to imply a sword once hung 'but we'll need to verify that assumption. No indication of forced entry, implying the attacker was possibly known to the victim.'

His bullet points run temporarily dry. A hammer clicking on emptiness.

I nod towards the table where the good Doctor Charteris's head is leaking its last, a table that boasts a mess of wires but no laptop, no phone, no iPad.

Charteris's faintly tutting aura disapproves of their loss.

'Theft?'

'Probably. We've not located any cash, cards, phone or computer hardware. But the value of that stuff . . .'

He shrugs rather than completing his sentence, but his meaning is clear. Yes, you might want to nick a few hundred quid's worth of computer junk from a single middle-aged woman. But no, you probably wouldn't want to go to the trouble of all this head-loppy-offy, spear-jabby stuff if your only reward was a second-hand laptop and a handful of bankcards.

He reloads and continues, 'We're obviously looking at some kind of maniac or some kind of ritual killing. If it's a maniac, he's probably local, otherwise why trek out here? So we need to ask around. Neighbours. Vicar. Doctor's surgery. Local mental health. Fiona, I want you to take the lead on that. You've got three uniforms to work with. Stay in touch. I want regular reports.

'Jon, I want you to look at the possible ritual aspect here. That's desk work. Take a look at the PNC. Call the National Crime Agency, see if they have any experience of anything like this. Check Interpol for possible overseas angles. OK? Got that? Yes?'

I think he wants us to yessir him and go trotting off like a pair of Spanish show ponies, but off and away I do not trot.

'Permission to familiarise myself with the scene, sir? I want to get a feel for the man we're pursuing.'

Jones gives me a look that somehow manages to take in me, the headless corpse, the corpseless head, the bucketfuls of blood, the sword, the spears, and imply, 'you want to *get a feel* for the man? You haven't already got some hints?'

But since he doesn't actually say anything, and since I don't curl up and start mewing, and since procedure does in fact require that key team members have a reasonable familiarity with the crime scene, in the end he nods.

'Five minutes, then brief your team.'

He heads off to annoy someone else.

Jon leaves, show-pony style, kicking his fetlocks and tossing his prettily braided mane.

Me, I start with the corpse itself, trying to avoid treading on any significant blood-marks, though that's easier said than done.

Gaynor Charteris's hands are clean enough, but have a pale tan, even here in a Welsh Marchtime, even under the pallor of death. Her fingernails, worn short, have the sort of scraped-out grey colour you get if soil has collected under your nails and you want to make a reasonable shot at tidying up. She has that sinewy, fifty-something, outdoors look which, out in villages like this, usually goes with dog ownership, but I see no sign of a dog. No leash in the hallway, no hairs on the sofa.

The incisions on the neck look interesting too. It looks to me as if the front of the throat was cut by something sharp enough to slice through the soft tissue in a single stroke. Beyond that, there are signs of multiple hacking blows, the ones that finally severed the head. It's hard to feel the edge of the sword properly through latex gloves, but it feels bluntish to me. A decorative piece, not a fighting one. And if that's right, it looks like my putative local maniac came here with a sharp knife, neatly slit Charteris's throat, then used the broadsword to complete the beheading.

And the spears? Either they were carefully made beforehand and brought here. Or Charteris happened to have a nice trio of antique spearheads conveniently fastened to some seriously non-antique broom handles. Or someone stole the spearheads from Charteris, turned them into actual spears, then came back to plunge them into the chest of a woman who was already dead.

That's not very maniac, if you ask me, but no one did.

I take a brisk gander round the rest of the house. Everything tidy. Everything orderly. Everything consistent with the age, sex and occupation of the deceased. With this quiet, leafy, sunlit street.

No dog.

There are a pair of very muddy gloves drying in the kitchen.

The garden shed has a few ordinary garden implements, all dry.

It's odd. Something I've noticed before. When a person dies, their presence in a home seems to swell initially. Everything exhales the dead person's personality. Their hopes, their fears, their loss. Then, as relatives and officialdom nibble at the scene – items removed for evidence, valuables packed and stored, utility accounts terminated, the house cleaned – the dead person starts to fade until you can hardly feel their print.

But right now is the peak of the peak. I feel Charteris in every speck of dust, in every bloody smear. When I'm not in the living room downstairs with her, I feel slightly weirded out, like someone is talking to me and I've simply turned my back. And when I am in the living room, it feels strange if I can't directly see her head, preferably her face itself.

11

I haven't yet got my usual feel for the victim. Partly, poor dear, that's because her head has been hacked off with a broadsword and those things can be unsettling. The set of her face – glassy, pale, unseeing, shocked – is, presumably, not standard-issue Gaynor Charteris. But it's more than that. This outdoorsy woman, with her short grey hair and practical hands, has some quality that eludes me. I might capture it, perhaps, if I had longer here, but I know I don't have long before Jones will toss me out.

And then I notice something that has been bothering me since I first came in. Or not bothering, but nagging.

One of those things you see, but don't see that you see.

Standing Charteris's head on that little corner bureau could be taken, in a way, as simple trophy display. 'Look what I've done! Here's the body, here's the head.' Except if you were aiming at some kind of triumphal display, this tucked-away corner is a hopeless choice. Better to place the head on the corpse. Or the coffee table. Or in the window. Or almost anything.

So perhaps the placement of the head was more accidental. More like: 'OK, that's sorted. Now let's grab the laptop and the iPhone. No, you dummy, you can't go out like that. You're still carrying the old lady's head. Yep, down there, that'll do. Now let's fuck off and hope no one notices we're covered with blood.'

That's possible. Murders are shocking to the perpetrator as well as to the victim. People do stupid things. Make mistakes. Botch the job.

But someone, probably, arrived here with three homemade spears and arranged them carefully in a dead woman's chest. That's not really stupid-mistake territory, so I want to bet that the placement of the head has its own dark significance.

But what?

Charteris's empty eyes are turned towards the wall, where

12

there hangs a piece of framed text, in that hard-to-read medieval script. I take a photo of the text for later reference, but try to read it anyway. It says, I think, something like this:

> *Agitio ter consuli, gemitus britannorum . . . Repellunt barbari ad mare, repellit mare ad barbaros; inter haec duo genera funerum aut iugulamur aut mergimur.*
> —Gildas, *De Excidio et Conquestu Britanniae*

I don't understand Latin – though '*Britannorum*' and '*repellunt barbari*' presumably mean something like what you'd think they mean – but I feel the tug of that ancient world, its torments and darknesses. Perhaps there, in that tug, is an important part of Gaynor Charteris herself.

I feel the flicker of her. Some stronger sense of the woman herself.

I'd like to stay with that flicker, sense her better, but Jones comes up behind me.

'Do you have a *feel* for the perpetrator yet, Sergeant? I said five minutes.'

He's one of those officers who deploys sarcasm the way Russian riot police deploy batons, but I don't care. I float above. I swim below.

'Yes, sir. May I ask, have we secured the victim's place of work?'

'Place of work, Sergeant? She worked for the Open University. She worked from home mostly.'

'I think she was working on a dig.' I mention the muddy boots, the gloves, the recently dirty fingernails, and the absence of a dog or visible gardening activity. 'She's an archaeologist, after all.'

That pauses the sarcasm assault. Procedure does indeed require that any scene potentially connected to a murder be secured as soon as possible.

'Good catch. When you're researching local angles, ask

around for any locations where she may have been working. We'll get officers there as soon as possible.'

'Yes sir.'

I make my exit, hopscotching through the blood puddles in my parachute-suit and my non-tear paper overshoes. The street is still sunny. Still catkiny. The ginger tom is still there, his parts now beautifully clean.

Gaynor Charteris is already maybe my third best ever corpse, runner up only to the beauties that were Alina 'Carlotta' Mishchenko and the ever-wonderful Mary Langton.

I wait four hundred and fifty-three days, then up pops a beauty.

3

I do my job.

Do it in a way that even Bleddyn Jones couldn't find fault with, not even if he were tramping after me, spitting bullet points and beardy irritation.

I've been given a team of three. One of them, Joe Harris, is a village resident of long-standing. He is quick to speak to two local vicars, the school headmaster, the people in the village store, the post office and the barber shop. The other two constables are, like me, native-born Taffs without local knowledge, but they troop sturdily from house to house, asking questions and collecting up answers. I stay on top of all that, but I also hit the phone, struggling through our beloved mental health bureaucracy, trying to locate any nutters with a known interest in swords, spears and beheadings.

Nada, nothing, nix.

No known nutters.

No one, except Charteris herself, with a fondness for broadswords and antique spearheads.

The local nutter hypothesis was never, I thought, excessively plausible but, fair play, you do have to test these things, no matter what.

We also, rapidly, ascertain where Gaynor Charteris was muddying her boots. The village name, Dinas Powys, means something like 'fort of the country-dwellers' and, sure enough, a short distance out of the village, in Cwm George, there's a low hill with the remains of an Iron Age fort. The site has been excavated before, back in the 1950s, but, it seems, Charteris was keen to re-explore it and enlisted a number of students from Cardiff to get the project started.

As soon as I have that information, I relay it to Jones, who sends a couple of uniforms up the hill to take guard.

An hour later, with my team ticking away nicely and no urgent leads emerging, I check in with Jones. Nudge him into sending me up the hill to Cwm George, which he does with only a flicker of irritation.

I drive up there.

A small parking area, mostly for dog walkers, I guess.

Walking boots from the back of my car. Fleece.

A stony path curves into a forest.

Beech trees, ivy, and a dark gleam of ferns. Noises muted by the trees. Further in, any connection with the outside world is lost completely. It's as though, round the next bend, a knight might come cantering up on a pale-grey charger. A jingle of spurs and a flutter of silk caparisons. The feeling is strong enough, and weird enough, that I actually call one of the uniforms. Check I'm heading in the right direction.

I am, and soon find what I'm after.

A rise of ground. The ramparts of a fort, still discernible. And, just below, a small green Portakabin, its door open to an indecisive breeze. There's a lock on the door, a padlock, but the hasp has been torn out of the flimsy wall and the thing just swings loose, screws dangling in space.

I enter the cabin.

The two uniforms are there, along with three others, students from the look of them. Two boys, both with longish hair, and a tall, skinny girl with pale, luminous skin. They all wear heavy boots, old jeans, warm coats. Mud on boots and knees.

The cabin has a few folding camp chairs. Some shelving

down one side, muddy, like everything else, but sort of clean too. Like someone's been taking care to wipe things down and sweep up, no matter how basically. There's a stack of heavy tools in one corner – spades, forks, mattocks – and some smaller tools – trowels, brushes, hammers – tidily arranged on the shelf beside them. There's an orange plastic washing bowl and two big plastic water containers, fifty litres, or something like that. The shelves are otherwise clear. On a portable gas-stove, a kettle is coming to the boil.

'Typical CID,' says the uniform nearest the kettle. 'Always arrive in time for tea.'

He makes tea, the regular sort. I always carry peppermint teabags with me, but just for today I think I'll face the big, bad caffeine monster.

The students introduce themselves. Katie, Mitch and Rob. Katie – complicated braided dark blonde hair, nose-piercing, a spray of star-tattoos behind one ear – seems like the queen of this little band and the others visibly defer.

They all have the jerky movements and speech rhythms of unfaked shock. Rob, reaching for a stool to sit on, misses it with his hand, stumbles and refocuses. When he reaches for the stool the second time, he's successful, but his face is tight with concentration. When he speaks, he does so with a clumsy, over-articulated clarity.

I turn to the non-kettle-occupied uniform, Rhys. Ask him to bring me up to speed. He tells me that he and his colleague have taken basic statements, the gist of which is that, yes, the three students all knew and worked with Dr Charteris. The dig was happy and productive. They all got along fine. No one knew of anyone with a grudge against the archaeologist, nor did she seem troubled or fearful in any way.

Just one thing.

Katie, gripping the side-shelving, asks, 'Do you know where all our stuff is? Our finds?'

The uniforms look at me to see if I know.

Nope. Nothing to do with me.

I ask Katie what's missing.

'Everything basically. Not our tools, those are all there, but everything else.'

Shocked eyes sweeping the emptiness and returning. Everything is just that little bit off. Her timing, her fluidity. Everything.

I say, 'OK, sorry, everyone please leave the cabin.'

I shoo everyone out. If stuff has been stolen, we have to presume there's some connection with the murder down the hill. That means that, forensically compromised as the cabin now is, we have to take it seriously as a crime scene.

We re-assemble on the grass outside.

I ask about the project and it emerges that the dig had only been going for three weeks, an exploratory excavation in preparation for a much bigger project in the summer. These preliminary works had already confirmed the basic richness of the site.

The braids-'n'-tattoos Katie says, 'What we've got here is a really good Iron Age hill fort. There are thousands of them all over Britain, many hundreds in Wales alone, and this one isn't particularly large. But it *is* well-defended.' She starts pointing out the natural slope of the hill, its multiple levels of ditch-and-rampart defences.

'OK, go on': my uncertain contribution to the discussion. It's hard to know what to ask because it's hard to see what could possibly be at stake.

Katie continues. 'So in about 43 CE – that's AD in old money – the Romans invade Britain. They don't reach south Wales for some time, but when they do, this area slowly Romanises. Although the Romans are technically in control of all of Wales, their rule to the north and west of here is military only. You only get real Roman villas and all the rest of it down here in Glamorgan.'

'OK.'

'But with the Romans keeping the peace, forts like this one fell out of service. You didn't need this kind of military wellie, when you've got Augustus's Second Legion a day's march away in Caerleon. So yes, the site was probably inhabited, but was no longer of particular importance.'

'And nothing valuable?' I ask. 'I mean no horde of gold and silver? Nothing to provide a motive for murder?'

'Not at all. I mean, what we found had *some* value. A few Roman coins. Some nails. Some bits of pottery. But you can pick those sort of things up on eBay for a few quid. There's historical value, yes, but monetary value? No. Nothing.'

'Oh.'

I feel disappointed. Our one little lead seems to be vanishing into nothingness. A candle flame flickering on the blue edge of extinction.

And yet the thefts: those were real. That broken hasp, it's real too.

Katie isn't done. She's eager to get to the next part, in fact. 'But look, the real glory of this site is what happened *after* the Romans left.'

'Go on.'

'OK. It's the end of the fourth century. The Roman empire is being attacked from the north and east. Large parts of the empire are using German troops anyway, and those troops start to think, the hell with this, we'll just grab everything for ourselves. So the Romans start to panic. First of all, they withdraw from the north and west of Britain, from areas like this. Then, in about 410 CE, they withdraw *all* their troops. All of them. They tell the British, sorry and all that, but you're on your own now. Goodbye and good luck.'

'Not brilliant news, presumably.'

'Not at all. All of a sudden, places like Dinas Powys become important again. They get reoccupied. Refortified. Once again, they're the safest places to be. And right here, where we're sitting now, is a fantastic site. It's got these great defences. It's in the richest part of Wales. It's right on the coast, close to an excellent harbour. If you were a British nobleman at the dawn of the Dark Ages, this site would give you everything. Security. Trade. Wine from Spain and Italy. An opportunity to keep the good times going. That's why Dinas Powys is so important. It's got the most important collection of early Dark Age material anywhere in Wales. There aren't many sites in England which come close.'

She starts telling me more about what they've found. Evidence that a jeweller was once busy here. Also a blacksmith. Animal stock-holding: an earlier dig found twenty-two thousand animal bones.

'And the stuff that was stolen. Was there anything there? I mean, anything that mattered historically, leave aside the financial aspect.'

Katie shakes her head. 'Not really. We're really only prospecting, remember. Figuring out our strategy for the summer. So, yes, we found enough to support our view that this site is going to be really great, but no, there was no individual piece which made us go *wow*.'

I ask, 'Did Charteris ever come up here alone. Did she ever dig by herself?'

Katie – and the others – all laugh at that, a little embarrassed perhaps.

Katie, tiptoeing round her answer, says, 'Gaynor lived on her own. Her kids are in Australia. She loved archaeology. Yes, I think she had plenty of friends, but maybe not so many in the local area. So, of course she came up here whenever she could. She loved this place.'

That's code, I think, for saying that Charteris was mildly obsessive. Perhaps more than mildly.

I think of that stern, outdoorsy, short-haired head in its little suburban cul-de-sac below. The way her gaze was fixed on that bit of Latin text. It makes no sense, no sense at all, but I have this stupid feeling that it was Charteris herself who, in death, swivelled on her stump of a neck to find that bit of Gildas again.

> *Repellunt barbari ad mare, repellit mare ad barbaros; inter haec duo genera funerum aut iugulamur aut mergimur.*

I feel that flicker again. That flicker which whispers somehow of the real Charteris. Our victim, our corpse, our head.

Tucking that thought away for later, I say, 'OK, and just say she'd found, I don't know, a Roman goblet. Gold, rubies, whatever. Who owns it? What happens next.'

Katie's answer is that it's the local landowner who would profit, not the person who found the object. And anyway, 'Gaynor didn't care about money. She'd have no interest in any of that.'

I try a few other questions. Get nothing of interest. Call Jones.

He, predictably, isn't impressed. The theft is significant enough that he wants to keep some police presence on site – which means the uniforms get to drink more tea, up here amongst these blowing trees, these ancient ramparts – but 'I want you back on the local angle. You can't keep an eye on your men from up there.'

As it happens, I *have* been staying in fairly close touch with my three guys throughout, the ten or fifteen minutes I've been talking to Katie my longest interruption yet.

But I'm a good girl. I do as he says.

Ask the uniforms to stay on site. Ask Jones to get some

forensics guys up here. Meantime, the kids want to get back to Cardiff. Katie, it turns out, is a postgraduate student, researching for her doctorate. The other two are undergraduates, hence Katie's air of authority.

We walk, the four of us, down the side of the cabin towards the path back to the parking area. Katie, I realise, is tearing up. I tell the other two to go on, and say, 'Katie?'

She wipes her eyes, the blue of old seas and far horizons, and says, 'I mean, who does that? Kill Gaynor of all people. And this dig. It's totally fucked now. It's just . . .'

Her lips tremble with unfaked emotion. Katie's clearly upset about her friend and colleague, but it seems like Katie is almost equally upset about the project. That seems like a weird thing to be so upset about, but violent bereavements *are* weird. People react in funny ways.

Her little squall of grief subsides.

At the corner of the cabin, there's a tangle of long grass and fallen leaves, black and heavy with damp. She kicks at the tangle, loses her footing and has to grab at the cabin wall to steady herself.

'Fuck it.' She pauses as she catches her breath, which is jerky and asthmatic. When she's ready, she jabs again with her foot at something in the tangle below her. 'Well, they didn't get *that* anyway.'

'*That*' appears to be a right-angled bit of stone, a stump of masonry, now very much corroded by time. It looks like the sort of thing which, if you found it in your garden, you'd throw on the nearest skip. Mossy, dirty, broken, useless.

I raise my eyebrows. 'Well, gee, Katie. It's lucky they didn't get *that*.'

She stares at me, then laughs.

'OK, I know it doesn't look like much.'

'But really it's a priceless . . . um, I don't know, help me out here.'

'It's old. We haven't yet had it tested, but the appearance is consistent with the early medieval period, possibly even the very start of the Dark Ages.'

'A lump of stone?'

'Yes, but it's not a lump, is it? It's carved.' She pushes back the grass so I can see better. 'It's probably the angle from a stone cross, or burial stone. I mean, that's a nice find, whatever, but it's better than that. Look.'

She gathers herself a second, then wanders a few feet away. Pulls an ordinary lump of stone out of the ground and lays it beside the possibly-ancient bit of cross. The two things are different. The stones aren't the same.

I see that, but don't know what Katie's getting at.

She stares at me, like I'm supposed to know. The click-click-click of a shocked brain figuring out ordinary human interactions.

Then she gets there. Restarts.

'It's basic geology,' she says. 'The rock here is all Triassic. If you're a Dark Age Christian wanting to carve a cross or even just build a house, you're going to use the stuff kicking around under your feet. This stone looks Silurian, possibly Ordovician. There's plenty of that stuff in north and mid Wales. Ireland too for that matter. But around here? Nothing.'

I shake my head. I can't quite believe I'm discussing Welsh geology as part of an investigation, but then again I don't know *what* matters or *why*, and until I do then everything has to matter.

I try to get my head round this latest nugget.

'So, someone brought a lump of rock here – by ship presumably – then carved a cross.'

'Or, more likely,' corrects Katie, 'carved the rock in north or mid Wales, then brought it here.'

'Which sounds like a lot of hassle, when there's plenty of stone right here.'

'Exactly. So why would anyone want to do that?'

I shake my head. The puzzles of the present day seem strange enough without bringing mysteries from sixteen centuries back.

We stare at each other a few seconds.

She has no answer to my puzzles. I have no answers to hers.

We walk down to the carpark and she's about to join her fellow students in a scruffy blue Ford Fiesta, when I say, 'Katie, how are you with spears? I mean, can you tell antiques from fakes?'

'In a laboratory? Yes.'

'And if I just showed you one?'

'Then maybe. It depends.'

I ask her to come with me. Promise her we'll get her back to town in a squad car, if we have to. She says yes, says fine.

We drive down the hill. I check in with my team of three. Joe Harris has been keeping things under efficient control and our Contacts Made list is already looking plump and healthily stocked. There are still a few gaps. Charteris sang in a local choir and we'd like to speak to as many of those people as possible. But we've done well and I say so.

Out on the concrete ramp in front of Charteris's garage, I report in to Jones. He's grumpy but not actively critical. Tells me to keep going.

'Yes, sir. Just one thing. I have an antiquities expert with me, a Katie Smith. I thought you might want her to take a look at the sword and the spearheads.'

Jones looks darkly suspicious, narrowing his eyes like a man considering a bet on a street game of three-card monte.

He looks for the con, can't find it, so tells me, grudgingly, that if the forensics boys are happy to let a 'member of the public in', he'll allow it.

I want to argue at that. Calling Katie a 'member of the public' makes her sound like she's a murder-scene tourist, instead of

24

what she actually is: an archaeologist offering us a free, instant and expert appraisal of a key aspect of the crime scene.

I don't actually say that, but I also don't do that prettily-maned fetlock-kicking thing, so I think I lose points anyway.

I get Katie.

'This will be rough, I'm afraid. It's not particularly pretty in there.'

A terse nod signals her understanding.

A CSI tells us that they've completed sample-taking and photography. He still gives us protective suits, overshoes, haircaps and latex gloves, 'Just to be on the safe side.'

We go into the house.

Someone has covered Charteris's head with a pale-blue cloth. The stump of her neck too. The room is bright with halogen task-lighting, rigged up for the photography. Already the old living room is vanishing, being replaced by something else. It's like those fast-forward films you see of life in the jungle. Animals dying and collapsing into carrion. Larger animals snatching the meat. Birds of prey cleaning the bones. Then ants and insects. Mould. The moss and the rain and the sunlight and the leaf-fall. And you watch those things, fascinated by the upthrust of new life, and you've forgotten, almost forgotten, that what you're watching is also a graveyard. A kind of burial.

I try to find the scent of the dead woman. Her presence. It's already fading.

Dry white bones in the undergrowth.

A life sketched in blood.

Katie stays close. The stains on the floor are dry now. I avoid treading in any of the larger marks, because it's now instinctive to do so, but Katie just treads where she wants. Blood rises in rust-coloured flakes as she passes.

I stop at the feet of the corpse, the body.

'Oh.'

Katie has the expression of any newbie. I watch her closely to see if there's anything else there – we can't exclude the possibility that she knows something more than she's reported so far – but her expression is faultless. Shocked, unsettled. Upset.

That jerky breathing again.

She pieces together the scene. Figures out what lies under the blue cloth on the computer table.

'May I?' she asks.

There's a CSI labelling up sample bags on the kitchen table. I pass the question to him with my eyes, and he shrugs and says, 'Just look, don't touch.'

I lift the cloth for Katie.

There's the head again. Familiar now. Settling.

That short grey hair. Those lightless eyes. The grimly disapproving mouth.

I feel a kind of chuckle rising in me. A feeling of recognition. Or more than that even. Friendship. Fellowship.

I'm pleased, in a way, that she has blood still spattering her hair. She liked her mud. The rhythms of the dig. The basic tools, the knees-down-in-the-dirtness of it all. She wouldn't have wanted to be too polished up in death.

As often, I want to put my hand out. Stroke the dead woman's hair. Trace the curve of her face with my finger.

Want to, but don't.

Katie looks at the head a few moments, says nothing, then I replace the cloth.

We turn to the corpse. The sword and the spearheads.

The sword she disposes of quickly.

'This is a modern reproduction of an Anglo–Saxon style sword. There are websites that sell these things. It belonged to Gaynor, it hung up there—' she points to the empty fixings 'and it's not old at all.'

26

The spearheads, though, are a different matter.

She kneels down to inspect them. Leans over. Wants to support herself with a hand on Charteris's chest. Avoids doing so. Then leans more and does it anyway.

She looks at all three spearheads up close and from every angle. Pulls away.

'So?' I ask.

'Um, no promises, and I could tell for you definite if I had these in a lab . . .'

'But . . .?'

'I think they're the real deal. If they're fake, they've taken exceptional care with things like the pitting, the patina, even the basic quality of the ironwork.'

She points to a slight kink in one of the spearheads, where the blade's lozenge narrows to meet the shaft.

'Ancient iron-making wasn't particularly sophisticated, so their weapons weren't particularly strong. It's common to see that kind of bending in spears that have actually been used in battle. Modern reproductions almost never have that kind of kinking because people don't want to buy something that looks wrong. I mean, I can't be positive without more work, but I'd say these are real.'

'Approximate era?'

'I'd need a lab. Sorry.'

'Wild guess?'

'Oh, Iron Age. Roman. If they're Anglo–Saxon, they're relatively early.'

She speaks casually about items that could easily pre-date Christianity.

I say, 'And they're not Gaynor's? I mean, you'd know if they were?'

'Not Gaynor's, no. She felt strongly about genuine antiques being stored properly in a museum. She'd happily have reproduction stuff or finds so minor no museum would want them. But those spearheads? No way.'

She stands up. And as her attention widens away from the specific technical questions, she remembers where she is, what she's looking at.

Silently now, and without asking my permission, she lifts the cloth over Charteris's head again.

Looks, and murmurs, '*Requiescat in pace.*' Rest in peace. She holds the dead woman's gaze, then reverently lowers the cloth.

I say, 'You read Latin, of course.'

'Yes.'

'Do you know what this says?'

I point her to the medieval fragment hanging on the wall. The one Charteris was looking at.

'Oh, that? It's Gildas. The groans of the Britons.'

I don't say anything, but my face probably does a 'Gildas who?' kind of look.

Katie: 'Gildas was a sixth-century monk. A saint, in fact. His writing is one of our earliest sources for the period.'

And, reading the Latin, she translates:

'To Agitius, thrice consul: the groans of the Britons . . . The barbarians drive us to the sea, the sea drives us to the barbarians; between these two means of death, we are either killed or drowned. Gildas, *On the Ruin and Conquest of Britain.*'

'And the barbarians in question . . .?'

'Northern tribes. Modern-day Scots and Irish basically.'

She answers the question, but the words drop noiselessly, pebbles vanished in a well. We both share a sudden sense that it is almost disrespectful to be talking about these long-ago conflicts when what we are dealing with is a very twenty-first century corpse. It's strange how this investigation, young as it is, keeps getting tugged under by the past, and the deep past at that.

Stolen Dark Age finds. Iron Age spears. Gildas and his Latin lament.

We leave.

The air is different in the homes of the dead, I've noticed.

Partly it's the smell. Blood baking under those bright halogen lamps. The smell of our paper suits, something like that of a newly stocked stationery cupboard.

But there's also something boxy, closed in. Like the deceased person's soul has mostly succeeded in clambering free of that old, messily biological contraption that now lies discarded on the floor, but hasn't yet had the nerve to take that final leap. To exit the room, the house, the street, the village. To fly forth upon the wind, glittering and free and for ever.

It's a relief to be outside again, in this bright, ordinary air.

I search around for a squad car leaving for Cardiff. Find one. Summon Katie. Her right foot drags a little as she walks towards it. When she notices, she looks angry and starts to walk with exaggerated care. I wonder if it's a drug thing. Something she doesn't want me to see.

She gets into the car.

Leaning down into the interior, I say, 'They never came, did they?'

'Who?'

'The Romans? They never came back.'

'No.'

'So the British were basically fucked, were they? The ones who were left behind.'

Katie laughs and says in her crystal Oxbridgey English. 'You tell me: you're Welsh. Those Britons were your ancestors, not mine. From your point of view, I'm just another hairy-arsed barbarian.'

She makes a hairy, scary barbarian face at me, then laughs. The awkward, coughing laugh of someone in grief.

The car departs.

Three ancient spears in a dead woman's chest.

A savage beheading.

An island deserted by its Roman protectors.

And a case that feels – almost – like it's been worth the 452-day wait.

4

We get nowhere.

We do everything right and we get nowhere.

The forensics are slow but they come. Prints, aplenty. DNA, aplenty. A long slow process of teasing out who had legitimately been in Charteris's house in the days before her death. But though there's still a load of work to do, we have nothing that looks suspicious. Nothing useful.

Also: nothing from cameras. Nothing useful on vehicle movements. Nothing from all my house-to-house stuff. No interesting local nutters. No recent killings with similar quasi-ritual elements.

The case has had a lot of media interest, inevitably, which means we get a lot of phone calls, but none of them helpful or even, mostly, sane.

One week on from our corpse discovery and we are not one inch further forward. The enquiry, given the macho title of Operation Blade, is already limping.

Jackson calls a Case Review meeting. These things do happen, of course. They happen in long, complex enquiries when the mass of data becomes almost overwhelming and everyone benefits from a deep breath and a fresh perspective. But one week into a murder investigation? With a single victim and no great torrents of data?

This is early for a Case Review, very early, and Bleddyn

31

Jones prepares for it like some kind of angry bluebottle. Buzzy, demanding, repetitious.

Obedient to that angry buzz, we all do extra work. Re-examine interviews, check lists, compile data, fill blanks.

Me, I don't mind. I like the activity. I have a photo of Gaynor Charteris's oozing skull as my screensaver and a six inch by ten inch shot of her spear-stabbed torso at eyeline above my desk. I put in long hours and I love each one.

The Case Review meeting is in Jackson's office.

Jackson and Jones are both there, of course. So am I, also Deryn Powell, the guy who's been leading the forensics, and Sian Ryder, our indexer.

Jackson kicks out his legs. Says, 'So Bleddyn, why don't you tell me what you've all been up to?'

Jones tells him, via a Powerpoint presentation, no less.

Maps with different coloured dots. Charts that assemble our not-very-useful forensic data into not-very-useful patterns. A team list with tasks and responsibilities. At one point, he's talking about our house-to-house work and I think I was probably meant to chirp up with some interesting observations, but although he stared at me hard and arranged his moustache and beard into ever-less-pleasing configurations as he did so, I didn't feel like chirping, so just stayed silent.

He ended up doing the local summary bit instead of me, then said, 'Is that right, Fiona?' I said, 'Yes, sir,' in a way that was intended to be positive, supportive and emphatic. His eyes glittered dangerously for a second, then moved off.

I think: *it's a prison officer beard*. That's what it is. If you imagine your worst sort of prison officer, all keys and rules and punishments, you'd garnish that nightmare with a beard like Jones's. Prickly and strangely black, as though dyed.

We run for an hour. I mean: Jones does. That's how long his Powerpoint thing lasts. Except for clarifying little points of fact, Jackson says nothing. His face is unreadable.

A north-facing cliff that glimpses sunlight only during the winter solstice.

When Jones is done, Jackson says, 'OK, good. That's very organised. Thank you.'

Jones, who doesn't yet know that Jackson's interrogation technique is mostly based around saying nothing at all, is a bit non-plussed. 'OK, good': *that's* the case review?

Jones darts off into another spatter of Action Lists and task management speak.

Jackson says nothing. Nods. Moves his eyebrows.

Once Jones has finally finished – though I'm near certain that there are bullet points still dribbling into his beard – silence finally enters the room.

Jackson rotates a thick finger round the rim of his empty coffee mug.

Eventually, he says, 'That *is* very organised, but we don't have a suspect, do we? Or any credible leads?'

Jones can't bring himself to agree. He hurtles off into a discourse about parts of the case that are still incomplete, where there is still more work to be done. Jackson does nothing to stop the hurtle and another five minutes of my life pass into dust.

Silence.

Jackson still unreadable. Jones reorganising his papers.

Jackson: 'So. No leads.'

He asks Deryn Powell for his comments. Powell says, 'Well, there are more bits and pieces still to come in, but I'm not expecting much.'

'How long till you'll have everything?'

Powell shrugs. 'About a week. Depends on the lab, mostly.'

Jackson and Sian Ryder have a short discussion of personnel, data and action management. A few niggles, as there always are. Nothing that can't be, and isn't being, sorted.

Eventually, Jackson's heavy gaze settles on me.

'Fiona, you are being uncharacteristically silent.'

That is, I realise, the sort of thing people do come out with, but they don't think it through, do they? If I say, 'Yes, sir,' then I'm not being silent, which means I'll be speaking a lie.

If I say, 'No, sir,' then I won't be trapped into lying to a superior officer, but I will be contradicting him for no good purpose. Between a rock and a hard place, that's me.

The barbarians drive us to the sea, the sea drives us to the barbarians; between these two means of death, we are either killed or drowned.

I stay silent.

'Fiona?'

I say, 'Um.'

'Are you able to do human-speak today, Fiona? Is there a translation available?'

'Well, um . . . the thing is.'

Then, since that is a broken-arsed non-sentence if ever there was one, I take one more run at it.

'Look, I think we *do* have leads here. It's just they're of a sort we're not used to, and aren't sure how to follow. Take, for example, those spears in the chest.'

Jones, uncomfortable at the fact that Jackson is allowing me to run free without bridle or bit, instantly starts flashing his Powerpoint charts around. RITUAL KILLINGS IN THE UK 1995–2015 and MURDERS INVOLVING SWORDS, SPEARS AND OTHER 'CLASSIC' WEAPONS.

No one says anything and when he shuts up, Jackson's gaze returns to me.

I say, 'Those spears, they weren't just any old spears, the actual spearheads are more than twenty centuries old.'

Sure enough, Katie, working with a lab here in Cardiff, has established that the spearheads are genuine Iron Age artefacts, probably from the first two or three centuries before Christ. Fancy things to stick into a body that's already dead.

Jackson says, 'OK, agreed . . .'

'And ritual killings? Is that really what we're looking at?' My finger circles the date on Jones's blessed Powerpoint chart. '1995–2015'. In a case that seems to hark back to the Dark Ages and beyond, I'm not sure that figuring out what some Middlesbrough weirdo got up to in 1997 is going to help us much.

Jackson: 'OK, so: alternative angles?'

'Um, something like the Kirkburn Sword, maybe?'

'What?'

'Well, this wasn't something I'd heard about either, but . . .' But I did some work of my own alongside all the boring stuff I was doing for Bleddyn bloody Jones, 'And, there's a sword they dug up in Yorkshire about thirty years ago. The sword was about the same age as those damn spearheads of ours and, according to the British Museum, no less, this sword is "probably the finest Iron Age sword in Europe". OK, now that in itself doesn't mean anything, only get this. The man they dug up with the sword had three spears buried in his chest. It wasn't a ritual killing, or at least that's not what people think. It looks like it was some way to bury an honoured warrior. But if you want to find a case that looks like ours – three Iron Age spears in the chest – then that Kirkburn burial is arguably as good a fit as we've got.'

We talk a bit more about that. The Kirkburn warrior appears to have died naturally and though he was buried with a fancy sword, no one had bothered to lop his head off with it.

Jones fusses around with his Powerpoint charts, but Jackson ignores him.

'Fiona, let's suppose you're right. Suppose this killing in some way references this Yorkshire thing, or even just Iron Age burials in general. What do we do with that? It's not like we've got people running around with woad on their faces any more.'

35

'No.'

'And we can't go back in time and arrest someone from twenty-three centuries ago.'

'No.'

He's right about that. Definitely correct.

Jackson: 'So?'

'So, um.'

Then, since I can see Jackson is about to do his translation-into-human thing again, I forestall him.

'So, look, I don't know. I don't have an answer. But I do think that our clues are going to come from the historical angle. Looking at the things Charteris was interested in. The things that the hill fort was starting to reveal. Somehow those things mattered enough to someone that they were prepared to kill Charteris. And not just kill her, but kill her *in this way*.'

I bite my lip.

Literally and figuratively.

The thing is, if you kill someone in these extravagant ways, you're usually trying to send a message. So when the Ku Klux Klan strung people up from trees, they were carefully sending a message. To black people: stay in your place. To white people: this is the way we run things here. None of that civil rights nonsense, or else . . .

A loathsome message, brutally delivered.

But clear. Horribly clear.

And if this stagey presentation of Charteris's corpse is aimed at sending a message, then who the hell is its target audience? And what's the message?

The single thing that disturbs me most about this enquiry so far is the idea that *we're* the intended audience: we, the police.

That's not a good thought. Like, beneath these dark waters, yet darker waters flow.

But I don't say any of that. Don't even finish thinking it, when Jackson cuts in.

36

'Bleddyn. Fiona Griffiths here thinks that we should examine the historical aspects in more detail. What do you think about that?'

When it finishes speaking, Jackson's face assumes a remarkable stillness. 'Glasslike': that's the conventional descriptor, I think, except that there's nothing of glass there at all. His expression has the solidity and impenetrability of rock. Cliff walls, rising into mist.

Jones spends a moment or two trying to read Jackson's face, but he might as well seek to read a slab of Snowdonian rhyolite.

Those crags, those mists.

And after a while, he visibly gives up the attempt. This is his enquiry, his decision. A decision shaped, perhaps, by Jackson's earlier terse summary. *That* is *very organised, but we don't have a suspect, do we?* What I offer is scarcely the type of lead that Jones would choose to pursue, but he wants to stay in the game. Maintain control of this enquiry in the hope that something turns up.

His face ripples and says, 'Yes, I think that it would be a good idea if Fiona . . .' He waves his hand at me, permissively but vaguely, then takes another stab at the end of his sentence. 'If Fiona maybe takes a look at – what? – Iron Age killings and things of that type . . .?'

He stares at me, not quite sure what I'm proposing and his confidence fading with every word.

Jackson waits for long enough to mark the fact that Bleddyn Jones himself has made his choice, and made it unforced and of his own volition, then he leans forward, grinning.

'Bleddyn, mate, you've no bloody idea what she wants. None at all. Neither have I. But if you want a word of advice from an officer who's had to work with this one in the past, then just give her her head. A little freedom of action. Only a little, mind, because before you know it she'll be running off

God knows where doing God knows what. But if she wants to look at Iron Age killings or, I don't know, old hill forts or whatever, then let her do it.'

Jones, still not quite understanding how he's been negotiated into this outcome, just nods.

Jackson, speaking to Powell and Ryder in turn, says, 'Deryn? Sian?'

They nod. Shruggy nods of the like-we-give-a damn variety.

Jackson pauses a microsecond, then opens out into a full-beam, full-wattage smile.

'Well, that's terrific. Splendid. Bleddyn, you and your team are doing a fabulous job. Keep it up. Well done all.'

We unstick ourselves from the fake black leather of Jackson's giant sofa and tumble out of his office into the wide open spaces of the corridor beyond.

Jones, still slightly dazed, says, 'So, Fiona, then you'll . . . You'll . . .'

'Yes, sir. Of course. I'll get going at once.'

5

The next day, a sparkling one.

A high blue sky. A buoyant sun. The sea a sparkle of silver and blue.

I sit on a damp green bank and smoke a roll-up. I'm not a smoker, not really, but I'm trying to reduce my appetite for cannabis, and for some reason the tobacco acts as a partial substitute, even if this particular cigarette does have a little Pentwyn resin crumbled along its length.

Sweet resin, Welsh winds.

I'm a little earlier than I said, but it's not long before I hear the sound of approaching feet.

Katie appears. Sees me up here on my bank. I raise a hand and smile welcome.

She approaches.

Impressively torn black jeans. Black cowboy boots, well-used. Dark vest-top worn under an almost military khaki shirt. A chunky necklace. One of those broad-brimmed Aussie-style hats with a leather band. Some multi-coloured wristband that probably communicates something to do with music or some charitable cause or event or something else that I would know about if I knew anything about that kind of thing.

The look has attitude and personality and toughness, without quite dipping into angry hippy counter-culture.

Also: she walks with a ski stick, a mobility aid not a fashion statement.

She comes up the bank towards me. Sits beside me.

I say, 'You hurt your ankle?'

'No.'

She volunteers nothing further. I say, 'Anything you want to talk about?'

'No.'

That's fine with me. I offer her my tobacco pouch, but she says, 'No,' more gently this time.

I put my pouch away and she loosens up a bit. Actually physically loosens. Stretches out, decompresses.

I continue smoking. We're close to the sea here, very close, but these hills, these trees are so enclosing, they create their own little world. Their own deep pond of time.

Katie: 'Have you guys got anywhere?'

'The official answer? We are actively pursuing a number of lines of enquiry.'

'But you have nothing? In reality, you have nothing?'

'That's right.'

'So you want to talk about Roman pottery? That's one of your "lines of enquiry", is it?'

There's something so needlessly snippy in the way she says that, I can't help laughing.

'Yes, yes, I'm afraid it is.'

Katie looks apologetic – then fierce – then juts her jaw at a green horizon.

While she's busy cycling through whatever twenty emotions she's picked out for the day, I get out my iPad and bring up the list of finds downloaded from the project website.

I say, 'Right, I know none of these things looked all that interesting to you when you found them, but that was before Gaynor was murdered. And since she *has* been murdered and your finds *were* stolen, we have to take a second look.'

So we do.

Start picking through the list.

> *Pottery fragment*, rim piece, 2cm x 5cm, prob. local
> manufacture
> *Pottery fragment*, 4cm x 9cm, possible southern Europe
> origin (?)
> *Nails* x 12, varying condition, Roman-style, poss local origin.
> *Button*, horn, 1cm
> *Seal box (lid)*, 3cm x 3cm. Figure of bear (?), wolf (?), heavily
> scratched and poor condition.
> *Coins* x 4. Varying dates 2nd/3rd century. (?) Variable
> condition.
> *Bronze wire*, 7 cm. Very fine craftsmanship. Probable use in
> jewellery. Post-Roman (?)

And so on.

Katie dismisses everything in turn.

'No. Look, these things aren't rare in themselves. They're just not. Take that seal box. If that had been in good condition – lid *and* box, no buckling, no scratching – then it might retail for maybe a hundred and fifty pounds, something like that. As it is, you couldn't even sell it on eBay. These things are of interest because of where we're finding them, not their rarity.'

All through the list, the same thing.

The only thing that gives Katie pause is the lump of rock down by the corner of the Portakabin.

> *Carved stone fragment*. Probable part of a cross. Condition
> consistent with early medieval period. Stone of non-local
> origin.

'I mean, that surprised us, the fact that the stone wasn't local. But still. You could think of any number of explanations.'

'Such as?'

'Well, these Dark Age British were Christian. Suppose that a

41

saint with important local connections had died in some other part of the country. They might want to relocate the relics. Bones, a skull, or a memorial cross. Something sanctified by the saint himself.'

I say, 'So, I don't know, let's say someone grows up here, then goes round the country healing the sick or whatever. When he drops dead, the people back here want a piece of him.'

'Exactly, yes. And of course there was plenty of fraud and forgery. The most popular medieval saints generated enough sacred bones to make two or three whole bodies.'

'And you know all this how? I mean is it just archaeology?'

'Digging up physical evidence is a key part, yes, but manuscript sources are just as important. Hopefully, when you put manuscript sources together with physical evidence, you start getting a reliable – or *almost* reliable – picture.'

I ask other questions, but turn up nothing of value.

I also ask Katie to show me the dig itself in detail. It doesn't take long. The main part of the site is only about sixty metres in either direction. The site has already been explored once, so Charteris's project was only ever about adding depth and texture to what was already well understood in scholarly terms. With Charteris dead, Katie tells me that the whole project is probably doomed.

'You can't take it over?' I ask.

'No.'

Katie's 'no' is abrupt, almost rude, but I don't enquire further.

Instead, she stands where a Great Hall once stood. Waves her arms as she reconstructs the way things were. She has her ski stick loose in her hand as she does so. Whatever her mobility issue is, it doesn't affect her each and every minute.

She shows me the dig too. Rectangles of ground pegged out

with orange string. One of the trenches still has little plastic markers showing where the most recent finds were located.

If there's a clue here, I'm not seeing it.

Back to the Portakabin. Look at that lump of old stone, lost in its tangle of wet grass. I ask why it, alone of all the finds, was left out of the cabin.

'It's heavy,' says Katie, doing her stupid-question voice. 'We worried it would break the shelves.'

'And if we get this thing into a lab, would you be able to tell me where it came from? I mean, specifically, not just "somewhere in north or mid Wales".'

'Well that's a question for a geologist, really. But yes, I can certainly find out.'

'Yes please.'

That leaves us the problem of how to shift the rock into Katie's car. I can't lift it on my own and she doesn't offer to help. So we wait around until a dog-walker passes by and we prevail upon him to do the manly thing, which he does, eyes crossed with effort. We thank him by smiling prettily in my case, and looking skinny but somehow warlike in Katie's.

Katie says she'll get the stone's origin defined as soon as she can.

'Thanks.'

'Sorry, by the way. I was a bit sharp.'

I shrug. Give her another smile: they're free.

And, strangely, for all Katie's jerkily variable fierceness, I think she's already helped. We've already checked the Police National Computer for other archaeologists suffering violent deaths.

Nothing.

Historians suffering violent deaths.

Nothing.

Thefts of archaeological materials.

Yes, a few hits, but nothing of interest.

43

But I wasn't thinking properly. Katie's earlier comment about the importance of manuscript sources made me realise there is a whole category of crime we just haven't looked at.

Thefts of manuscripts? Piles of old paper? I never thought to check.

I drive, too fast, back to the office.

The rest of that day, a Thursday: nothing.

Friday, ditto.

Work Saturday and Sunday, both. Take orange juice and some vaguely healthy salad box into the office at nine. Sip, work and nibble, till the streets outside are sunk into some neon orange gloom.

Sip, work, nibble – and get nothing.

On Monday morning, frustrated and losing confidence, I try a search I've tried before, wanting to double-check myself. The screen fills with results and, up at the top, this:

CRIME: Burglary
VICTIM: Diocese of Bangor
ADDRESS: Bangor Cathedral
DATE: 7 March 2016
PROPERTY STOLEN: Old papers, various.

For a moment, I can't figure out why I haven't seen this before. I might, in my tiredness, have missed something lower down the list, but I wouldn't, surely, have missed the topmost result.

Then I realise the North Wales Police have only just uploaded the data. And why not? On the polician Richter Scale, the theft of 'old papers, various' hardly rates a tremor.

But the date. That's what really catches my eye. The burglary took place just a week or so before Gaynor Charteris's head was made so bloodily separate from Gaynor Charteris's body. I feel the tingle of the discovery. A wash of cold that dances in my cheeks and fingertips.

I call the officer who logged the crime.

He's not interested. He says, 'The papers? I don't know. Just junk, I think. The cathedral people were pissed off because someone broke a lock. They had to report the incident to claim on their insurance.'

Junk.

But the thefts from Dinas Powys were junk too and I get my not-very-interested Gwynedd copper to give me a number for the cathedral librarian, Aled Owen.

Call him.

Owen is probably a good human being and one more likely to be summoned before the Holy Throne than I am, but, Lord help me, the man is boring. Just talking to him makes me want to push plastic forks into my eyes.

'The papers that were stolen. Do you have a detailed catalogue of what was taken?'

A long answer. One that tells me about trying to get funding to computerise an old card-index system.

'Sorry. I don't care about your funding issues. I asked if you have a detailed catalogue of what was taken.'

'Well, *no*, as I was telling you, we were hoping to *get* the funding so we could start to *build* a proper record-keeping system. Because the project *wasn't* completed, we have only the card-index system that was here before.'

I had one of those fruit salad boxes for breakfast and the black plastic fork is still there, a dark little devil-trident that winks evil at me.

I pick the thing up and start pressing it into my left hand.

'That card-index,' I say, as the tines of the fork bend whitishly back. 'It listed each one of the documents that was taken, yes? And you have the index cards themselves, yes?'

'Yes, the index cards were filed away. You know, the old-fashioned little wooden drawers. They're nice to use,

45

actually, if you're present in the building. But so much research now takes place online—'

'Do you have the cards, yes or no?'

'Yes, we do, but—'

'OK, and do the cards record every single one of the documents that had been present before the theft? That's another yes-or-no question, by the way.'

'Well, it's *not* quite like that. It's *partly* yes, *partly* no. It's the diocesan system, you see. The way documents were originally collected.'

'Mr Owen, I'm investigating a murder. A woman down here had her head cut off by someone wielding a reproduction broadsword. The victim also had three Iron Age spears plunged into her chest and her head was left sitting on top of a table in her living room. The murderer is still at large. OK? Now I'm going to ask you a question and you're going to answer it with a "yes" or a "no". No other words allowed. Do you understand?'

'Look, I don't think you have to be like that. I'm only—'

'You mean, "Yes." The answer to my question was "yes".'

It takes a little longer, and I have to go on pronging my hand until I get my answers, but the upshot is that the cathedral library had a complete catalogue of all its own materials, new and old. But there'd been a recent programme of retrieving older documents from the various parishes in the diocese, so that everything could be held and accessed centrally. Those parish documents had, in most cases, never been indexed in any way. Many of them were still sitting in the same stacks that they'd arrived in. And it was the parish documents, some of them, which had been stolen. The cathedral documents – the more obviously interesting targets – had been left untouched.

'Good. That's helpful,' I say, gingerly removing the fork and looking at the three dark-purple blood spots that it's left behind. 'And do you know which parishes had their

46

documents stolen? That's another "yes" or "no".'

'Yes.'

'Good. And are you able, please, to supply me a list of those parishes?'

'Yes.'

Owen has been so good for so long that he lets himself off the leash again and starts promising to get a letter to me as soon as possible.

I tell him to fuck off with the letter. Tell him to use email like everyone else.

I don't use the phrase 'fuck off' but I do get close.

I say that 'as soon as possible' has to mean he starts work right now this minute and means he doesn't finish until he actually sends me the email.

He tells me about some bit of diocesan business which is going to occupy him for most of this afternoon. I start telling him, in detail, about the way our pathologist thinks Gaynor Charteris's neck was first cut with a sharp-bladed knife, then hacked off with a sword. Tell him how many litres of blood we estimate are still gluing up the pile of Charteris's hand-knotted Persian carpet. Ask him if his stupid meeting is more important than finding the killer.

'No.'

'No? Your meeting is less important?'

'Yes.'

'Good. So you will tell your colleagues that your assistance is required in the course of a murder investigation and you will not be able to help them, not in one single detail, until we have what we need. Is that agreed?'

It is. Hosanna and hallelujah, it is. He promises to work on my list and get it to me as soon as possible.

Promises and delivers.

A list of parishes, in north and mid Wales. In most cases, very little data on what documents were stolen but – helpfully

– names and contact info for the relevant local rectors, who presumably know a little more.

I'm about to start hitting the phone, when another thought comes to me. I turn to Wikipedia, the source of all fine detective work, and start looking up individual parishes.

And when Katie phones, at four that afternoon, with news of what her geologists have found, I say, 'Let me guess.'

'What?'

'I'm going to take a wild guess and say your cross comes from Llanymawddwy. That village, or somewhere close by.'

'How do you spell that?'

Katie's English ear takes a moment to process my impatient answer, and I can hear her typing the place name into her computer.

Then she chuckles softly down the phone. Says, 'The upper Dyfi valley. That's where my geologist buddies place this stone. This Llanywhateveryousaid is slap bang in the area they were talking about.'

There's a shocked pause. A pause lit by the dull amber glow of a dead trail turning live.

Katie: 'How did you know?'

I tell her. About the cathedral theft. 'Nine different parishes saw their records vanish, but some of those were Victorian churches in urban parishes, or rural churches that go back further but not *that* much further. But the church at Llanymawddwy is old, old, old.' I click around until I get the Wikimedia entry on the church, double-checking what it says. 'Saint Tydecho established the church in 525 AD,' I say. 'That's just a century after the Romans left. That's pretty much the same time as your Dark Age nobleman was sitting in Dinas Powys worrying about hairy-arsed barbarians.'

I don't know what the hell is going on, but the Dark Ages are alive again. Alive and killing.

6

I ask Katie if she's happy to accompany me up to Bangor. She says yes.

We're to leave first thing in the morning and Logic, that noble angel, says that I should finish up my ordinary office tasks, get myself home and washed and packed and ready.

And I love Logic, her and Sweet Reason. Those two good angels once helped me out of a deep, dark trough of illness. Held my hand through three difficult years at Cambridge. Have walked with me throughout my career in CID. I owe them love and fealty, and I honour them both.

But, poor dears, they can be simpletons.

Logic says 'Go home, get ready,' and Sweet Reason, nodding, agrees. But they've forgotten who I am, what I need. And, before I even really know it myself, I'm zooming up North Road. To the hospital. To the mortuary.

Arrive just before the place starts to close for the night. Flash my warrant card around. Sound all grim and policey. 'Sorry, some further investigations are needed,' I say. 'Yes, I know it's last minute,' I say. And, 'Yes, of *course*, this has been sanctioned by the SIO,' I say.

People want to go home and I tell them, 'Go home.' I'll lock up, no problem. Watch as a mortuary attendant, treating me like an idiot, shows me not once but twice how to turn the main lights off, how to operate the door-exit button.

Someone lays Gaynor Charteris out on a gurney. Both

parts of her. The head and the body. Like a brutally explicit demonstration of Cartesian dualism.

Other people clatter with keys and lights and coats and desk drawers and procedures. Someone, a new person this time, comes again to check that I know what to do on exit.

I do. *Yes.* I do, I do, I do. I do.

Please go away, or better still – sorry, and all that – just fuck off.

Eventually, blessedly, everyone fucks off.

Logic and Sweet Reason depart sadly, their bare feet pattering away down the hospital corridor, wings bright beneath the halogens.

I'm alone with Gaynor Charteris.

I'm not here to examine her. To ask tedious questions of her remains. I just want to be with her.

Silent, together, and alone.

I get a wheelie chair. Adjust the height till I can sit up close to Gaynor's chill arm, her bloodless chest.

Swivel her head so it's looking at me. Tilt it back and wedge it with a wad of paper towels so she's looking up into my eyes. Hold her hand. Feel that bloody stump of neck. Stare into her glassy, unseeing eyes.

Feel the peace of it. This infinite peace.

That, and the infinite strangeness.

Was there a *moment*? I always wonder that. Is there ever an exact moment of death? One microsecond you're there, the next you're definitely not? People, even doctors, always talk as though that partition exists, but personally I doubt it. I suspect that death creeps over us more gradually than that: an ever-dimming sunset, not a sudden rush into night.

When I die – die properly, I mean – I'd want to feel the whole process. I'd want my ordinary seconds to expand, suddenly, to hours, so that I could watch, one by one, as my cells figured out that things weren't working any more. As, one by one, they drew the curtains, flipped the lights, slipped quietly away into the dark. It seems wrong, somehow, that you wait your whole life for this one unimaginable lightshow, this never-to-be-repeated magic trick – and then, *biff, bam, boom!* – the show's over, leaving nothing but the night that has no morning.

I sit and think these thoughts.

Don't always think, even. Just sit.

Me and Gaynor Charteris, her head and her stump. Watching a violet evening fade to indigo. Wait till no light enters except a vague starlight, the glow of neon.

Charteris and I merge a little. Become one and the same.

Dead nobodies in this palace of corpses.

I feel something of Gaynor herself, of course. I always do. Less sadness than I normally get. More a brisk *tsk* of annoyance. An impatience at being kept rudely away from her precious dig. Someone has cleaned up her hair, unfortunately, but we don't mind too much.

We share a sense of bustle. Love of the past and the open skies.

But that's not the biggest thing, the most insistent. The feeling that keeps on intruding is an odd one: a sense of fakery. Of fraud.

That swift, sharp slitting of Gaynor's throat was done with some modern implement. A very sharp kitchen knife, even. That was the stroke which killed her.

The pathologist confirmed as much in his report, but I saw it for myself when I first encountered the corpse. See it clearly now, even in this neon-tinted dark. The clean, effective slit. The brutally repeated butchery that followed.

The sword, the spears, the severed head: that set-up had a superficial grandeur to it, but the closer you look, the cheaper it seems.

A designer dress remade as a high-street cheapie.

Costume jewellery in place of diamonds.

Increasingly, I realise, I feel angry and disappointed on Charteris's behalf. If you're going to do a job, then do it properly. The spears, we both like very much. (Except: why the broom handles? Why old spears on such tactlessly modern shafts?) And the sword itself: well, perhaps we can forgive a reproduction. But a kitchen knife? A *kitchen knife*?

No, we can't allow that. Don't accept it at all.

I'm troubled enough by that damn knife that I can't settle. Can't tumble into that dreamless union with the dead which has been central to most of my cases.

By ten o'clock, I simply feel angry and unsettled. I give Charteris a parting kiss on her stony forehead, then tuck her up again in her body bag. Shove her back in her stainless steel fridge.

A little row of green lights tells me that everything's fine. This meat won't spoil.

I think briefly about meeting some of the other corpses here. Getting to know them. I did that before once, when I was young and foolish, but I'm wiser than that now.

Or, if not wiser, then hungrier.

When did I last eat? Did I actually have lunch today? Or breakfast?

It is possible that I forgot.

I close up and let myself out.

Don't get lost. Don't walk into any walls or mistake broom cupboards for exits.

Find my car surrounded by empty asphalt and a skitter of night.

Switch on. Heating up. Mortuaries are cold and I never remember that before I enter.

Turn my phone on. A shower of texts. Missed calls. Voicemails. Most are boring. Some aren't.

Chief among the non-boring ones: a succession of texts

and calls from my friend, Ed Saunders. We were meant to be having dinner tonight. He'd cooked for me. Waited in for me.

I am a terrible person.

I am a useless, stupid, forgetful idiot who favours a slightly unsatisfactory communion with the dead over what would have been a highly satisfactory communion with the living.

I call Ed. Tell him I'm an idiot. (He knows.) Tell him I'm a terrible human. (He knows.) Tell him I'm very sorry and if it would put anything right, I'll come over right now and let him tell me how terrible I am to my face.

'It never makes any difference, Fi, no matter how much I tell you. But sure, why not come over for a swift drink?'

Twenty-five minutes says my sat-nav. A mere eighteen says I and, sure enough, eighteen minutes later, I arrive in Penarth, Alfa Romeo friskily panting, to be greeted by a slice of homemade stilton and broccoli quiche with a fresh-tossed salad and some buttery new potatoes.

I say sorry again.

Ed says, 'You told me you had a case.' He means a murder case. 'And I know what that means.' It means I become more than usually terrible.

It's good having friends. Good, in particular, to have friends who don't desert you just because (a) you were once their former lover and (b) they've hooked up with a perfectly nice, if annoyingly glossy, woman called Jill who is looking increasingly settled and like The One.

Ed and Jill and I socialise together reasonably often and Jill's mostly got past her early territory-marking prickliness, presumably because she's sniffed me over, tossed me between her paws, scrutinised her mate through slitted, lethal, emerald eyes, and determined that I'm no threat to her glossy loveliness. But, though Jill has mostly accepted me, our new trio – things aren't the same as, or as good as, our old Ed-'n'-Fi evenings and it's nice to have a scrap of the old times back.

I scrunch my eyes up, trying to remember why Jill isn't here tonight.

'Business trip?' I say, voice rising into uncertainty.

'Spot on, Fi.'

He does a look at me which, I think, is asking me to remember anything else about what he told me two days ago when we set this evening up.

'Um, New York? She's . . . meeting someone?'

It's stupid, but when I was sitting with Gaynor Charteris, I had problems connecting with her properly, because the pair of us were too annoyed about that damn kitchen knife. Now here I am with my oldest, bestest friend, and I'm having trouble connecting properly with him because I keep missing Charteris, her physical presence. That way that children sit with a teddy bear on their lap or pulled into their tummy: I want the same, except with Gaynor's head. Want to feel that stony chill against my skin.

I find myself looking from side to side, checking vaguely to see if that head is somewhere in the room. As though in my absent-mindedness I might just have brought it along with me, leaking slightly through an old plastic shopping bag.

I don't know if Ed notices, but if he does, he doesn't mind.

'Yes, New York. She's looking to set up an office over there. Exciting stuff.'

Is it?

I spend my time sitting with corpses and chasing murderers. *That's* exciting.

Ed, a clinical psychologist of insight and compassion, spends his life helping child and teenage crazies. I don't know if his job is exciting exactly, but rewarding, certainly.

And Jill, a psychologist herself, quit her clinical work to set up a business that – and I never quite understand the details – uses psychometric data to help big companies understand what sort of workers to hire, which ones to reward and (I guess) which ones to fire. She lives in Bath, has an office in London, travels a lot and is now, obviously, trying to replicate her success in the United States.

Is that exciting? I don't know. Maybe for Jill, but definitely not for me. Not for Ed either, I wouldn't think, but maybe when you get this close to someone, you have to merge your values a little.

Anyway. I say what I think are the right things and Ed says things back and asks about my case and I tell him about severed heads and kitchen knives and Iron Age hill forts refortified against the barbarian tide.

I tell him, 'You're English. An Anglo–Saxon. If I were a Dark Age Briton, I'd probably want to lop your head off. Sorry and all that, but that's just the way it is.'

Ed nods gravely and gets Welsh goats' cheese and a cold pear from his fridge and we eat both things and watch a bit of TV, then Ed yawns, and I take the hint, and stand at his door saying sorry, again, for messing up this evening, and he says, again, not to worry and closes his door.

I drive home. In my dreams that night, Gaynor Charteris and I keep looking at the neatly incised soft tissue at the front of her neck and saying, 'A kitchen knife! They used a kitchen knife!'

7

The next morning. Pick up Katie, from a student-share house on Cathay's Terrace. She doesn't seem weird today. No foot-draggy thing. No ski stick. No pointless snippiness.

I start driving.

Katie fiddles with her phone and says, 'In current traffic, we'd probably better head out east. The best route goes via Shrewsbury. Or, actually, it's probably fastest up the M5/M6. Just hammer up the motorway, then the M56 to Chester and on from there.'

I don't say anything. Drive north.

When Katie figures out that I'm not driving east, she says, 'This isn't right.'

'Katie. I'm Welsh. We're driving from the capital of Wales to what is, effectively, the capital of north Wales. You hairy-arsed barbarians might think it's fun to go driving through your Anglo–Saxon lowlands full of our plundered villages and stolen cattle just because your roads are a bit faster, but I'm going to follow a route that stays in my own country and I don't give a damn if it takes a little longer.'

Katie laughs and shrugs.

After a bit, she says, 'Slave.'

'What?'

'Slave or foreigner, but I prefer slave.'

'What?'

'You say you're Welsh, but *Welsh* is an English word,

deriving from the Anglo–Saxon *wealas*, which means *slave* or *foreigner*. So if I'm a barbarian, you're a slave.' She glances at me to see if she's annoyed me enough, then adds, contentedly, 'And your cattle tasted really nice.'

I don't have a genius answer to that, so we just drive up into the hills that once stopped the hairy-arses from driving my people into the sea, and the beauty calms us, and Katie fiddles around until she's got her phone plugged into the car music system and has it playing stuff much cooler than anything I ever listen to.

We chat.

She tells me about herself. Home Counties parents. Girls' private school, then Oxford. Two brothers doing boring jobs in the City. She had no interest in any of that, her passion for archaeology shining bright and clear.

'And after your Ph.D.? You'll become an academic, is that the plan?'

'The *plan*, slave? Yes, that's the *plan*.'

I don't know why that question gets a snippy response, but I don't care.

We drive – slowly – through our green hills until even Katie's eccentric temper is softened by the drive.

We get to Bangor.

The cathedral, the library, Aled Owen.

He takes us to the site of the break-in. There's some security, yes, but cathedral quality only, which means a thick oak door with an elderly, and now broken, lock.

I inspect the cupboard from which the papers were taken. An ordinary wooden cupboard. Bare pine shelving, whitened with age. Papers sitting in stacks above little handwritten labels, denominating the diocese's various parishes. Saint Afran, Saint Beuno, Saint Cwfan, Saint Cybi, Saint Edern, Saint Iestyn, Saint Illtyd and so on.

Tydecho, the poor brute, occupied a fair chunk on the

lowest shelf, and it was the bottom one, plus most of the one above it that got stripped.

I say, 'How much paper was there here? How high were the piles?'

Owen blathers.

I only half-listen, but it seems that Tydecho's piles would, together, have amounted to perhaps three or four feet high in total. The other piles were all lower and often much lower. Tydecho had so much, just because the church was old and remote. The various disasters which swept so regularly over Bangor's stony walls never really bothered the good citizens of Llanymawddwy, so it just stood there and accumulated documents as thrones tumbled and centuries passed.

'How often is this room used?' I ask. 'How often is someone physically present?'

That's not a yes/no question, so Owen's answer starts to bore me before the end of his first sentence, but it's as you'd expect. Papers are stuffed in here to get them out of the way. Almost no one ever looks at them.

I inspect the shelves closely. On hands and knees.

'When you reported the theft, did the police dust for prints?'

'Prints?'

'Fingerprints, fingerprints, fingerprints. Did the police dust for prints?'

Owen, looking scared, does his good-boy voice again. 'No. Not that I know. And I would, yes, yes, I would have known.' He pauses. Realises that wasn't a one word answer and adds – low, humble voice – 'Sorry.'

'Are these shelves cleaned? On the inside, I mean. Does a cleaner clean the interior of these shelves?'

Owen doesn't know and doesn't know how to express his not knowing in a way that won't make me bite, but I sniff the shelves up close. Nose touching the bare wood. There's some fake honey-wax scent there and an undernote of bleach.

'Before the break-in. Was that outer door normally locked? During an ordinary working day, I mean.'

'No. It was locked at the end of the day, then opened again when people came in in the morning. The thieves came overnight.'

The window looks out on to a little courtyard. A young curate is talking to a middle-aged woman on a bike. An electrician leans against his van, phone to his ear.

There are some modest attempts at security that I can see – a burglar alarm, a camera – and I go to talk to whoever looks after those things. Katie stays behind, fiddling with her phone.

I get nothing useful.

We leave. Eat sandwiches.

Katie asks, 'Why did you want to know about cleaning?'

'DNA. Cleaning products will destroy any traces. Especially bleach.'

'So. No clues?'

I find a bit of roasted aubergine in my sandwich and eat it with my fingers.

Katie may know a lot about archaeology, but she knows bugger all about detective work. Who would break in to that apology for a library, when you could just walk right in? No lock, no staff, no valuables, no security.

'Clues don't always look like clues,' I tell her.

We take the coast road to Llanymawddwy.

8

Caernarfon.

Porthmadog.

Dolgellau.

Katie uses her phone to give me her version of a briefing on Saint Tydecho.

'*Formerly one of the most venerated saints in Britain.* Humph, don't know if that's true. *Strongly associated with his Mawddwy heartland.* However the hell you pronounce that. *Sixth-century saint*, yes. A tough cookie too. *Said to have been present at the battle of Camlan* . . . blah . . . Lots of stuff about holy maidens, sacred wells, giant oxen, mountain fairies, some dodgy links to King Arthur, healing statues.' She looks up from the screen. 'Do you actually know what we're looking for?'

'No.'

Welsh hills, slow roads.

The purple-rust colour of dead bracken and cropped bilberry bushes. Frost-whitened grass. Grey rock and falling water.

Katie finds a number for the vicar of Llanymawddwy, George Bowen. Asks him to meet us at the church. He says yes.

We arrive after six on a rain-sodden evening. In the west, rainclouds and gleams of silver. A low grey church. A churchyard shaggy with grass.

In the church itself, a light is on.

I say, 'Bowen's here, is he?'

Katie: 'No, ten minutes, he says.'

A tarmac path leads to the church's main door, but there's a line of footprints in the long grass round the side. Stems bent. Their beads of silvery rain trodden into the deep green-brown of the root.

People are allowed in churchyards, of course. And though this would be an odd time to lay flowers on a grave, people sometimes choose odd things. Or perhaps there's a shortcut through to something at the back. Or—

We walk round the side of the church, following the footsteps.

The trail leads up to the vestry door, which has been forced open, wood splintered at the lock.

I see it before Katie does. Halt her with a hand on her arm. Silently gesture her back.

We move rapidly to the mouth of the churchyard.

I make a call. North Wales Police, using the 999 operator.

'I'm Detective Sergeant Fiona Griffiths from South Wales. Requesting an Armed Response Unit immediately to the church at Llanymawddwy.'

The operator maintains her professionalism, but a note of surprise creeps in anyway.

'Confirm, you want an ARU?'

'Yes. Suspects may be armed and very dangerous.'

'ARU requested for you.'

'How long?'

'To Llanymawddwy? We'll do what we can.'

'Which means?'

'Hold please.'

I hold.

A mountain breeze blows. Some rain falls. Clouds move and change shape.

Then: 'We've got nothing in Dolgellau, sorry. We're looking at forty minutes, minimum, from Oswestry.'

'*Forty* minutes?'

'Minimum.'

'Well, make sure they've got their clown noses on and their squirty bow-ties. I mean, we wouldn't want to scare any fucking criminals, would we?'

'Sergeant, we don't have units any closer. Do you want to cancel the ARU?'

'No.'

'We can get regular uniformed officers to you in maybe fifteen, twenty minutes.'

'Please, yes.'

Another short hold, then: 'Two patrol cars *en route*. Do you require other services?'

She means fire or ambulance.

'No.'

She takes some more details and I ring off.

As all this is happening, a dirty Land Rover has pulled up in the lane beyond. From it: George Bowen. Dirty jeans. Boots. A waxed coat, worn open. A thick woollen jumper, that you'd call green, in theory, except really you can't describe it except by calling it the colour of moss and wood bark and lichen and old gates and Welsh valleys and damp springs. A clerical collar mounted in a black shirt peeps, just about, from the top.

Fifty-something, perhaps. Stocky. That Welsh build that runs to girth more than height. Grey-haired, but sparkling eyed.

He bounces up to us, checks his hands and wipes them a couple of times on the wet grass before delivering a bone-crunching handshake.

'Sorry,' he says. 'You caught me lambing. I'm sometimes smarter than this. At least, that's what I tell my bishop.'

I interrupt. Tell him about the break-in.

'A break-in? There's nothing to take.'

'I'm not so sure.'

The churchyard gate has a few steps leading up and a stone entrance arch too narrow to admit a vehicle.

I say, checking my memory, 'The vestry door. It opens outwards, yes?'

'Um, let me think,' says Bowen, as his arms remember the motion. 'Yes. Yes, it does.'

'Is there any way to get a vehicle into the churchyard?'

'Round the back, there's a hedge that's not so amazing. You could probably just go through it.'

'Good.'

My Alfa Romeo isn't going to love anything involving Welsh fields in March, but Bowen's Land Rover won't give a damn.

I gesture at it and say, 'Do you mind? Katie, please get back in my car and do nothing.'

She stays where she is and says, 'It's OK,' like I was inviting her to shelter from the weather.

'It's not fucking OK, Katie. I am a police officer and my first duty involves the protection of civilians. Get into that car, with the lights off, and do nothing.'

She rolls her eyes at me, but does as I ask.

Bowen fires up the Land Rover. Drives round the back: not the fastest process, because we have to fiddle with a couple of gates that want to stay glued up with mud and bailing twine.

When he gets us to the bit of hedge that he was talking about – some thin hawthorn saplings protected by a poor bit of wire fencing – I say, 'OK. I'll take it from here.'

'Gears are a bit cranky. I don't mind driving.'

'If I get hurt, I'm doing my duty. If you do, I've messed up.'

He gets out. I slide over into the driver's seat.

I go at the hedge with a bit of speed and it's not man enough to stop me. I can feel a tangle of wire dragging on something beneath the car, but it's not my car and I don't care.

I drive in low gear over the hummocky churchyard, trying to miss the graves. At some point, there's a hideous metallic twang and jolt, but the drag of wire is no longer present.

Still don't care.

Roll up to the vestry door.

Ram it shut.

In the split-second before impact, the door moves as though to open. That could be the wind, but I don't think so. I think whoever's inside heard the sound of my motor and wanted to know what was happening. There's the smallest of small chances that I managed to trap or disable the arm of whoever was opening the door, but I somehow doubt it.

I slide down beneath the dashboard in case any bullets come blasting through the door, but no bullets, no spatter.

Feeling a bit foolish, I get out of the car. Bowen, tramping over the wet grass, comes to join me.

'What now?'

'We wait. See if the intruders can get out faster than we can get reinforcements.'

We stand at the church's west end. Bowen looks down the north wall, while I keep an eye on the south.

Nothing happens on my side. Then, after a minute or two, the sound of breaking glass summons me over to Bowen's. A window has been punched through. Someone is beating out the jags of remaining glass with a leather-gloved hand.

I say to Bowen, 'Your voice is stronger than mine. Can you yell "Police"? Tell them the building is surrounded and they're to remain where they are.'

Bowen does so in the kind of bellow that could carry over two hills in the blast of a westerly gale.

Whoever's inside takes no notice.

Bowen's look is thunderclouds cut about with lightning.

64

'Technically,' he says, 'that's my bloody window.'

A metal ladder lies alongside the church wall. Staying low, Bowen goes to get it.

From the broken window, a man's head emerges. Bowen brings the ladder hard down over his shoulders, a good old bash that yields a dull metallic clang.

The man swears, disappears, then the snout of a shotgun emerges, and Bowen comes back towards me a lot faster than he left. We shelter behind the slab of a tombstone.

'What now?'

I shake my head.

Nothing.

Shotgun versus shouting: shotgun wins. They teach you that in the police.

Two men climb out of the window. One gun between the two of them. Dark jeans. Dark coats. Their faces are uncovered, though they keep their hands up to their faces. One of them wears a small black rucksack. Aside from very short, darkish hair, approximately medium build and height, I can't really tell anything useful.

The two men look uncertain of their next move.

Bowen, idiot man, leaps up and roars, 'Get the hell away from my church. And drop the damn gun while you're at it.'

He tugs the front of his jumper down and juts his chin up to make his dog-collar more visible.

The shotgun swivels again, towards us, towards Bowen. He freezes a moment, but doesn't move.

The gun fires, but it's a warning shot, nothing more. A blast over his head and into the night.

The two men run in the opposite direction. Towards the broken hedge, the fields and hills beyond. Bowen still doesn't move and I stand up next to him.

'That was stupid,' I say, but in a way that says I'm pleased he did it anyway.

He shrugs. 'Better them in the hills than waving that damn thing in the village.' He grins at me, white teeth in the gloom. 'Anyway, no one shoots a vicar. It's one of the rules.'

I call the Emergency Control Centre again. Update them.

Bowen gets Katie and unlocks the church.

By this time: some actual police cars arrive – with lights and everything. Another ten minutes and we have some armed policemen, stabbing torchbeams into the dark and hoping beyond hope they get a chance to play with their toys.

I do what I have to do, but all this activity comes too little, too late. In the absence of some real fluke, the men are gone.

I enter the church.

It's small and cold, the chills of winter preserved in thick stone walls. Even with the lights on, the place is dim, clerical.

Katie is up by the altar, somehow suiting this setting better than either Bowen or me. She flashes an unreadable look down the nave. Bowen calls attention to a smear of blood on the broken window and I get one of the uniforms to call in forensics.

Which leaves the question of what the hell the men were doing here in the first place.

The church seems tidy enough, but also empty. There's just not much here.

'Anything missing?' I ask Bowen.

'Not that I can see, no. Church doesn't get much use now.'

Behind a curtain at the back, we find a clutter of empty vases and flower arranging stuff. An elderly Christmas crib collection that looks like it would frighten more children than it would entertain.

We go to the vestry.

An overhead light. A peg with clerical robes and an old scarf. Ecclesiastical clutter.

'Do you know what we're looking for?' asks Bowen.

'No. Just anything old.'

'Fifth or sixth century,' says Katie. 'Tydecho's era, basically.'

'There's nothing here like that. There was a lot of stuff when I arrived here. Old papers and the like, just kept a heap in that box.' He points to a polished wooden box, nineteenth century maybe, that hangs on the wall. 'They seemed in reasonable condition, but I worried about moths or woodworm, or I don't know, whatever eats paper. So I got some plastic storage cases, added some silica gel – you know, to protect against damp – and bunged them up on that cupboard. The theory was I was going to sort through them at some point, but . . .' He shrugs, the way you shrug if you're the rector of a parish now approaching the end of its fifteenth century. 'I was happy enough when the cathedral people said they'd take the lot.'

Katie, taller than me, stands on a chair and looks on top of the cupboard.

'Dust,' she says. 'Spiders. A little piece of cornice.'

'Anything down the back?'

Bowen shifts the cupboard away from the wall and we stare at the filth behind. A thick web of cobweb, fallen plaster dust and flaking paint, dead insects. Some fragments of wood.

Inside, everything clean and tidy enough, but nothing of interest.

We look in the box where the documents had been stored before Bowen moved them.

Nothing.

A sheet of newspaper covers the bottom. The paper is a local thing dated 1953. The front page story: a fire at a local fish restaurant.

A theft of Tydecho's papers from the cathedral and now a second break-in here. You'd have to guess that they were after documents here too. Either because the cathedral documents were missing something, or because the thieves just wanted to double-check they'd got everything there was to be found.

And on Bowen's account, there was nothing here.

Dust. Spiders. A bit of cornice.

We go back into the church itself.

The forensic guy has his blood samples.

'Do you want me to look for prints?' he asks, in a voice that implies the answer 'no' would be welcome.

I shake my head. 'They were wearing gloves.'

A uniform sticks his head through the main door. Tells me that they're close to abandoning the search 'for your suspects'.

I shrug. The light now has failed almost completely. The two men won't be found unless they're the stupidest or unluckiest criminals this side of Oswestry.

The uniform goes. The forensic guy goes. The church lighting somehow just emphasises the darkness. It thickens the air into something yellowey-orange. Gluey.

We regather in the vestry, just because Katie's left her coat there.

Bowen lifts the 1953 fish-restaurant newspaper out of the wooden wall box.

'I suppose that can go.'

He looks glumly at the mess behind the cupboard, knowing that it'll be his job to clean it. Katie looks into the box, now missing its newspaper floor.

Glances once, then looks more sharply.

'No, that's not right,' she says, and starts picking at the bottom with a fingernail.

I already looked under the newspaper and saw just the pale, bleached colour of old pine – pine that has never seen the sun – but that was me being dumb. Me not knowing how to see.

Katie picks at the bottom and it comes away.

A sheet of paper, blank on the upper side, but with writing in clear purplish-black ink on the lower.

Latin text.

A hard-to-read medieval hand.

Bowen stares. I stare. We all stare.

'Katie,' I say, 'This paper? We can get it dated, presumably?'

In the gluey light, she shakes her head.

'No. No, we can't.'

'We *can't*?'

There's something about this light, this thickened silence which makes everything seem slow, unnatural.

'We can't test this paper, because it isn't paper. It's vellum. A dead sheep, basically, scraped clean and stretched out thin.'

She takes the vellum and places it under the best of the light.

'What's this? . . . No, it's nothing. This doesn't look helpful. It's just a record of a grant of some land to the church.' She reads to the end, then confirms her diagnosis. 'What we've got is an old bit of vellum, with some really boring text.'

That leaves us with our original mystery – why would armed robbers come to a place like this? What were they searching for?

But it leaves us also with something more tangible. Something helpful.

Our piece of boring vellum tells us, for sure, that there were once old documents stored in this church. Documents that are now, presumably, in the hands of the thieves.

I still can't tell what's going on here, but I'm now more certain than ever that this strange path is the right one to follow.

Shotguns and vellum.

Churches and saints.

And Gaynor Charteris's severed head watching on with grim pleasure as we pluck at her riddles.

9

There's no more that we can do here in the dying, rain-murkened light. I want to get back to Cardiff, but Bowen insists on giving us something to eat.

Katie, who's hungry, is quick to accept. Bowen extricates his Land Rover and we follow him two miles down the Dyfi, before turning up into a valley, Cwm Cywarch, to a cottage-cum-smallholding hard up against the jut of the hill.

'My wife's place, really, this is. But we prefer it to the vicarage, so we stay up here most of the time. Sixty ewes, she's got, nothing much, but it keeps us busy. *Her* busy, that is. I've got a full-time job and never have to help with the lambing.'

He says that with his 'at least that's what I tell my bishop' face on.

He tells us also that his wife is away at the moment, but he promises us a teenage son whose presence is marked by an audible heavy-rock thumping from upstairs.

Tea, toast, eggs, bacon.

Katie sits at table, with that awkward breathing of hers, intermittent but clearly discernible when it comes. She inspects the vellum as closely as she can, angling it against the light.

I don't know what she's looking for. Don't ask. But I do say, 'The vellum itself. Can we get that dated?'

'Hmm? Yes. Radiocarbon. We can date the vellum and there are things you can do – ink analysis, some palaeographic

70

techniques – to date the text as well.'

I put the vellum, carefully, in a large evidence bag.

Between mouthfuls, I tell Bowen about Charteris. What happened to her. The reason we're here.

'The things people do,' his only comment.

When I'm done eating, I go outside to bring the car up to the front door. In the dark and the rain, however, I fail to see a drainage ditch and, turning the car, drop a wheel into it. Rev stupidly and angrily, knowing that I'll need to be pulled out.

'That damn ditch,' says Bowen, who comes out with a torch. He'll pull me out in the morning, he says but, 'No use trying now.'

Back inside, Bowen says, 'There's a spare room upstairs. If you don't mind sharing.'

We don't and, pinned here for the for night, we talk. Not just about Charteris, but about the investigation more broadly. Its central puzzle: Why would anyone behead Gaynor Charteris for something that happened fifteen centuries ago? For that matter, why would anyone break into a church that has nothing in it?

I don't know. I have no ideas.

I ask Bowen about Tydecho. No reason particularly, except that Tydecho lived long ago and this whole case seems rooted in that dark past.

'Tydecho? Half-saint, half-mad, probably. He was a hermit. Plenty of legends about him, but no question he had a big following in these parts. He's got a few churches dedicated to him round here.'

He shakes his head. Slurps his tea.

Does those things, and adds, 'But look, I know I'm on Tydecho's team and all, but I don't suppose anyone's still interested in him. I'd have to guess they were more interested in his uncle.'

'His *uncle*?'

71

Katie darts a rapier look at Bowen, then says, 'Oh, no. For fuck's sake.'

Bowen looks at Katie, at me, then grins.

'Tydecho's mother was Anna Pendragon. That's not formal history, I suppose, just oral tradition, but oral tradition means something in these parts.'

I'm slow here. Five or ten metres behind the pace.

'Sorry. Tydecho's mother was Anna *who*?'

'Pendragon. Arthur's sister.' Since I'm still not getting it, Bowen adds, 'King Arthur. My Saint Tydecho was King Arthur's nephew.'

My jaw drops, or I think it does. At any rate, I'm dumbstruck and saying nothing, when Katie chips in with her own thoughtful genealogical contribution.

'Yes and, you know, Tydecho was also brother to Robin Hood, father to Cinderella, and grandfather to the fucking Tooth Fairy.'

Bowen looks at me, indicates Katie, and says, 'She's English, isn't she? A little bit *Saesneg*.'

''Fraid so,' I tell him. 'A hairy-arsed barbarian, that's our Katie.'

Bowen grins and pulls at his neck. He doesn't mind Katie's outburst. He's enjoying it.

I say, 'Look, stupid question, but was King Arthur real, yes or no?'

It's Bowen's house. He gets first dibs.

'Yes, probably. We don't know for sure. We don't know *anything* about that period for sure, but Arthur's existence is one of the more solid facts we have.' He shrugs. 'I'm not expert exactly, but since I took over Tydecho's parish, among others, I got interested in our early history. Made a bit of a study of it, I suppose.'

Katie nods in slow agreement, the academic historian joining forces with the skilled amateur.

'Yes,' she says. 'That's about right. King Arthur, Snow White, all seven of the dwarves – including Dippy, Dopey, Loopy and Crazy – that lot, plus the bloody Tooth Fairy. All real.'

'I'm sensing some disagreement here.'

Katie: 'Look, where do you want to start? The Lady in the Lake? The Sword in the Stone? The Knights of the Round Table, for fuck's sake. It's all just medieval invention. I mean, is it pretty? Yes. Romantic? Ditto. Real? No chance. The only people who believe any of that stuff are – sorry, George – cranks and obsessives.'

As Katie talks, Bowen brings wine and glasses. Sets one in front of Katie.

She looks fierce, then apologetic, then turns all Home Counties polite as she says, 'Yes, a glass of wine would be lovely. Sorry for swearing.'

Bowen shrugs. 'I've got a sixteen-year-old son who's into video games and heavy metal. I've got a wife who's an upland sheep farmer. And I've got a parish full of Welsh countryfolk who aren't afraid to voice their opinions. I've heard worse than your swearing, Saxon. I've heard worse.'

I say no to wine, but the others clink glasses and drink. The mood changes. Bowen says, 'Here, let's go through to my study. We'll be more comfortable there.'

We go through. Not huge, but nice. A wide view of a light-twinkled valley. Two walls lined with floor to ceiling bookshelves.

Katie starts looking at book titles. No reason, except that's what people like me and Katie do when we walk into a room with books. After a few seconds, she pulls up abruptly. Darts a sharp look at Bowen.

He says, apologetically, 'I know. A crank and an obsessive.'

I take a look at the titles myself. It takes me longer to figure it out than Katie did, but realise that one whole wall of books is devoted to Dark Ages history and all things Arthurian. Serious books too. Scholarly. Facsimile manuscripts of Old Welsh, Old English and Latin sources.

I'm impressed. Like Katie, I want to know more.

Pointing at the two book-lined walls, Bowen says, 'That wall's reserved for Arthur. That one for God. I try to make sure that God gets more than half my attention, but there are times when Arthur wins.'

Katie says, 'This is a serious collection. Have you published anything?'

Bowen nods. 'A few pieces, yes.' He names the scholarly journals where his work's appeared. 'Early Welsh legend, that's my specialist area, but there's history behind the legend – or so *I* think, anyway.'

Katie realises that, whatever her theoretical differences with Bowen, she hasn't been arguing with an idiot.

She says as much, and we end up divulging everything. About the bit of stone cross which brought us up here. The theft from Bangor.

'And I guess we were right about how that cross came to be in south Wales,' Katie says. 'Tydecho probably wasn't originally from this area. It's more likely that he came from further south. So if, say, Dinas Powys was Tydecho's birthplace, the folks back home might well have wanted a cross to remember him by.'

Bowen nods. 'That's one theory,' he says, in a voice which implies it's a rubbish one.

'What? So you've got anything better?'

Bowen says, 'Well, let's suppose a famous warrior died. The most famous warrior-general of his era or, come to think of it, any era whatsoever. No doubt *he'd* have memorial stones of his own. And personally, I'd say those things were more likely to travel cross-country than if they belonged to a somewhat obscure local saint.'

'What, now you're hypothesising that King Arthur happened to fall down dead in your backyard. *That's* your theory?'

Bowen: 'No, that's not *my* theory. It's in the history books. The *Annales Cambriae*, the Welsh Annals.' And, quoting from memory, says, 'In the year 537, the Annals tell us "*Gueith camlann in qua Arthur et Medraut corruerunt.*"' For my benefit, not Katie's, he translates. 'That's the Battle of Camlann in which Arthur and Medraut – or Mordred – perished.'

'OK,' says Katie. 'OK. So let's suppose that's real history. Let's just say that it is. No one knows where Camlann is supposed to be. There are people who claim it for the River Camel in the West Country. In the north of England, there was a Roman fort, Camboglanna, which—'

Bowen interrupts, swigging wine and enjoying himself. 'Or maybe the Battle of Camlann happened in Camlann. I mean, that has to be quite a strong possibility, doesn't it?'

Katie says, but uncertainly now, 'There *isn't* anywhere called Camlann.'

'Well, it's lost an N, that's true. It's just Camlan, with one N, these days, but you'll find it about two miles down the road there,' Bowen says, jerking a thumb through the kitchen wall. 'You drove past it today.'

Katie, for once, is lost for words.

In the silence that follows, I creep out on a little bridge of conjecture.

'OK, let's just say that Arthur existed—'

Bowen – stirring – nips in to add, 'As all the earliest histories agree he did—'

'And let's say he died here, or somewhere around here. That damn cross might well have been carved from local stone and transported to some other part of the country. Somewhere that had an association with the guy. Yes?'

Katie says grumpily, 'Yes. I mean, if you believe any of that stuff, then yes, that's a plausible theory.'

'And Dinas Powys?' I ask. 'Is there any evidence that links Arthur to that hill fort? Or even just south Wales?'

Katie shakes her head.

Bowen does the same, but he adds, 'Look, the very earliest reference to Arthur is in Welsh. Some of the earliest historical references link him to places in south Wales. I mean, those things fall short of proof, definitely, but if you were betting? You'd bet on him being Welsh. And yes, you'd probably guess he originated a good bit south of here.'

'For example, Dinas Powys?'

'No reason why not.'

Katie, grimacing, says, 'I hate to agree with you, but it would actually be quite a plausible site. You wouldn't get to be a successful warlord unless you were born into the nobility in some way. And that Dinas Powys fort was wealthy, well-connected, well-fortified. If you grew up there, you'd have a strong family recollection of the good times under the Romans. So yes, it's a plausible site.'

Katie and Bowen are thinking about Arthur, but my thoughts are all with Gaynor Charteris.

An archaeologist, brutally murdered.

Some stolen finds.

A burgled library.

Two men – *armed* men – breaking into a church.

This isn't about whether or not Arthur existed. It's about what those men want and why.

I say, 'Katie, what did Gaynor think about all this? About Arthur—'

'Oh, she loved all that. *Loved* it. That picture in her hallway?'

She starts describing it, but I remember it anyway. A pissed-off woman at a loom, a big circular window behind.

Katie says, 'That's the Lady of Shalott. Only that wasn't

a window she was looking at: it was a mirror reflecting the beautiful world of Arthur's Camelot. I mean, that part *is* a myth, of course, but Gaynor loved all of it. The history. The myths. All of it.'

We talk a bit more, but it's bedtime. Bowen takes us upstairs. Shows us a pretty bedroom, with a rose-sprigged double bed and the same roses on the curtains.

Bowen yanks some bedding out from under the bed. 'One of you will have to sleep on the floor, I'm afraid, but you've got everything you need here.'

He shows us the bathroom. Leaves.

The room we're in is built up into the roof and we can hear the drumming of rain on slate, just a foot or two above our heads.

Katie says, '*I'm* not sleeping on the floor.'

I don't care. I really don't. I'd already sort of assumed that, since Katie only came on this trip as a favour to me, I should be the one to take the floor.

But there's something about her needless prickliness that makes me prickle back.

'*I'm* not sleeping on the floor,' I tell her.

She glares at me a second, then says, 'So,' as though we've just come to some sensible adult arrangement.

We get ready for bed.

Katie has a tattoo down the inside of her left arm. In squirly writing, it reads, 'YOLO,' and then, in a very slightly different ink and style, 'If you're lucky.'

I say, 'YOLO?'

Katie: 'You Only Live Once.'

I nod. It wasn't quite like that for me, as it happens, but I'm not going to quarrel.

We head peaceably for sleep in a bed that is easily big enough for the pair of us: the tall, skinny and crabby Katie, the short, skinny and ornery me.

Once in the night, I think, I hear Katie crying softly into her arm. She doesn't know that I'm awake and doesn't seem likely to want my help, so I say and do nothing.

Tomorrow is another day.

10

The next day.

We wake early, rise early. An hour later, I'm on the road again with Katie, porridged up and in a good mood.

Llanbrynmair.

Caersws.

Llandrindod Wells.

Green hills slide past us, a grassy lullaby.

My route is a slightly circuitous route, avoiding Rhayader, for no good reason except that I have some uncomfortable associations with that area.

As we squeeze down Llandrindod High Street, with its weirdly out-of-time collection of Victorian hotels and places of entertainment, I ask about something that's been puzzling me.

'When you told me about the Romans leaving Britain, you said that the native British were afraid of attacks from the Picts and the Scots. The *northern* barbarians, basically.'

'That's right.'

'But that's not where the problems actually came from, was it? I mean, it was your lot we should have been afraid of.'

Her lot: the Angles, Jutes and Saxons. A group that has come to be called 'English' in her language. A group that's still called 'Saxon' in mine.

Katie laughs. 'You don't know? You don't know the story?' Then, seeing my headshake, continues, 'You Celtic–British *were* afraid of the Picts and the Scots. So one of your kings, a guy called Vortigern, decides to take action. He looks around Europe for the hairiest, scariest soldiers available and invited a bunch of them – a bunch of *us*, I should say – over to help. Mercenaries.'

'Ah, and let me guess. That idea didn't turn out so well.'

'Not so brilliantly, no. The Anglo–Saxon fighters looked around, decided they liked this new country and would rather like to have it.'

'Which is exactly what happened?'

'Yes.'

'And Arthur, assuming that he existed . . .?'

'Led the Celtic–British against the Anglo–Saxon invaders. He probably wasn't a crowned king, in fact. Something more like a commander-in-chief . . .'

She trails off, like she's just been bitten by the Thought Wasp.

I keep the car moving. Escape Llandod's sticky traffic and pick up speed again on the road south.

'Katie . . .?'

'Do you have your iPad here? The one with our finds on it?'

I say yes. Where to find it.

She rummages. Finds it. Pulls up the relevant material.

I drive.

Caravans and cottages.

Roads dark with the wash of recent rain.

Wipers on, when passing lorries kick up spray.

Then Katie says, 'Holy fuck.'

Says, 'Can you stop the car?'

Says, 'There's something you need to see.'

I stop.

Pull over onto a bit of verge that isn't quite wide enough for us, so we're sticking out into the main carriageway. I put on my hazard lights, but an approaching horse-transport honks me anyway.

Katie says, 'Are we OK here?'

I wave my hands. Like I care.

Katie does a little double-take, then decides she doesn't care either. She shows me the iPad. Shows me, specifically, the photo of the little seal-box lid, that thing that might be worth £150 if attached to a whole box in good condition but which, as it is, is little more than ancient junk.

Katie says, 'What do you see?'

'Um, I don't know. We thought a bear probably. A wolf maybe, but it's more bear-like, isn't it?'

'I think it's a bear, yes. And over its head? Those marks . . .?'

Marks that look like scratches. Marks that *are* scratches, but is it possible that the scratches conceal some piece of the original artwork?

I look more closely. The photo isn't brilliant. These pictures were only ever taken on phones for easy upload to the project website. The proper analysis and cataloguing hadn't yet begun.

Above the bear's head, there's a kind of horizontal groove and then some deep vertical slashes. I cast my mind back to what Katie was saying just a moment before the Thought Wasp got her.

He probably wasn't a crowned king, in fact.

I say, 'You think this bear is wearing a crown? Yes, you could be right. Now that you say it, I think you're right.'

Katie says in a hollow voice – hollow, shocked, aghast – 'The Bear King. Maybe that's what we found. The seal box of the Bear King.'

I shake my head. A help-me-out-here kind of shake.

'The Bear King. In your language, slave, the language as it was in post-Roman Britain, that would have been *Arto-rīg-ios*. *Arto*, bear. *Rīg*, king. It's thought that the name *Arthur* derived from that root.'

I say, slowly catching up, 'You found Arthur's seal box? That's what it was? The lid to his seal box?'

'And somebody stole it. Killed Gaynor and stole her find. And she never even knew. She never even fucking knew.'

We feel, both feel, the press of something dark and old. Like those ancient Dark Age conflicts have come to life. Are, once again, stalking these damp valleys, leaving bloody footprints behind.

I say, quietly, 'But Arthur never existed, you said. You bracketed him with Snow White and the Tooth Fairy.'

'Yes, but . . .'

'But?'

'Look, most people who go on about Arthur are cranks. I'm not talking about George, just . . . there isn't enough hard historical fact to go on, so people who say Arthur did definitely exist are basically willing themselves into it.'

'But, you're saying, Arthur *could* have existed?'

'Oh yes.'

'Could have, maybe did?'

'Look, think of this courtroom-style. Can you prove his existence beyond reasonable doubt? Answer: no way. But on a balance of probabilities? Is there a reasonable possibility?'

She tails off, not answering her own question. Perhaps she's remembering her over-combative tone last night.

I say, 'Katie?'

She says, whispering, 'It's perfectly possible. People like George would say actually probable. The best explanation we've got. And look, we just don't know much about this era. Truth is, we don't actually *know* much about major figures, even centuries later. Alfred the Great, for instance. I mean, he certainly existed and we know some of what he got up to. But beyond that?' She shrugs. 'We just don't know much. That's not weird. It's history.'

'So King Arthur *could* have existed and *could* have left seal

82

boxes kicking around the fort at Dinas Powys?'

'Yes. He probably wasn't a real king, but yes.'

'And, just possibly, the person who found the first hard evidence of Arthur's existence was beheaded with her own sword?'

Katie doesn't answer but the light of fear and wonder shines in her eyes.

We drive to Cardiff, pursued by Arthur.

11

Work hard.

Collect fragments.

Data that starts to drift in, like those flakes of burned paper that come floating down from a bonfire.

The blood we retrieved from Saint Tydecho's: it was easy enough to retrieve the DNA, but there's no match on the system. No easy wins.

Photo analysis of that seal box: good news. Our analysts think they're able to divide the image into 'original artwork' and 'later scratching'. It's not a perfect job by any means, and these things only ever give you a sense of the probabilities, but when we look at the image with the 'original artwork' only, it's clear what we have. A bear with a crown.

Arto-rīg-ios.

Arthur.

That doesn't prove that Charteris and her team found the seal box of King Arthur. It doesn't even prove she found the seal box belonging to some other person called Arthur. Back then, bears and crowns could have all sorts of other meanings now lost to us.

All the same: Camlan, Tydecho, the crowned bear, that bit of broken cross. A chain of lamps is beginning to light up.

Fragments starting to form a picture.

And one more thing: that vellum. A lab in Oxford has dated the dead sheep in question to some time in the ninth century.

That's not as old as those finds at Dinas Powys, but it certainly confirms that Saint Tydecho was once home to some very old material indeed. Whatever the thieves escaped with could have been even older again.

I remember, too, Bowen's comments about the oral tradition in areas like Mawddwy. Is it not possible that a collection of ninth-century documents could have recorded oral traditions that stretched much further back? Perhaps not merely possible, but *likely*?

I don't know.

I'm still trying to make sense of all this, when Jones calls another case review. No Jackson this time. This one is Jones's gig all the way.

I get ready.

Ready in a Jonesian sense.

Ready with bullet points and executive summaries and – God help me – Powerpoint slides.

I carefully mangle my English too. I concoct excrescences like: 'Reshape current tasking procedure to introduce specific skillsets (e.g. archaeology, antiquities) into overall case management.'

I download and include in my pack as many pointless, pointless, pointless, stupid, stupid, stupid charts and maps and diagrams as I can. Charts that plot the acquisition, theft and sale of antiquities from across the world. A trade that is reckoned to be worth some six billion dollars globally. A trade that, in the Olympics of global crime, stands in bronze medal position, bested only by the superpowers of arms smuggling and drugs.

And pattering behind in the wake of all that money, all a-skitter in that dollar-tossed breeze, walks violence, bloodshed and murder.

Murder in Syria. Murder in Iraq. Murders aplenty in the badlands of Pakistan and Afghanistan. In China and India too, no site too holy or too old to be exploited, robbed or pilfered.

At ten o'clock sharp, we gather. Six of us, plus Jones.

Jones sits formally at the head of our conference-room table. Back straight. Tie knotted into a fatly silked triangle. He has four piles of paper in front of him. Neatly rectilinear, both the piles and their spacing. Also: I suspect the honourable Bleddyn Jones of being a man who likes to make sure that his nails are manicured. They have a palely even gleam I do not love.

He does his stuff.

Bloody Bleddyn, he blithers and blathers.

The blundering Bleddyn, he blubbers and blusters.

That blabbering Bleddyn, he blurts and he blares.

Billows of bullet points –

'Fiona?'

'Sorry?'

'Fiona!'

'Sir?'

'You're paying attention, are you?'

'Yes, sir.'

'You're not taking notes.'

I look around the table. My five co-meetingees have all been writing busily. Their pads all contain at least two or three pages of blue-inked writing. My pad, a very nice feint-ruled yellow pad with pleasingly perforated tear-off sheets, has nothing on it except a little red doodle of a flower-head, which was there before I came into the room.

'I find it's more important to get the major issues straight up here,' I say, pointing to my head. 'I can always fill my notes out afterwards.'

I think Jones would have a go at most subordinates telling him that, but I am somewhat protected by an office reputation which credits me with an almost freakishly good memory. Jones, however, isn't done.

He narrows his eyes in that nasty chemistry-teacher way and says, 'So you could give me a quick summary of what we've just been talking about?'

'Yes, sir.'

He widens his mouth in what is meant to be a be-my-guest sort of smile, except that smiles are meant to be nice things, all peach trees and sunflowers, and this rictus of his looks more like a beast of prey debating whether to start with a leg or a liver.

I smile back. Put as many peaches and sunflowers in there as I can manage.

'So . . .' he says, which is definitely not a sentence.

I say – still peachily – 'Sir?'

So, Fiona, please give me a quick summary of what we've just been talking about.'

'Oh. Oh, I see. OK, um . . .'

I screw up my eyes in a trying-to-get-my-memory-straight sort of way. Beside me, Jon Breakell, an ally, has tilted his pad towards me. He's tapping his pen on the bit I need to read.

That's helpful, certainly, but the truth is that I wasn't entirely successful in blocking Jones's discourse anyway. There's a sort of painful throb in my head which I'd been trying to avoid but if I approach that throb, I find that it's stored much of what Jones was yabbering on about anyway. Between Jon's helpful tapping and my own sort-of recollection, I give enough of an answer to Jones that he's either satisfied or (more likely) doesn't have sufficient grounds to bleat publicly about his irritation.

On we go.

Blurt. Blabber. Blare.

I do take one or two notes now, but mostly extend my red flower into a whole garden of red flowers. Bulbs mostly. Crocuses and daffodils and the elegantly sexy tulips which are just starting to nose up above the ground in Bute Park.

We cover forensics.

Local angles.

Traffic mapping analysis.

Jones talks us through a psychological profile of the murderer which states that 'the perpetrator should almost certainly be regarded as highly disturbed,' and makes me think, *We paid money for that advice. We actually paid money.*

Then it's my turn.

Jones says, 'Fiona. So. You're going to update us on . . . the "historical" angle.'

His tone and his look throws as many inverted commas round the word 'historical' as it can bear before outright collapse.

'Yes, sir.'

I do my stuff.

Start out by summarising the scale of the trade in stolen art and antiquities. 'It's a multi-billion-pound industry,' I say, 'yet there are only about two or three specialist officers in the whole of the UK. Only perhaps five or ten per cent of stolen art or artefacts are ever recovered, and a lot of specialists put the proportion very much lower than that. The internet has made it easier than ever to connect buyers and sellers.'

Jones: 'You're saying that Charteris may have found an artefact of real value? This seal box thing?'

'Um, yes and no.'

Jones: 'What does that mean? You're saying that seal box belonged to Arthur?'

'No. Not that it did. That it could have done.'

'It "could have done"? Seriously?'

'Yes. Look. There's a massive question mark there, obviously, but is it *possible*? Yes.'

'So Arthur existed? You *are* saying that?'

I shake my head. 'That's just not known. It's uncertain. But there are senior historians who'd say, yes, balance of probabilities and all that, but Arthur probably existed. Gaynor Charteris, for one, would have said he most likely did.'

And the stone cross. And Tydecho. And Camlann. And the seal box. And a Dark Age British nobleman sitting amidst the ramparts of Dinas Powys and thinking about the world that was lost.

Jones has no real idea how to pursue this line of questioning. For once, I can't blame him.

So he tries, 'So let's say your man Arthur existed. And let's say this *is* his seal box . . .?'

I shake my head.

I have no answers.

I say, 'Look, if we could be *sure* that this seal box *actually* belonged to Arthur, then of course it would be valuable. Maybe insanely valuable. But . . .' I shrug, and here's the rub. The hard knot of difficulty that lies at the heart of this puzzle.

'Fiona?'

'But without a secure provenance, who's going to pay for the damn thing? I mean, who would pay, I don't know, even fifty grand for something that might well prove to be a piece of junk?'

And that's not even the end of the problems. If you wanted to steal the damn thing, then just steal it. Why kill Gaynor Charteris? And why kill her like *that*?

Jones: 'So you're saying this seal box has no value?'

'Correct. Not unless someone has a way to prove provenance. A way that isn't known to us.'

'And how could anyone prove provenance? I mean, you think that somewhere there's a document that says, "King Arthur's seal box is lying on a hillside above Dinas Powys."?'

'No. No, I don't think that.'

'So you think this "historical angle" can be safely discarded?'

I gape.

No.

No, that is not even remotely what I'm saying.

I say, 'Sorry, sir. The opposite. We followed a trail from Dinas Powys to a churchyard in north Wales. When we got to that church, we found an armed robbery in progress. A robbery which, almost certainly, had ancient documents at its heart.'

'So, in your view, the motive for Charteris's murder?'

'Don't know.'

'Likely perpetrators?'

'Don't know.'

'Actionable next steps?'

'Don't know. Probably wait. Probably . . .'

And I realise, I'm speaking lies. I think I *do* know what's going on here. There are still lots of murky areas, yes. Some huge don't-knows. But these are early stages, and I do, I'm sure, see the thread that connects this whole thing up. You have to look at it all backwards to see it, and I am troubled with a boss who has difficulty even finding the forward view.

'So: two "don't knows" and one "probably wait"?'

I can see I'm losing this. Can see that, almost no matter what I next say, I'm losing this.

I say, 'I think our view of the Charteris murder needs to answer six questions. One, why was she beheaded? Two, why did she have three Iron Age spears plunged into her chest? Three, why were the main archaeological finds stolen? Four, why was the bit of broken cross, the piece that led us to Llanymawddwy, left behind? Five, why was the lock broken at Bangor Cathedral? Six, why were the Llanymawddwy thieves armed with a shotgun?'

'Those are the key questions? In your opinion?'

'Yes, sir.'

'OK, well I can answer two of them right now. Charteris was beheaded because someone wanted to kill her. The lock was broken up at Bangor because someone wanted to obtain entrance. Oh, and here's a third. The thieves were in possession of a shotgun, because they were bloody thieving.'

Jones does his beast of prey, leg-or-liver grin again and rotates it round the table to ensure he gets a harvest of answering smiles. He gets his smiles but, I notice, the smiles are more dutiful than sincere.

I find myself murmuring, 'A press release might be helpful, sir. We could put these historical matters out into the public domain.'

'That's your "actionable next step"? A press release?'

'Yes. See if we get any useful leads from the academic community.'

'And if we do that, you will be content to drop active investigation of this "historical angle"?'

No.

No, no, no, no, no, no.

That's what I think. What I say is, 'Unless new evidence comes to light. Yes.'

He stares at me. There is something cold and dead in the light of his eyes. Something like the touch of a fish belly. The chill of marble.

I think, *Jones actually hates me*. And so soon. I'm used to people disliking me, but it normally takes longer than this. And I don't actually think I've done anything to earn this hatred. Haven't, for once, screwed up my ordinary work, turned up late, sworn at the wrong time, or done any of those other terrible things I too often do. This hatred is just earned by me being me. Or worse: me being a good version of me. The version that Jackson likes, not the one that makes him want to tear my head off.

Ah well. Since me-being-me is, short of a brain transplant, an issue I'm unlikely to fix, I just let Jones's opinion go.

With a hey and a ho, I let it go.

Off we rumble to other things.

Jones has replaced his early Local Nutter theory with its close replacement, the Reasonably Local Nutter theory.

So, instead of looking at nutters within a short drive or bus-route from Dinas Powys, Jones wants to expand the search to all of south Wales. 'Basically, any individual with a history of mental illness and possible violence. If there's psychosis there – hearing voices, that kind of thing – then so much the better. That's our target group. We just need to start mapping movements, interests, Facebook pages, that kind of thing. So, assignments . . .'

He blathers, blurts and burbles on.

I don't listen. It occurs to me that I'm Reasonably Local and have a history of psychotic mental illness mixed in with plenty of violence.

No beheading though. No interest in spears. That's my defence and I'm sticking to it.

We break up.

I tell Jon thanks for helping me out with his pen-tappy thing earlier.

'No worries,' he says. 'I don't think Jones likes you much, though.'

'Not so much, no.'

'Hope he doesn't take over long term.'

'What?'

'From Jackson, I mean. Short term is one thing, but—'

'What?'

He explains. Jackson is going off on a six-month sabbatical but office rumour says it's fifty-fifty whether he comes back at all.

I want to ask how come I don't know about this when Breakell – and apparently everyone else – does, but then the detective in me notes (1) I never read boring adminy email circulars, no matter what the subject line, and (2) I've not always been in the flow of office gossip because, especially recently, I'm often too bored or too irritable to make the effort.

The detective in me draws the obvious conclusion and takes the prompt and necessary action, which involves running straight to Jackson's office. He confirms the worst.

'Something I always wanted to do before I got too old. Rent a boat. Float around the Med. Eat properly. Swim. Lose some of this,' he says, patting his not-very-prodigious belly.

I'm appalled. Genuinely am. I wait four hundred and fifty-three days for my first proper post-Llanglydwen corpse and Jackson has to go running off to some stupid sailing boat. Like, the man prefers floating around in the sun to finding murderers, and *interesting* murderers at that.

I give him my what-am-I-to-do face, complete with hand and arm gestures. If I had a spontaneous expressive dance to match, I'd probably do that too.

I've had only two real, close allies amongst my superior officers, Jackson himself and a senior DI, Rhiannon Watkins. Until about eight months ago, we were, all three of us, working on a major enquiry. An enquiry that I initiated and christened: Operation April.

We had our hands, almost, on a conspiracy so broad and ambitious it took the breath away. And, after a lot work, we secured the evidence that allowed us to bug a major planning session held by the chieftains of that conspiracy.

The meeting took place in summer last year. The setting: a German Schloss-turned-luxury-hotel planted on a windy North Sea coast.

There were six men present. Their names: Owain Owen, Ben Rossiter, David Marr-Phillips, Nick Davison, Idris Prothero, Trevor Yergin. Two of those men – Rossiter and Prothero – are certainly crooks. Rossiter directed a nasty and violent series of kidnaps. Prothero set up a weapons-smuggling enterprise that we busted wide open, only for the damn thing to turn 'legal' at the last. A scatter of murders were involved in both cases, but nothing we could prove.

The six men turned up in casual clothes, bringing the rich man's sporting clutter of golf clubs, tennis rackets and the rest. But they also booked a meeting room, confident in the belief that German privacy laws and their own extraordinary security prowess would make it safe for them to talk openly.

Their confidence was misplaced. We had recently been able to provide the Bundeskriminalamt – the German FBI, effectively – with evidence that enabled them to bug the fuck out of that meeting room. Audio, video. The meeting room the restaurant, the men's bedrooms. Everything.

And we almost got them. That's the thing. We almost got them.

They turned up to their precious meeting room. Faddled around with teas and coffees and sparkling mineral water. Then one of them – Marr-Phillips – said, 'Well, we'll get started, shall we? A couple of apologies for absences – you know who I mean – but we've got enough people here to work with. We'll run everything as normal. Review current investments, then discuss any new enterprises any of us might wish to bring to the group's attention. Who wants to go first? Ben, maybe you? Your Russian millionaire farming scheme hit some bumps recently. You were going to look at restarting, maybe?'

Millionaire farming scheme: a nasty, nasty kidnap operation that ran for years until we broke it. The man behind it, until now, untouched and untouchable.

Jackson, Watkins and I crouched like beasts around the speakers transmitting that conversation. Stared at the video like we could burn our way through it.

They were about to divulge everything. We were about to capture every last one of those fuckers. Convict them using their very own words from their very own mouths.

And then—

A man came into the room. Didn't enter, even. Just hovered in the doorway, where our cameras couldn't quite pick him up. He said, very distinctly, 'I don't think we'll be going swimming today.'

All the faces in the room swivelled.

The man repeated his sentence. Distinctly, forcefully. In a way that brooked no dissent, no interruption.

It was twenty-eight degrees Celsius outside and a perfect day for swimming.

And from that moment – nothing. Rossiter's millionaire farming scheme was dropped and never mentioned again. The men just knocked listlessly around their meeting room for twenty minutes, talking about golf or travel arrangements.

Then left.

Played golf. Ate. Drank. Swam. Walked on the beach. A couple of them donned wetsuits and did some windsurfing thing.

Just that. For the whole weekend.

The German BKA were good to us. They tested the limits of the laws constraining them by keeping the surveillance active until the very last. But not once, not once, did the conspirators breathe a single word of their conspiracy. That little snippet of Marr-Phillips's the only quasi-useful fragment we secured.

And then—

Nothing.

Our operation collapsed. It had run a long time. Generated nothing. Soaked up resources that were better used elsewhere. After being reprieved once before, this time it enjoyed no second chances.

The budgetary plug was finally, decisively pulled.

A few months later, Detective Inspector Rhiannon Watkins – a fiercely excellent detective, feared and respected in equal measure – was headhunted. Went off to lead the Major Crimes unit in Dyfed-Powys's Carmarthen Headquarters. She's a detective chief inspector now and will soon, I'm sure, make it to superintendent.

But Carmarthen has no major crimes. If a hay lorry gets stolen, that's a big deal in Dyfed-Powys. Watkins has essentially – my view – abandoned serious policing in favour of a nice pay rise and a comfortable life with her delightful wife, Cal.

All that's background. The failed story of my life in CID. But the thing that appals me now is that, having lost Operation April and lost DI Watkins, I may now also lose Dennis Jackson.

That would be a threefold loss I almost couldn't bear.

I try to squeeze all that into my face. My arm and hand gestures. The spontaneous expressive dance that, alas, didn't quite come in time.

Jackson rubs his face. A weary rub.

'Fiona, look. Bleddyn Jones is a perfectly good copper. He's a bit by-the-book maybe, but the book is there for a reason. I suggest you do your work, add your tuppence worth, and trust that ordinary police procedures will get there in the end.'

I give him my pained look.

He gives me his what-do-I-care-I'm-going-on-sabbatical look.

Our looks wrestle for a moment. Then, in a sort of matter/anti-matter thing, they just go pop and disappear.

I leave.

Leave-leave.

Go home.

Smoke one joint angrily, then a second one slowly. The second one is where the thinking happens.

Forwards, backwards: two ways to view this case. Forwards, backwards. Forwards, backwards.

I can't get the pieces to line up in a forwards direction, which means that the backwards one has to take priority.

But the backwards thing is aiming at what exactly? What lies at the dark and mercenary heart of this whole thing? I don't know.

My thoughts dissipate, swirl, regather.

I suggest you do your work, add your tuppence worth, and trust that ordinary police procedures will get there in the end.

What did Jackson mean by that? I mean, really?

The surface meaning is plain enough. He was saying, 'Do whatever Bleddyn the Blitherer tells you to do.' Except that Jackson knows me well. When he said 'add your tuppence worth', I think he was encouraging me to operate the way I operate best. A little more entrepreneurially than Jones would like. A little more imaginatively.

I think about smoking a third joint, but decide I'm done at two.

Sitting outside in a pale April sunshine, I fetch my laptop.

Open a browser.

Search 'Tor'.

Wikipedia tells me, '**Tor** is <u>free software</u> for enabling <u>anonymous communication</u>. The name is an acronym derived from the original software project name *The Onion Router*.'

I read for a while, then open a new browser page and type 'Agora'.

Wikipedia again: '**Agora** is a <u>darknet market</u> operating in the <u>Tor</u> network . . . After <u>Evolution</u> closed in an exit <u>scam</u> in March 2015, Agora replaced it as the largest <u>darknet</u> market.'

I read on, but then am troubled by a further thought. Click around online. Medical stuff this time. The National Institute of Neurological Disorders and Stroke.

Find what I need. What I more than half-expected. But this little puff of thought blows further than mere diagnosis. It blows all the way to a dead woman's corpse.

I pick up my keys and leave the house.

12

Katie's not home, but I'm sitting in my car, wondering whether to call or wait, when I see her coming round the corner.

Ski stick. Shopping bag. And, unless I'm making it up, something drawn in her face. Taut. Pained.

I watch for a moment, then hop out of the car. Go bounding over to Katie just as she arrives at her front door. She puts her ski stick and shopping down. Gets her key. Leans against the wall as she unlocks. We say hi.

I pick up the bag and reach for the stick.

'I'll get that,' I say.

Katie, with that sudden ferocity of hers, says, 'I think I can get it for myself, thank you, slave.'

'Can I come in?'

'You want to *help* me in?'

'Katie, I don't think you killed Gaynor Charteris and nor do my colleagues. But you are the person who worked with her most closely in recent weeks and I can't rule out the possibility that you have some connection, even unwittingly, with Charteris's killers. So yes, I am happy to help you inside and upstairs with your bag, but I am also professionally curious to see where you live on the off-chance that I might learn something of value to the investigation. It was as a detective that I came here this evening, not as a friend.'

'Oh.'

'Hairy-arse.'

She opens the door. Goes inside. Leaves bag and ski stick for me to pick up. I watch her from behind. Her gait. That unevenness that comes and goes.

The house is a student-share but, Katie tells me, her housemates are all post-graduate women and the house therefore lacks the stink, disorder and unhygiene which marks the true student house.

We put the food away, then go upstairs. Katie's room.

She makes nice, sort of.

I don't see anything that tells me about Charteris's killers, but I do see something that I more than half-expected to find: a book, titled *Living with MND*, on the top of the reading pile by her bed.

I sit on the bed. Shift the book.

Say, 'How long, Katie? Since your diagnosis, I mean.'

She looks at me, gapes, then bursts into tears.

Normally that word 'burst' doesn't really fit. People might crumple a little, or sob, or pat their eyes. But Katie bursts. Throws her head up, her chin back, and tears actually fly outwards as she does so. And there are sobs, yes, but these are darker, deeper: the howls of some fierce animal caught in a trap. A fox with a shattered leg, a stag with the press of a bullet between his shoulders.

I let her cry. When she tries to ask the 'how did you know?' question – but can't because she's still too busy yowling – I say, 'Your foot, your gait, your breathing. Your attitude, too. Those things had to amount to something, so I fooled around online and made a guess.' I gesture at the *MND* book – MND: Motor Neurone Disease. 'When I saw that, I knew I was right.'

Katie cries with the energy of the newly dying.

MND kills most people within about three years of onset. Stephen Hawking, the disease's most famous sufferer, is also that rarest of rare exceptions: someone who survived its ravages. If Katie's disease follows its normal progression, she will gradually lose control over her hands and feet, legs and arms. She will become unable to eat, walk, talk or swallow. Eventually she will be unable to breathe without mechanical assistance and then, shortly afterwards, she will die.

Katie is twenty-three years old and could have expected to live to eighty years or more.

She cries, then chokes, because the crying has been too much for her failing musculature, then cries again because the choking is a bleak reminder of what lies ahead.

I go downstairs, make tea, bring it back.

And as I stand over the kettle, feeling the heat gathering in my fingertips, hanging my face over the spout to feel the rising warmth, I suddenly become aware of a sudden pop, a vanishing. Like, without even moving, I've suddenly crossed from one world into another, a world entirely like the one I just left, but without feeling. Without sound or smell or taste or feel.

I still see the kettle. Still know I'm standing there. But that's all: it's knowledge without participation. Without membership.

Because I'm dealing with this sudden transition, I'm slow to remember the logic of where I am: fingers clasped around a heating kettle, face hanging over its spout. It's literally only as the world blurs with steam that I connect everything up: the kettle is boiling, I should move my face, my fingers.

Move them I do. Then stand unsure what to do next.

I think: *tea. I came here to make tea.*

I make two cups of tea. Peppermint for me. Ordinary caffeinated stuff for Katie. She prefers coffee, I think, but I never really know how to make coffee, so tea it will be.

Then think again: Tea. Kettle. Steam. Fingers. Pain.

I don't have pain, or don't think I do, but I look at my

fingers and see that they're brightly, angrily red at the tips.

This puzzles me. It all puzzles me. The evidence that lies, literally, at my fingertips speaks of scalding. Of pain. Of bodily injury. But try as I might, I can't find any trace of sensation that joins up, that makes sense of the available data.

For a while, I stand unsure of what to do. Then, a voice in my head, a police voice with first aid training, says, 'You have to put your hands under cold water.'

So I do. I obey the voice. Plunge those scalded fingertips beneath the cold tap. Wait for something to happen. A feeling of cold. A feeling of pain. A feeling of something healed.

I get none of those things, but my fingers do change colour. My police eye watches the clock on the kitchen wall. Counts one minute. Two minutes. Three.

The voice tells me it's OK to remove the hands from the water. So I do. Turn off the tap, go upstairs. Walk carefully, because I can't feel or sense my legs. Have to actually watch my feet onto each stair because I can't trust that they'll find their own way there.

Into Katie's room. Put the drinks down without spilling them.

I think I must look wooden. Almost puppety. Legs like poles of hollow pine. Joints of knotted elastic.

I sit down on the bed.

I assume Katie will say something about my awkwardness, but she's too pre-occupied with her own departing gusts of feeling to notice anything awry in me.

She wipes her face.

'It's a bit of a fucker,' she says.

'Yes.'

And as she speaks and as I answer – *pop*! It all returns. Feeling, ordinary sound, everything. The whole world back again, just as it was, except that my fingertips can now feel the afterburn of that scald.

101

I don't say anything. Don't try to figure any of this out. Just listen to Katie as she continues.

'Diagnosis was six weeks ago. My age should count in my favour, but so far . . .'

She doesn't finish the sentence but makes a downward-plunging motion with her hand.

I nod.

'And when Charteris died . . .'

'It was another kick in the teeth. I mean, I really liked Gaynor and was sorry for her anyway . . .'

'But you also needed her.'

'Yes. It's stupid, I know, but I made up my mind that I'd get my Ph.D. before I died. I'd give up on everything else but, fuck it, I'd at least achieve that one thing.'

'Then Charteris dies. The project looks like it's going to fail. Yes, in theory you've got the capacity to take it over, but you're going to be losing mobility and a lot else, and you just can't see yourself running the dig, monitoring your team, and writing a doctoral thesis.'

Katie snorts.

'Thank you, slave. You have an uncanny knack for pointing out quite how thickly enshitted I am.'

Katie's naturalness with me helps. So too does the glow in my fingertips. I say, 'And Charteris knew? She knew about your diagnosis?'

'Yes.'

'The others?'

'No. They knew something was up, but not what or how bad.'

That brings me to the niggle that brought me here. The little puff of thought that blew all the way to murder.

'Katie, did you ever talk about the issue with Charteris by email? Email, text, anything like that.'

Katie nods. Says yes. Tells me they needed to plan how to

manage the dig if Katie was progressively more disabled.

I say, 'But not on her Open University email address. Not on her BT one.'

As far as we know, Charteris had just those two email addresses. A work one, and a home one.

Katie says, 'She had a Gmail address as well. She wasn't very tech-savvy. Liked to curl up in the evening with her tablet and chat online . . .'

She continues, but I interrupt.

We need that data and need it soon. I ask for the email address.

Katie laughs. 'I can't pronounce it, but I can spell it.' *Gwenhwyfar@gmail.com*.

Gwenhwyfar: the Welsh spelling of Guinevere. Arthur's wife.

There are a few possible answers to that. A few questions, rather. But what I actually ask is this: 'Katie, how much do you know about ancient metalwork?'

'*Metal*work?'

'Jewellery, goldsmithing, blacksmithing. That kind of thing.'

She tells me what she knows, and what she knows is plenty.

13

Leave Katie's house. Drive up past the cemetery, to the green languor of Roath Park, the troubled turpentine of its lake.

I park there, watching the waves.

That moment in Katie's kitchen.

Fingers clasped around a boiling kettle, face hanging over the spout. The world clouding with steam and me so removed from it that it took real mental effort to figure out what was happening.

I think, *it is happening again. My illness is coming back. I will never feel safe. I will never sleep again.*

My illness.

It's not something I speak about much, but the simple facts are these. When I was fifteen, I became mentally unwell. Spent two years, on and off, in mental hospitals. My condition was diagnosed as Cotard's Syndrome: a state in which sufferers believe themselves to be dead.

For two years, in the most literal way possible, I thought I was dead. A walking corpse.

I did, eventually, recover. Make friends, go to college, get a job, build a life. But I've never felt secure. Never felt that the illness was gone, never to return.

And now?

It is happening again. My illness is coming back.

I am so scared I almost don't know how to move.

After a while, I don't know how long, I call Bleddyn Jones.

Tell him about Charteris's third email address.

'She had a secret address?'

'No, not secret. Just something she only used for particular times and particular people.'

I give him the name, Gwenhwyfar.

'What's that? In English, that would be Jennifer, right? Do we have any Jennifers in connection with the case?'

'Sir, I don't think she had any Jennifers in mind.'

Tell him about Gwenhwyfar/Guinevere.

'Ah.' He doesn't like that answer. Changes tack. 'Gmail, you said?'

Yes.

And Google holds its data overseas, where a regular British search warrant has no legal force. But there are processes which unlock even Google's vaults and Jones tells me, a bit gruffly, that he'll deal with them. His chore, his headache.

I hang up.

Drive, slowly, up the hill to my parents' house.

My parents.

My booming pa, my changeless ma, my two younger sisters.

Today, I'm in luck. I score my mother (expected), one out of two sisters (Kay, the older one, not usually around these days), and my father (a rarity on these Friday evenings).

Dad does his usual bear-huggy crush. His holding me at arms-length thing, that inspection.

My mam rushes out to welcome me, then races around the kitchen, laying out everything that is edible and tempting.

Plates, food, chatter.

Kay appears.

Hug. Kiss. Genuine affection.

That exchange of glances between grown-up sisters that says, 'Parents, huh?' and answers, 'Yeah, parents!'

There's a bottle of brown beer for my pa, who doesn't actually drink much these days. Water for the rest of us, water that's had a long squeeze of lemon juice because – this is Kay's latest thing – the lemon juice helps you lose weight, cleanse your system, boost immunity, remove impurities, eliminate caffeine, and does something with potassium, Kay isn't sure what, but after hesitating between three major options (increase potassium, decrease potassium, or just balance the stuff), she opts for the third with a flourish of confidence.

I say, 'Your skin *is* looking really nice,' and Mam starts telling me how long she's been free of colds and flu.

We eat. We drink. We finish. We wash up.

Kay ghosts upstairs and comes back down in a vaguely metallic dress, dark blue and moody bronze-gold. Her lemon-juiced good looks are now lipsticked, blushed, mascaraed and eye-lined to a point where they're at or beyond weapons grade. A hemline rides high on her thigh. A clutch-bag, loaded, lies on a hallway chair.

Kay has a lingering desire to spend a bit of time curled up between me and Mam on the sofa, but her huntress instincts prove too much, and her gold stilettos carry her, clicking, across the parquet to the front door and whatever waits for her beyond. A sweep of perfume, duskily sexy, the only lingering trace.

The house feels emptier without her.

I spend half an hour with Mam in front of the telly. We watch enough of a period detective drama together that she's happy. Then pop into the kitchen to make myself a peppermint tea, get waylaid by Dad, allow myself to be ushered through into his studio, his world.

We talk. We chink around. Dad's got a thing for lovespoons at the moment – ornate carved wooden spoons, a Welsh tradition. He tells me that he's bought a six-foot lump of lime wood and is commissioning a giant lovespoon for Mam.

It's good patter, Dad's, it always is, but his heart isn't quite in it. Nor is mine.

Without thinking about it, without premeditation, I ask, 'Do you want to come for a drive?'

That's a strange question to ask at ten in the evening, but his response is delayed by a micro-second only. No more.

'Yes, love, of course. I'll just tell your mam.'

He does.

We leave. Take my car, not Dad's. Head out of town. Hit the motorway. Turn west.

Dad says nothing, but I feel the prick of his gaze on me. We talk about anything or nothing, but mostly we're just aware of this thrum of road, the passing miles.

We sweep past Bridgend. Past Neath and Swansea.

It's now gone eleven, and for the first time I see Dad kick his legs out, relax. There's a chuckle rippling in him now, a secret entertainment. We get out beyond Carmarthen. Nothing much beyond us now but a few sheep-bitten fields and the wide blue Atlantic. We drive on through a dark and empty Haverfordwest. Take the lane that leads to Walwyn's Castle and St Ishmaels, the last scrap of land before the ocean.

This is the tip of infinity, the edge of oblivion.

I park on a grassy verge. Turn the engine off.

Still that tremble of pleasure from my father, whose old night-time adventures now lie largely in his past.

He says, 'You had a case here once, didn't you, love? Back when you were starting out.'

I tell him yes, sex trafficking, but add, 'Brendan Rattigan. He was the guy behind all this.' I gesture forward into the night.

'Oh, I know that. It was in the papers, you know, love.'

'And Brendan Rattigan was mates with people like Idris Prothero, David Marr-Phillips, Owain Owen, Galton Evans.'

I list the men who were the primary targets of Operation April. Who escaped from us, from our enquiry.

Dad shrugs. 'Rich men . . .' he murmurs. His implication

being that in south Wales the club of the super-wealthy is small enough that they all know each other.

'Yes, but they weren't just friends, they were colleagues too. Were, are. The ones who are still alive and out of jail.'

Dad doesn't respond with words, but even his silence is a kind of response. I don't think his merriment has altogether vanished, but his silence now has a watchfulness to it. An alertness.

'You used to know them,' I say. 'That gang. Not just know them. You used to work with them.'

Dad's silence now is absolute. He doesn't know if he's sitting here at midnight with his daughter or with a detective. If he's listening to a helpful disclosure or the prelude to a formal charge.

I help him out. 'My colleagues don't know this. I haven't told them and I won't. I *do* have proof of your acquaintance. I *don't* have proof, not courtroom proof anyway, of your working relationship.'

And it's true. It took a long time but I found a photo that showed my father at the races with another man. The photo of that other man showed only his arm, but that arm was distinctively clad in a blue Prince of Wales check. By working print by print through the archives of Chepstow Racecourse, I was able to find the owner of that arm: David Marr-Phillips. By working even harder, I was able to place Rossiter and Evans at the same racecourse on the same date. Eventually found enough overlap of dates and people to prove beyond reasonable doubt that this little group were using the races as a place to meet. Those meetings reached a peak in the mid-'80s.

Around the time that Cardiff Bay was being redeveloped.

Around the time that some already-rich men became even richer.

Around the time that I was found – a penny dropped from a silver heaven – in the back of my father's Jaguar.

I was about two years old at the time. Mute. Didn't speak my name, didn't speak at all for a couple of years. Went untraced by the police and was formally adopted by this man, Tom Griffiths and his wife Kathleen. Technically speaking, they're my adoptive parents, but they're the only true parents I've ever had.

My dad is still silent, so I add, 'I'm not wearing a wire. I'm not recording anything.'

And, as Dad probably knows, my relationship with him is such that any evidence I acquired in this way would be pretty much trashed in court. Too conflicted to be of any evidential weight.

Dad says, and the chuckle is still just about there, 'They're bastards, that lot. Every last one of them.'

I say, 'Gina Jewell.'

Killed in 1985. A road accident, or that's what was believed at the time. That's how the death was reported. But Jewell was also a redoubtable campaigner for the rights of local residents. A woman who threatened the profits of those selfsame property developers.

A credible source, a man in the City Council Planning Department at the time, told me that my father arranged the killing.

Dad says, 'Gina Jewell.'

I say, 'As far as any of my colleagues are concerned, she died in a road accident.'

Dad says, 'Gina Jewell.'

I wait.

Let silence do what silence does.

I can almost feel my dad deciding what to do with this unexpected line of enquiry. Considering his options.

And eventually, after thinking them through, all he says is, 'You didn't bring me all this way just to ask about Gina Jewell.'

'No.'

In truth, I don't quite know why I brought him. Company mostly, but also something I've noticed before. Dad opens up more when's he's a little excited by the setting. I came to him once – working undercover, employed by gangsters, braceleted with an audio device that recorded everything – and he told me more then, typing silently into a laptop, eyes sparkling with merriment, than he ever has done before or since.

But if he doesn't want to tell me more, then he doesn't.

I shrug slightly. Reach into the back of the car for my fleece. Change my pretty scallop-edged black-suede flats for a pair of thick walking boots. Get a torch from the glove box.

Dad gets out. Stretches. Pulls on his jacket and zips up.

'It's fresh,' he says, facing the wind. 'You can smell the salt.'

Can you? I never really know. But I twitch the torch at a field gate and we clamber over.

Cropped grass and lichened limestone.

Fields that slope down to the sea.

A little cliff that I once rolled a man over. A lighthouse where I shot three men, killing one and wounding two.

Happy days.

But we're not going to the lighthouse. Not going to the cliff.

Up behind the lighthouse, there's a stone sheepfold. We go there.

Dad holds the torch while I root around at the back. I shift some stones around, wondering why I didn't come when it was light. Then see the blue gleam of an old fertiliser sack and yank at the plastic till it comes free.

Inside the plastic: a gun.

I take the gun. Shove the fertiliser sack back where it was.

The gun is a bit big for me, but it'll do. A gun's a gun.

Dad peers at it. 'That's not the one . . .'

110

'It's not the one you gave me, no.'

He opens his mouth to say, 'I didn't give you a gun.'

The default denial. The automatic response of a man who has spent half his life avoiding police surveillance.

But then – the wind, the night, this gun. He's in a deserted field at midnight, watching his daughter retrieve an illegal handgun from the place she stashed it.

He waves his hand, implying that the denial is there if needed. His denial-hand is also his torch-hand, and the beam of light swings briefly up to a star-filled sky before returning to us. Anyone watching us from Alpha Centauri will, in a few years' time, see that little flash. Wonder what it meant.

'Do you have ammo?' he asks.

'Yes.'

We start to walk back.

'Are you in danger?'

'No. I mean, I've got a case on at the moment and I don't know how that'll turn out. But no. Mostly, I just wanted a gun.'

So I can sleep. Because the only time I've ever slept really well, I had a gun within one short arm movement of my bed. There's no logic in that. I don't need a gun. I live in a quiet suburb of a quiet city in one of the world's quietest and safest countries and I have no need of this gun. But here I am, in the middle of the night, with an illegal handgun in my pocket and I feel almost safe for the first time since that moment in Katie's kitchen.

'You want to watch out for those things,' says Dad primly. 'They're bad things, guns.'

Says the man who was prosecuted twice for armed robbery, once for possession of a firearm with intent, and once each for kidnap and arson.

I shake my head in the wind and night. Say nothing.

Back at the car, I shove the gun in the glovebox. It's two hours back to Cardiff and neither of us feels like climbing back into the Alfa Romeo's lamplit cockpit just yet.

I say, 'Do you want to smoke?'

Dad doesn't smoke normally, but the wind and the stars call for something, so we sit on the verge and smoke. A tobacco-only roll-up for Dad. A rather more herbal version for me.

Dad says, 'Gina Jewell.'

I look at him. Say nothing.

He smokes. A glow of orange at the tip. Another tiny clue for those watchers from a distant star.

He says, 'She was killed, yes, and on my patch. But not by me or by any of my lads. That's when everything started to fall apart. We had . . . we had different ways of operating.' He laughs. 'I was never ruthless enough. Too nice, me.'

I grin at him, accepting his answer.

I say, 'And I don't think you just "found" me in the back of your car. I don't believe that.'

He laughs again. Freer in this night, this wind, than I've ever seen him in Cardiff.

'Love, if you want to find stuff out, you'll need to find it out yourself.'

I nod. I'm OK with that.

'Just . . .'

I look at him. Asking him with my eyes what that word might mean.

He tells me. Says, 'Just if you *do* insist on finding out, don't do it by halves. Those fuckers are dangerous, dangerous men. You either win completely. Or you'll lose your life. You can't go at it half-cock.'

Dad almost never swears: one of the unexpected things about him. But he's more or less confirmed what I was more or less certain of anyway: that my tangled origins lie in whatever dark dealings my father had with those men – the Rattigans, the Evanses, the Marr-Phillipses and the rest.

I say, 'I don't do anything half-cock. You know that.'

Dad's big arm comes round my shoulder. Crushes me into him. And I'm a seven-year-old girl again. Never been ill. Never seen the inside of a mental hospital. My future nothing but a golden road snaking into a rose-washed infinity.

That, just that, for a moment or five.

Then Dad pulls away. We drive back to Cardiff. Long miles, but nice ones.

I drop Dad and go on home.

I do all the things you're meant to do.

Shower. Teeth. Change.

And somewhere along the way, for no reason at all, that whole thing happens again. The dissociation. Water running hot or cold over my hands and I can't tell which or why or what.

I know I'm alone in an empty house.

I'm wearing pale-blue pyjamas and for the moment can't remember anything else. When did I put them on? Did I buy these things and if so why? Why this pattern, this colour, this anything?

A face moves in a mirror. A pale balloon on a blue pyjama body.

I place the gun, loaded, by my bed. A box of ammo on the floor. Practise a quick snatch in the dark.

There is no reason for this gun. I have no reason to be afraid.

Light off.

Sleep.

14

Sleep, and in the morning, all the joys of Saturday.

A world where I'm meant to stay away from work. Meant to pretend that I have things to do that are better than catching murderers.

So. I clean my house, sort of. Remove things that are fizzy, mouldy, empty, dried-out, or otherwise icky from my fridge. Call friends. Actual human beings who are pleased to hear from me, or make out that they are.

Arrange social things. Swimming with Bev. Accept a drinks thing timidly arranged by Essylt. Invite Ed Saunders and Glossy Jill round to mine for supper.

Ed says, 'Oh cripes,' when I say I'll be cooking, but he says it nicely.

Midday.

Midday, and I've been good.

Ticked the cleaning box. The food box. The making-nice-with-humans box. There are a couple of boring boxes unticked, but phooey to them, for dirty laundry ye have with you always, but high-quality murder victims ye have not always.

I fool around on the prison service database. The probation service one.

Get what I need.

Write an address down on the inside of an old chocolate wrapper, then fold it so the address doesn't show.

Rummage through my wardrobe.

Find an old pair of black jeans, much washed, and one pocket starting to come away at the back.

Boots, worn long enough that the soles are starting to get papery and thin.

A gym T-shirt from the laundry pile and an old jumper worn above. The jumper's old, but in reasonable nick, but I pick at the elbow till I get a pleasingly sized hole appearing.

Jacket. Bag. A horrible grey scarf I'd forgotten I ever had. No make-up.

I collect together a few papers – an out-of-date library card, an in-date bus pass, a Post Office savings book, a receipt for something, a letter still in its envelope, two ten-pound notes folded into eighths. Bind those things together using an old black hair-tie and put them in my inside jacket pocket. Add my chocolate wrapper address. Put some actual money in my jeans pocket too: fifty quid, just in case. A tin of stuff to make roll-ups with.

Go to the coach station.

Buy a ticket, one way, for the next coach to London. There's one leaving in twenty minutes and the journey is advertised as taking three and a half hours, or at least an hour longer than I'd take if I drove.

Ah well.

Buy the cheapest and nastiest sandwich I can find. Tear off the thin plastic film from the top and stuff it in my jacket pocket. Eat the sandwich, or some of it. Drink water from the taps in the ladies' toilets, even though there's a sign saying, for some reason, do not drink this water.

Get on the coach. Someone's left a magazine in one of the seat pockets, a TV listings thing mostly dedicated to soap opera. I read that. Then read nothing. Fields and trees, towns and bridges slide past.

London.

Try to take buses to where I need to be. Make a mess of it

and end up walking nearly three miles across north London to correct my errors. At some point it starts raining and I remember why I no longer wear these boots.

On the way, I pass an off-licence. Buy a bottle of Algerian wine for £3.49 which I assume – I don't know about these things – means it must be really terrible. The shopkeeper, an Algerian, puts the bottle in a plastic bag for me.

I say, 'And some crisps please,' and he puts those in a bag too.

I pay.

Keep the change in my pocket, but tuck the notes remaining from my fifty pounds into my boot. Actually take my boot off, shove the money down to the toe, put the boot back on.

Continue.

Arrive at the right address.

A flat over a place that calls itself the Harlesden International Trading Centre. The trading centre has a metal grille over its windows and a grimy plastic sign that says 'Importers – Distributors – Wholesalers – Household Goods'. Someone has kicked lumps out of the wooden boarding beneath the metal grille. Some graffiti has been there so long it has moss growing on it.

A side alley leads to a door. A selection of buzzers.

I press one that says 'Mason'. A rain-smeared label written in blue biro.

A voice comes through the buzzer. 'Yes?'

I hold my head away from the microphone. Mumble something.

'What? Who's that?'

I hold my head a bit closer and mumble something that ends with, 'Steve Mason.'

The voice on the other end mutters something angrily as he pulls back and disconnects. But footsteps come downstairs.

The door opens to reveal a man dressed in jogging bottoms

116

and an old T-shirt. He hasn't shaved today. Maybe not the day before.

I don't think he's guilty of overusing the shower either.

He's forty-something. Short dark hair. Reasonably lean, but with something compressed about him. Primed for discharge.

I say, 'Hi.'

'Yes?'

'Are you Steve Mason?'

'Yes.'

'Hi.'

'And you are?'

'I'm Fiona. A friend of Ian Shoesmith's.'

'Ian?'

'Yes.'

Mason's eyes take me in. Up, down. A proper inspection.

I say, 'He's dead. I know that. That's what you were thinking.'

'Yes.'

'I was a friend of his from before, obviously.'

Mason doesn't reply to that. He's wondering why I'm here, I imagine, but since it would be easy enough for him to ask and he doesn't ask, I don't see why I should help out.

I hold out the plastic bag I'm holding with its bottle of terrible Algerian wine. Say, 'I brought you this,' and make a sort of *please* expression on my face.

He takes the wine, nods, starts walking back up the stairs.

I follow.

Mason's room is a bedsit. A real shithole. Two single-paned windows that open out on to the high street below. Grimy net curtains. The room smells of cigarette smoke and male sweat and whatever don't-even-think-about-it odour is produced by recently watched porn.

A low table holds a laptop, some papers, and a takeaway curry in a foil tray.

My jacket is wet through. I peel it off, almost literally having to unstick its sodden polyester lining from my arms, my back.

I hang it out over the back of a chair. Sit on the chair. Legs together, arms in, not leaning back.

'Sorry,' I say.

'You're Fiona?'

Nod.

'Welsh Fiona?'

Nod.

My accent is distinct enough that you hardly have to be Sherlock Holmes to figure it out, but I think Mason meant more than that. Which is good. It means Shoesmith mentioned me.

'I thought you were caught up in all that too,' Mason says.

'I was. I just got out.'

Shoesmith: an IT guy who got mixed up in something nasty and ended up being murdered for his troubles. Prior to that career-ending mistake, Shoesmith was partnered up with Mason in a complicated little technology fraud. The scam was busted. Shoesmith was never convicted, but Mason got five years inside, and a criminal bankruptcy on top. He is even now working his way through a post-jail term of probation.

He unscrews the bottle of wine. Finds a glass, a mug.

Rinses the glass in a basin and offers it to me.

I say, 'I don't drink.' Ask for a glass of water instead.

He gives me water.

Stares at me.

Stares at me the way a recently released ex-con does. Stripping me naked. Stretching me out on the bed.

'Why are you here?' he asks.

I tell him. Say that I've got some stuff I want to sell.

'So sell it on eBay.'

'It's not that sort of stuff.'

This is where Mason ought to tell me that he knows nothing

of the darknet. That involvement in that kind of computer activity is an explicit breach of his probation licence. That he'll need to ask me, please, to leave his room.

He doesn't say any of that.

Just stands up. Reaches for my jacket and twirls it from the back of my chair. Goes through my pockets. Finds my little hair tie with its wad of goodies. Goes through those things one by one.

Fiona Grey. That's the name on my Post Office book, my library card. They're left over from my old undercover identity. I've kept the various bits and pieces reasonably up to date. The letter in its white envelope is from a homeless hostel in Cardiff telling me about new out-of-hours access arrangements.

Mason looks at everything, including the letter. Tosses most of it on the table. Keeps the two ten-pound notes.

I say, 'That's mine,' meaning the money.

He says, 'How do I know you're not wearing a wire?'

I think, *fuck's sake, this isn't the 1980s.* A modern audio recording device is so small it can easily be inserted into a button. You don't need wires and gaffer tape and little boxes the size of old-fashioned Sony Walkmen.

But he wants to do the thing. Jerks his head upwards, in a sign that he wants me to do the thing.

So I stand up. Take my jumper off. Roll my T-shirt up above my bra. Face him. Turn round. Turn back. No wire.

Mason points his finger at my chest.

'Come on, pet. Do it right.'

I lift my bra. Show him. Front and back. No wire.

Get dressed again, under the low gunfire of his gaze.

He thinks about getting me to repeat the rigmarole below the waist, but my jeans are tight enough that they couldn't conceal much and he contents himself with making me empty out my pockets.

'So. You want to sell something. Drugs?'

'I just want to know how it works.'

Mason's eyes flick around the room. He goes to the window and watches the street outside.

And even as he's there, holding back the net, looking for watchers in parked cars, re-enacting scenes from movies that have no actual relevance to contemporary police operations, he says, 'I give you an hour. You give me a blow job.'

'No. You've got my twenty quid.'

'OK, first hour for twenty. After that . . .'

Mason has a black Dell laptop, not very new-looking, lying in the clutter on the table.

He doesn't reach for it. Goes out of the room. Does something. Comes back with a glossily new MacBook Pro. Fifteen inch screen. Two grand's worth of computer, or near enough.

He pings it awake. Connects, I notice, not to the router sitting in the corner of his own room but to the Harlesden International Trading Centre beneath us.

'OK,' he says. 'Tor.'

Tor.

The. Onion. Router.

Gateway to the dark web.

Called 'onion' because it has a thousand layers of encryption and if law enforcement happens to peel one back, there are nine hundred and ninety-nine still waiting. The system is, even to the intelligence agencies, all but uncrackable.

We don't work for one hour. We work for eight. Don't stop until a pinky-orange dawn leaks into the grey streets, their tired shopfronts and their uncollected bags of rubbish.

Mason keeps my money and the wine. He doesn't get a blow job or anything better than thanks. I think he works with me because he enjoys being expert in something. Because he is in fact very good at this stuff and has few opportunities now to share it.

120

I am duly grateful. Duly admiring.

And, when I leave, I leave not expert exactly, but proficient. Good enough.

Take the bus back to Cardiff. Back to Cardiff by bus. Sleep curled up over two seats.

Home.

Bath and a joint.

A long bath, a fat joint.

Those things and a mug of peppermint tea and a tin of tuna, eaten straight from the can.

It's early afternoon, Sunday.

A basket of dirty laundry murmurs at me. My running shoes remind me that they've not been used for a few days now. But those things can wait. There's one more person I need to meet. The only person who's really central to this case of ours.

Arthur.

King-commander of the Dark Age Britons. A man who fought the invading Anglo–Saxons. Flung them back for a generation or more.

A man whose historical existence has never been proved. Never been certain.

I rush off to Waterstones. Buy all the books I can there. Rush to the library, to Katie's, to borrow the other things I need. And start work.

Arthur.

Vortigern.

Ambrosius Aurelianus.

Hengist and Horsa.

Old names. Old wars. Old enmities.

At one point, I call Katie to check a particular point about the spread or non-spread of Anglo–Saxon cemeteries across England, she gives me the answer in a quiet, competent voice, then adds, 'It's two in the morning. You knew that, did you?'

'Uh. Sorry.'

'That's OK.' Pause. 'Do you think you'll catch them? The people who killed Gaynor?'

'Yes. Or rather, I'm hoping *you* will. Or rather, I'm hoping they'll catch themselves.'

That's not a helpful answer, I realise, and it kicks off a long pause, silvered and moonlit. The ghost of Katie's own mortality stalks the space between us, scattering frost and starlight in its trail.

She says, 'Good luck, slave. And goodnight.'

I turn back to history and the cemeteries of the dead.

15

Monday.

Bleddyn Jones hasn't yet got that Gmail data but he says, with a carefully managed insouciance, 'Oh, it's with California now. I'm expecting it to be actioned first thing in the morning, their time.'

I get that thing I get when people take abstract nouns and turn them into verbs.

I draft a press release. One that solicits 'any information concerning the theft of antiquities from Dinas Powys'. I mention a possible ('speculative') connection with a theft of documents from the cathedral library at Bangor. Also a possible connection with a break-in at Llanymawddwy.

Nowhere do I mention Arthur but, in a deliberately underwhelming section entitled 'Notes for Editors', I write:

> Antiquities stolen from Dinas Powys include a seal-box lid engraved with the symbol of a bear and crown, and a stone fragment, believed to be from the upper Dyfi valley, near Camlan/Llanymawddwy. The vellum located in the church of Saint Tydecho's dates from the ninth century. It is believed that the documents stolen from Bangor Cathedral/Saint Tydecho's may include material of similar or greater antiquity.

That's all.

Jones approves the release. I get the press office to issue it. Then poke around on the internet. Find a few Arthurian message boards. The kind of sites where King Arthur fans exchange ideas, projects, theories, chat. I set myself up a fake online identity. Call myself *FrenhinesGwenhwyfar*, Queen Guinevere. Get a Gmail account in that name.

Then I just stroll around on the message boards. I write, 'interesting' or 'Well, well, well . . .' or 'Look what someone dug up.' Then add a link to the press release we've just put out.

Ten minutes. Six forums. Done.

If Charteris was killed in order to send us a message, I think it's important to let the bad guys know that we've heard them loud and clear. *It's OK, guys. We've got the picture. No need to cut anyone else's head off.*

For a little while, I try doing some work, some actual proper work, but that doesn't feel very satisfactory so, before long, I give up.

Go to eBay. Search 'Antiquities'. Select 'Roman' and 'Celtic'.

And buy stuff.

Some ancient Roman glass. Some beads. A Celtic bronze brooch. Two dozen stones of Whitby jet, probably Romano–Celtic in origin. A tiny silver bell, about the size of an acorn. I have a little buying frenzy, and pay less than £150 in total for the pleasure.

Late that afternoon, I drift by Jones's office.

It's nine in the morning at some sunny Californian Googleplex, five o'clock in a gloomy Cardiff. Outside our windows, a sudden fierce scatter of sleet.

I say, 'Anything?'

Jones shakes his head. 'I'm pushing.'

I grimace.

Jones has his keyboard pushed away. A fierce black doodle is taking shape on his notepad. I observe this, then observe Jones observing me. Two detectives reading each other for clues.

'If anything comes in . . .' I say.

He doesn't say yes, but he nods.

I return to my desk. Do nothing much. Look at pictures of Charteris, mostly. Her headless body, her bodiless head.

Jones turns up eight minutes before seven. Dark grey suit. That weirdly black hair and beard.

'Still here?' he says.

I blink, which is one eyelid movement more than the question warrants.

He says, 'I got a call from California. They've given us a password. We're in.'

He shows me the password.

MynyddBaddon960.

Jones scrutinises my face, seeing if it means anything to me. It does.

I say, 'It's a reference to Arthur's decisive battle, Mount Badon. That "960" isn't a date, it's the number of men he killed.'

'He killed nine hundred and sixty men?'

I've got a couple of my Arthur books in my bag. Get one of them – Nennius's *Historia Brittonum* – and pass it over.

'This is Nennius, one of the earliest historians to mention Arthur. Chapter fifty-six is the bit you want.'

Jones doesn't read the text out loud, but I know it well already.

At that time, the Saxons grew strong by virtue of their large number and increased in power in Britain . . . Then Arthur along with the kings of Britain fought against them in those days, but Arthur himself was the commander-in-chief. His first battle was at the mouth of the river which is called Glein. His second, third, fourth, and fifth battles were above another river which is called Dubglas and is in the region of Linnuis. The sixth battle was above the river which is called Bassas. The seventh battle was in the forest of Celidon, that is Cat Coit Celidon. The eighth battle was at the fortress of Guinnion, in which Arthur carried the image of holy Mary ever virgin on his shoulders; and the pagans were put to flight on that day. And through the power of our Lord Jesus Christ and through the power of the blessed Virgin Mary his mother there was great slaughter among them. The ninth battle was waged in the City of the Legion. The tenth battle was waged on the banks of a river which is called Tribruit. The eleventh battle was fought on the mountain which is called Agnet. The twelfth battle was on Mount Badon in which there fell in one day nine hundred and sixty men from one charge by Arthur; and no one struck them down except Arthur himself, and in all the wars he emerged as victor.

Jones looks perplexed.

'This is real, is it?'

'It's a real history book, yes.'

'And this battle, Mount Badon? That was real?'

I shrug. I'm a detective, not a time traveller. I say, 'Historians on both sides mention the battle, including some who were writing within living memory. And there's archaeological evidence that *something* halted the Saxon invasion at around this time. So a decisive battle of this kind? Well, yes, it certainly looks likely.'

Jones takes my pad and writes. 'Mount Badon. 960 men. Major battle.' Tears the sheet off and pockets it.

One of those things that police officers do for no reason I can possibly fathom. Like if you take a note of something, you've trapped it. Clapped handcuffs over an idea.

He says, 'He killed nine hundred and sixty men? With what? A machine gun?'

I don't reply.

We go to Jones's office. Go to Gmail. Enter Charteris's

126

address and password. There's a momentary pause, then –
emails. Hundreds of them. A busy, well-populated account.

We call out for pizza.

Work.

16

To: MyrddinEmrys@gmail.com
From: Gwenhwyfar@gmail.com
Subject: Quondam futurusque
Date: 3 January 2015

Phew, what a night that was – I'm getting too old! And look, just to put in writing what I said (more than a bit tipsily) then: YES. I think we should go for it. From my point of view, it's only about actually getting proper attention back to the amazing work we all do. I've been working in this field for thirty years now and the hard fact is that funding is actually decreasing. (Yes, yes, I know: should have been a particle physicist.) I suppose I think of it like those doctors using defibrillators: a short sharp shock to get things moving again. A PR stunt, really.

    Anyway. Yes. I'm in.

    Gosh. I think I'm still hung over!

    Gwen xxx

To: MyrddinEmrys@gmail.com
From: Gwenhwyfar@gmail.com
Subject: Quondam futurusque
Date: 6 May 2015

M, just wanted to say that I was in Oxford today for a lecture and dropped in on Uthyr afterwards. Yvain + Medraut were there too – already a bit pissed, I think, even though I only arrived about sixish.

I didn't stay long – back home now – but just thought I should say, Medraut seemed really dark. Maybe it's just one of his phases – with a past like his, it's hardly surprising! – but I thought you should know. I sort of rely on you to keep this whole thing on track. Someone's got to.

Gwen xxx

To: MyrddinEmrys@gmail.com
From: Gwenhwyfar@gmail.com
Subject: Quondam futurusque
Date: 18 June 2015

M??? I think I want to say that this has all gone too far. I thought at first it was a fun idea to play with. Something halfway between a prank and a real exercise in scholarship. And now? I just don't like any part of this. Medraut's obsession with getting the 'right gold' is taking us into dangerous areas. I mean, if he wants gold, why not just get some gold? Personally, I feel like I want to stop this whole thing.

Oh God! I was so excited when we started and already it feels like the worst mistake of my life.

Gwen xxx

To: MyrddinEmrys@gmail.com
From: Gwenhwyfar@gmail.com
Subject: QF and all that
Date: 11 October 2015

Oh gosh, M – I feel relieved. I'm sitting here, feet up, watching a late-night weepie, and you know I think I feel OK for the first time since our whole idea got serious. With hindsight, the whole thing was a terrible idea and I don't quite know how we all got seduced into it. But at least we abandoned ship at the right time . . . or I think we did.

So, anyway, I just wanted to send you an extra big hug to say thanks for everything. Will you come over at Christmas maybe? We

could tramp around my favourite fort and talk about what might
have been.

    Thanks again.

    Gwen xoxoxox

It's midnight. We've printed and read 721 emails. We've
been into Charteris's inbox, her sent mail, and her deleted
folder.

The vast majority of those emails are ordinary nothings.
Chit chat with Katie. Sorting little work niggles. Making
arrangements with her choir-buddies.

But that still leaves about three dozen emails that seem
interesting. Those emails are mostly to or from MyrddinEmrys
– Merlin Ambrosius, the wise man or wizard of Arthurian
myth. Those emails have only one subject header: 'Quondam
Futurusque'.

Early on in the evening, Jones's pizza-holding hand tapped
the phrase.

'Latin.'

'Yes.'

He looked a question.

I said, 'It refers to the supposed inscription on Arthur's
tomb.' Explained that the inscription was said to read *Hic
iacet Arthurus, rex quondam, rexque futurus*. In English:
'Here lies Arthur, the once and future king.'

'A once and future king? What's that? Some kind of riddle?'

'Not exactly. Legend has it that King Arthur never really
died. He lies below ground but will return again if and when
Britain is in peril. The king-protector of these islands.'

'So why didn't he come back to fight Hitler then?'

Jones smirked for an audience that wasn't there, wasn't in
this room. An audience that he left behind in Bridgend.

And I remember thinking: *well, maybe he did*.

Maybe, somehow, that spirit of Arthur returned to win

130

the Battle of Britain, to stumble victorious from the mud and slaughter of the First World War. Perhaps Arthur was on the field at Waterloo, swayed on *Victory*'s quarterdeck through the smokes of Trafalgar, manned the guns at Blenheim, sailed with Raleigh against the Spanish Armada.

If you're dealing with myth, you're dealing with myth, and who knows how those things work?

We put the *Quondam Futurusque* emails in a chain, linked by date.

It seems clear enough that a group of like-minded people conceived some secret project. Secret, illicit, some whiff of danger.

There was initial excitement, then a darkening. A gathering sense of risk or failure. Then the whole thing was abandoned – or at least, Gaynor Charteris *thought* it was.

The group of conspirators, if that's what they were, included:

Gwenhwyfar: Guinevere/Gaynor Charteris.

MyrddinEmrys: Merlin Ambrosius, the wise man or wizard of myth.

Medraut: Mordred, Arthur's illegitimate son.

Yvain: a knight of no particular interest, as far as I know.

Gwalchmei: ditto.

Uthyr: ditto.

To judge from the tone of her emails, Charteris herself never intended any serious harm from the scheme. Myrddin seems to have been central to the plot, at least from Charteris's perspective. If there was a ringleader of the 'dark side', then Medraut was probably that person. We don't know who the 'Medraut and co.' signifies.

We don't know what the conspiracy was, except that gold was somehow involved.

The pizza is now stone cold and greasy, but I nibble at it anyway. Jones re-reads the emails. His lips don't move as he reads, but he has this habit of moving his thumb down the page, paragraph by paragraph, as though pinning the things down, preventing flight.

'There's not enough here,' he says.

'No.'

'For a search warrant, I mean.'

'I know.'

Google will respect a British search warrant, but no British court would give us a warrant for reading the innocent emails of third-parties not clearly connected with any crime.

So we can't persuade Google to show us the Medraut/ Myrddin/Yvain emails.

So what we have, for now, is a tantalising dead end.

I say, mouth full of pizza, 'We arrange a meeting.'

'What?'

I take Jones's keyboard with a flourish. A conjuror about to perform a brand new trick.

Get up a fresh Gmail page.

Compose a new message.

To: MyrddinEmrys@gmail.com.
From: FrenhinesGwenhwyfar@gmail.com
Date: 5 April
Subject: Rex quondam, rexque futurus.'

Can we meet? Gwenhwyfar.

I don't hit send.

Let Jones lean over me, over the computer, stroking his beard and thinking.

Lose the beard, lose the beard, lose the beard, I think, trying to pummel the message into him by mind-power alone.

'Why do you have a Queen Guinevere Gmail account?'

'It's one I made earlier,' I say.

Lose the beard.

'It can't hurt can it?'

He reaches over my shoulder. Clicks send.

'Why do you have a Guinevere Gmail account?' The second time he's asked.

A truthful answer would be: 'I used that name to circulate our antiquities-themed press release to about ten thousand Arthur fanatics, and chose not to mention that to you.'

But it's gone midnight and the rules say that you don't have to answer annoying questions after midnight. I yawn to remind him.

We're alone in a room with an empty pizza box and 721 emails.

17

A week later.

The Bear Hotel and Restaurant, Bath.

I'm alone. Half-past midday. On the table in front of me, I have a lunch menu and a glass of fizzy water. Those things, plus a small brown teddy bear and a plastic crown.

To: FrenhinesGwenhwyfar@gmail.com
From: MyrddinEmrys@gmail.com
Subject: Re: Rex quondam, rexque futurus.
Date: 5 April, 2016

Where? When?

Here and now, the answer to those questions. We've got audio recording on the table. Video from two angles. Outside on the street, there are some guys repainting a green telecoms unit. A man changing a tyre. In a nearby cafe, a couple of women chatting over cappuccinos. They're our people, all of them. The man changing his tyre will find that his spare tyre has gone flat. Will have to call for help. Will be able to stay out there for two hours if need be.

Jones – positioned up the road in a van stuffed with electronics – calls me.

'All units in place,' he says. 'Stand by for contact.'

'"Stand by for contact?" This isn't Afghanistan, you know.'

'Fiona – just. Just be ready, OK.'

'I *was* ready. I'm actually less ready now because you keep talking like we're expecting an attack of the Taliban.'

A waiter approaches. I wave him forward.

With Jones listening, I say, 'I'll have the pan-fried chicken livers, please. Then the fillet steak.'

Jones says, 'Don't go crazy, Fiona. That steak's the most expensive thing on the menu.'

I say, 'No, not unless you get the Béarnaise sauce as well.' To the waiter, I say, 'And I'll have the Béarnaise sauce as well, please.'

Jones says, 'Fiona!' which isn't either a question or an order.

'I'm getting in role, sir. I just think Guinevere would have the steak.'

We ring off.

Nothing happens.

A waiter comes with my chicken livers. Pan-fried, because as far as I know there is no other way to fry the things.

I eat some of them. They're nice. Garlicky, and lemony, and fatty, and yum.

The waiter clears my plate.

The restaurant is reasonably busy now. A bit of business custom. Some men in grey suits. A woman in a cream dress talking to a salesman type in a silvery-lilac tie. A family birthday party. A group of women, two of them with babies in prams. A few men at the bar.

A waiter brings my steak.

I don't think I've ever had Béarnaise before, but it's nice. The steak is a bit much, though, after the chicken livers, so I only peck at it. Give the side salad most of my attention. Finish my water.

The family birthday party breaks out into Happy Birthdays and the dad hops around taking photos.

One forty-five. No Myrddin.

I order peppermint tea, because I can't face pudding, not even to annoy Bleddyn Jones.

135

Make the tea and bill payment last until two fifteen.

Then Jones calls.

'OK, let's wrap this up.'

I go. I keep the teddy bear but leave the plastic crown as part of the waiter's tip. Walk half a mile in towards the centre of Bath, before an unmarked white van pulls up beside me.

I yank at the back door and climb inside.

'How did we do?' I ask.

'Yeah, OK.'

He shoves some print-outs at me. Stills taken from the restaurant video feeds.

The business guys. The cream dress woman. The birthday party. The barman's buddies. The various other people who came and went while I was there.

Most of the print-outs have vehicle plates scribbled on them. Some have names as well. Other names will follow shortly.

The family birthday party isn't yet tagged with either vehicle registration or name.

I say, 'This guy. The dad. He kept taking photos. I was definitely in some of them.'

Jones nods. 'They arrived on foot. Then took a taxi to the station.'

Which is strange in itself. Birthday parties of that kind are normally taken round the corner from home, or at least in the same town. And trains are expensive: a family like that would normally travel by car.

Jones makes a call. Aidan Jenkins, the guy who'd been busy with his thwarted tyre change.

'Aidan, any update?'

'Yep, I've got them in sight. They're buying tickets. Time on the clock is two forty-eight. Left-hand window. The person making the sale is a blonde thirty- or forty-something woman, shoulder-length hair. You want me to follow onto the train?'

'How did they pay for the tickets?'

'Card.'

'OK, just watch them onto a train. That'll do.'

He rings off.

'You're paying for that damn steak. I won't authorise it.'

I don't argue.

We wait until Aidan Jenkins calls back. 'Train to Reading and London. They're on it.'

We drive to the station.

Flash warrant cards at the ticket office. Jones comes over all detective inspectory. Talks about, 'Pursuing a suspect on a current murder enquiry.'

The blonde woman lets us look at her payments screen. The father bought tickets to Oxford, with a change at Reading. We take a print-off of the card receipt.

Jones calls the card numbers through to Cardiff. Holds the line. Scratches his beard.

Then, 'Yeah, OK, give me that again.'

Writes: 'J. P. Oakeshott. John Phillip. 15 Halifax Road, Oxford.'

'OK. Get everything else you can. Bio. Photo. Facebook. Phone number. All that.'

But I'm half a step ahead of him. Use my phone to search, 'John Oakeshott Oxford'.

The first result: an Oxford University web page. John Oakeshott, with photo – the guy in the restaurant.

Senior Research Fellow at Worcester College. Area of interest: Late antiquity and early medieval history.

Bingo.

18

Oxford.

Buildings in gently honeyed stone. Grassy lawns and deep flowerbeds. Tulips and daffs.

We drove here, to Oakeshott's college. Arrived before him. Have been waiting an hour and more for him to turn up. I come back from a toilet break to find Jones standing well back in this gathering dusk.

He points to a lighted window.

'He's in there. Just turned up. Two students in with him.'

I nod.

This next bit. Do we do it police style or Guinevere style? That was always the question but we, the police, have almost nothing to frighten Oakeshott with. No hold, no squeeze of information.

We could just enter the room and hope that Oakeshott chooses to volunteer whatever information he has. But those childish pseudonyms? His attempts to avoid recognition? Those hardly suggest a man inclined to tell us all.

So Guinevere it is.

Jones doesn't like that, but he has nothing better to suggest.

So Guinevere, Arthur's queen, leaves the two men in their violet shadows and marches up to Oakeshott's door.

I don't knock, just enter.

Oakeshott's room is an Oxford don's room of the sort that an unimaginative set designer might have built. Lots of white bookshelves. Lots of books. A tumble of paper and more books on the desk, the floor, side-tables. Side-lamps with silk shades. Some old prints and maps in frames. A Georgian fireplace, unused. A little sideboard with decanters and glasses.

Also two students, both women. One dark-haired, one blonde. Pretty. The dark one has an extravagant loose polo neck and complicated jewellery. She's either one of those people who gives off sex-drive under all circumstances or, equally possible, she half-fancies Oakeshott.

I say to Oakeshott, 'Hi.'

He says, 'Ah!' Doesn't look thrilled to see me, but thinks he needs to explain my entrance to his students. Says, 'This is, uh . . .'

'Gwenhwyfar,' I say. And to the students add, 'And you are?'

Felicity and Emma, they tell me.

I say, 'Felicity, Emma, would you mind fucking off? Like, right now.'

They glance at Oakeshott who nods OK.

'We'll pick this up later,' he tells them.

Once they're gone, he says, 'Look, I don't appreciate—'

'*You* don't appreciate? *I* don't appreciate being stood up by a dick who thought it would be funny to drag me out to some random place in Bath, just so he can take photos of me and not actually step over to say hello.'

'OK. I'm sorry. I just needed to find out who you were.'

'Oh, and how did that go exactly, dickbrain? Work out for you OK?'

'No, but I haven't yet—'

'You haven't yet distributed my photo to Uthyr, Medraut and the rest.'

'No.'

'Dick.'

I thump my bear down on his desk and glare at him.

139

My bear and my crown were my way of identifying myself in the restaurant, but the bear's plasticky little nose happens to contain an audio transmitter which will beam this conversation through to the various boxes of tricks in the back of Jones's surveillance van.

Oakeshott stares at me and asks, 'So who are you?'

'I'm Queen Fucking Guinevere. Here to replace the one whose head was cut off a few weeks ago, or have you forgotten that?'

'No.'

'So?'

'So?'

'So what the fucking hell is going on?'

Oakeshott twists the bear round on his desk. A really professional criminal would distrust that bear. Distrust me. Want to sweep us for transmitting devices. Want to avoid any possibility of recording. But you've got to be a pro to do those things right and Oakeshott's day job is, after all, that of early medieval historian.

'You followed me here?'

'Yes, that's right. I followed you back here using my superspy surveillance skills. Either that, or I recognised you the moment you walked into the fucking restaurant.'

'You're a historian?'

'Yes.'

'A medievalist?'

'No. I'm really interested in the battlefields of the Second World War. That's why I call myself Guinevere.'

The early-medieval history community is small enough that, if I were a historian working in that area, I could well have recognised one of our little firmament's brightest stars.

Oakeshott scrutinises me, trying to place me. I look young for my age, but still older than the dewily new Emma-Felicity.

'Graduate study?'

'Yes.'

'Where?'

'Fuck you.'

'What if you're police?'

'Then you're fucked.'

Which isn't in fact true, but he might think it is. His distrust doesn't vanish, though, so I choose to help him.

I go over to his little decanter area. Pick up one of them. Sherry, I'd guess. Dry or sweet or whichever is the more up-yourself middle-class version of that up-yourself middle-class drink. The decanter is about half full. It's got the heaviness of lead crystal. It's probably antique or belonged to his grandmother or was hand-cut by some overpaid craftsman in Donegal.

I lift it.

Drop it.

The thing doesn't, unfortunately, break, but it does leak middle-class sherry all over his middle-class carpet.

I pick up one of his matching glasses. Hold it over the decanter.

Drop it.

The glass breaks, with a pleasingly explosive shatter.

Oakeshott looks at me, furious and appalled.

'Not police,' I say placidly. 'See? I bet they'd get told off for doing stuff like that. Or sent on a course or something.'

I'm not quite sure what Jones's attitude will be, in fact, but it's a chance I'm happy to take. And of course we *do* need to force the issue. Everything about Oakeshott's behaviour tells us that he's hiding something we need to know but we don't yet, in narrow police terms, have enough to force him to divulge.

I pick up some more glasses.

'Put those down.'

'Gaynor was a friend of mine. And someone cut off her

141

head. And I don't care about your fucking glassware.'

Drop them.

Break them.

The glass makes a wonderful sound, percussive and deep, but with a lovely tinkling overlay. That's what you get from using those top-dollar Donegal craftspeople. What you get from all that lead in your crystal.

'I didn't kill Gaynor.'

'I'm not saying you did.'

Get a meaty paperback from his shelves. A social history of women in England, ending in 1500. It looks interesting. I make as if to rip it down the spine.

'Stop that. Just stop it.'

He comes over. Looms over. Is physically threatening.

I make a peaceable movement of my hands.

'OK.'

Back away.

Sit in the chair that Emma or Felicity or Venetia or Charlotte or some other long-haired lovely last sat adoringly on.

'All right. I won't break anything else. I'll just call the cops.'

Get out my phone. Start to dial the Cathays switchboard.

'Don't do that.'

'You're always telling me not to do things,' I complain.

Hit the call button.

The call is picked up after a couple of rings. I ask to be put through to the Major Crimes team.

Oakeshott can't stand it. Can't stand the pressure.

He grabs for me, the phone.

Gets the phone and bends my fingers sharply back as he takes it. My fingers hurt and I yelp a loud *ow!* for the microphone, but I'm pleased he's getting aggressive. It shows his decision-making is starting to deteriorate.

Also: Oakeshott is bigger than me, but I'm nastier.

With my free hand, I grab at his testicles.

Grab, squeeze, twist, pull.

That's the correct order, I'm told. And since the person who told me used to teach unarmed combat in the Spetsnaz, the Russian special forces, I'm fairly sure he knew what he was talking about.

I expect that, if Oakeshott had the leisure to consider the matter, he'd agree too.

At any rate, he's doubling forward in that delightfully easy to access male agony, when I grab his tie, hook my foot around his ankles and shove.

He falls hard, hitting his head against his desk on the way down.

I keep my hand bunched up on his tie and pressed tight against his Adam's apple.

'If you lay a hand on me one more time, I will call the police and report assault. If you ask me to leave the room, I'm happy to do so. If you want me to pay for your broken glass, I'll do that too. But if I leave the room without knowing what the hell happened to Gaynor, I will call the police and tell them everything I know.'

I say that first part about the assault for the listening microphone. To place on the record that Oakeshott assaulted me and to mark the total absence of denial from him. Ditto the thing about my being ready to leave and pay for any damage.

I keep my hand up tight against his neck until the fire of anger changes in his eyes. Becomes something more like the smoulder of defeat.

I move my hand. Pick up my phone.

Get the Cathays number back up. Hover over the call button.

'Well?'

'I've done nothing illegal.'

'Fair enough.'

I make the call.

'Major Crimes, please.'

'Who's calling?'

'Gwenhwyfar.'

'Can I have a full name, please, caller?'

'Sorry, no, I'd prefer to remain anonymous.'

'Putting you through now.'

Calling Major Crimes after hours is a little chancy in all honesty. *I* often work late. So does Jones. Aside from us, though, most of my dear colleagues pelt out of the office by six o'clock at the latest, and we're already past that hour.

But I'm in luck. Mervyn Rogers picks up grumpily.

'Major Crimes,' he says, as though asking me to order something from a takeout menu. 'This is Bleddyn Jones speaking.'

Good man! I was a little worried about making the call because, assuming that anyone was there to pick up, any of my colleagues would certainly recognise my voice. Rogers, in particular, would be likely to arse around if I called up pretending to not be me. Giving his name as Bleddyn Jones is his way of telling me that Jones already phoned ahead to warn him that I might make this call.

I say, 'I'd like to remain anonymous for the moment, but I have some information regarding the recent murder of Dr Gaynor Charteris.'

Rogers starts to answer that, but Oakeshott has levered himself up from the floor and is making a vigorous horizontal chopping motion with his hand, asking me to cut the call.

Interrupting Rogers, I say, 'Just a moment,' and mute the phone.

Oakeshott says – croaks – 'Come back here tomorrow. I'll tell you what you need. It's just – there are – look, there are people I need to talk to first. There are others in this too.'

I say – phone still connected, still muted – 'Tomorrow evening? Six o'clock? No bollocks?'

He nods.

'Is that a "yes"?'

'Yes.'

I unmute the phone. Say, 'Sorry I'll need to call you back. Expect a call from this number at seven o'clock tomorrow evening.'

Cut the line. Turn the phone off. Open the back and remove the battery. Drop the bits in my pocket.

Oakeshott, meanwhile, has put his desk between himself and me. Keeps plucking at his collar, adjusting things around his crotch, rubbing his head where he banged it.

My teddy bear is still on his desk. I leave it right where it is.

Standing up, and gesturing at the broken glass, I say, 'Nice room, but you should tidy up the crap.'

Leave.

In the green shadows and violet light of the gardens, I see Felicity and Emma still hanging around. Curiosity, perhaps, but also a mild concern for their tutor's well-being. Perhaps they heard the smashing.

I walk past them, heading for the exit, heading for the street.

19

Three of us in the van. Jones on the audio controls, crouching over them like an anxious sound technician.

Sounds of Oakeshott clearing up. A swearword as he cuts himself on something. I laugh. Jones glowers.

Then women's voices, checking on their wounded hero.

'Those are the students,' I say. 'Felicity and Emma. I didn't get surnames.'

Oakeshott says something that's meant to be calming. He calls me 'a troubled young woman': an entirely accurate description. He says, 'It's sad, really,' and says, no, he's OK tidying up on his own.

The students go.

More tidying.

In the van, Jones says. 'That was totally unprofessional, what you did in there. I'll have to review this.'

That annoys me. Review what? He knows what I did in there. If he wants to give me a bollocking, he should give me a bollocking.

I say, 'Undercover officers are encouraged to think on their feet in what may well be dangerous and fast-moving situations.'

'You're not undercover-trained.'

'I am.'

'What? You did the course? That Undercover Training thing?'

'The Undercover Training and Assessment Course. Yes.'

'And passed?'

'Yes.'

Jones digests that. The course in question is specialist and hard. Few officers put themselves forward, and the vast majority of those who do fail to complete it. He tries to figure out how that information might or might not affect matters.

Decides it's still safer to be antsy.

'Even so, it was totally unprofessional. This could be a disciplinary matter.'

'So I'm not allowed to protect myself if I'm assaulted?'

'No, I'm OK with that. It's the—'

'I broke four glasses for which I offered to pay. *Four glasses*. Are you saying that is not a proportionate measure to be taken in the context of an active murder enquiry? An enquiry where we are currently short of leads and where the subject is clearly withholding information and frightened of police involvement?'

'No, look, all I'm saying is I might need to review this.'

I shrug.

Don't care.

Moron.

We turn the audio feed up, leaning into that crackling silence.

Whatever Oakeshott has been up to, he clearly has co-conspirators and ones he now feels pressured into communicating with. That's the good news.

But there was bad news too. He said, in so many words, *I've done nothing illegal.* That, and *I didn't kill Gaynor.* Those statements basically kill any chance we have of getting an interception warrant on Oakeshott's phone. Surveillance that invades the privacy of an innocent third party is not totally outlawed, but the case in favour has to be exceptionally strong and what we have isn't strong enough.

Knowing all this, Jones is twitchy about continuing our teddy-bear-based surveillance. He's in a Jonesian nightmare. On the one hand, a high-profile enquiry without adequate leads. On the other, a possible breach of the Regulation of Investigatory Powers Act.

Rock. Hard place.

Moron.

We listen in, willing him to make a call. Willing him to make the kind of call which will permit our continuing surveillance.

But when he picks up the phone, it's his wife he calls.

'Darling, it's me. Sorry, I'm running a bit late, but . . .'

Fuck it.

Jones kills the connection. The van fills with the burr of traffic outside. The creak of our elderly seating.

So. Tomorrow evening. We wait till then.

We drive back to Cardiff.

Green shadows. Violet light.

And the sweet, sweet sound of breaking glass.

20

Jones, the pillock, spends the night thinking about what to do and decides that his butt would be best covered by giving me a formal written warning.

'On due consideration, I have come to the conclusion that your behaviour in relation to John Oakeshott was excessively confrontational and not in keeping with the standards to be expected of the South Wales CID.'

Blah, blah, blah.

He gives me a letter and yaps at me.

I don't read it. Don't even listen, or not properly. I've had plenty of first-stage disciplinary things in the past and I can't see that this one is going to turn into a second-stager.

I say 'Yes, sir,' for a bit and try to look like a newly beaten puppy but, when I get bored of all that, I interrupt to say, 'So, this evening, how are we going to play it?'

'Well, as you'll gather, I think a more measured approach—'

'I'm thinking maybe I should apologise for yesterday and write out a cheque for the stuff I broke.'

'I think you do need to compensate him, yes.'

'But I should also make it really clear that no adverse consequence will befall him if he chooses not to tell me anything. I mean, it's important to remove that sense of pressure.'

'No, no, I wouldn't go so far as—'

'I'll give him some cash, apologise for swearing, call him

"Mr Oakeshott" or maybe "sir", and ask very politely if he wants to tell me anything. Make it clear that it's OK if he doesn't.'

Jones does that hatred look again.

Narrow eyes. Cold lips.

I don't think I have any more second chances with the good Inspector Jones. He says, very coldly, 'I will give you written instructions.'

We exchange smiles made of ice and snow.

Japanese martial artists bowing over tatami mats.

But, as it turns out, Jones never writes his instructions. I never get to make nice to Oakeshott – or smash up more of his things – or anything else.

Because, as we turn to our databases, start to research the guy in more detail than was possible yesterday, we come across a crime report, dated today.

Not long after dawn this morning, a corpse, three stab wounds in its side and belly, was recovered from the canal that skirts the western edge of Oxford. No cash, cards or telephone were found on the victim, but an identification was quickly made via a Missing Persons report, lodged the evening before. The victim's wife has already identified the corpse as John Phillip Oakeshott. While theft is being considered as a possible motive for the attack, it is noted that an unknown woman entered his room in Worcester College the evening before and appears to have been responsible for some broken glassware, which is currently under examination by Thames Valley forensics.

I don't quite know how I feel on encountering this news. On the one hand, I didn't kill Oakeshott: his murderer did. On the other hand, I was among the very last people on earth to see him and I deliberately frightened and upset him. My intrusion was, presumably, connected to his death. I deliberately chose to destabilise a wall, not knowing that a man would be killed by its collapse.

Those things weigh on a person, even me.

Jones dobs me in, of course. Picks up the phone to his Oxfordshire counterpart, Stuart Carr, and identifies their mystery woman.

Carr's sort of pleased, because it's resolved his major lead, but sort of annoyed, because his nice little murder now dangles from the coat-tails of someone else's enquiry.

Carr asks us to send him whatever we've got. Asks to see us.

So off we go. In Jones's car, a BMW 1 Series. Not the newest model, but scrupulously clean, inside and out. The damn thing, in true Jonesian style, is funereal black and glossy.

Miles and minutes pass us by.

I notice how, viewed from the motorway, the countryside always looks the same. Pressed into some universal shape by this frame of tarmac and concrete.

I say, 'Funny how everything looks the same when you're on a motorway.'

Jones doesn't respond to that interesting observation. Instead he says, 'It's not the first time. I know that. I looked in your file.'

I don't answer. Look away, rolling my eyes.

No, it's not the first time I've troubled my superiors. But it's also not the first time I've worked undercover and the last time I did that, I did so for nigh on eight months, in a highly perilous situation and ended up forcing a successful – or almost successful – conclusion to the whole adventure. If Jones wants to play file-wars with me, he's welcome.

We drive on in silence.

The miles and minutes go on passing, but they go more slowly now. Heaving their way past in a tense, embarrassed silence.

Past Oxford to Kidlington. An unlovely suburb that houses the Thames Valley Police HQ.

Carr's office.

Bland, cheap, unmodern.

Carr himself: one of these fifty-something DIs who'll never, for some reason, make it higher up the ladder. It's often a matter of choice as much as competence. Some detectives just like the chance to get their boots dirty.

He listens to our audio recording of last night. Listens to my entrance. My glass-smashing.

Chuckles.

'That's old school, that is.'

At the bit where I yell 'ow!', he stops the recording. 'He did hurt you, did he?'

'Yes. I mean, I *was* being arsey with him.'

Jones says, 'It was unprofessional behaviour. I've spoken with her about it already.'

Carr says, and his gaze is on me, cutting out Jones altogether, 'When you went in there. Last night. Did you have any reason to think your intervention would place Oakeshott at risk?'

'No.'

'And he was a key witness, was he? I mean, potentially?'

'Yes.'

Carr looks at me a little longer. Then shrugs. Restarts the tape.

We hear the woody thump of Oakeshott's head hitting his desk. Carr says nothing. The chuckle is still there in his eyes, but something more serious too.

We listen to the end.

Carr asks, 'You believe him?'

Believe, that is, that he hadn't killed Charteris. That he had done nothing illegal.

'Yes. He was mixed up in something, but not that.'

'So, whoever killed your Charteris woman killed Oakeshott. Maybe killed him for something he was about to disclose.'

Probably yes, is the upshot of the discussion that follows.

Carr – white hair, glasses, something a bit forward-leaning, a bit greyhoundy in his manner – takes a new pencil from a plastic holder and drums on the desk with it. Holds it up, ceremoniously. Displaying it to us. Then snaps it. Drops the pieces in a mug decorated with a child's handprint. Puts the mug back on a shelf.

'My good luck ritual,' he says. 'Always do it in cases of murder. Happened by accident the first time, then . . .'

I stare at the mug, horrified. There are six pencils in it.

I say, faintly, 'How long have you . . .?'

'Eighteen years ago the first one.'

God save me from policing in Oxford, I think. And I'd thought Cardiff was bad.

As I'm thinking this, the grown-ups are putting their Serious Masculine Faces on. I can't match those faces for seriousness or masculinity, so I just smile becomingly.

Carr points at me and says, 'I might need to keep a hold of this one, if you can spare her.'

Jones: 'Far as I'm concerned, you can have her on a ninety-nine-year lease.'

'And we'll need to kick this upstairs, of course,' Carr says, referring to the audio recording.

Jones mutters something, but whatever he says is too boring for my brain to process, so instead the syllables get shredded and recycled and will turn up again as an interesting remark about waste collection or the best ways to organise desk-stationery.

Jones goes. I stay. Carr talks to his boss. When he returns, he says, 'Grieving widow time. Prepare to make nice.'

Oxford.

A row of brick houses, rattly Victorian things. Front gardens with bulbs and magnolias, bicycles and bins.

The grieving widow – Lydia – is forty-ish. Slim. Shortish dark hair. Black trousers. A pretty floral tunic thing, roses on black, notched at the front. It's the kind of top you might see

153

on a much younger woman, but which looks good on her. Cool, even. All that, and a cardigan that doesn't button or tie, just hangs and swings in a cooler way than it would ever hang or swing on me. The woman got dressed this morning not knowing that her husband was floating face down in a canal. Would she have dressed less cool if she had known? Or do you just wear the same clothes as you always wear? Finding that the weirdest thing about sudden bereavement is that the whole world goes on, much as it would if you hadn't lost your beloved.

Lydia Oakeshott's home backs on to a canal. We sit at the end of the kitchen, looking through some french doors to where a weeping willow bends its fronds over the petrol-grey waters. An old rope-swing hangs motionless. It reminds me, for no reason, of an uncompleted suicide.

In the living room, the couple's two kids – a boy and a girl, six and eight – sit with a grandmother and a family liaison officer, supplied by Carr's force. I recognise the kids, and Lydia of course, from the restaurant in Bath. If circumstances were different, I suppose they might even recognise me.

The FLO flurries around with coffee. Knows where the biscuit tin is and puts it out.

Early in my career I was offered training in family liaison. Female officer: good with tea and sympathy. That was the logic. Then my colleagues got to know me better and the offer was never repeated.

Carr says, 'Mrs Oakeshott. We've got information. New to me personally, and new to you too. That mystery woman. Last night's intruder.'

He stops. Some muscle in his jaw moves in a way that indicates, I think, he wants me to take the stage.

I do so.

'Mrs Oakeshott. I was that woman. I'm a police officer, a detective, in the South Wales force. We were pursuing an active investigation over in Cardiff and we believed that your husband was withholding some key information. I entered his room—'

Lydia Oakeshott hardly hears me.

'You?'

'Yes.'

'You broke his glasses?'

'Yes.'

There's a movement in the woman's face which seems almost relieved.

'You weren't . . . I mean, you and he hadn't . . .'

'We had never met before. There was no sort of relationship, no sexual relationship, involved.'

She puts her hand to her face. Pushes back hair which hadn't been in the way. Silver bracelets rattle at her wrist. Different shades and expressions of grief compete for houseroom.

I think: all those Emma-Felicity-Venetia-Charlottes, their long hair and dewy eagerness. Of course there were infidelities, perhaps many of them. It's one of the things we neglect about grief: its unyielding complexity. A puzzle that never simplifies no matter how often, how obsessively, you turn it.

I continue, 'Our investigation is still at an early stage. But at this point, we *do* think that your husband was withholding information. We *don't* think that he was involved in anything illegal, or not significantly illegal anyway. And we are *not* aware of any outside sexual relationship, or certainly nothing linked to our case.'

That last comment elicits a short, sharp toss of the head, but nothing more.

Carr, speaking carefully, says, 'In cases like this, we always institute an internal investigation. We will keep you closely in touch with the—'

'You were doing your job, yes? You broke some – some glasses.'

155

Shrugs. A like-I-give-a-damn shrug.

Lydia Oakeshott is so impeccably middle-class, she can't even bring herself to insert the word 'fucking' where it naturally belongs.

I say, 'Mrs Oakeshott, we suspect that your husband's death was linked to whatever it was he was withholding. Whatever secret he kept. If you can help in any way . . .'

'I don't know. Nothing. I mean . . .' She wonders whether to talk about those infidelities. Realises she can't. Moves on. 'Nothing. He had this stupid Arthur obsession, but . . .'

Her braceleted hand waves all that nonsense away. Away from the table. Away through the french doors. Down the slope of that tidy-lawned garden to the rope and the swing and the weeping willow and that dark unmoving water.

With a half-smile, I sweep the nonsense all the way back again.

'Ma'am. Sorry. Believe me, we know how hard this is. But our Cardiff investigation centres on the murder of another historian. An archaeologist. Someone who also had an interest in Arthur. Someone who may well have died as a result of that interest.'

She stares at me. Doesn't know how to respond.

From next door, there's a sudden wail from one of the children, the boy, I think. The wail summons the mother's attention back from wherever it is. I'm struggling to reach her.

I say, 'Mrs Oakeshott, we'll leave you as soon as we can. Just – do you have the names of others who shared your husband's interest? We think there was some quite close circle of friends and associates—'

'Oh God, no. He was all secretive about that stuff. His Round Table, he called it.'

Her old annoyances encounter the rocks of her grief, their

unfamiliar upthrust. For the first time since we've been here, there's a quick wash of tears. Salt drops glinting in a blue, marine air.

We ask what we need to ask. Leave as soon as we can.

The widow's story is this.

Oakeshott came straight home last night. He was perturbed, clearly, after my intrusion into his chambered life. He snatched a quick supper. Helped bath the kids, but inattentively, distracted, unlike his usual self. Then raced out again, 'with his stupid Round Table phone. He never used his regular mobile for those calls.'

He left the house about half past eight. When he wasn't back at midnight, and hadn't called or texted, Lydia Oakeshott called the police, somewhat embarrassed, but anxious all the same. Her call wasn't treated with any great seriousness: in the absence of child protection concerns or the like, no police force will treat someone as missing without a gap of at least twenty-four hours.

'But,' the widow told us, 'I just had this awful feeling. He wasn't the way he normally was. I just thought . . . I just thought . . .'

What she thought, I don't know, but her instinct was horribly right. The corpse was found not long after dawn by a man cycling down the canal towpath.

Lydia: 'Oh yes, he used to walk there all the time. If he had calls to make, he'd often go outside. Walk and talk. He had a big fresh air thing.'

If we could trace those calls we'd quite likely be able to close the case fairly speedily, but there's no trace of the phone, no record of its number.

Email the same.

We get on to Google immediately, of course. It took one long and tedious weekend last time but, given the newly accelerated circumstances, we manage to get access to

Oakeshott's MyrddinEmrys@gmail.com data by eight o'clock that evening.

And—

Nothing.

Everything deleted. Not sitting in the deleted folder, but deleted-deleted.

Not just that, but when I send test emails to Uthyr@gmail.com, Medraut@gmail.com, and the rest of that crew, the emails bounce.

We talk to someone at Google about it. He sounds like a real human being – albeit a Californian one whose hair is probably full of sunshine and organic hair product. But he confirms that, *real sorry*, the data has actually gone.

Gone as in gone-gone.

Gone as in irrecoverable.

John Oakeshott was many things. A man, a husband, a father, an adulterer, a historian, an Arthurian obsessive. But he was also, crucially, our most promising lead on the Gaynor Charteris case and, so far, that lead is as dead as the man who was carrying it.

Two corpses. No leads.

And a mystery that darkens with every turn.

21

So we work.

Forensics, of course, though that muddy and well-travelled canal path is hardly promising.

Data analysis. Phone calls and car movements and all that.

And interviews. A million of them.

Our interviews take in all the medievalists in the Oxford history faculty. *Where were you on the night of the 11/12 April? Were you engaged in secret phone and email communication with John Philip Oakeshott? Or with Gaynor Charteris, lately of Dinas Powys in the county of South Glamorgan?*

We ask the right questions in the right way.

Push hard, get nowhere.

It's not even that we get no answers. We don't even get a frisson of concealment, that sense of fear.

On the contrary. We find the opposite. Tweedy dons, earnest graduates, all shocked by what happened. Anxious to help. Offering advice and information that is anywhere from hopelessly irrelevant to endearingly barmy.

We go through Oakeshott's known professional contacts. Oxford graduate students working in the same field. We look at his personal address book, his work emails, his conferences, everything.

Do that, and get nowhere.

Yes, we find evidence of Oakeshott's infidelities. The lovely Felicity – she of the extravagant polo neck and complicated jewellery – was one such. But she, winsomely tear-stained and repentant, knew nothing to help us. From Oakeshott's point of view, she was an available shag, nothing more.

Jones doesn't want me in Cardiff and Carr does want me in Oxford, so I'm part of that whole busy whirl. Interviewing. Note-taking. Report-writing. Briefings. Reviews.

The Kidlington HQ has a block that provides accommodation for visiting staff. The place is clean enough, but still horrible, so I call an old friend of mine from Cambridge – a Junior Research Fellow in philosophy at Christchurch College. She, Rosemary, offers me a berth on her floor, and I spend my days working up at Kidlington or co-interviewing with Carr's team. Spend my evenings snuggled up on Rosemary's sofa, stockinged feet buried amongst her abundant cushions. We sit talking till late.

After she's gone to bed, I generally pass a pleasant hour or so checking out those Arthurian message boards.

My press release and my stirring has done the trick.

People have noticed that the seal box could be the first ever true Arthurian artefact. That stone from Camlan, or nearby, seems to confirm it. The thefts from Bangor and Saint Tydecho's suggest that there's more to come and there's intense speculation as to what that might be.

And what is that thing?

I don't yet know. I need to find out.

I talk endlessly with Katie, speculating about the case. Talking about blacksmithery and jewellery and what life was like back then. The Romans gone, the Saxons coming. *Repellunt barbari ad mare, repellit mare ad barbaros; inter haec duo genera funerum aut iugulamur aut mergimur.*

Katie comes over to Oxford a couple of times too. Not for work reasons, or not really. We've become friends, I think. That friendship started somewhere on the road up to Bangor and has slowly settled in to place thereafter. And it's true, certainly, that Katie's loss of her Ph.D. leaves her at a loose end, and this case is the most interesting thing to fill it. But also – we like each other. We enjoy our time spent together. It's a good feeling.

At one point, I have to go back to Cardiff to receive my Formal Written Warning from Bleddyn Jones and some pretty blonde bob in Human Resources. And when that happy ritual is complete, I head home for some fresh clothes and find, waiting on my doormat, some padded envelopes with my eBay treasure.

My Roman glass. A silver bell. Some beads of Whitby jet.

When I go back to Oxford, to interview more academics or sit across a table as Oakeshott's grieving students explain to me how utterly surprising and mysterious and inexplicable his death was, I keep one hand in my pocket, where I keep my two dozen beads of Romano–Celtic jet.

Roll those beads round and round, little emissaries from a distant age, and I remember that nothing is for ever.

King Arthur was not for ever.

His defeat of the Saxons was not for ever.

Inspector Jones of the Irritating Beard: he too is not for ever.

When Katie tells me that she's arranged for the dig at Dinas Powys to be re-opened, just for a week or two, just so the initial exploratory project can be completed as planned, I give her six of my Whitby beads. She will scatter them into the trench and cover them over with soil. When they are 'found', they will be logged, analysed and uploaded to the project website.

Eighteen beads left.

And nothing is for ever.

22

In Oxford, our investigation tapers to a point where I'm no longer needed, so – unwanted everywhere – I end up back in Cardiff.

Jones doesn't want me either, but he knows that his limping enquiry needs whatever help I bring, so I'm allowed to continue working, although 'on a short leash', as Jones creepily puts it. He makes a gesture as of a beardily annoying man jerking a dog lead, and I have this horrible idea that that's how he likes to imagine me. On all fours. Collared, leashed and muzzled. Thighs and buttocks a-tremble at the sight of my master's boot.

We maintain a chill politeness, but barely.

It's clear enough now, even to Jones, that the Reasonably Local Nutter theory is dead. We have two historians, both murdered. A whole web of other clues, other data, which murmurs of conflicts past. Dark Age battles against a Dark Age foe.

We failed to find Oakeshott's Round Table associates in Oxford, but they're out there somewhere, so we look everywhere we can. Historians and archaeologists. Anyone with an interest in early Dark Age Britain. Our interviews take in Cardiff and Oxford, but also Cambridge, London, Durham, York, Bangor, Bristol, Kent.

Carr wants me to lead those interviews, and Jones agrees, accepting that I'm the right person for the job. That's good

162

enquiry management, that is, except that because he doesn't trust me, he hobbles me. Orders me – in writing, no less – to 'avoid confrontation and to maintain a polite and professional demeanour'. In the event that I actually discover something like a lead, I am to 'take no further action without consulting the Commanding Officer'.

Moron.

But still. Even working in this Jonesian way, our data accumulates. Working sometimes with a DC up from Cardiff, at other times with a DC supplied from Oxford, I collect universities like postage stamps. Stone quadrangles and church bells. Modern campuses and artificial lakes.

Door after door. Face after face.

Bland, unprobing questions. Bland, unhelpful answers.

And then – Durham.

It's a sodden May day. Rain chases us up the A1, with me impatiently at the wheel. An almost painfully eager DC from Oxford, a Paul Compton, is in the car with me, an Interview Plan on his iPad, a bunch of research notes in a bundle on his lap.

We reach Durham. The cluttered streets and puzzling topography of what is claimed to be England's third oldest university.

Find a place to park.

Search under the falling rain for the right door to the right building. By the time we find it, Compton and I, both underdressed, look like a pair of Jack Russells scattering water after a walk.

Our interviewee, Alden Gheerbrant, has a cheerful, Georgian, book-lined room. Bookshelves and panelling. Everything white. A busy enough desk, but also a carpet, a fireplace, sofa and chairs. The guy is a specialist in early medieval warfare. Weapons. The archaeology of violent death.

He has long, dark, curly hair. A wide smile. Greets us with

a public schoolboy's easy, elastic, dislikeable charm.

'Find me all right, did you? Here, do you want to put your wet things down? There's a towel in there if you want to dry off. Tea OK? Or do detectives always have to drink strong, black coffee?'

He manages, somehow, to convey that our wetness is amusing. The sort of solecism that chaps like him would never commit.

I hesitate a moment.

Stop still, trying to catch the scent.

Some politeness is just affable. Some automatic. Some genuine. And some plain deceitful.

The smiler with the knife under the cloak. The cattle-shed burning with the black smoke.

Do I smell smoke here? Or am I just too hungry for a breakthrough?

I don't know. But that comment about detectives tells me that he's a little on edge. And that laughing, too-confident politeness: I don't trust that. Don't trust it at all.

So I ditch Compton's stupid interview plan. Form a new one of my own, which I proceed to implement in a manner which will 'avoid confrontation' and 'maintain a polite and professional demeanour'.

I use the little shower room that Gheerbrant indicates. Dry my hair off with a towel. Go back into his room, still fluffing. My hair is short enough that, if I don't use a comb, I end up looking like a punk princess on Valkyrie Night.

I don't use a comb.

'Do you have a radiator I can use? These things are soaked.'

Kick off my stupid black court shoes. Put them on a radiator. Pick at my wet tights. Grimace.

Say sorry.

Get out my voice-recorder.

Drop it.

Say sorry.

Try to set the recorder up. Can't. Ask Compton to help. Watch as he does it. Mouth 'yikes' at Gheerbrant and pull a face.

We get started, or sort of.

Compton starts off introducing time, date, names of those present for the recorder. Thanks Gheerbrant for his time. Starts to ask the most basic questions. Things to do with Gheerbrant's current position. His research interests. His degree of acquaintance with the two murder victims.

As Compton talks and Gheerbrant answers, I look through Compton's notes, which are well researched, well put together.

Look through them.

Drop them.

A page falls into my mug of tea and I fish it quickly out, popping the dripping corner into my mouth so as to keep drops from the carpet.

Thanks to my bold and resourceful action, the carpet is spared any drips, though my skirt is not quite so lucky. I stand up, dabbing at the tea with Gheerbrant's towel. Poor Compton, unprepared for any of this, sits there with his hand shielding his mouth and a look of alarm in his eyes.

We soldier on.

Compton follows his interview plan, which sounds like it should be the right thing to do, except that if you adhere to these things too closely, you can't help getting overly mechanical.

Which is good. Which is ideal.

I want to see Gheerbrant relaxed. Confident. Unguarded. If he sees me as an idiot and Compton as a junior officer robotically ticking the boxes on some pre-made interview sheet, he'll be less defended. Less cautious about offering up any micro-tells.

And the tells are there. The tells are there.

His easy charm is interrupted by darting eye movements. His eyes hold smilingly on Compton, before flicking attentively to me, then smilingly back again. But his gaze is shot through with a wintry calculation. No smiles, no warmth, no summer.

That, and one other thing.

Compton asks, as his Interview Plan requires him to ask, 'And you knew Gaynor Charteris, of course. When exactly did you last see her?'

Gheerbrant does nothing exactly wrong. Nothing. But he puts his hand to his mouth, a gesture of self-reassurance. And then – artificially, I think, with awkward timing – stands up with an apology for not having offered us more tea. Stands with his back to us, banging around with kettle and teabags.

Time-wasting, I think.

Gathering his thoughts.

I make a circling gesture to Compton, telling him silently that we're to swap roles. He nods, relieved to see that his buffoon of a boss isn't quite as inept as she appears. I point to my eyes, then at Gheerbrant's back. I mouth, 'Watch him. Watch him.'

When Gheerbrant turns again, he sees that we've swapped roles. A look of caution dances in his eyes. A temporary hesitation before that muffling, blanketing charm returns.

I find the wrong place in the Interview Plan and start about five questions back.

'Didn't we already go through that?' asks Gheerbrant.

I gape.

Consult briefly with Compton, then announce, 'We just want to double-check some things. Sorry.'

So. We burble through some of the things we've burbled through before.

Gheerbrant, who started this interview leaning forwards, long fingers nervously moving over coffee cup, paper and cushions, is now thrown back in his sofa. He has his hand over his mouth again but this time, I think, the hand conceals amusement, not insecurity. Amusement at me. My incompetence.

If he had any anxiety before we started all this, that anxiety has all but evaporated. In its place, confidence. The single most dangerous emotion he could have. The rope that will snare him.

We get to The Question.

I ask The Question.

'So, we've caught up with ourselves at last.' Little laugh. Apology-smile. 'I think you were about to tell us when you last saw Gaynor Charteris.'

His answer comes out as smooth as poured cream. French silk gliding over a naked thigh.

He tells us something about a conference. An academic get-together. 'It would be easy to check,' he says.

'And that was your last contact with her?'

A momentary pause. Then, 'Yes. Yes it was.'

'No phone calls. Email. Nothing like that?'

'No. I didn't know her *that* well. And of course, she was down in Cardiff. I'm up here. It's quite a drive.'

'Of course.' I roll my eyes at the drive. The roadworks and the rain.

As I do that, I write two dates on a sheet of paper. The date of Gheerbrant's last conference sighting of Charteris and the date of the latter's death.

I pass him the sheet. Not because he needs the information, but because I want his hands occupied and away from his mouth.

I ask, 'And did you talk *to* anyone about her? In the period between your conference and her death?'

'Uh – that's a question. I'd have to think.'

He thinks.

Holds my stupid sheet of paper in both hands and thinks.

When dogs look at human faces, they exhibit what's known as 'left gaze bias'. That is, their eyes drift leftwards, because the right side of the human face is more likely to display the person's authentic emotion, while the left side tends to be under closer conscious control – which is to say, more likely to lie.

Because I know this, I'm careful, when interrogating, to display left gaze bias myself. I try to filter out the deceitful left side of my subject's face and watch only the truthful right.

On this occasion, Gheerbrant wears a crooked smile. The left side of his mouth has a sort of fixed grin. A kind of default, holding-at-bay politeness.

The right side isn't like that. It's ruler-straight. And his eyes have an almost frowning intensity.

The moment doesn't last more than a second. Gheerbrant almost shakes himself. Puts the paper down. Wipes his forehead with the back of his hand. Grins – but still lop-sidedly – and says, 'Gosh, you know, it's hard remembering exactly.'

Having given himself permission to pause, he pauses. Thinks hard. There's no dissembling in his face now. It's a frown of concentration. More concentrated, more effortful than anything he's done so far in this interview. Beside me, I feel the prick of Compton's glance. He's seeing what I'm seeing. Wondering what I'm wondering.

I put no more pressure on the question than Compton had placed on any of his – and when Gheerbrant didn't have a ready answer to one of Compton's questions, he would just toss his hand and say, airily, 'Oh, I don't know, I should think . . .'

This time, he thinks hard. Too obviously. Then he says, still cautiously, 'I don't believe I did, no. But I do speak to a lot of colleagues. It's possible that I'm missing something.'

We continue.

In other circumstances, perhaps, I might lean on

Gheerbrant's exposed weakness. Apply pressure to see if I could force the break. But my throat is still circled by Jones's invisible leash and, in any case, it's sometimes better to hold your knowledge of a lead away from the suspect who's provided it.

But, of course, I don't believe his answer. He knows perfectly well whether he spoke to anyone about Charteris. Knows perfectly well that he *did*. What drove him into that frown of concentration was his attempt to figure out whether we'd be able to detect his lie. What the consequences would be for him if we could.

Professional criminals handle those things better. They're less stressed by lying. More aware of police resources and limits. But Gheerbrant is no professional criminal, no more than Oakeshott and Charteris were.

He told us a lie. Got stressed by lying. Let his stress show. The first wrinkle of an edge we've found since Oakeshott's murder.

We bumble on.

I play the goof a little more. Drop papers. Get flustered. Accidentally stop recording and have to go back a couple of questions when I notice the error.

Gheerbrant is almost openly laughing at me now. Exchanging smiles and wrinkled eyebrows with Compton.

And when we, properly this time, switch off the voice recorder, collect shoes from the radiator, thank Gheerbrant for his time, and make ready to go, he's laughing, joking, thinking he's won.

Because he's a warfare- and weapons-man, he has various knick-knacks around the place. An antique spear-tip. A notched bone. A fragment of leather. Something which I think may have been chain mail.

Also a blade. A knife.

Clearly modern, unlike the other things. A strangely

patterned surface, like some map of deep-sea contours. Depths and shadows.

I pick it up. No investigative impulse there. Just curious.

'Damascus steel,' says Gheerbrant, his mood still up, ebullient. 'Pattern welding, to be strictly correct. This is a modern piece, but the Celts used similar techniques. You fold alternating layers of steel into rods, then twist them together as you forged the blade. It's those different layers of metal which give you that contouring, and if you were really good at it, you managed to lay hard steel over a softer iron core. That way your sword combined the springiness of iron and the sharpness of steel.'

He encourages me to test the blade for sharpness and I do. Run my fingertip across it. The edge has that whisper of evil that all really sharp objects possess. That tracks each ridge and valley of my fingertip. That could open a flesh-wound with the merest twitch of the handle.

'Who made this?' I ask, just to say something.

And then – a weird, temporary hesitation. A sudden sucking-in of that ebullience.

The change in mood is sharp enough that Compton, packing up our papers, glances across to see what's up. And I don't know. Don't know what's up. Gheerbrant collects himself and bats away the question. 'Oh, I'm not sure. Probably American.' He starts telling me about the American Bladesmith Society which is, no doubt, a fine institution, but is not, I think, an outfit that should cause Gheerbrant to get flustered.

I realise something.

Dummkopf.

Ich bin ein Dummkopf.

I almost laugh at the obviousness of the whole thing. The crudity of the clues that were laid. Truth is, I think I've been slow in putting this whole thing together, but it doesn't really matter. Not if you get there in the end.

We gather our things. Say goodbye.

By the time we get outside, the rain has ceased, at least briefly, and a rainbow's temporary shine gilds the streets.

I walk away from Gheerbrant's building. Not to the car, just away. I don't want him watching us.

When we're out of sight, I stop.

Compton says, 'The car's that way,' raising his voice at the end of the sentence to make it sound like a question more than a statement.

'Yes.'

He says, 'Maybe get a sandwich before we go back?'

'Yes.'

Above us, a couple of pigeons perch heavily on a cherry tree, sending a shower of silver raindrops onto the black asphalt below. I don't move.

Compton says, 'Is it me, or was that a bit weird?'

I have one of those things. Out of body. Out of time.

We're in sight here of Durham Castle. An eleventh-century fortification built over an older original. For the moment I can't tell where I belong. What month, what year, what hurrying century.

A modern blade.

Hardened steel over springy iron.

Pigeons showering silver in the rainbowed air.

I don't try to force anything. Don't try to find the right century. Don't try to figure anything out. Just stand here knowing that castles and rainbows, pigeons and centuries will all find a way to settle in the end.

And when they do – when, finally, I become aware of Compton's tediously twenty-first century presence chattering at my elbow – I know that everything's going to be OK.

Charteris. Oakeshott. Arthur.

Everybody.

I feel a sudden closeness to Gaynor Charteris. I've not felt her close to me for some time, but I have that sensation now and it's a good feeling. Comforting.

I want to tell Katie. I didn't know what the thing is and now I do. And it was always obvious. *Duh*!

I tell Compton, yes, that *was* a bit weird.

We eat a sandwich and drive back south.

23

Compton writes up the interview. He concludes:

> Subject seemed mostly at ease and relaxed, except in relation to two questions (see above) where subject appeared tense and concentrated hard before answering. Interviewing officers were of the opinion that subject was concealing information of relevance to the enquiry. <u>Recommendations</u>: consider possible follow-up.

It's not that we suspect Gheerbrant of being the killer. Apart from anything else, his two alibis are rock-solid: a faculty meeting in Durham that ran all through the day of Charteris's death. Lecturing in Edinburgh the night that saw Oakeshott stabbed and drowned.

And yet, and yet . . . there's *something*.

I think it. Compton thinks it. And Jones and Carr, bless their sainted inspectorial heads, think so too.

We do the basics. Get metadata on Gheerbrant's phones, his email accounts. Peek at his bank statements. His tax returns.

There's nothing strange, nothing awry.

But, because I make a pest of myself, we also get the phone companies to provide us with data on calls made from the area covered by the masts local to Gheerbrant's cottage, a few miles outside Durham.

We look at calls made or received by unregistered, no-contract phones.

Only one such number shows up. Just one. The call location appears highly consistent with Gheerbrant's cottage.

And that phone, that very phone, made calls to Oxford and to Dinas Powys.

On the very night of Oakeshott's death, the phone received a call from, it would seem, that same bit of dirty canalside where Oakeshott met his end.

The evidence is undeniable.

It looks like Gheerbrant used an unregistered mobile to call both Charteris and Oakeshott. He received calls from them both, including one from Oakeshott just an hour or two before he was murdered.

All this amounts, in police terms, to a big, fat, golden gotcha. Carr thinks so and Jones does too. So we're all ready to hit Gheerbrant hard, fast and nasty, when—

Good news. Bad news. Good news. Bad news.

Bad news.

We find our killer.

Or, to be more precise, he finds us. A local Oxford thug. Known to the police. Previous convictions for assault. Suspected involvement in low-level drug-dealing, car-crime. Tattoos running from neck to ankle.

Shaven head. Heavy brow. Gold rings. Leather jacket.

He's picked up by regular uniformed police for a suspected domestic assault against his black-eyed, badly bruised girlfriend. His T-shirt is stained with her blood and, as part of the routine forensic follow-up, his jacket is also analysed.

And yes, that jacket is caked in the blood of his beloved, but the side-seams hold traces of other veins, other injuries.

Oakeshott.

The man, Antony Wormold, is cautioned and interrogated on suspicion of murder.

He has no alibi.

He makes a sworn statement that he wasn't down by the

174

canal that night of 11 April. Not that night. Not any time that he could remember. A sturdy 'no' to any questions that mattered and lots of silence to the ones that didn't.

But the canal terminates in central Oxford, an area well covered by ordinary city centre CCTV. And we have footage of him walking to and returning from Hythe Bridge Street, at the butt end of the canal. Thames Valley's own, really good, forensics lab also manages to extract mud from one of Wormold's shoelaces. You can't normally tell much from mud, except that there used to be an ironworks fronting the canal and that particular section of footpath is notably high in various industrial by-products. Lo and behold, the mud on Wormold's shoe shows strong traces of just the right mixture of by-products to place him on that particular section of footpath.

In Carr's pithy summary, 'The lad's fucked. The blood alone would almost do it. The CCTV and the mud are clinchers.'

Wormold is charged with murder.

Bail refused.

Court date set.

The clanking machinery of justice, that strange steampunk conveyor, starts to roll Wormold down a road that will terminate with the iron door of a maximum security cell.

Which is where he belongs.

Carr, feeling he has his man, pulls back from everything else. He says, 'Those interviews with academics. They didn't actually lead anywhere, did they? And if we've got our killer, we've got our killer.'

That kind of thinking makes me want to hit my head against something thick and hard. I assemble my evidence. Pat it into a metaphorical pile and shove it across a metaphorical table at Carr and Jones.

The seal-box lid.

The Dyfi stone.

The thefts from Bangor and Llanymawddwy.

The phone calls made to Dinas Powys and Oxford by a phone surely belonging to Alden Gheerbrant.

And those other things too. The decapitation. The Iron Age spears. These damn Round Table conspirators, middle-aged professors playing at spies. The fact that one of those professors was killed on the very evening that I burst into his room and started smashing his glassware.

'What,' I want to yell, 'do you *think* is going on?'

Carr, who knows me better now, says calmly, 'Who, in your opinion, stabbed John Oakeshott and threw him into the canal?'

'Wormold.'

'Do you have any connection between Antony Wormold and this guy Gheerbrant.'

'No.'

'And there might be any number of legitimate reasons why a Durham historian should be talking to his colleagues around the country, yes?'

'Yes.'

'I mean, that is in fact what you would expect a Durham historian to do? It's his job, right?'

'Yes, but . . .'

No one is interested in my buts.

Obviously, we do what we can to check Wormold's whereabouts on the day of Charteris's murder, but Wormold was at work, in a mail sorting office, on both the fifteenth and sixteenth of March. It's certainly possible that, sometime during the night of the fifteenth/sixteenth March, Wormold tootled down from Oxford, murdered Charteris in that bizarrely exotic way, before returning to Oxford to punch his girlfriend, sort mail, deal drugs and do all those other things that made for a satisfying Antony Wormold day. But if Wormold drove, he didn't drive his own car, which doesn't

176

appear to have left Oxford. And then – why? Wormold *could* just have killed Oakeshott for a pocketful of cash. A stupid late-night argument. But the whole exotic staging of Charteris's death doesn't seem Wormoldian in the slightest.

So, as Carr's Oxford enquiry detaches from us and steams away, Jones and I are left with all the questions we started with. All the questions and none of the Wormolds.

I persuade Jones that we need to take a second crack at Gheerbrant. He has nothing else to run with, so he agrees.

We make a date with Gheerbrant. Drive north.

Three hundred miles. A five-hour schlep, by far the longest time we've spent together since the whole written warning, short leash thing.

We can't bristle at each other the whole way, so we maintain a taut, unimpeachable politeness. If we talk, we talk mostly about the case.

Birmingham.

Nottingham.

Sheffield.

Stop for fuel. Coffee for Jones, a crumbled blueberry muffin for me.

Leeds.

Durham.

Tilting sun, pale skies, and the Durham Constabulary HQ. A gleaming white building with glass enough to catch this sloping, northern light.

We find Gheerbrant in the lobby. He, like us, is collecting a stupid plastic badge. He introduces us to a woman next to him – grey wool dress, glasses, an air of intelligent self-possession.

'This is Miranda Speyman. I'm a bit of a novice with these things, so I thought I should get a lawyer. I hope that's OK.'

Jones and I exchange glances. Short of some really strange circumstances, no entirely innocent person ever hires a lawyer. But we say nothing.

A uniform takes us to the interview room. Sorts out drinks. Arranges the recording equipment.

I lead the interview, so that Jones can stay silent and observe. Come storming in, if the need arises.

We get started.

This time, Gheerbrant doesn't fool around. Doesn't bother to try out his charm, his flighty ebullience. Because he's more cautious, those micro-tells, so interesting in the first interview, aren't really available for inspection today.

But we have a job to do and do it.

'Dr Gheerbrant, you told us that you last saw Gaynor Charteris at an academic conference in Norwich that ran from the seventeenth to the nineteenth of February. Is that correct?'

'Yes.'

'Dr Charteris was murdered on or around the fifteenth of March, approximately one month after that conference. Did you see Dr Charteris at any point in that time?'

'No.'

'Did you speak to her by phone in that period?'

'No.'

'What about email? Text? Anything else?'

'No.'

We go over the same questions in relation to John Oakeshott. Ask repetitiously enough that Gheerbrant won't be able to squirm away from his answer later.

Then, 'How many mobile phones do you own?'

An uncomfortable pause, terminated by Gheerbrant's terse, 'One. You have the number.'

'Can you tell us anything about a mobile phone with this number?'

I show him the number of that unregistered mobile, the one that's made calls from somewhere near Gheerbrant's house to both Dinas Powys and that Oxford canal.

'No.'

That answer is clearly rehearsed, but still seems to cause him anxiety.

I confirm his answer. Snap away at the same issue, pinning him down.

Then, 'Can you explain why a mobile phone with that number made calls to Dinas Powys, Gaynor Charteris's home area, from a location at or very close to your home?'

'No.'

His lips move in a circle, pushing that round 'O' out into the space between us, but no actual sound emerges.

I say, 'For the benefit of the recording, can I confirm that your answer was "no"?'

He nods. 'Correct.'

It is a ghost of Gheerbrant who speaks the word.

'The same mobile phone was used to make and receive calls to and from Oxford. To a part of the city that included John Oakeshott's home and the canalside where he was killed. Do you still claim that the phone was not yours?'

His mouth moves on emptiness.

A dry silence. A whisper of dead grass.

He tries to speak – can't – sips some water – says, 'Can I have a moment, please? I'd like a private word with Miranda.'

Jones and I exchange glances. We don't have Gheerbrant under arrest. If he chooses to get up and walk out of the room, we can't actually stop him. His alibis for the two relevant dates remain as solid as the rock under Durham Castle.

Jones says, 'Fine. Take your time.'

We leave. Find the canteen. I get water and a salad box. Jones gets something designed to clog his arteries, poison his gut and silently devastate his liver.

'He's going to break,' says Jones.

Maybe.

Gheerbrant having a lawyer isn't all bad news, because lawyers have a dual role. Yes, they are there to protect and defend their clients, but they are also, always, officers of the court. That means they can't lie or collude in a lie. Gheerbrant can certainly use Miranda Speyman to choose which parts of the truth to present. He can use her to help him figure out how to present it and understand what the consequences may be. But she can't knowingly lie to us or help him to do so.

An hour passes. Jones adds two cups of black coffee to the various calamities already facing his liver. Then we get a call from Speyman inviting us back.

We go down.

Speyman says, 'My client would like to correct aspects of his comments so far.' Then, with a sharp nod at her client, tells him to proceed.

He does.

Speaking clearly, but jerkily, Gheerbrant says, 'That phone. It's mine. I spoke to Oakeshott and Charteris. I was not involved with their murders. They were my friends. Friends and colleagues.'

There are tears in his eyes. Some self-pity there, for sure. A release of stress and the relief of truth-telling. But perhaps there's something left over for his dead colleagues.

Decapitated and speared. Stabbed and drowned.

I say, 'You spoke to them about what?'

'Academic matters mostly.'

'Matters relating to Britain as it was in the Dark Ages?'

'Yes.'

'Matters in which you all had a shared interest?'

'Exactly. Yes.'

'And what specifically? What exactly was the topic of those conversations?'

'That's confidential.'

I jerk my head upwards in surprise. Jones the same.

I pull back a bit from the table. It's Jones's call how to respond to that.

He says, 'Sorry, Dr Gheerbrant, just for a moment there, I thought you said, "That's confidential".'

Good old-fashioned police sarcasm. I always like that.

Gheerbrant doesn't react. Just, 'That's correct.'

Jones: 'You are aware that your two friends were murdered? Nastily, brutally, savagely murdered. The information you hold is quite likely key to locating, arresting and prosecuting their murderers. You understand that?'

'Yes.'

'I mean, I'm not a clever man, myself. Not university, like you. But killing people is bad, right? It's a good idea to put killers behind bars, yes?'

'Yes.'

'So now might be a good time to help out. Tell us what you know.'

Gheerbrant just deflects that question, if it was a question, sideways and down. He says nothing.

Jones pauses. Tries to read Gheerbrant's face. Speyman's too.

'Just a minute.'

He beckons me with him out of the room.

'Get a search warrant,' he says. 'Home, office, car, everything. Get a team together and have them move as fast as possible. I don't want Gheerbrant disposing of anything when he gets out of here.'

I nod.

Our liaison in the Durham Constabulary is a DI Paul McGinn. I brief him swiftly. He assembles a team – by sticking his head into a kind of common room area and yelling – and dials through to the duty magistrate.

We do what we need to do to get the warrant – sensible applications are seldom refused and certainly not in a case with a double murder dangling at its heart. We're all done within about thirty minutes. McGinn's team moves out.

I go back to the interview room.

Jones says, 'All done?'

'Yes, sir.'

'Search warrants OK?'

'Yes.'

This is theatre, of course. I've kept Jones informed by text and he knows the state of play perfectly well.

'Home, office, car, everything?'

'Yes. The teams will be arriving any minute now.'

'Instructions to be thorough, yes?'

'They'll rip everything to shreds if they have to.'

Jones looks at Gheerbrant. 'I'll have your phone, please.'

I flip a copy of the warrant across the table at Speyman, who inspects it, then nods. Gestures her client into handing over his phone.

'And your wallet.'

He passes that over too.

'And please turn out your pockets.'

Gheerbrant does.

Receipts. Some loose change. Keys. A length of string. A folded letter, with a Durham University letterhead.

Jones takes the receipts, the keys, the letter. Gets Gheerbrant to identify each key. Calls a uniform from outside to have each key checked against the relevant lock.

There's meant to be a written record of what we seize, but Jones just spreads it out on the table under the video camera's gaze, lists each item in his tiresome monotone, then sweeps it all up again and hands it to the waiting officer.

Gheerbrant watches his keys, wallet and documents leave the room. He pockets the change and the string.

Silence. Drained and empty, like the concrete bottom of an old pond.

Jones turns a disappointed face on Gheerbrant.

Says nothing. Does nothing. Just looks.

Maybe Jones sports that horrible beard as an interrogation tool. Perhaps suspects end up confessing simply to avoid its stare.

'Home *and* office,' says Jones sadly. 'Uniformed officers. Squad cars. Everyone watching. Neighbours, friends, colleagues, students. Maybe the local paper too, you never know. Those things can destroy people, you know.'

Jones lets the silence press at Gheerbrant.

Under the old common law of England and Wales, a prisoner couldn't be tried unless that prisoner voluntarily submitted themselves to the court's jurisdiction by entering a plea of guilty or not guilty. If a prisoner refused to enter a plea, he was forced to submit to *peine forte et dure*, an Old French term meaning 'hard and forceful punishment'. That punishment consisted of being stretched out on a hard floor, loaded with weights of iron and stone, as much as the body could bear. The punishment was continued until the prisoner entered a plea, or died.

I think of that old, merciless system now.

There's something crushing Gheerbrant.

This weight of silence. This press of questions. The knowledge that even now his life is being broken apart under the public gaze.

That weight of stone and iron, and still he tells us nothing.

'Aren't you frightened?' asks Jones. 'Scared that someone will do to you what they did to your friends?'

Gheerbrant doesn't answer.

'It's OK to say yes. We're here to protect you. But we need to know who we're protecting you from. We need those people behind bars.'

Nothing.

Those subjected to *peine forte et dure* were given a modest amount of barley bread to eat for the first day of their punishment, but no water with it. Thereafter, they were given nothing but foul water, as much as they could drink.

Gheerbrant has no bread, but he fiddles with a horrible plastic cup of coffee, still two-thirds full.

He suddenly stares at the coffee as though baffled to find himself still here.

There is no iron weight pressing on him. No cords spread-eagling him on a hard prison floor. It's as though he's suddenly stunned by his own liberty.

'Sorry,' he says. 'Sorry.'

He stands up.

Leaves the room.

Goes.

24

McGinn's search teams report back, excited.

The team at Gheerbrant's house have found a stash of weapons. A working crossbow. Various swords and blades. A couple of axes. Numerous arrowheads. Spearheads, very like those plunged into his former colleague's chest.

'We've got your killer,' concludes the team leader. 'It's like a warehouse for psychos.'

Alas, not. We inform him that since Gheerbrant is the country's leading expert in ancient weaponry, his collection is nothing more than we'd have expected. Sorry.

The data offers more hope of breakthrough. The Durham guys are straight to work on phones and hard drives. Promise to share everything as soon as they've extracted files.

The early excitement dwindles out into the hard grind of slow, detailed work.

It's six in the evening.

McGinn says goodbye to us, as we stand by Jones's car in a slant of evening sun. We all say the right things. Things with a general motif of 'We'll get the bastard yet.'

And maybe. Maybe we will.

Jones and I drive home, gathering back those long unspooled miles. Five hours in Jones's blackly glossy nutshell of a car.

We don't talk much.

Somewhere near Nottingham, we eat a hamburger. Dead food under a dead light.

Back in Durham, Jones had fired up the sound system with country music and said, 'Do you mind?'. I didn't answer and didn't mind, but by the time we pass Birmingham, I reckon I'd sooner push drawing pins into my eye sockets than listen to another damn singer telling me about whiskey and dirt roads and that l'il ol' sweetheart waiting home for me.

As we swing, finally, on to the M4, Jones says, 'Almost there now.'

I say, 'His phone data, sir. Would you mind if I had a crack at that?'

He turns to stare.

The car, inevitably, has black leather seats and Jones creaks a little as he turns. I keep my eyes on the road, because someone ought to.

'You want to take charge of the phone data?' he says.

He asks not because he misunderstood my, relatively simple, question but because ploughing through phone data is notoriously the most boring job of the many oceanically boring jobs it is our pleasure and duty to perform.

'Yes, please.'

He creaks back round in his seat. Eyes front once again.

'Yes, of course.'

It's touching midnight when he drops me at my door. Says good night.

'And, look, I thought your behaviour up there was very professional. I'll make a note of that for the record too.'

I'm just temporarily speechless. I suppose this is him trying to compensate me for that written warning. Recompense paid in the same coin. But, *Himmeldonnerwetter*, the man is patronising.

I stand there, by the open car door, gaping. Finally manage a, 'Thank you, sir. Good night.'

Then Jones's mutt – collared, leashed and muzzled – wags her tail, licks her chops and trots obediently in to bed.

25

Gheerbrant doesn't crack. Doesn't talk.

McGinn put pressure on him all right. Went straight to the university authorities. Explained that Gheerbrant was withholding information from a murder enquiry. The authorities asked Gheerbrant if that was true. Found that it was. And suspended him.

Jones is now of the view – which isn't an idiotic one, just a wrong one – that Gheerbrant is somehow the mastermind of the two killings. So he Joneses around. Tries to connect Wormold with Gheerbrant. Visits Wormold in custody. Does things with vehicle registrations, CCTV, and Lord knows what else.

When he talks to me, which is still delightfully rare, he is mostly anxious to know if I can find anything that links Gheerbrant's damn phone with Antony Wormold. He thinks that's what I'm up to.

I say, 'Not yet, sir, but I'm on it.'

He pats my head and gives me a dog biscuit.

I work hard, but my best work is done outside the office, with Katie for the most part.

We know what we have to make now.

We've already found a jeweller. A blacksmith. Have started to source materials.

Those things aren't easy and Katie's expertise is essential at every stage. To take just one example: the blacksmithery needs to be done by someone working with the exact right tools and techniques of Dark Age Britain. Not just that, but we need to work with actual Dark Age iron that hasn't been corrupted by any later, foreign material. What's more, because soot from the fire may affect the chemical composition of the metal, the furnace has to be fired with logs sourced from south Wales, using only trees that were native in the fifth century. Katie even gets the blacksmith to dress as she wants.

'No cotton. No modern fibres. Wool, leather, or nothing, I'm afraid. You get one bit of polyester in the metal and some trace of it *could* show up if you looked hard enough.'

Our blacksmith, owning no woollen underpants, tells us he works dressed in leather boots, a leather apron and nothing else.

He sends us a sample of his furnace ash and Katie tests it against the ash found in Dinas Powys. When the first set of results comes back with some anomalies, she tweaks the venting arrangements of the blacksmith's fire to get a better carbon balance. I don't even understand the detail, but she does and that's all that matters.

We get a design too.

A drawing of what the final piece will look like.

It looks good to me, but I know nothing.

I ask Katie for her opinion.

She says, 'Yes. Good. I think good . . .'

'But?'

'We need to ask George. This isn't just about history, is it? Not just about archaeological precision. We need this to be right in terms of the oral tradition. The myth.'

I laugh at her. Tell here that she's backtracking on all that early hostility to the idea of a historical Arthur. Tell her she's going to lose her professional reputation completely over this.

She laughs. Shrugs. Doesn't deny it.

And, ten days after that second Gheerbrant interview, we drive north.

Brecon.

Builth.

Llanidloes.

Camlan.

A din of swords, a clatter of shields.

Up the Abercywarch valley to Bowen's farm.

It's a proper Welsh spring day. Blue sky alternating with sparkling silver showers.

I sort of expected Bowen to be in farmer-mode, but today it's his wife, Janice, who's out in the fields and her husband – dark suit, clerical collar, and shoes that, but for a crusted tidemark of mud, are almost smart – meets us at the door.

Because the sky is blue and the sunshine brilliant and the fields aflare with buttercups and dancing lambs, we don't go inside straight away. Just stand outside and gaze.

Katie has given up the ski stick for a crutch now. Bowen looks at it, wondering if he should ask.

I say, 'Katie is in the early stages of motor neurone disease, but she doesn't like talking about it. Best thing to do is say, "That's really tough, Katie. That's awful," then leave it there.'

He does say that. Uses those exact words, but he hugs her too. Gives her ever-thinner frame a big, squashy, lifting-the-feet-off-the-ground hug. When he's done, he has to settle her carefully back again, because her balance isn't good.

She grimaces a smile, but is touched, not upset.

We go in. The hurly-burly of Bowen's study. Books and papers and old sermons and a sheep's skull and a green baize writing table.

Bowen looks at us. Says, 'Well?'

So.

So.

I clear my throat and tell them what I'm thinking.

Who killed Gaynor Charteris and why.

189

Who killed John Oakeshott and why.

What I think Alden Gheerbrant is up to.

I say, 'It was reasonably clear what all this had to be about, but I didn't know what the actual *thing* was, the *object*. Now I do and, to be honest, it was blindingly obvious. But of course, my job is to find the actual killers. I don't really see a way to do that, so I think we need to go at it in reverse. Get *them* to find *us*.'

Katie, who knows most of this, sits there with her hand over her mouth, a shine in her eyes.

Bowen says, 'Get the killers to find *you*? A police officer?'

'Yes. I mean, I probably won't shout about the whole police officer thing.'

'So – what? – you're going to put an ad up somewhere?'

Katie laughs.

'George, you have to understand that this woman is batshit crazy. I mean, think of the craziest person you've ever met. The craziest person and the craziest idea. Then double them both, cube the result and what you've got is sitting in front of you.'

George stares at Katie. Stares at me. And back again.

'Do you mean what I think you mean?'

Katie nods. 'Exactly. Yes. She wants to make—'

I interrupt. Say, 'Caledfwlch.'

Katie: 'What?'

'*Caledfwlch*. The damn thing is Welsh, not some fake Latin, medieval French knock-off.'

Katie says, 'Crazy: I told you. The High Princess of Planet Nuts.'

That's more accurate than Katie knows, so I just accept the orb and sceptre of my new realm.

Bowen: 'Katie's right, is she? You want to make Caledfwlch?'

'Yes.'

'And Katie's going to help you?'

'She *has* helped and *is* helping. But you're the Arthurian. We need you too.'

'That's why you're here?'

'Yes.'

'Well, bloody hell. I'm in. I'm bloody in.'

We turn to detail.

The make or break.

The art and science of top-end fakery.

Katie tells us about the massive industry now dedicated to churning out fake Chinese antiquities.

'The big auction houses routinely test pottery using thermoluminescence, a method of dating items with a high degree of accuracy. Trouble is, the fakers have taken to re-using old-clay – basically material discarded by the Ming dynasty potters, or whoever. So when that stuff is tested, it shows up as old, because it *is* old, yes, just completely fake. And if they can't get enough old clay, they irradiate the clay they do have, until it performs the same way under a thermoluminescence test. Same thing with the minerals used for the paints. The fakers go to the exact same spots that the original craftsmen once used. Mix their paints in the exact same way. You can get the best expert in the world to examine those pieces and they'll most likely be fooled. The result is that items are being sold for a hundred thousand dollars and more that might have been created just a few months previously. There are *way* more fake Ming vases being sold than actual real ones – and no one can tell the two apart. There's no difference.'

Bowen asks about metal. 'Is it the same there?'

Katie: 'Pretty much. We're being really careful to use ancient source materials, and ancient manufacturing techniques, and all that. People will be able to do all the spectography they want. What they'll see will look Dark Age through and through, and that's not surprising. It *is* Dark Age.'

We talk design.

Katie, working with her blacksmith and her jeweller, already has a design drawn up like an architect's blueprint. Life-size, so we have to unroll the paper on the floor. Weight it down with books and, on one corner, Bowen's blessed sheep skull.

Laid out like this, and even in outline, the thing looks beautiful.

Jet and glass and horn and patterning.

A dark and dangerous beauty.

We talk details. Adjust the draft.

And Katie's right. Bowen's knowledge is essential. Every suggestion he has, every tweak, enriches the design. And I realise: this isn't just about history. It's about Bowen's side of things too. The myth. The tradition. The beliefs.

We begin to shape our Caledfwlch until it starts to feel absolutely right.

Right for the age. For Arthur.

Then Bowen says, 'And gold. There has to be gold.'

'Katie?'

She nods. 'I suppose so, yes. I mean, really, this is a utilitarian item and one that's quite likely to get broken in use. So normally, sure, you'd expect some decoration, but only involving relatively cheap materials. Maybe some type of copper alloy. But—', sighing, 'on the other hand . . .'

Bowen nods and completes her thought. 'Exactly. This *is* Caledfwlch. This *is* Arthur.'

'Yes, yes, it is. So, we should probably have gold in there. Unfortunately.'

I say, 'OK. And sourcing gold? How do we do that? Where would the gold even have come from?'

'Really, slave! Your man would have got it from Wales, of course. The old Roman gold mines at Dolaucothi.'

'And that's still going, is it? The gold mine?'

'Hardly. The mine was abandoned shortly after the Romans left. Gold *was* mined in north Wales until quite recently, but that's the wrong part of Wales and, anyway, modern methods of extracting gold are way too sophisticated. You need proper fifth century Dolaucothi gold. Sorry.'

'So we can buy some?'

Katie grimaces. 'I doubt it. Even from north Wales, where the gold was more abundant, prices are ridiculous. For Dolaucothi gold?' She puffs out. 'Don't know. It's extremely rare. Like, crazily rare. The Queen probably has some. The British Museum. I wouldn't even know who else.'

We talk about that for a bit. Get nowhere.

I remember that email of Charteris's.

Medraut's obsession with getting the 'right gold' is taking us into dangerous areas. I mean, if he wants gold, why not just get some gold?

I didn't understand that at the time. I understand it now.

And Medraut/Mordred was right. We don't just need gold. We need the right gold.

Damn.

Bowen goes away. Makes some phone calls. Parish stuff. He starts fiddling with tomorrow's sermon.

When he returns, he brings bread, butter, cheese and a dish of soft new asparagus. 'From one of my parishioners,' he explains. 'Bribing his way to the Kingdom of Heaven.'

We eat the asparagus with our fingers. Butter, pepper, nothing else.

Bowen, I think, believes we're done. He wants to turn to his sermon. But we're not done. We're not even halfway.

I say, 'George, it's all very well to *make* it, but where do we *find* it?'

'What?'

'We need to "find" the damn thing, remember. We can't just dig it up in someone's back garden.'

'Oh, now there's a point,' Bowen says, his eyes agleam, his sermon forgotten.

I say, 'Camlan? Arthur's last battle?'

Bowen thinks about that, but a first gleam of excitement fades into a heavy shake.

No: the site has never been excavated.

No: there's never been solid evidence of a battle there.

No: there are no digs scheduled there, so any 'find' would need to be truffled up by a local farmer, which is hardly the kind of thing we're going for.

We rule out Camlan.

I say, 'Well, what about, I don't know, Camelot? Where's that?'

Bowen says: 'No, no good. That place *is* a myth, nothing more.'

'What about his burial site? Avalon?'

Katie snorts. 'No way. You'll find the Tooth Fairy sooner than you find Avalon.'

'George?'

'Sorry, Fiona. The Saxon's right. The name "Avalon" derives from the Old Welsh for the Isle of Apples, but it's probably just invented. The Glastonbury associations are all piffle.'

So Camlan is a bust.

Ditto Camelot.

Ditto Avalon.

That leaves just one site. Perhaps the best one. The site that, for perhaps two or three short decades, seemed to have changed the course of history.

Badon Hill. Mount Badon. *Mons Badonicus.*

The battle in which Arthur, reputedly, slaughtered the Saxon host. Halted the English advance by a generation or more.

I say, 'So Badon Hill. Where is it?'

Katie says, 'No idea. None. No archaeological evidence for the battle has ever been found.'

I look at Bowen. Push the same question at him.

'Yes, look, Katie's right in a way. There's nothing solid, but . . .'

He starts to talk. *His* version of history, not Katie's. Intelligent conjecture based on the scraps and fragments available.

'Look, very roughly, the Anglo–Saxon invasions started in the south-east and spread outwards from there. So if you want a decisive battle, it's most likely somewhere on the curve of that outward spread. That rules out anywhere in the north or west and of course, the battle is often referred to as a *siege*, an actual siege. So: who would besiege a *mountain*? Answer, no one, unless there was a fort on it. And given the era, that's going to mean a traditional hill fort, something like Dinas Powys, in fact. And then you have to remember, this was a *big* battle. Big enough that it destroyed the Saxons for a generation. So this isn't some minor hill fort we're talking about. It's got to be a big one. Important.'

Katie sighs. 'God. Yes. OK. I agree with that. That's all sound logic.'

Bowen grins. Gets a map. And they start to work. Pencilling in possible locations. Crouching over the map adjusting the lines.

Because the Celtic–British – my ancestors – were Christian, they had different burial rituals from the pagan Anglo–Saxons. As a result, the spread of pagan graveyards across the country gives one of the best clues as to the spread of the invaders themselves. The curve of invasion mapped out with corpses.

Bowen and Katie bicker gently, but start to build a list of possible locations. It takes time but, already, a few names start tumbling into our lap.

Maiden Castle.

Cadbury Castle.

Poundbury Hill.

Bathampton Down.

Forts. Battles. Sieges.

And – somewhere here, on this much-pencilled map – lies the fabled Mount Badon.

Where the Saxons were slaughtered. Where Arthur reigned supreme.

Where this case will meet its climax.

26

I'm good with corpses, but don't offer much when it comes to ancient battlegrounds.

I listen to Katie and Bowen for a while, but end up wandering outside. I spy Janice mending a hedge in a field up the valley, so pull my boots on and walk over.

Janice greets me in a friendly way. The collie, Tidy, sniffs, then disregards me.

To his aristocratic sense of hierarchy, I rate a little lower than dachshund.

I help out.

A lot of leggy taller trees have been sawn back to chest height and, to fill any gaps, Janice is planting saplings of hawthorn and field maple. She plants them, stakes them, winds those odd plastic protector things around them.

Me, I tug the cut wood into a pile and start a fire, using a scrunched-up copy of the north Welsh *Daily Post* and a box of matches. Soon get a thin grey smoke and the fierce tremble of heat. Sweat happily in the chill sun.

We work hard. Work happily.

By five o'clock, we've done enough and, for five minutes or more, we rest. Lean up against the Land Rover. Drink tea from a thermos. Watch the fire.

Janice asks, 'You'll be staying tonight?'

'If we can,' I say.

She says yes. Says of course. Zooms off in the Land

Rover, Tidy bounding along behind.

I walk back to the little farmhouse.

And on the way – *boof!* – it happens again.

It.

The dissociation. The emptying out.

One moment, I'm walking across this late spring field. The next moment – what?

Someone is walking across this late spring field. A person who, from the outside, to an ordinary observer, probably looks and sounds and – I expect – tastes, feels and smells like me.

But I'm not there. No one is.

Where there should be a bustling consciousness, all full of, I don't know, a wood-smoked, sunny-eyed satisfaction at a day gone well – instead of all that – nothing.

The person walking over this green Welsh grass is a marionette. A wooden toy.

I can't feel my legs or hands or body. Can't feel the wind on my face. The sunlight on my skin.

There are thoughts, I suppose, but they seem disembodied. Belonging to no one.

I get back to the farmhouse, waiting for that little *pop!* of return. A sense of me returning to me.

But there's no pop. No me.

By the farmhouse wall, a small wooden marionette sits on a wooden bench.

Eases her boots off, eyes closed.

I aim to look like someone casually relaxing in the sunshine. Someone you wouldn't particularly choose to interrupt or disturb.

I think I become a little less disembodied than I was, but that's like trying to measure which is bigger, a flea or a louse. You want to say, the hell with it, they're both tiny.

I go back inside.

A ghost-thing blown on a ghost-wind.

Bowen and Katie are, luckily, both so deep in work that they don't notice that the High Princess of Planet Nuts has gone completely barking.

They both, mildly euphoric, wave a list at me.

A list of forts. Their 'strong possibles'.

Maiden Castle, Cadbury Castle, Poundbury Hill, Bathampton Down.

Danebury.

The castles at Uffington, Barbury, Liddington.

Bindon Hill and Solsbury Hill.

Badbury Rings.

Bowen says: 'We're not the first to think all this through, of course. Some good scholars have argued for Liddington Castle as the probable site. There's also tradition linking the battle to Badbury, Bathampton Down, Solsbury Hill. A few other places too.'

And I listen to him and I nod and I feel the sudden dart of Charteris's presence. Her toughness. Her impatience and seriousness.

I think, *she cared about these things too. These things mattered intensely to her as well.*

And – not with a *pop!* exactly, but something softer, a *ping*, a *puff*, a slow exhalation – the clarity of that thought returns some clarity, just a little, to me too.

I'm still not right. I still feel clumsy. Makeshift, perhaps, but at least a makeshift version of myself.

And I find myself thinking a new thought, *This search for Mount Badon. Weren't we meant to be given a clue? Why is this so hard?*

Also: *That theft from Saint Tydecho's. What* was *that, really?*

For the first time, almost, I wonder if I've got this all wrong.

27

That night – a nothing thing. Really nothing.

After supper, Katie and I go upstairs. We don't have any more stupid fights over who's sleeping where. Just share the bed as we did before. Except that Katie kicks occasionally, it's a nice enough way to spend a night.

But before bed, one of those Katie moments. We were in the bathroom. Me, doing my teeth. Her, fiddling at her hair.

She had her hair up in one of those complicated hair-knots. A double twist, a bun within a bun. I watched her fiddle, partly because we were together in a tiny bathroom and where else was I supposed to look? Partly too, because I have a vague curiosity about those long-hair styles and wanted to know how this one worked.

But Katie's right hand kept letting her down. That whole intricate hair-thing relied on pins and Katie's right hand no longer had the deftness required to extract the damn things. She managed it with her left hand in the end, but her face wore that grim look it gets. Peering into its ever-darkening future.

'I'll cut it all off soon,' she announced. 'Shorter than yours.'

Short hair doesn't seem to me one of the biggest losses there is, so I shrugged. Just helped with the last of the pins and the night-time pony-tail.

The next morning, I stand with her in the bathroom again. Say, 'What do you want?'

The answer, when I understand it, is a plait that starts with the long hair above the left eye and curves over the forehead to disappear behind the right ear.

I've never had long hair myself and have never had enough hair to braid. On top of which, I'm an almost total incompetent in matters which, to some women, seem to come as naturally as breathing. Nevertheless, I do as Katie asks. Get quite into it, actually, and end up making a second plait that starts somewhere over the right ear and slides round behind the other plait towards the other ear. The whole thing takes me several attempts and close to twenty-five minutes, but I'm quite pleased with the outcome and tell Katie she looks like an Anglo–Saxon warrior princess.

'All ripe for slaughter,' I say.

'A household slave,' she says. 'That's what you are. I'll keep you as my household slave.'

And so, happily bickering, we go down to breakfast.

I'm no longer wooden. I feel myself as well as I ever do. Not brilliant, but OK. Warning lights reset to their ordinary low amber.

But I realise this.

The dissociation. The me-losing-myself thing. That's happened twice recently. Both times when I was around Katie.

And that's not coincidence.

She's dying. A real, properly biological death. Unstoppable. And while I've never died, not biologically, I have had my Cotards. Have lived long with my own death. My own internal version of that dark state.

And these recent episodes of mine, I'm having them because of Katie. This new proximity to someone dying. That doesn't make me want to shun Katie. The opposite. I think, *I have to be able to do this. Stand close to death and not go crazy. Step on that edge and feel its wind. But stay stable, stay standing, stay me.*

201

I don't know if I can do that, but I know I have to try.

It feels like the biggest challenge of my life. The only one that really, truly matters.

28

My weekends and evenings, I find I'm spending increasingly with Katie or, by phone, with Bowen too.

But that still leaves my regular work. My police work.

Boring, repetitive, pleasant, necessary.

We have the call log of Gheerbrant's 'Round Table' phone and we know too the locations of the phones he was calling:

Dinas Powys – surely calls made to and from Gaynor Charteris
Oxford – we presume calls made to and from John Oakeshott
Usk in Monmouthshire – no idea who is involved here
Holborn in London – ditto
Hathersage in Derbyshire – ditto

If we knew who he was calling in Usk, Holborn and Hathersage, we might well have a swift closure of the entire case. But oh my gosh and oh my golly, those numbers do not easily reveal their secrets.

Holborn is by far the hardest of the three locations. The mast which handled the relevant calls covers a broad urban area that includes shops, offices, underground stations and the like. I get lists of addresses and try to check if any of those names are the kind of people I'd expect Gheerbrant to be calling. Academics. Archaeologists. Jewellers. Metalworkers. Antiques dealers.

I get nowhere. I mean, yes, I find some possible matches –

everywhere has jewellers for example – but I find nothing that suggests a possible connection. I try Google, the PNC, the Electoral Roll, various business directories, and more.

Nothing.

Try the same kind of thing in Hathersage and Usk. There are fewer possibilities there, but still: nothing.

Jones, who is still trying to get his Wormoldian theories to fit the uncomfortably unWormoldian facts, is also getting nowhere. The whole case has a doomed, career-killing feel to it.

As it happens, I'm pretty confident that the crime – the *real* crime, I mean – hasn't yet unfolded. I want to say that to Jones. Tell him not to worry. But though he needs me, he does not love me, and I keep my darker thoughts strictly to myself.

So we work hard. Work efficiently. Accomplish nothing.

Two weeks pass.

I drive up to Carmarthen a couple of times.

See Rhiannon Watkins, my former boss, and her pretty wife, Cal, and let the pair of them treat me like their adopted daughter. We eat and talk and go on walks and don't talk about policing much, not least because Cal is fairly close to the opposite of a police officer and that kind of conversation ends up excluding her completely.

It's just nice to see them both.

And meantime, well, I'm happy enough. A warm May is turning into a golden June. Work hard with Katie and Bowen. And I have to say it, our joint project is going very well indeed.

Design: finalised.

Iron-making: well in hand.

Jeweller: all tooled up and ready to go.

Our iron, jet, horn, glass and other bits and pieces are all properly ancient and Katie is running a battery of spectrographic and other tests to make sure they will pass any plausible analysis.

Everything that should be going well is going well, except, except . . .

'The gold?' I ask. 'The gold?'

'Still trying,' says Katie brightly.

'But . . .?'

'My best plan currently involves an armed attack on Buckingham Palace.'

'Katie—'

'Plan B is an arson attack on the Tower of London.'

'An arson attack on the Tower of London? Excellent. Brilliant. We'll go with that then.'

'Or go Irish? I *can* get some Irish gold of the right age.'

She makes a *pretty please* face at me. Trying to coax me into acquiescence.

I say, 'Katie, honestly now, suppose that we actually had Caledfwlch in front of us right here. The real thing. Not a medieval forgery. Not some romanticised idea of what the damn thing might be like. Would you expect to find gold on it?'

She nods, glumly.

'And, Katie, that gold . . .'

'. . . would be Welsh. Yes. I mean, with an Arthur from Dinas Powys. He's only – what? – fifty miles from a functioning mine. Even if those mine workings had decayed since Roman times, there would still have been people alive who knew how it all worked. Who could extract gold if they needed to. It would have been his closest, easiest source and then as well—'

'Yes?'

'Well, these things never just operated at a single level, did they? I mean, the gold would have been there for its symbolic meaning, not just because it looked pretty. The gold wouldn't just say "I'm rich" or "I'm important". It would also say, "I'm British. I'm a proud Christian Celtic–Briton, the inheritor of that old Roman civilisation." And to

205

communicate those things you'd need *your* gold. Gold from your own culture. Mined by your own miners. Refined by your own metalworkers. Worked by your own jewellers.'

'So we need *Welsh* gold.'

'Yes.'

'Fifth-century gold from Dolaucothi.'

'Yes.'

'And we don't have any.'

'No.'

'And your best plan is an armed raid on Buckingham Palace.'

'Or the Tower,' says Katie with an it's-not-as-bad-as-you-think shrug 'n' grin combo.

I grimace.

I'm annoyed, but I'm also puzzled. If *we* can't get the right kind of gold, then *they* can't. And if they can't, then . . .

Once again, I have the feeling that I'm missing something. There's something I haven't yet fathomed.

I don't sleep much but when I do, I keep my gun, fully loaded, within a short arm-reach of desire. I don't use it. Seldom even touch it. But I like knowing it's there.

I smoke too much. Work too hard. Eat badly. Sleep worse.

29

And then – and then—

Finally. One of my problems is solved. No stroke of genius on my part. Just life choosing to deliver something that had seemed out of reach.

It's early June. Trees are wearing their happy green. That frolicking new summer youthfulness that is a wilful forgetting of every cold October, every cruel November.

It's Saturday.

I'm wearing a floaty pink skirt and a striped pistachio-and-coffee top that's on the older side, but still a favourite. The weather is warm enough to permit such things, and mine are not the only pair of white Welsh legs to think the same.

I've spent a morning shopping with Kay. I bought nothing. Kay returned two dresses and bought one. Of the two she returned, one had been worn for an entire night, with the store tag carefully tucked down the back. ('You have to put cling film over the tag,' Kay explained. 'That way it doesn't get stained and they can't say anything.' She told me that, like it was some kind of law.)

I'm meeting Bev down at the pool later but, for now, I have a sandwich, a bottle of orange juice, and a floaty skirt, and I intend to deploy those assets where and how they are most effective: in Bute Park, under a tree, with my nose in a good philosophy book.

I *intend*.

I have an *intention*.

If you intend to do a certain thing and then don't do it, even though you are entirely free to do so, was it ever an intention in the first place? I've got to say not. Intention is a matter of action, not just state of mind. If you 'intend' to give up smoking but don't go so much as a day without lighting up, then your intention was a nothing. It never existed.

But, but, but.

What if you intend to do a certain thing – in my case: sit in Bute Park with a floaty pink skirt and a philosophy book – and then don't do it, because something else comes along? A thing that doesn't *prevent* your executing that intention, but does suddenly, swiftly and totally re-order your priorities? A thing such as – just by way of example – the sharp yap of police sirens. A movement of people. A sudden tremble in this urban atmosphere.

In that case, the hell with it. I say, allow the girl her intention. It was a good intention. A sound intention. An intention that may yet come into being.

But priorities change

I walk not to the park but away from it. Down the Boulevard de Nantes, then cutting across Gorsedd Gardens – *hurrying* across Gorsedd Gardens – *running*, actually running, across Gorsedd Gardens to the National Museum Cardiff.

Squad cars.

Police tape.

A scurry of armed officers.

Exiting the museum: people. Visitors and staff. An armed officer standing guard, radio bleating on his shoulder.

At the police tape, I show my warrant card. Step through. Ask what's happening.

The answer: armed intruders have stormed the gallery. Are stealing art. Have taken hostages, maybe as many as sixteen.

The guy who tells me this is barely able to conceal his

delight. His tone and his swagger say, 'Oh? What? The rifle? Yes, semi-automatic, a SIG 516 actually. Annoying thing to carry around, but—', nonchalant shrug, 'Armed raid, hostages: what you going to do? Honestly, some days, it's just work, work, work.'

These guys try to affect a kind of nonchalance, but they bloody love it.

And me?

Well, I don't like armed coppers on the streets of Cardiff. And I definitely don't like weapons in the hands of bad guys. And I seriously, seriously don't like the sound of sixteen hostages. That news casts a grim and midnight shade, red-fringed with danger.

But inside all the bad news, I think answers may lurk. Answers and solutions.

So I carry my juice, my philosophy book and my thwarted intentions to a low step near the museum's south-east corner. I'm still within the perimeter of the police tape, but at a distance from the main entrance. Twice, a uniform comes over to shoo me away, but I show them my warrant card and act sticky and in the end everyone has something better to do than get rid of a fairly small orange-juice-drinking detective.

Time goes by.

The building is cleared.

After that first flurry of activity, there's not much to do and I slowly tease out the story of what actually happened, piece by piece, from my fellow-officers.

What happened was this:

Three men wearing dark clothes entered the museum, separately, at around eleven o'clock. The museum operates a security search at the entrance, but it's hardly airport-quality. A few instances of minor vandalism aside, the museum has simply never experienced major problems. In any case, it seems like the men managed to walk through security carrying two pistols, a few packets of firecrackers and a bagful of smoke grenades. Those grenades sound like fairly high-end equipment but, it turns out, you can buy them from Amazon for a few quid.

The pistols, however, appear to be real.

Not fakes. Not drilled-out replicas. Real.

Procuring weapons in Britain isn't either cheap or easy, so the presence of genuine firearms suggests a measure of forward planning. On the other hand, the rest of the men's 'plan' – if you can call it that – appears to have been simple. They rendezvoused in the room that normally houses *La Parisienne*, an early portrait by Renoir and one of the museum's principal treasures. Alas, the painting – all ten million pounds of it – was away for cleaning. The men, captured on good quality CCTV, seemed to be bemused by its absence.

For about twenty minutes, they seemed frustrated. Appeared ready to just walk away. But then, the hell with it, those bold heroes decided they were here to steal, so steal they would.

Standing away from the main view of the cameras, using what concealment they could, two of the men started to detonate their smoke grenades. The third man lit firecrackers and started to produce a series of loud bangs.

Once the smoke 'n' bang operation was well underway. One of the men started to cut some smaller, and relatively minor, Impressionist works from their frames.

It appears that the men hoped to blind the cameras and cause enough chaos that they would be able to smuggle their trophies out in the confusion. And, to be fair, that's the sort of plan which works well in the movies. The kind of idea which sounds plausible when cooked up over booze and drugs in a grimy Cardiff flat.

And maybe it could work. Maybe, if you tried that kind of thing ten times over, two or three times out of ten you'd succeed.

Or maybe not.

The smoke grenades worked all right, but they worked slowly and didn't remotely fill the large and high-ceilinged room. A gentle draught wafted most of the smoke through the gallery doors and away. Consequently, the room was never really obscured and – in peaceful Cardiff – no one mistook the firecrackers for gunshots. The CCTV shows an elderly woman tutting and wagging her finger at the three men's commonplace vandalism.

What's more, the gallery staff responded by running towards the scene, not away from it. The whole 'escape in the chaos' theory quickly became transformed into a 'get trapped by well-ordered and swift security response' reality.

Whoops.

Nothing daunted, the three men adapted rapidly. They drew their weapons. Fired two shots to prove their seriousness. Grabbed their paintings and a group of hostages – now known to number only eight, not the sixteen first advertised – then fled down some emergency stairs to the basement. The three paintings they managed to take have, a curator has told us, a market value of perhaps three or four hundred thousand pounds.

Now, of course, the game is to end the siege without bloodshed. Police marksmen are on the scene but, with no lines of sight, they have little to do.

A communications van is acting as command centre and trained negotiators are doing their thing. There are enough people trickling in and out of the van that I can always find someone to tell me what's going on. Situations like these are instantly resourced to the max – over-resourced, in fact – with the happy result that there's always someone happy to come over and chat to small pink-and-pistachio detectives.

The gunmen's first request: a helicopter and ten million pounds in cash.

The negotiators' first response: yeah, sure. Coming right up.

Three of the hostages are security guards, all male. Four of the five remaining hostages are female, two of whom are elderly, one of them a diabetic. The negotiators want to get both of those two, but especially the diabetic, out of there as soon as possible.

No progress so far.

I've been kicking around for almost two hours when Bleddyn Jones arrives on the scene.

He sees me. Is less than thrilled.

'You're here,' he says.

'I am, yes.'

The conversation starts so scintillatingly, we neither of us have the heart to drag it out, so we do a semi-polite nodding thing, then Jones struts off, to make sure everyone knows how important he is. Before long, he struts back, as it turns out no one cares.

He has a coffee from somewhere. Drinks it.

Says, 'Nice having a crime where you know who the bloody criminals are. Who they are and what they want.'

I adjust his statement in my head, so it reads, 'It's nice having a crime when you have video footage of three of the men involved. And it's nice knowing what they want, so long as you recognise that what they want is most unlikely to be those three stupid pictures.'

Having adjusted his statement, I agree vigorously.

Meantime, negotiations trickle on.

The gunmen's second request: a helicopter and five million pounds in cash. Everything to be ready by dawn. Hostages to be executed hourly from six in the morning if things aren't ready.

The negotiators' second response: OK, OK, we can talk about that, but first we need to check the hostages are all right.

The gunmen's response to the response: Uh, OK, but bring pizza.

Pizza.

The pizza request is, classically, the moment in any negotiation when you know you've won. The helicopter-and-bagfuls-of-cash idea melting into the dream it always was. The urgency of food and fizzy drinks assuming ever greater importance to those hunkered down in their stone and carpet-tile basement. I'm personally not so sure that this pizza moment is, in fact, The Pizza Moment, but no doubt we'll soon find out.

A couple of ambulances wait patiently in case of carnage. A tall, good-looking woman doctor stands, slightly impatiently, by the open door of one of them.

More to and fro.

The medical team idea finally gets the go-ahead from a gunman calling himself 'John', but in exchange for what is basically a very lengthy order for take-out. Mostly pizza, but also doner kebabs, fried chicken, hamburger, chips and drinks. John is quite specific about which outlets should supply each of those fine foodstuffs. His meticulousness, his detail, reminds me of those Death Row inmates in the US with their last meal wish-lists, their gargantuan appetites.

Some uniforms go off to buy the food.

Nothing happens too fast, of course. Operations like this are all about timing. The purpose is to gradually narrow the gunmen's range of ambitions, until they want nothing more than a hot shower and a cosy prison cell. Even our worry over medical care is mostly overcooked. Most people will do fine sitting uncomfortably for a few hours or even days. The two elderly hostages *are* a worry, but even there, the two women are only in their late sixties. They wouldn't necessarily be more at risk if stuck on a train.

Gradually, a heap of fast food is assembled. Someone's

found a white plastic crate to put it in. Anna Kerrigan, the doctor, has a red nylon equipment bag.

I make myself helpful.

Bring bottled water to the negotiators. Find a techie guy called Steve when there were some problems with the audio recording.

I sidle closer, crabwise, to the heart of the action.

Inside the ambulance, a small nurse sits drinking tea or coffee. She looks down at her sensibly shod feet and does not seem particularly happy. Telling the difference between her and a ray of sunshine: not so hard, I think.

The negotiators are on the line again. Explaining in detail what food they have. The crate it's contained in. The medical team that'll be coming.

No surprises. That's key to this next bit. If the gunmen are expecting a female doctor and a male one arrives instead, the possibility of panic shooting increases exponentially. Same thing with everything. So the negotiator, Mark Wetherby, goes over everything in painful detail, not just once, but two, three, four times.

The crate mists up with the steam of chip fat and pizza grease.

The nurse finishes her drink. She looks pale. Almost ill.

My crabwise sidling is now less a sidle. More a full-on assault.

'I'll go,' I say.

Kerrigan looks at me.

'And you are?'

'Detective Sergeant Fiona Griffiths.'

I show my warrant card, to give me the authority that my floaty pink skirt and pistachio-striped top do not supply.

Kerrigan snaps, 'You're not medically qualified. I need a nurse.'

'Really? What are you doing down there? Temperatures,

214

blood pressures. Maybe an insulin shot? It's not like you need a full range of nursing skills.'

The nurse – the actual one – grabs her chance. With a firmness she's not previously shown, she says, 'She can go. I'm not going down there.'

Two against one.

I give Kerrigan my two-against-one smile. Gracious, but with a core of steel.

But this isn't Kerrigan's call. Wetherby, the chief negotiator, gets involved. Also Hermione Peters, one of his side-kicks. Bleddyn Jones too, frustrated at the lack of opportunities to meddle, now tries to peddle his meddling for all its worth.

All around me, grown-ups talk about things in grown-up voices.

I say to the nurse, 'What size shoes do you take?'

Four, like me.

Her scrubs will fit too, partly because we're much the same size, but also because those scrubs never really fit anyone anyway.

The grown-ups come to a decision, the right one. They concur that the risk of sending a reluctant and frightened nurse into battle is greater than the risk of sending down an unreluctant non-nurse. Also, of course, no one's employment contract forces them to enter a room full of dangerous morons armed with guns.

The nurse and I swap clothes.

'I always wanted to be a nurse,' I say untruthfully, 'but I wanted one of those little caps. I don't know why they don't do them any more.'

The nurse agrees with vigour. We don't know why they don't do them any more.

Kerrigan shows me the ear thermometer. How it works.

I say, 'I know how a thermometer works.'

She shows me the blood pressure cuff. How it works.

That's slightly more novel but, you know: blood pressure cuffs, rocket science – not so hard to tell the difference there either.

She shows me the insulin pen. Uncap. Push. Discard.

I say, 'Uncap. Push. Discard.'

Kerrigan says, 'In the sharps bin. Here.'

She shows me a small sharps bin which is bright yellow and says sharps.

I say, 'Oh, that's lucky. It says sharps.'

Kerrigan scowls, but she'd rather go down with someone who's not frightened.

Wetherby says, 'And, to be clear, neither of you are armed in any way? No pocket knives. Nothing sharp? No aerosols? No phones. No cameras. Nothing?'

I say no, no, nothing. I'm wearing just one layer of cotton scrubs. Hardly concealment wear.

Kerrigan discards her phone, but says, 'There are scalpels in the medical bag. Also scissors and spray.'

Those things are communicated to 'John', but he's getting hungry now. Just yeses everything.

Wetherby: 'The medical team comprises a doctor and a nurse. They're both women. They will show themselves at the top of the stairs. They will not come down until you specifically instruct them to.'

John: 'They need to come down with their hands up.'

John: either not-very-good-at-his-job John or remarkably-proficient-at-his-job John.

Eeny-meeny-miny-mo.

Wetherby: 'They will be carrying a crate of food and a red medical bag, remember. They will need their hands.'

'OK, but no sudden movements.'

'They will make no sudden movements.'

Jones tells me, 'You will take orders from Dr Kerrigan. You

will do *exactly* as she instructs, yes? I don't want you taking the initiative here. Is that understood?'

I do a sit. Give him my paw. Pant obedience.

Wetherby – slightly surprised by Jones's heavy-handedness – raises an eyebrow.

Jones says, 'She can be erratic, this one.'

I woof my assent. Jingle my chain. Roll over and play dead.

Wetherby says, 'Steady', but nothing else.

I tell everyone – and this isn't the first time – that we need to check *all* possible exit routes. Say the helicopter plan is so ditzy we should regard it as a bluff.

Everyone tells me that all exits *have* been sealed. They roll their eyes and Jones does his 'What did I tell you?' face.

Kerrigan says, 'Ready?'

'Yes.'

Kerrigan is taller and stronger than me, so she takes the crate and I take her medical bag, which makes me look like the doctor and Kerrigan like the support staff.

I think of making a merry play on the subject, but don't.

We walk up the steps to the museum.

TV cameras watch our backs. Ditto the eyes of the few dozen spectators who are still bothering to watch proceedings. Ditto the eyes of the increasingly bored police marksmen.

We enter the museum.

Echoey, empty halls.

Kerrigan has shoes with a bit of a heel and they make really good clicks as she walks. My shoes are soft-soled and make a squashy squeaking sound. When we walk we go click-squash, click-squash, click-squash.

Kerrigan: 'Are you OK?'

'Yes.'

We walk on through to the French Impressionists gallery. A gallery that now has three empty frames. I notice that one of the pictures left intact was a Pissarro landscape. Next to

217

it: a nice-looking portrait by Paul Signac. I'm hardly expert, but if I was stealing pictures from this gallery, I'd have taken the Pissarro and the Signac, not the three non-entities that actually vanished.

As we enter the gallery, a posse of firearms officers and an emergency response medical team scurries over to assist. Two buff-looking paramedics help Kerrigan with her crate. I try to look like my red bag is really heavy, but no one rushes over to help me.

The senior firearms officer holds open the fire door at the top of the staircase.

Says, 'Good luck.'

That sentiment is seconded by a grunt of masculine, gun-jingling assent from the posse.

We go through to the staircase. It's a double-winder, so we have to go down a few steps, before making the turn onto the landing. At the top, we can be seen from below, so we halt. Put down our stuff and raise our hands.

We can just about see, through the partition below us, a dark-clothed man.

Given where we stand, he can probably only see our feet and maybe a chunk of leg.

The man bends round and down, until he's bent over, looking up.

We go down a step or two so he can see us better. Make 'OK to come down?' faces.

He stops us with a hand. Disappears. Reappears again in front of the glass.

'You've got the food?' he asks.

He has a gun in his hand. Doesn't make any big play with it, but that's the thing about guns. You just have to have them. You don't need the big play.

Kerrigan says, 'I'm Dr Kerrigan. This is my nurse, Fiona.'

I do my best nurse face.

'OK. Come on down. One at a time. You first.'

I'm the 'you'.

I walk down, slowly.

The big red bag has a shoulder strap, so I let it dangle free and keep my hands out in front of me, like I'm about to catch a giant, invisible beach ball.

Get to the bottom. Put the bag down.

Let the guy search me. Hands right up my leg to the knicker line. Then the other leg. Then my hips, including my crotch. Then the rest of me, including my breasts.

He's shortish for a guy. Five foot eight or nine. Dark hair, very short. Not broad, but fit. Neck tattoo in blue. Dental hygiene with scope for improvement.

I don't say anything until he's finished. When he is, I say, 'In that bag, there are medical supplies including scalpels, scissors and sprays.'

He tells me to open it. Stands back as I do so.

I show him the bag. Its many-velcroed compartments.

Even the gunman gets bored as he watches me. His gaze keeps drifting upwards to the box of food. Before I'm finished, he tells me to go inside with the hostages. Tells Kerrigan to come on down.

I do as I'm told.

It's a staff rec room. Easy seating in pale blues and greys. Coffee machine. A vending machine with crisps and things. Someone has obviously tried to smash the glass, but it wasn't very smashable, so the machine looks dinged and unhappy, but basically intact. Some posters advertise recent exhibitions. *Adventures in Archaeology.* An Impressionists thing from a few years back. *Maps and Manuscripts: our hidden past.*

Eight hostages, not visibly harmed.

They are bound with packing tape, but not ankles and wrists. Instead, they're bound one-and-one, in a sort of three-legged-race-type arrangement. So one hostage's right leg and right arm are taped to the neighbouring hostage's left leg and left arm.

That strikes me as odd for a moment, until I realise that people, even hostages, need to go to the loo. This one-and-one method gives enough mobility to each couple that they can just about manoeuvre themselves around toileting and that kind of thing, but still makes any escape attempt effectively impossible.

Neat. Almost too neat for the blundering smoke-grenaders who got themselves into this pickle.

The two elderly women are taped together. One of them looks fine, actually. Robust and defiant. Not quite the war generation, but cut from that same durable khaki serge.

Her partner, though, is visibly unwell. Her colour's bad. Forehead both white and sweaty. She sits with a hand on her chest. Barely responds to my arrival.

Kerrigan joins me.

She looks composed. Coolly professional.

The first gunman is joined by two others. Both bigger. Short hair. More tattoos. The same general mould as the first.

Conveniently, one of them has blond, almost gingery, hair. The other is mouse-brown. I don't know which one 'John' is, but they can be Dark Hair, Ginger and Mousy.

The three of them start to snarf into their food, except that Dark Hair guy tells Mousy that someone has to 'watch out'.

'Watch out' means pointing a pistol at us and looking generally menacing, while still using a left hand to pick chips from their paper wrapping.

Ginger says, 'Hey, Nursey, there's not enough vinegar on the chips. Nip out and get some more, would you?'

Mousy laughs and nods and laughs some more, the perfect audience.

Kerrigan introduces herself, to the gunmen but also to the hostages.

'I'm Dr Anna Kerrigan. This is Fiona. We're going to examine each of you, especially you, love.' This last bit to the diabetic who we think may be called Lorraine Biggar. 'We've got supplies here including insulin.'

She talks and moves slowly.

Before diving into the medical bag, she holds her hands over it, asking for permission to delve inside.

Mousy nods.

Kerrigan and I head straight for the diabetic, who confirms her name is indeed Lorraine.

'OK, Lorraine, we'll take a reading right away. A few other measurements too.'

Kerrigan takes a blood sugar reading, which isn't good at all. She calculates an insulin dose. I inject it.

Alcohol swab. Uncap the pen. Push. Discard into the sharps bin.

I wriggle my eyebrows at Kerrigan in a *ta-daa!* sort of way, but she doesn't wriggle back.

Kerrigan listens to Biggar's chest with a stethoscope.

Grimaces.

Tells me to get going with the thermometer and blood pressure cuff.

I do so. Don't cock anything up. I should think, to the three watching gunmen, I look very much like a not-excessively-large nurse doing my not-excessively-challenging job.

I give Kerrigan the measurements she needs in a low mutter. Biggar's systolic blood pressure score is well over one seventy, which is way too high. She's running a fever too. Not much of one, but a bit.

Biggar complains of headache and we give her aspirin. Kerrigan takes the woman's shoes off and inspects her feet, I think because circulation problems often manifest there first. Kerrigan lightly touches Biggar's toes. Asks if she has normal sensation there.

Biggar's answers are slow and unconvincing, but that's as likely the result of anxiety as from any kind of nerve failure.

At one point, she vomits slightly. She doesn't produce much and I wipe her up as best I can with paper towels.

Kerrigan doesn't comment, but her face is grim.

As she continues to examine Biggar, I take readings from everyone else.

No other fever. A couple of the security guards have lousy blood pressure. One of them pats his tummy with his free hand and says, 'Biscuits. That's my downfall.'

I note names, dates of birth, temperature and blood pressure readings on a pad, then go round again with Kerrigan, noting other observations, mostly heart rates, as she gives them.

When we're done with the hostages, we turn to the gunmen, now shinily greased around their mouths.

Mousy has yielded the gun to Dark Hair, and is stuffing his gob with hamburger.

Kerrigan says, 'I'd like to examine each of you, if I may. This is a highly stressful situation for everyone, including you, and I'd like to check for any problems early.'

Mousy and Dark Hair treat that idea with contempt.

Ginger the same, except that, ever the humorist, he rolls his sleeve up his well-muscled arm and says, 'You can do me. So long as you do it topless.'

I don't know if that was aimed more at me or more at Kerrigan, but we don't offer a topless medical check-up service, not even with guns in our faces.

Ginger hesitates a moment, but decides his witticism is too good to leave, so he gets Kerrigan to listen to his chest and has me take a blood pressure reading, as he writhes around and breathes heavily and makes horrible little grunty noises.

I've a nasty feeling we're getting glimpses of Ginger's real sex face.

Bending over his arm, as I operate the inflation bulb for the pressure cuff, I note that his hands smell of soap, but have a whitish dust under the fingernails.

When we're done, Kerrigan straightens. Flicks her long, dark pony-tail behind her.

'OK. Everyone's fine, except for Lorraine here. She's on the edge of hypertensive crisis. She needs proper medical attention right now. That means hospital.'

Dark Guy says, 'You just gave her insulin. I watched you.'

'Her blood *sugar* will soon come back to normal. Her blood *pressure* is on the edge of crisis. You can see it.'

Dark Guy studies Biggar, then shakes his head.

'Sorry. We didn't cause those problems. She'll just have to take her chances.' He gives a look that adds, *her fault for being a fatty*.

Kerrigan: 'This woman needs immediate transfer to a hospital.'

'OK. Once there's a chopper on the roof with a bag full of cash.'

Kerrigan, I think, is going to continue to argue, but Biggar chooses that moment to vomit properly. A full-on, head-forward, moaning gush.

I do my nurse bit to the full.

Check her airways. Start cleaning her up – an almost impossible job. Talk soothingly, bending close to her ear. She's not really with me, though. She's foggy and unresponsive.

Kerrigan, hand on Biggar's pulse, says, 'Hospital. She needs a hospital *now*.'

Dark Guy: 'All righty. One in, one out.'

He means one of us.

Kerrigan flashes a look at me.

I say to Dark Guy, 'Can we talk? In private?'

He shrugs. Kerrigan and I go to the far end of the rec room, which is hardly private, but probably good enough.

I tell her I don't mind staying. Tell her some other things

223

too. Things to do with a smell of soap and a whitish dust. Tell her what to communicate to whom.

She shakes her head with impatience. 'No. I'm the doctor. If anyone stays, I do.'

That's a crap argument if ever there was one. I say, 'Yes, and I'm the "nurse",' wrapping as many inverted commas round that word as one low whisper can manage. 'Aside from Biggar, this is a room full of healthy people. My skills are more relevant here.' Since Kerrigan is still hesitating, I look pointedly down at her left hand, where a wedding band twinkles on her ring finger. 'Also, I'm not married and I have no kids.'

Kerrigan thinks a second and says, 'OK, fine.'

Turns back to the grinning gunmen and says, 'My colleague, Fiona, has agreed to stay. I need your word that she won't be harmed.'

Dark Guy shrugs and agrees. Just adds the itsy-bitsy rider, 'Unless we need someone to execute.'

Ginger cuts Biggar out of her packing-tape casket. He and Kerrigan help her up. Biggar's eyes still have the madness and vacancy of shock but, I assume, she'll be OK the further she's able to get from this place.

Kerrigan, supporting the woman's weight, starts to lead her away.

That leaves me.

Me. A splatter of puke. A pile of paper towels.

Ginger wants to put me into Biggar's place right away, but I gesture at the mess. At me.

'Can I clean up first? Is there a bathroom?'

Dark Hair nods. The place stinks and none of the gunmen want to perform the clean-up.

At a nod from Dark Hair, Ginger escorts me out of the room and round a corner. I'm carrying a plastic waste bin that I'll use to fetch water. Ginger is carrying a gun, but not pointing it, particularly.

224

Further on down the corridor, just in front of a sign saying Numismatics, Palaeography and Codicology, there's a spot where some ceiling tiles have been removed. Stacked up on the floor. From the hole that's been left, I can see the glimmer of what is presumably an air duct. A portable CD player sits a bit randomly on the floor below.

Ginger sees me looking at this set-up and pushes my shoulder towards the bathroom. So I stop staring and go obediently inside.

Codicology, I think. *Codicology*.

Fill my bin with water. A few squidges of that weird pink soap. Lots more paper towels.

Go back to the room.

Hands and knees clean-up. Do a reasonable job, given the tools at hand. Then Ginger leads me back to the bathroom to get rid of the water and the stinky towels.

Once done, I ask permission to use the toilet. He says fine.

I enter a cubicle, close the door and pee. The air duct thing. Is that real or a red herring? The corridor floor was carpeted, but I dab carefully at the sole of my shoe. Find a little white stone dust, gritty under my fingertips.

Dust then that didn't come from outside. That didn't come from upstairs.

These are either among the worst museum-breaker-inners in the world, or among the best.

I think about that CD player. Why have that? Only one reason that I can think of.

Also: *numismatics. Codicology*.

Ginger starts moving about impatiently outside my stall, so I finish my business and exit.

Move towards the basins to wash my hands, when I glimpse movement in the mirror.

Ginger has swung his pistol up and is pointing it, in a

two-handed grip, at the back of my neck. The barrel of the gun is maybe six inches away from me.

Because he's now directly behind me, we can't see each other's eyes in the mirror and that appears to bother him, because he changes stance, rotating round me, so the gun's cold glare is now fixed on a spot at the side of my neck.

I don't move. Just watch Ginger in the mirror.

Watch him watching me.

He has pale-blue eyes, white skin, and his mouth is just a little parted. The wet interior of his lips slightly exposed.

Under these bathroom halogens, the gun has a steel-blue quality. It seems like the only durable object in the room. My neck, me, Ginger: all temporary, soft, disposable.

Through all this, I've kept my hands down and slightly away from my sides. Remain like that, completely still, as the gun traces lines on me. My head. Neck. Then chest. Special mention for my breasts, the line of my arm, then the barrel rises again to settle on my ear.

My mouth is completely dry.

Ginger says, 'That doctor was quite hot, maybe an eight or nine. You're probably only a seven, but I bet you're one of those girls who goes batshit crazy in bed.'

I don't enlighten him. Try not to look batshit crazy.

I say, slowly, 'I'm going to step forward and wash my hands.'

I do that.

Before I turn on the tap, I say, 'I'm going to turn on the tap.' Before I squidge soap from the dispenser, I say, 'I'm getting soap.'

My movements are slow. Like a mime artist breaking each motion down into its smallest components.

If Ginger was dividing womankind up into deciles, I don't see how he could rate Kerrigan at anything less than ten, but I don't argue. I suspect that with people like Ginger the lower deciles are more heavily populated than the upper ones.

As I wash and rinse my hands, Ginger moves again. Places the snout of the gun against the back of my neck. Leaves it there just long enough that I can feel its metal chill. That conversation between barrel, bullet and flesh. Then the gun moves.

Traces the line of my spine, vertebra by vertebra, through the thin cotton of my nursing scrubs. The gun catches a bit when it reaches my bra – a catch that stopped my breath, stopped time itself – but it moves on.

As the water still gushes from the tap, the gun moves down to my waist. My coccyx. Then, horribly, between my legs. He actually pushes his fist in between my thighs far enough that I have to part my legs to make room. The gun barrel slides between my thighs, pushing up.

Pushes hard enough that I find myself lifting slightly. Legs slightly spread, standing on tiptoe, wet hands resting on the basin for support.

We stand like that for a moment. Frozen in this moment.

Then he jabs upwards. Hard. Nastily. I let out an involuntary *ah!* of pain and shock. Mouth open. Attention not in my head, or in the mirror, but down below where the action is.

I think that cry of pain gives Ginger what he wanted. Perhaps he thinks he's seen my sex face. And maybe he has. I wouldn't know.

In any case he removes the gun.

I come down from tiptoe. Stand normally again.

'A biter,' he tells me. 'I bet you're a biter.'

I say, 'I'm going to rinse my hands.'

I do so.

'I'm turning off the tap.'

Do so.

'I'm moving over to the drier now.'

Do so.

227

My gait is a little awkward, I think. The dark upward jab of that bruise is still widening. Still the centre of things. But Ginger's not pointing the gun now. Just dandling it around the way he was before.

I stand there at the drier, slowly calming.

Codicology.

'Codicology', I assume, derives from the word *codex*, which means book. So: the study of books as physical objects, something like that.

I'm not too sure about 'palaeography', but I think *palaeo* must mean old, as in *palaeolithic*. And *graphy* might have a connection with *graphic*, or something to do with writing. And if the damn word is stuck on a door next to codicology, I'm going to take a wild guess that palaeography is the study of old writing.

Codicology, palaeography, numismatics.

The drier clicks off.

My hands are actually dry. For possibly the very first time in my life, I have stood by a hot air drier long enough to actually dry my hands.

I turn around, still slowly, but not with the extreme, exaggerated slowness of before. I say, 'All done.'

Ginger says, 'OK, Nursey,' and motions me back outside.

He takes me back.

His games aren't quite over. He enjoys stroking the gun barrel in wide curves over my back and I walk slowly enough that he can, more or less, keep the gun in steady contact with me. But the gun doesn't drift down to my bum or spend more than a moment or two at the back of my neck.

Small mercies.

We get back to the rec room. As we draw close, Ginger holds the gun away from me, down by his side. Assuming that Dark Hair is the head of this particular crew, I suspect he'd be pissed off with Ginger for his fooling around.

I feel the tension of that pointing gun slowly, and only partially dissipate.

I sit where Lorraine Biggar sat. Ginger tapes me to my new neighbour, Molly.

Brown packing tape that crackles when you move.

'Hello, Molly,' I say. 'Hello everyone.'

I'm hellooed back. One of the security guards says, 'You swapping places with Lorraine there. That showed real guts, love. They should give you a medal.'

I bloody hope they don't, but sit there and nod as people say nice things.

Talk flickers and flares.

I look at the posters. *Adventures in Archaeology*. A boring photograph of bones and churned earth. I like bones, of course, but I prefer them fresh.

Maps and Manuscripts. That one has an image of that old, medieval writing blurring into and overlaying an old map. Two images superimposed.

Mousy stays in the room. He has his gun next to him, but mostly he's just sitting with his feet up, flicking at a magazine. The other two go off somewhere.

Rock music starts playing, from the CD player beyond the bathroom. I try to listen for sounds beyond the music, but can't, or don't think I can.

I hope Kerrigan passes on my message. I hope someone acts on it.

With my free hand, I rub my eyes.

'You all right, Molly?'

'Oh, don't you worry about me, love.'

I don't.

Just sit there. Rub my eyes.

And time goes by.

30

Time.

The fourth dimension.

One of my favourite dimensions. One that brings all the good stuff, even if she brings more than her share of the crappy stuff too. But there are times she's out of her depth. Times when she shunts one second into the void, over the edge of the present and away – then, blow it, the next second to come along looks exactly the same. And the next and the next.

Thousands of seconds, all alike. Yes, they come with minor differences of colour and tone. Sometimes it's one gunman at the table. Sometimes another. Sometimes the fattest of the three security guards snores as he snoozes. Sometimes he doesn't, or he blinks himself awake, or looks around the room with a kind of incredulity.

But still: it's samey.

The crate of food is passed around and we, or some of us, eat cold chips, fallen hamburger.

There's a bit of chat, but not much. Flickers of conversation that spurt for a minute or two, but don't ignite. Out in the corridor, that stupid CD player plays the same CD over and over and over again.

When we move, we crackle with packing tape.

It was about three o'clock when Kerrigan and I came downstairs. It's eight in the evening now.

Five hours. Eighteen thousand same-coloured seconds.

Maps and Manuscripts.

Codicology.

Palaeography.

And then – I stare one more time at that stupid poster and laugh at myself. My second *Dummkopf* moment of the case.

The thing that I was missing is missing no longer. The clue is shoved almost literally in my face.

Palimpsest. That's another cracker of a word, even if it doesn't get much airtime these days.

A second food crate arrives. I'm not sure how it came or who brought it. I can't see from my position and whoever's making those 'John' phone calls to the negotiators isn't making them from any place we can hear them.

We eat some food. Drink some drink.

No one has much appetite, not even the gunmen. They seem tired, actually. Like men most of the way through a long and arduous job. Arctic trekkers two days' short of the Pole.

The men's hands are grained in dust now. They're not bothering to wash off properly even. There are marks on their jeans where they've wiped them. Their faces too. Sweat streaked with white. One of the guys, Mousy, has a dark graze ruling a line down the inside of his thumb. He picks at the injury. Eats chips.

We're getting close, I think. This drama is nearing its denouement.

When I get the chance, I use my free hand to slip off my earrings. One goes in a pocket. The other in my mouth, lying in the channel between gum and cheek like the world's tiniest dagger.

One of the security guards, munching burger, says, 'Free food, eh? It's not all bad, then.'

Molly says, 'Oh, I don't usually eat anything like this. I always like to cook from fresh.'

She tells me all about her philosophy of food. I adhere

to my normal policy on small-talk and agree with whatever proposition has just been put to me.

At nine o'clock, Mousy and Dark Hair come into the room.

'Photo time,' says Dark Hair.

Molly and I are made to stand up. Walked three-leggedly to a wall. We're turned around, facing out into the room.

Mousy holds a gun to my head. Dark Hair takes the picture. The same thing with Molly.

Multiple pictures of both views. Molly and I hold hands tightly in our packing-tape cuffs, but I feel her shaking, literally shaking, as she stands. For the first time, I think, her stoic calm is collapsing into real shock.

'You're OK, Molly,' I tell her. 'You're doing well.'

Then Dark Hair yells for Ginger. ('Mate,' he calls, nothing helpful.) Ginger comes in and Dark Hair takes a picture of Molly and me at the same time. Two heads. A gun at each.

I think we're all thinking of those awful *jihadi* hostage pictures. The executioner and the axe. The black robes and the hatred.

I wonder what I look like.

Hair unbrushed. Stone-faced. Empty-eyed.

A gun to my head. Its own blank stare equalling my own.

But I don't know. They don't show me the images. And then, anyway, Dark Hair shifts to video.

He steadies the picture on Molly and me. They get their, now classic, heads 'n' guns shot. Then the camera tracks up from us to the clock that hangs on the wall above.

Dark Hair says, for the benefit of the recorder, 'It's just gone nine o'clock. At six o'clock in the morning, we execute our first hostage. Then one an hour from there on. You know what our demands are. You know what you have to do.'

He clicks off.

Plays back the video to check it. I assume he'll upload the thing to YouTube or email it to the BBC. The aim will be to grab the headlines for the ten o'clock news. Pressure the police side into compromise.

I wonder where they've got to with the helicopter and cash.

I also note that a helicopter is of no use, unless you've also got a couple of hostages on board and can't help realising that petite, healthy, female hostages are more portable than most other sorts. And if you want to conduct your negotiations through the media, then petite, young, prettyish hostages will get you instant access to the front pages. A gap-toothed six-year-old would be even better but, *faute de mieux*, I'm the best they've got.

We wait, standing, till Dark Hair nods an OK. Then orders us, crackling and shuffling, back to our seats.

Molly's posture of defiant firmness remains intact, but I can still feel the shaking.

'You're OK, Molly,' I tell her. 'You're OK.'

Dark Hair says, 'Right, it's nighty night. Anyone need to use the loo?'

A couple of people do. The 'loo' in question is just the waste bin at the end of the room. Dark Hair waits with a brisk impatience for them to get back to their seats.

'OK. It's lights off till six. You better hope that someone out there is going to play sensible.'

Ginger and Mousy start taping us all into our seats. Ankles and wrists. Keeping us from moving at all now. And Time, to be fair, has upped her game, I notice. All those long, identical seconds have become nicely jumbled up again. Plenty of action and variety.

A bit of gunplay. A bit of threat.

This long dread of night.

The two men tape us in. Dark Hair comes along to check bindings. Tugging at arms, kicking at legs. Not particularly gentle. Not particularly aggressive. Just getting a job done.

But we're OK. Packaged up like two rows of brown, crackling mummies.

They put tape over our mouths too. Wind it a couple of times round the head, leaving the mouth closed, but the nose free.

Not nice. That doesn't feel nice at all.

Ginger and Mousy leave.

Dark Hair hangs on the doorpost. Delivers his farewell address.

'OK, if you move, you die. If you leave this room, you die. If you shout for help, you die. If you piss us off in any way at all, you die. Is that clear enough? Like, completely fucking clear?'

It's completely fucking clear.

We nod assent. Dark Hair kills the light. Closes the door.

We are left in silence and darkness.

We have eight hours till the first execution.

31

Silence, yes, but one soon interrupted. Rock music again, played as loud as that crappy little CD player will go.

We hostages rustle and itch in our bindings. Try to figure out the best available solution to our discomforts. Head this way or that. Back straight or semi-slouched.

Molly and I still hold hands. Use our eyes to ask each other if we're OK. Use them to say, yes, fine, never been better.

In the gaps between tracks, I listen into the silence. That silence which is never really silent.

I hear the snores and breathing of my fellow hostages. Their crackling movements. The tick of the clock. Little beeps of distant electronics. The ticks and shifts of the museum as it settles into its night-time temperature.

Something similar is true of this thickened darkness.

It's dark here, but not pitchy. There's that part-glazed partition behind my head, and some of the light from the stairwell above filters down to us. I can see the dark shapes of four sleeping shadows opposite me. The clock on the wall. The slow, luminous circuit of its hour- and minute-hands.

The music finishes and starts again.

Finishes and starts.

In the gaps, I listen as hard as I can for the kind of sound that I'm expecting. Maybe hear something. Maybe don't.

Numismatics. Palaeography. Codicology.

At about half past one in the morning, the music reaches its final track – again – and melts into silence.

A minute goes by.

Five.

Ten.

One of my fellow hostages, mutters through his gag, 'Thank fuck for that.'

He says that as though the only thing standing between him and a good night's sleep had been a troublesome neighbour and their late-night party.

I let an hour go by.

Pass it through my hands, second by second. Time Future becoming Time Past.

I spend that whole hour listening as intently as I can. Listening hard into this non-silent silence. Trying to hear any human sound beyond this room.

Hear nothing.

Showtime.

I manoeuvre the world's tiniest dagger to the front of my mouth.

Pop its little blade through the packing tape, then lean down and start pecking at my bindings.

The shaft of my earring won't *cut* anything, but it'll pierce cellophane tape no problem.

Peck. Peck. Peck.

Make a series of puncture marks. Wiggle my wrist until the damn tape starts to part. Then work back along the length of my arm to the elbow.

Peck. Peck. Peck.

I wake Molly, of course.

She gag-mumbles, 'They told us not to move, dear.'

That's Brits for you. Someone in authority tells you to do something and people get all anxious if you take a little initiative.

I gag-mumble back, 'I'm fine. Don't worry.'

Peck. Peck. Peck.

The hardest part is the elbow. I sort of thought that once I'd got my hand free, the rest would be simple, but it turns out to be the other way round. But hey ho. I've got plenty of time.

I get one arm free, and from there on it's easy.

I rip my gag off, which hurts a bit but is basically fine. Then free my other arm. Then my legs.

I feel achy and sore and sticky, but I'm in one piece.

In one piece and ready to rumba.

Take some latex gloves from the medical bag. Go to the door.

A couple of gag-voices wish me mumbled good luck. I don't answer them. Just flash a smile, raise a thumb. Stand listening into that many-toned silence.

Ticks and clicks. A slight shuffling sound, perhaps from above. An electronic thing doing its annoying beepy thing in some far-off office.

Listen for ten minutes, then ease the door open.

Stand. Listen. Gaze out on a dark corridor.

A corridor that stands wide and empty.

Shoes off, I walk out of the room. Not back up the stairs that brought me here. Not to the merry police officers and their merry little assault brigade. But to the door that intrigued me from the first.

Numismatics, Palaeography and Codicology.

I think I may have some business, soon, with the palaeographers and codicologists of this world, but for now the numismatists have all my attention.

Numismatics. The study of coins.

I stop at that closed door, barefoot in this whispering silence.

Listen hard. Listen for my life.

Hear nothing. Hear no one.

No men. No violent gingers. No snoring. No mutter of low voices. No kicking around in anyone's sleep. No nothing.

Just this almost darkness. This almost silence.

I take a deep breath. A silent prayer.

Shoot me quickly.
Shoot me dead.
Silver bullets in my head.
Kill me gentle.
Kill me brave.
Arthur's sword in Arthur's grave.

Say my prayer and open the door.

32

Open the door and—

No men. No guns. No hail of bullets.

No brief, brief opportunity to reflect that I don't always know as much as I think I do.

Instead – silence.

Darkness eased by a distant bulb. Those things and an empty corridor and, on my right, a door marked Numismatics Stores – Private. That door would have caught my attention in any case, but does so doubly right now because the door has been jemmied open. A useless lock in a splintered frame.

I enter.

Find a small storeroom. Drawers like safety deposit boxes. Lamps and a workbench.

Those things and also a socking great hole in the wall. A hole big enough to take three men and three crappy paintings that were never really worth this amount of effort. A hole that carves its way out of the museum's external, but underground, wall and through to a well-made tunnel beyond.

The tunnel snakes beyond the limit of my light. That thing wasn't constructed overnight. This whole heist must have been planned for months. Carefully planned and perfectly executed.

There was, though, one wrinkle in the men's plan: the very last part. Tunnelling right up to the museum wall itself: that must have been time-consuming, certainly, but wasn't much harder than any ordinary digging.

But pushing the tunnel through this two-foot thick foundation wall: that would have taken plenty of time and made plenty of noise.

So: how to do it?

The answer our three heroes came up with was to clear the museum. Remove the security guards. Distract the police. Blather about helicopters and sacks of cash and executions starting at dawn.

Do all that to give themselves the space and time to puncture this final wall in quiet and peace.

When I saw the stone dust, I was fairly sure how this was going to play out. Told Kerrigan what to expect and what my brothers and sisters on the force needed to do. I don't know whether anyone took any notice of me, but suffice to say that if my colleagues had got the thieves in custody by now, my stockinged explorations of this ticking dimness would already have been cut short.

So our three hostage-takers have flown this muddy nest. Are even now ripping into the first beers of the night and pissing themselves with laughter.

But I don't mind too much about that, or not for the moment.

After all: I didn't come here to look. I came here to steal.

The drawers and boxes in this numismatics room are mostly locked, but the real security down here was the lock on the main door. That, and the whole museumful of security above it. These drawer locks are no harder to open than any ordinary filing cabinet and a fair few locks have duly been smashed and drawers opened.

Not pillaged, though, or not systematically. A few pocketfuls taken, I'd guess. But most of what the museum owns is left behind, still intact.

I rifle through the battered drawers, until I find the one I want. Late Roman, Welsh.

A scatter of coins. Unpolished. Dim.

Gold. Silver. Bronze.

I take my latex gloves. Put them on.

If you're going to steal something, you need to do it properly. They teach you that in the police.

There are twelve gold coins in the drawer. I take four. The same number of silver and bronze. My nurse's pockets are cut fairly loose, so I slip my thievings into my bra.

It's late o'clock and I'm exhausted.

I walk back to the hostage room, and stick my head in.

'All done, folks. I'll go and get help now.'

Walk up the stairs. Tired as a dog.

Tired as a very tired dog.

That ache in my crotch, where Ginger jabbed me, is a slow bruise. Crusting over into the dimness of an old, unwanted memory.

At the turn of the stair, I call up.

'This is Detective Sergeant Fiona Griffiths. I'm coming upstairs now and I'd really, really appreciate it, if no one shoots me.'

Keeping my hands well above my head, I ascend slowly to the top.

Eight men. Eight rifle sights. Eight laser beams dancing on my chest.

A buzz of fireflies.

But no one fires.

33

Sunday morning.

Gethin Matthews's office.

He's a detective superintendent, which is exactly the rank I'd be if my bosses were stupid enough to promote me, reckless enough to promote me again, then dangerously incompetent enough to do so for a third time. From my bargain basement depths, Matthews appears to live on a kind of Olympus. Remote. Powerful. Possessing thunderbolts.

He says, 'Help yourself.'

Pushes a tray of baked things at me.

Croissants. Danish pastries. Some muffins already beginning to speckle and shine in their own grease.

I peer at them closely. Like Sherlock Holmes examining footprints. Then, because I'm meant to take something, I take something.

I'm wearing a dress in pale forget-me-not blue, printed with a white fern design, except that my sister would admonish me, because (I've learned) it's not a white-white, it's more a natural white or a lime white or something else which is very pale but still lacks the snowy brightness of actual white.

Anyway, the point is, I'm wearing a nice dress.

I'm wearing it because it is ten thirty on Sunday morning, because I like the dress, because the weather is warm, because I spent last night taped up as a hostage, and because nothing says, 'Not dead yet', like a forget-me-not-blue dress printed all over with sweet not-quite-white ferns.

I'm wearing it for all those reasons, yes, but also this: I'm wearing the dress because it looks too flirty and summery and unprofessional for the office and I want to remind everyone that THIS IS MY DAY OFF and what with debriefings and the like, I didn't get to bed until almost seven o'clock this morning and was out of that bed less than three hours later so I could be here on Olympus with a tray of rapidly ageing pastries.

I hold my croissant aloft, look at my as-yet-unbecrumbed dress, and say, 'There aren't any plates.'

There are, in fact, some plates neatly stacked on a sideboard, and I can see them clearly from where I'm sitting. But I assert my various privileges – young woman in pretty dress, survivor of scary museum siege, person who is a good few hours short of sleep – and pretend I haven't.

Matthews – Jove-like – gets a plate and passes it over.

I place the croissant daintily on the plate. I'm not sure if I like croissants, but they do look nice. The pale gold of the croissant looks extra-nice against the soft blue of the dress, which is such an amazingly girly thought that I sit for a moment stunned by my own girliness.

Matthews, prompting: 'So.'

That doesn't mean anything, so I counter with, 'Yes sir,' which doesn't mean anything either.

Matthews: 'This whole tunnel thing. I understand you had an idea something like this might be happening.'

He waves a hand towards the only two other people in the room: Bleddyn Jones and Hermione Peters, Wetherby's sidekick on the negotiation team.

'Yes.'

Matthews: 'So three idiots walk into a museum. It looks like they've come to steal a Renoir, only the Renoir isn't there. They decide to steal some other stuff, except they make a complete pig's arse of the job in every way you can imagine.

You know all this and you decide you're seeing some top-level criminals engaged in a carefully planned heist.'

'Well, I wasn't sure. I mean, it all depends what you think they were stealing.'

Matthews stares.

Jones rubs his face. A 'here we go again' look hovers in his beard.

Peters – who can't have had much sleep either, but looks cool as ice in a grey skirt and crisp white shirt – gives me an encouraging smile. An all-sisters-together one.

Matthews says, 'Well, they were looking for that Renoir, weren't they? If they'd got their hands on it, they'd have had a painting worth somewhere north of ten million quid.'

I say, 'Worth that through an international auction house, yes.'

'OK, so maybe ten per cent of that. It's still a haul.'

'Ten per cent *maybe*, and *only* if you know your way around the criminal art market. But if these guys were as moronic as they appeared, they probably didn't have buyers lined up.'

I don't mention it, but most of these art-world heists have at least one person working on the inside, providing details of CCTV and that kind of thing. That person would presumably have had access to the museum's cleaning and restoration programme – those things are hardly secret – in which case you'd have to believe that these guys were world-class either for their stupidity or for their cleverness.

Matthews stares again, but the quality of the stare has altered.

Jones mutters, 'Look, Fiona.'

We battle away a bit. Me with my antiquities theories. Everyone else with their 'Look, they were there to take the bloody Renoir' theories.

Not much was taken from that numismatics store. About fifty coins in total. I took about a dozen. The thieves took the rest. The things we stole were rare, certainly. Impossible to replicate. But their open market value was nothing at all in relation to the Renoir. Melted down, that quantity of precious metal might buy you a cheap second-hand car in poor condition. Perhaps not even that.

So I lose. My theories discarded, again.

Matthews shifts the focus of discussion.

'OK. So then you get down to the basement. You see evidence of stone dust. You hear music being played continually, which suggests to you that some noise-generating activity is being concealed.'

'Yes. I assumed a tunnel, but couldn't be certain. They made a vague show of pretending they had some air duct thing going, but I didn't buy into that. In any event, I communicated my suspicions to Dr Kerrigan.'

Kerrigan, I now know, did come out and report my observations in full to the siege team. That team decided to take the intelligence at face value. Even Blathering Bleddyn, I understand, advised strongly in favour of taking the tunnel hypothesis seriously. For all the problems I've had in working with him, he's never been stupid or lazy or incompetent. Really, my problems with him amount to just two: his by-the-bookishness and that damn beard.

Matthews again: 'OK, and the team do everything they can to find the mouth of that tunnel. But . . .'

But: they didn't find it.

The National Museum sits in a little cluster of capital city-type buildings. Our own police headquarters for one, but City Hall, the crown court, the university and so on. It hardly seemed credible that the crown court had been used as a base from which to dig, but nothing was ruled out. So every sewer was investigated. Every building. Whole warrens of underground storerooms and cleaning cupboards were searched and checked. In the time available and working partly at night, my colleagues tried to scope out every square metre of ground in an ever-widening circle round the museum's eastern boundary.

That circle reached to around more than two hundred and thirty metres by the time I, so wearily, climbed those stairs to meet the fireflies dancing on my chest.

Alas, the thieves had gone more than seventy metres better. The tunnel exited in the cellar of an ordinary terraced house in Llanbleddian Gardens, the far side of the railway line. Another day's work and we might have cracked even that, but – it was not to be.

Matthews continues with the debriefing.

We check e-fits.

Go through distinguishing marks, accents, any inadvertent communications.

We went through all this last night, but here we are, going through it all again.

There are alerts out everywhere. We've alerted the Metropolitan Police's 'art-fraud unit' which acts as a national centre of expertise. Since, however, that unit comprises one full- and one part-time officer, I suspect that the depth of national expertise may not be very great.

We're winding up.

I have, I notice, eaten most of my croissant, without even making much mess. I lick my finger and lift one golden patisserie flake from my skirt. Hermione Peters catches my eye and squeezes a smile at me, I don't know why.

Then Jones says, 'Just one other thing.'

One other thing.

Not a phrase to strike dread, really, except that when it emerges from that mouth, that beard, I feel an internal clenching, as if my internal organs, my soft viscera, were all suddenly huddling for comfort.

Jones: 'Fiona, I'm sorry to raise this, but feel I have to. When you requested permission to act as Dr Kerrigan's nurse, I gave you explicit instructions. Do you remember what they were?'

I nod.

He says 'Well?' – or, actually, says nothing, but his beard and eyebrows collude in a kind of 'well?'-like thing.

I say, 'You said, "You will take orders from Dr Kerrigan. You will do *exactly* as she instructs. I don't want you taking the initiative." That's not quite word for word, but not far off.'

'Yes. And what actually happened?'

'We were faced with an unexpected situation. We weren't expecting to evacuate a hostage.'

'Fiona, did you do as Dr Kerrigan instructed?'

'No.'

Peters, who looks somewhat startled by this interchange, says, 'Bleddyn, I think Fiona showed a lot of courage—'

'Oh, she has courage, all right, I don't doubt that.'

'And she *did* get the hostage out.'

'Dr Kerrigan also offered to take the place of that hostage. She showed as much courage as Fiona did and I placed *her* in command.'

I say, 'Sir, Dr Kerrigan is married. I'm not. And as a police officer, it's my duty to protect civilians, Dr Kerrigan included.'

There's a temporary stalemate. But it's a three against one thing and – for once in my career, for maybe the first time in my whole blessed career – the three are on my side, not against me.

I don't gloat. Don't dance around the room shouting *Olé*! Just fix a mild smile on my face, look modestly downwards, and smooth the fabric of my forget-me-not dress.

But Jones doesn't accept his defeat. Doesn't buy in to my whole mild-'n'-modest shtick, which is a shame, really, as I so seldom get it out.

He says, 'Fiona, you are in many ways an exceptional officer. I'm happy to state in front of these—' he waves his hand at

Matthews and Peters and, I think, wants to say 'gentlemen', except that Hermione Peters's presence forces him to retreat to an awkward-sounding, 'good people.'

'I'm happy to state that you have always shown yourself intelligent, committed, hard-working, resourceful and courageous. But you are also erratic. You are not governable. You do not reliably obey explicit commands and I'm not sure you and I will be able to continue working together.'

There's a moment of shocked silence.

Hermione Peters actually does a kind of double-take. Like, she needs to check that she is indeed watching Bleddyn Jones reprimand a junior officer who gave herself as a hostage to a trio of dangerous gunmen and who also, almost, thwarted their extravagantly planned get-away.

She even starts to say, 'Bleddyn, what Fiona did was—'

But he interrupts. There's something slightly shaky in his intensity, like this is the final eruption of a lava flow that has been boiling underground for too many weeks.

He says, 'Fiona, I think you went over to the museum yesterday *wanting* to engineer an opportunity to get in there. I think you took advantage of the situation to make it happen.'

And this time, the shock is palpable.

The various armours I wore at the start of all this – young woman in pretty dress, siege survivor, person generally short of sleep and TLC – are somehow incompatible with the shell he just lobbed.

And, I realise, he's gone too far. My armour is stronger than his shell.

I could swat him down. Possibly even make his acting headery of Major Crimes impossible to sustain.

But what I find myself saying is, 'Yes, sir. You're entirely correct. I thought we needed a set of police eyes down there. I thought that was the easiest way to make it happen.'

Jones, triumphant, says: 'And did you, in any way – in any

way at *all* – discuss that with me first?'

'No.'

'And you had in mind, did you, that you have already received from me a written warning that drew explicit attention to your erratic behaviour?'

I say, 'No,' then clarify. 'I mean, yes, I know you gave me that warning, but no, I wasn't particularly thinking about it when I decided to go down into that basement.' I shrug. Pretty off-white ferns rise and fall on my shoulders. 'I just thought it was important to go, that's all.'

Matthews exchanges glances with Peters, who has her eyes wide with surprise.

Matthews, who, back when he was a mere DCI, had some past experience of me, gazes at me thoughtfully. Then says, 'OK, Fiona. This is a serious issue. It'll need discussion. But not now. You've had a tough night. So go home. Get some sleep. Take tomorrow off. And, both of you, we'll pick this up on Tuesday.'

Nods of assent from me and Jones. Two combatants circling towards their final showdown.

I go. As the door softly closes, I hear the swift buzz of adult conversation rise behind it.

But phooey to all that. Today is my day off, is it not?

HEROIC SIEGE SURVIVOR CELEBRATES
FREEDOM WITH BLUE DRESS
EYEWITNESSES REPORT 'OFF-WHITE FERNS
AND FORGET-ME-NOT BLUE'
Dress Said to Remain Unflaked Despite Croissant Encounter

Go to the lifts. Am about to hit the button that says, 'Ground floor. Exit. Home. Bath', when I think, *the hell with it*.

Codicology and Palaeography.

I move my finger down an inch and hit the button for the basement.

34

The basement, that loathsome place.

No gunmen in this one, but something almost worse: the exhibit rooms, where evidence collected from crime scenes is securely retained. I used to work down here once and hated it, but I do still keep on good terms with Laura Moffatt, who runs the place. Thanks to that friendship, and a little judicious thieving, I know the access codes.

I locate the room I'm after. Enter it. Check the log. Locate the evidence bag that contains the Llanymawddwy vellum.

Take it.

There's a forensic light kit knocking around as well. Grey plastic carry case. ALS lamp. Full set of filters. CSIs aren't allowed to leave equipment in a vehicle overnight, so they often use the exhibits rooms as secure dumping grounds instead.

More fool them.

I take the box.

Leave.

Walk up to Katie's house. One of her housemates lets me in – they know me fairly well by now – and I go on up.

Katie's there, lying on her bed, reading. She's wearing many-pocketed light khaki trousers and a none-too-new singlet in a very pale green. Her version of hot-weather wear.

She rolls to greet me. Says, 'So. They found a Plan C.'

'Yes.'

'Raid the National Museum of Wales.'

'Yes.'

'Probably easier than Buckingham Palace, when you think about it.'

'Much easier, yes.'

'And they *did* find gold, did they? All the TV could talk about was the paintings.'

'The paintings were minor. Worth a few hundred grand, if that.'

'And the gold?'

'The tunnel went out through the numismatics store. And yes, they helped themselves.'

'Bugger it. *Sod* it. They're one step ahead of us.'

'Not exactly.'

I open my bag. Dig around amongst the travel-deodorant and the tissues and the teabags and keys and the phone. Retrieve a dozen ancient coins, four of them gold.

'Plan D,' I say. 'Like Plan C, except without the guns.'

'You took these?'

'Yes.'

'Stole them?'

'Yes.'

Katie clambers off the bed. Goes over to her desk. Puts the coins on a sheet of white paper. Brings the desk lamp up close. Inspects them under a magnifying glass. Presses the tip of a pair of compasses into the metal.

'This looks like the real deal,' she mutters, but continues to check each coin one by one. Both sides. The unmilled edge.

When she's done, she pushes back. Stares.

She's happy about the gold, but there's a sadness there too.

I ask her about it, and she says, 'Well, the fucking Ph.D. is finally fucking fucked.' She tells me that she hasn't been able to find a senior archaeologist to lead the Dinas Powys dig. The dig has been cancelled. And she's ditched her Ph.D. too. Given up. Dropped out.

'So: the number one item on my do-it-before-you-die bucket list is a fail.'

I ask her if she actually keeps a list. If she actually has one written down.

The answer to that is yes. She shows it to me.

'Get my Ph.D.' is the first item on the list. Ringed and underlined. Other wishes include 'Live independently until I really, really can't.' 'Don't cut my hair off.' 'Have amazing sex with someone I won't hate afterwards.' A few other things, mostly boring ones, like 'Go to Venice' or 'Read Tolstoy.'

The book on the bed is *War and Peace.*

I read the list. Ask if Katie wants tea.

She says no, coffee. I say I'm crap at making coffee. She tells me exactly how to make it and I repeat, like an imbecile, what she just said and she stares at me, as though I'm an imbecile, and says, 'Yes. Like that. Coffee.'

So I go, imbecilicly, downstairs. Make coffee the way she says. The whole cafetière and ground coffee thing. Peppermint tea for me.

I don't freak out. Don't dissociate. Am neither more nor less nuts than my general average.

Go back with the drinks.

Say, 'Do a different Ph.D.'

'What?'

'Well, the Dinas Powys one is screwed, I can see that. But I don't know if your bucket list thing has to mean that particular Ph.D. thesis or if it could be some other one.'

'What? Like retrain as a nuclear physicist?'

'Well, no, you're an archaeologist, obviously. But what about something on the illegal antiquities trade?' I point down at the glitter of coins. 'That's got to be a hot topic.'

Katie stares at me.

'Like a case study? You mean, use all this? Everything we've been doing?'

'Yes. A case study. Exactly.'

She looks tigerishly at me for a moment, thinking hard. Looking for an objection and finding none. Then she punches me quite hard, but also nicely, on my upper arm.

'That is a fucking good idea, Fi.'

Her breath comes out jerky for a moment, before she gets it back under control.

I say, 'I can be your criminal investigations consultant. I've never been a consultant before.'

That remark recalls herself to herself.

She says sharply – correctively – 'You can be my slave, slave.' Then adds, agreeably. 'But you can have an honoured place in my household.'

I bow at her graciousness.

Eye her Anglo–Saxon neck for the coming chop.

We talk about coins and gold and early Celtic techniques for spinning gold into wire.

Our jeweller is an amateur archaeologist in Ipswich, Marianne Hadleigh. She's close friends with our blacksmith, Peter Burnham, and Katie swears they are both totally trustworthy.

I've met them both and I agree.

I do wonder, out loud, if I should have taken more gold.

Katie says, no, I took enough.

Her attention starts to turn to the things I brought with me. My forensic light kit. The vellum.

'Slave?'

I tell her about the maps and manuscripts poster. The design that overlaid one image with another. Handwriting lying over a map.

'A palimpsest. What if our vellum is a palimpsest?'

Katie stares at me, open-mouthed.

There really is something of the warrior queen about her. Her cargo pants. Her almost military singlet. She's skinny, yes, and getting skinnier, but if you subtract the disease from the human, you're left with someone intensely physical. Like those flyweight or bantamweight women boxers. Bare-armed, clean-muscled, small-breasted. And always, always those frank, unfrightened eyes.

She reaches for the evidence bag with her right hand. Her grip fails, so she tries again, more carefully. She still doesn't have a proper grip, but swivels her hand so that the bag is rolled round her hand as much as it is held by it.

I could help, but don't.

She opens the bag. Spreads the vellum.

Desk lamp. Magnifying glass.

She peers at the damn thing as close as she can. Up close, at an angle, through the glass and not. We did all that stuff before. Saw nothing then. See nothing now.

She pushes back.

'Look, I can't see anything, but there *is* an oddity here.'

I look a question and she explains.

'OK, so vellum is animal-skin. Stretched out, scraped, cleaned. It's a good writing material, but expensive. From about the twelfth century, paper mills became more common. They could mass-produce their product and you didn't need to kill a sheep or a calf. The price of paper fell and supply boomed.

'But that wasn't the only technological development. In the remoter parts of Europe, the standard ink was, for centuries, pretty simple. You took soot from a lamp, whisked it up with some animal glue – boiled horse, basically – then mixed the two together. The glue kept the soot stuck to your vellum and, with luck, your writing would remain clear for generations.

'Those were the plus points, but there were negatives too. The glues involved just weren't that good and they *especially* weren't much good in damp or humid climates. If the vellum was damp, the soot could just fall off.'

She gazes at me, checking I'm following her reasoning.

I think I am.

I say, 'And Llanymawddwy. I mean, lovely place and all, but . . .'

She says, 'But a Welsh church? In the hills? That's about as damp as you can get without actually being in a river. Those old-fashioned inks would have had a terrible time. So, from about the twelfth century onwards, the carbon blacks came to be replaced by inks made with iron gall. Those new inks kept forever, damp Welsh churches or no.'

She gestures at our bit of vellum. Its iron gall writing still glows bright and clear a full eight hundred years later.

'So,' I say, slowly following her logic, 'that's the oddity, right there. We've got *old* technology vellum, but a *new* technology ink.'

Katie nods. 'Yes. You can't be too linear about these things, but on the whole I'd expect to see vellum marked with carbon blacks, paper marked with iron galls. This particular document has those things the wrong way round.'

I say, 'So let's say I'm a vicar at Llanymawddwy. I need to write something, but I'm in a remote and relatively poor part of the country. So yes, I could go out and buy some paper.'

'But that's expensive . . .'

'Or kill myself a sheep and turn it into vellum.'

'Lots of hassle and also expensive.'

'Or I could just take an old document and clean it.'

'Exactly,' says Katie. 'Exactly, exactly, exactly.'

Palimpsest.

A manuscript page from which the text has been washed or scraped off to permit re-use. One text overlaying another. A palimpsest.

Codicologists like that sort of thing. Palaeographers too.

That Maps and Manuscripts poster plus those words – *codicology* and *palaeography* – gave me the nudge I needed to figure this thing out.

Katie stares at my grey plastic carry case.

'What's that?'

'It's an alternative light source lamp. Our CSI guys use them to find organic remains. Semen. Saliva. Sweat. Urine. That kind of thing. Anything which goes fluorescent under strong blue or UV light.'

Katie stares. 'Organic remains?'

'Yes.'

'Like boiled horse? Those sort of remains?'

I shrug. Don't know. But it's got to be worth a try.

We darken the room. Pull curtains across the windows. Kill the light. Throw a pillow at the door, so no light filters in from below. You don't have to make a place totally dark, but it does help.

I get the flashlight. The filters. Hand some safety goggles to Katie.

I try first with visible blue light, seen through an orange filter.

I think we get flickers, but it's hard to tell. The vellum itself is organic, so we need to find a light source that successfully differentiates between sheepskin and animal glue.

I fool around a bit. I know the basics, but I'm no expert.

Say, 'We'll try UV.'

I switch things around.

Cock it up. Get it right.

Point the torch beam.

Point the beam and – *shazam*!

The vellum damn near bursts with light. A storm of phosphorescence. Because the lamplight is actually invisible to the human eye, that phosphorescence is the only bright thing in this darkened room. It looks almost glaring. Almost too bright.

And that brightness isn't random. It's patterned. *And the pattern does not correspond to the ordinary visible text.*

We have found a new layer of writing lying invisible beneath the first.

A palimpsest. We have a palimpsest.

And the thing that was missing is missing no more.

35

It's not even hard.

We go back to the same lab that originally dated the vellum for us. Say we think there's some older text buried under the newer one.

And there is. Not one text even, but two. A single Welsh sheep doing threefold service over the centuries.

The scientist who comes out of his office to report is Italian. Young. A Ph.D. researcher recently scooped up from the University of Padua.

He's nice-looking. Biceppy and fit, but in a way that suggests casualness, rather than hours working in an over-mirrored gym. He wears a dark-blue shirt, designer glasses and has skin the colour of creamy coffee.

He says, 'You are police? You need these images fast?'

I say, 'It's a murder enquiry and we need them yesterday.'

'Yesterday, I'm not so sure. And if you want good quality result, I need a few days. It's not one text, only. It is three.' He layers his hands like a sandwich. 'But for quick version – "quick and dirty", yes? – I can do right now. Maybe come back at four, five o'clock?'

Katie and I go in to town. Sit in a café, then go for a walk by a murky Oxford river. Water under willows. A scurry of moorhens.

At four o'clock, we go back to the lab, which lives in a rattly Edwardian building on Banbury Road. Katie goes for a pee.

Comes back wearing lip gloss. A dab of colour on her cheeks.

She looks at me looking at her and says, 'Well?'

Well nothing, but I laugh anyway. That bucket list. *Have amazing sex with someone I won't hate afterwards.* And why not, Katie, and why not?

'He's probably got a girlfriend.' Katie says.

I tell her he has a fat and violently tempered Italian wife, to whom he is unreasonably devoted.

'Not devoted enough to wear a wedding ring,' says Katie.

'Well, he's probably Catholic. No sex before marriage.'

'So he'll be unbelievably horny. He won't be able to stop himself.'

We sit in a little waiting area and look at stupid magazines.

Outside the window, an Oxfordy rain falls on Victorian slate and chimney pots. I think of Oakeshott lying face down in that sullen canal. Floating there in that gently rocking mess of sticks and drink bottles and broken polystyrene.

I suddenly realise: Gaynor Charteris. I don't know what's happened to Gaynor Charteris.

Has she been cremated? Buried? I don't know.

I wish I had her here now. Her head only, in that leaking plastic shopping bag. Position it somewhere that she could see her palimpsest. The careful lab work. The text emerging from the past.

What thoughts occupy Katie, I don't know, but I just clasp Charteris's stony presence to me. Feel its chill comfort. Its impatient approval of our work.

At five, the Italian guy – Matteo – brings the best images he's been able to extract. The hard thing wasn't finding the buried texts, but separating the two.

He promises more work and better texts, but rolls his eyes when I ask for timing.

'I work hard, but . . .'

He waves his hand aerially.

Katie laughs and holds his eyes longer than she needs to.

I keep saying everything's urgent and Katie says we need Matteo's help, so he agrees to stay late.

We work till seven, then go out to a restaurant with an urban coolness so intense, it's almost desperate. Its menu includes a wagyu burger, whatever that is. Lots of things that involve broad bean salsas and wilted chard and pomegranate molasses.

The waiter wears an apron in brown suede and I ask him if the pomegranate molasses is organic. He goes back to the kitchen to find out. When he returns and says, 'No, sorry, it isn't,' I look faintly surprised and what-kind-of-place-*is*-this regretful and order the fish pie that I was always going to have anyway.

Once, as she grips the menu, Katie's hand fails and the menu falls. Matteo looks startled and Katie says brusquely, 'It's a stupid nerve thing.' She shrugs, dismissing it.

Matteo lets it go.

We turn to the images we brought from the lab.

I'm of no help here, but watch the two experts as they slowly start to piece together that lowest script, the oldest of our vellum's three layers.

They work letter by letter.

G. W. Y. R.

Space.

Then something which looks like an *A* and another space.

Then *A. E. T. H.*

The food arrives. Food and a bottle of Italian red wine. But Matteo's not happy.

He says, 'This can't be right. That's not Latin. It's not English.' He mutters about redoing the imaging.

'Welsh,' I tell him. 'It's Welsh.'

Bit by bit, our text emerges.

Gwyr a aeth gatraeth veduaeth uedwn.
fyryf frwythlawn oed cam nas kymhwyllwn.

The language is Welsh, certainly, but not as it's spoken now. This is Old Welsh. Ancient. A language both familiar and deeply strange. It's as though I'm reading through the greenish glass of an old bottle-end. It's not just the words themselves that are shifted and distorted, it's the thought too. The world that gave rise to the text. A world of warfare and bloodshed, four-square and direct. Without euphemism, evasion or compromise.

I attempt a translation into modern English.

'*Men went to* – I'm not sure. A place name. Catraeth, I suppose. I'm not sure what that would be in English. *Men went to Catraeth, nourished with wine*? Or *mead*, maybe? I'm going to go with mead. Then *sturdy and strong, it would be wrong not to praise them.*'

As I speak, Katie shows a sudden frown of concentration. Recognition even.

She says, 'That place. Catraeth. It's Catterick. In Yorkshire.'

'Catterick?'

I'm not sure what I was expecting, exactly, but I don't think Catterick fits into anything. I'm taken aback and probably show it.

Katie says, 'This poem here. It's the *Y Gododdin*.'

'No it isn't. It's either *The Gododdin* or *Y Gododdin*. It can't be *The The Gododdin*.'

Katie gives me her slave look.

I give her my fuck-off-out-of-my-country-and-leave-my-cattle-just-where-you-found-them look.

When we're done glaring, Katie explains. 'OK. This manuscript. If the rest of it matches up, what we've got here is a copy of *Y Gododdin*, a well-known praise poem written in early Welsh. The poem tells the story of a British–Celtic assault on an Anglo–Saxon stronghold in Catterick. The attack failed and the poem is one of praise and lament for the fallen warriors. The battle took place in about 570 AD, or about seventy years after any battle at Mount Badon. As far as we know, the events of the poem are basically true.'

I'm puzzled by this. Puzzled enough that I, once again, wonder if my reading of this case has gone wrong somewhere. But Katie is still talking. Still explaining.

'OK, so the most interesting thing about the poem is its date. Some scholars put the date of composition right close to the battle itself, so some time in the late sixth century.'

I say, 'So, OK, so we've got a really old poem. What I don't get is . . .'

Katie interrupts, so quietly that both Matteo and I have to lean in to hear her.

'This poem is famous, because of a few lines near the end.'

So famous, in fact, the poem has its own page on Wikipedia.

Katie brings up the page on her phone and says, 'OK, so here the poet is talking about a warrior called – bloody hell, you guys have stupid names – Gwawrddur. Is that right? Anyway, the relevant bit goes like this.'

She recites:

He fed black ravens on the rampart of a fortress
Though he was no Arthur
Among the powerful ones in battle
In the front rank, Gwawrddur was a palisade.

I stare.

Matteo stares.

Quite by chance, the restaurant enters one of those momentary silences where everyone happens to reach a conversational pause at the exact same time. But that's not what it feels like. It doesn't feel like a chance thing. It feels like that name, the magic of that name, has reached through time, through the centuries, and left a little thumbprint of silence. A little pool through which we feel the pull of those years, those battles.

I say, 'So this poem is talking about real events?'

Katie: 'Yes.'

'And this guy, Gwawrddur, he's a real person?'

'As far as we know, yes.'

'And the poem is ancient. Perhaps even written within living memory of Arthur?'

'Yes.'

'And the poem says, it says right here, "OK, this guy Gwawrddur, he was a really awesome warrior. He wasn't as good as Arthur, but he was still pretty damn awesome."'

'That's what the poem says, yes. And, if you're a George Bowen-type, this poem is about the strongest proof we have that Arthur was a real guy. This poem isn't about myth-making. There's no legend here, just history. And a poet, talking to his audience, seemingly certain that they'll all know who Arthur is.'

And we found a copy of that poem in a church sacred to Arthur's nephew and built just a few miles from the scene of Arthur's last battle.

I have that sense, click click click, of tumblers falling into place. Things finally starting to line up properly for the very first time.

I say, 'Sorry. The other text, we need to look at that.'

The other text. The middle layer of this palimpsest.

And we do. But I can't read that strange medieval script. Katie and Matteo can do the business there. So I leave the two of them to do their stuff. Leave them to their food, their drink, their flirting.

Go to my car. Get a joint. Smoke.

Walk randomly through this mild Oxford night.

Street lamps and cars. Shop-fronts and pedestrians.

I sit on the crumbly brick of an old Edwardian wall and blow ganja smoke at these neon-lit stars. I miss Charteris again. Wish I knew if she'd been buried. I normally hear about funerals. I'd have certainly gone to hers.

When I go back to the restaurant, Katie and Matteo aren't bending over Matteo's print-outs. They're gazing into each other's eyes and laughing.

Katie's bucket list. Looks to me like she's only an hour or two from notching up another item ticked.

I say hi and they move apart. Share their good news.

That middle text was simple. Clear and easy to decipher.

'We think this is late eleventh century,' says Katie. 'Written not long after the Norman Conquest. And it looks like a document granting permission for some Welsh warriors to make a visit to a place called Swine Hill. It's not clear why the warriors wanted to make this trip, but it appears they were willing to pay some real money for the privilege, as the document makes reference to a payment having been made.'

I say, 'Swine Hill?'

Katie: 'Well, the document refers to the place as Suinedune. That's how it appears in the Domesday Book. It's grown a bit since then, mind you. It's the city we call Swindon.'

Suinedune.

Swine Hill.

Swindon.

Just outside Swindon, there's a prominent chalk hill and on that hill, a fort. Liddington Castle, long claimed to be a possible site for Mount Badon, and one of those sites that Bowen and Katie identified as a leading contender.

I say – hear myself saying – 'We've done well. Very well.' Have one of those out-of-body moments, as I say thank you, say good night, and drive home to Cardiff.

Mount Badon. The mother of all ancient battles. And the place where this case will reach its climax.

36

Tuesday.

Bleddyn Jones and Gethin Matthews.

Matthews is of the opinion that you can't really yell at someone who voluntarily took the place of a sick hostage.

Jones is still of the opinion that he'd rather boil and eat his own leg than work with me any longer.

I listen to them go at it, then say, 'Look.'

Pause.

Am I really going to do this? Am I really going to say this? I think I am.

So I go ahead and say it.

'Look, I do know I'm a pest. Dennis Jackson used to tell me so on a weekly basis and he was right, I know he was. But recently – I don't know, I suppose it's all got a bit much. It all gets to me sometimes. Maybe I just need a few weeks off? Do something relaxing. Get myself into the right headspace again. Come back to work fresher. More disciplined.'

Jones receives this speech with startlement to begin with, then with strong and increasingly emphatic support. His nods become massive headswaying things, beech trees in the first gusts of a thunderstorm.

He believes, I think, that this is my breakthrough moment. The moment when, thanks to his own firmness and wisdom, I finally see myself for who I am. See myself and seek change.

Gethin Matthews knows me a little better than that, and he looks suspicious.

'This is real, Fiona, is it?'

'Yes, sir.'

Humble head. Humble voice.

'And how many weeks are we talking exactly?'

I stare at him. How the heck would I know?'

'I don't know. Just . . . a few weeks.'

Matthews looks at Jones, seeking his view.

Jones says, 'I think it would be a great idea. Fiona's really taking responsibility here.'

Matthews stares at me, then shrugs. 'Fine.'

Jones offers some patronising words of advice that I don't really hear. Just put in the syllable recycling bin.

Matthews tells me about some bureaucratic hoops that will need to be hopped through. I promise to hop through them all.

Then, Matthews: 'So, what will you do with your break? Any plans?'

'I don't know. But I've got quite into archaeology. Maybe find a dig to get involved with.'

We sit for a minute or two ticking off the most obvious conversational topics – amazing what they find, fresh air good for you, that kind of thing. And, once we've completed our whistle-stop tour through the realm of cliché, I walk – slightly dazed – to my desk.

Indefinite leave.

Leave that, however it's dressed up, follows a formal written warning and then a further, emphatic challenge from my commanding officer. Truth is, I've never been closer to losing my career in policing. Never closer to that shivery brink.

I do check with everyone I know – Watkins, Matthews, Bev, Rogers, everyone – that Jackson is coming back and yes, they say, as far as they know, he most likely is. But no one has a date. And everyone puts in those worrying little qualifiers. *Most likely. Should think so. Can't see him staying away from all this (little chuckle, change of subject).*

I have already checked, of course, that an archaeological dig has been scheduled for Liddington Hill. And yes – O surprise almighty – a dig has in fact just got underway. These things generally rely heavily on skilled volunteers, so I get Katie to recommend me and they're happy to accept my help.

I drift round the office. Say my see-you-soons.

And wander out into a future unknown.

37

Liddington Castle.

A high, blowy, chalky knoll. Grass-covered and windy.

And it's strange, in a way. The M4 motorway churns below. Swindon's busy industrial heart – all vast warehouses and sleek offices – a long stone's throw beyond. But you don't have to be up here long, within these ramparts, these ditches, before the modern world just blows away from you. Vanishes into the long grass, the hiss of chalk.

And as this new world goes, old ones rise to take its place.

The world of those Iron Age Celts, my ancestors.

The world of the Romans. Those southern invaders with their tunics, their wines, their strange, ungainly tongue.

And then the world that came after. Bloodshed at every border. Picts to the north. Those muscled blond mercenaries to the east.

Were these ditches redug? These ramparts refortified? What councils were held in low voices, behind these earthen walls, around these huddled fires? And was it here – on this high land, upon this windy hill – that the greatest battle of ancient days was fought? The battle that, for one golden generation, seemed to drive those eastern invaders back?

I don't know. No one does. But this dig might yet find out.

Our team consists of three or four proper professionals. A pair of lecturers – one from Reading, one from Southampton. Two graduate students using this dig as part of their Ph.D.

research, the way that Katie had wanted to in Dinas Powys.

The rest of us – a dozen at most, just three or four when the wind is sharpest and the rains keenest – are volunteers. Students or committed local amateurs. One intense girl who tells me (too often and too earnestly) that this is a mindfulness thing for her, you know? That London is, like, really intense? She tells me, if I let her, about ley lines and sacred fountains and the deep vibrations of Mother Earth.

She wears a lump of black tourmaline on a leather cord around her neck and wants me to do the same.

We dig.

Sometimes, in fact, that does mean pushing a spade into the ground and just humping it out, the way a builder would.

But it's not mostly that. Once we've cut a trench or pit, once we've cut through a millennium and a half of history to expose a Dark Age soil, we go slow. Our tools are little trowels. Scrapers. Stubby brushes and buckets of water.

I don't really understand why one trench is planted in one place and one in another. There's a logic to these things, I suppose, but what that is, I don't know. Just do as I'm told.

Work hard. Get muddy.

And, as the sun slopes down for its evening rest, I walk down the hill with the others, enjoying the ache that speaks of a day gone well.

After work, at first, I would shoot back to Cardiff, a commute that takes not much more than an hour. But, this dig has its own rules, its own little social system. So, increasingly, I don't just zoom off to my warm bath and comfortable bed. I head to the pub with the others. Or go to barbecues hosted by one of the locals. Or sit in a campsite with some of the London students and gaze into their bonfire and smoke cannabis of a strength and potency my pinkish Celtic lungs are quite unused to.

We talk of a hundred things, of course.

Food. The best clothes to wear. Our colleagues.

And the dig. We talk about the dig.

The stated goals of this project have to do with all those good things that Katie and Gaynor Charteris were looking at in Dinas Powys. Evidence of trade. Of lifestyle. Of diet. Of ironworking.

Good, sober, dutiful research.

But it's not those themes that we talk about as we gaze into the flames of our fire. Not what we talk about as we blow ganja smoke up into the sky above. We talk – daily, earnestly, obsessively – about Arthur. It's well known that Liddington Castle is a possible candidate for Mount Badon. No evidence for the theory has ever been found, but then again the site has never been properly excavated. That sounds strange, yet it's true nevertheless. Britain just has so many ancient sites that only a fraction of them have been fully explored, Liddington Castle included.

That said, it's known that in the centre of the castle there is a large pit one and a half metres across and at least two and a half metres deep. But the archaeologists who found that pit never explored it fully. On the contrary: a preliminary soil bore conducted last year, showed that the thing descends at least eighteen metres. At Wapley Hill in Herefordshire a similar structure – a 'ritual shaft' – goes fully thirty-three metres down.

What treasures might our own shaft hold? What treasures might we come across in one of our criss-crossing trenches?

No one knows. That's the beauty of the quest.

Our two lecturers – Simon Tifford from Reading University and Ann Wisbech, an acid-tempered Londoner – take care of strategy. We just do as they tell us. Dig carefully. Live our muddily contented life under this sun, these stars.

I get to know the area too. Not just the few acres occupied

by the actual hill fort, but the fields and farms and footpaths around.

On one of my excursions, I see a little construction site, fenced off and hung about with 'considerate contractor' notices. The site lies about four hundred metres from the Castle.

No one's present. A small digger – sporting a phone number and address belonging to a plant hire company in Cwmbran, Gwent – sits idle.

I am very happy to see it. So happy, indeed, I have to sit down on the grass and smoke a joint, right then and there. I take a photo.

And as I sit, a man comes past, walking his dogs.

I say hello.

He says hello.

Because I'm polite, I say hello to his dogs too and they say hello back in doggese, licking my hand and smelling my ankles.

I ask the man if the construction site has been here long. What it's for.

He doesn't know. 'Some drainage thing,' he thinks. They were here about a month, but are mostly packed up now.

I tell him thanks.

Lie flat out on the earth, feeling a pale sun push at my eyelids.

One evening, I finish work early and zoom back to Cardiff. I promised Ed and Jill that I'd have them round to mine for supper, and I'm making good on my promise. I've invited Katie too, because I think everyone will get on with everyone and because somehow four is a less weird number than three.

Katie arrives, bringing news.

Our Caledfwlch is finished. She has pictures. Shows me them all.

And Caledfwlch looks awesome. Genuinely stunning.

'We have to bash it about,' says Katie. 'Rust it. Age it. All of that. But doesn't it look great?'

It does, and I say so, and I mean it.

Then I take her phone and delete the pictures. 'Better safe than sorry,' I tell her.

Then Ed and Jill arrive.

I do the introductions. Unleash the meal. Beef stew, which is hardly summery, but which is so easy to do that even I can't mess it up. Proper wine. Eight pound a bottle stuff, which is pricey enough that I figure it has to be non-crap. A supermarket pudding, but from their premium range. Cheese served with grapes and celery because I couldn't remember which one you were meant to serve with cheese, so played safe and offered both.

And I don't cock anything up and Ed says, 'You cooked this, Fi?' and I fess up about the supermarket pudding but bask happily in the deserved glory of my stew.

And everyone does indeed get on. And we have a nice time. A genuinely nice social thing that I arranged and that happened under my roof and in my kitchen. I feel stupidly proud.

And at one point, after the cheese but before the coffee, Ed engineers a moment of privacy. He says, 'Jill and I are going out to Sicily this August. A fortnight's break.'

And I say, 'That's nice,' and try to remember what you're meant to say about other people's holidays.

And he says, 'I think that's when I'm going to do it. I mean, that kind of thing is corny, but you're allowed to be corny sometimes, I reckon.'

And I think: *Do what? I have no idea. I don't understand why humans can't speak more directly.*

And then I think: *Oh. He means get engaged. Pop the question. Do that thing with rings.*

And I say, 'Great,' and 'Oh, wow,' and 'I'm so happy for

272

you.' And I think I mean each one of those noble sentiments, but a part of me feels huge and hollow and cavernous and empty, and my head feels high and light and a very long distance from the ground. There is a thin rushing sound, like air leaking from a punctured tyre.

What does that mean? I don't know. I have no idea. It probably means nothing at all except that I am not a very grounded human being and I lose my bearings with remarkable ease.

At eleven-thirty, everyone filters out into the night.

I try to think about the Ed thing, but can't really. Just can't seize hold of it. Instead I go to my iPad and spend an hour or so looking at those crime scene pictures of Gaynor Charteris.

Her corpse.

Her head.

That ragged stump of neck.

I tell her that finally, finally, the real crime is coming. The one we've been waiting for. The one for which she, poor dear, was only ever a messenger.

She tells me that she understands. She understands everything.

I have my gun by my bed all night, fully loaded and safety on. But for once it brings me no comfort. Even holding its chill metal against my forehead, I can feel no rest.

I can't cry. Have only cried once in my adult life. But there is something jammed and choking in my throat. My eyes. A sort of dry heave of emotion that seeks to release something, but can't.

So I half-sit, half-lie through these night-time hours. Jammed with a feeling I can't describe. Holding a gun that brings no comfort. Lying beneath covers that bring no sleep.

38

My days: digging. My nights, increasingly, at the campsite near Liddington.

This life enfolds me. Binds me to its rhythms. I have so little anchorage of my own, that I'm quick to lose myself to other seas.

Even so, I do, of course, keep in touch with Operation Blade. Log in to the system most days. Call Jones.

The news: nothing much.

Alden Gheerbrant has been pulled in for another round of fruitless questioning.

The team chasing the museum robbery has nothing helpful. Plenty of DNA and fingerprints, yes, but nothing that shows up on the system. The e-fits have been widely distributed, but no useful identifications have come in.

The one titbit of real interest to me is that it looks as though the tunnel into the museum was professionally built. Literally, I mean. Not just by blokes with spades, but trained professionals who knew exactly where and how to support the tunnel.

I send Jones a photo of that Cwmbran digger. Tell him where I found it.

He emails me back, thanking me, and wishing me well 'for your recovery'.

My *recovery*.

Tosspot.

Meantime, Matteo and Katie have finished their work on our palimpsest.

I get the two of them to write up their findings. Nudge them into co-authoring a blog, which goes on the laboratory's regular website. Then, as Gwenhwyfar, I hop around a few Arthurian chat sites, linking excitedly to the Katie/Matteo blog. I don't comment much. Just say things like, 'Look at this. It's massive!' Then vanish.

The internet does the rest. The response on the message boards is little short of feverish.

Partly, there's a genuine historical interest in the vellum. Although the *Gododdin* poem was well known, that Llanymawddwy manuscript looks like being the earliest known version of the text. *And* the poem was found in a church founded, it's said, by Arthur's own nephew. Those two things alone guaranteed some kind of internet sensation, albeit that the sensation is limited, mostly, to Arthur nuts.

But, but, but.

That later text – the middle layer of the palimpsest.

That text tells us: *Warriors from a place associated with Arthur paid good money to travel to a place long associated with his most famous battle.*

It's a huge fact. Huge enough that it gets a glancing mention in one or two of the national newspapers. One blogger reproduces photos of that bear-and-crown seal box from Dinas Powys above a caption that reads, 'Is this King Arthur's seal box?'

The chain of clues that I've pursued so long is flashing bright red now.

The seal box. A lump of carved stone that seems to connect Dinas Powys to Arthur's final battlefield at Camlan. An old poem, mentioning Arthur, discovered in the church founded by Arthur's own nephew. All that plus a document that seems, surely, to suggest that something of vast worth is to be found somewhere in the immediate neighbourhood of Swindon.

What, after all, *could* those things mean?

We don't know. No one does. But the interest among enthusiasts is intense.

If our little dig was averaging six or eight volunteers before, we're never less than fifteen strong now, and our project leaders turn away five or even ten helpers for every one they accept.

We get used to spectators too. Never very many, but sometimes five or six at a time, wielding binoculars and cameras and thermoses of tea.

Our trenches do in fact find some arrowheads. Some crumbled leather. Broken buckles. Coins. Not enough to say that yes, a battle did take place here, but not so few that you could say no, it didn't. In those days, bits of iron had real value, so battlefields were carefully picked over for their leavings.

We haven't yet completed our criss-crossing trenches, but work has already started on that central pit, the ritual shaft.

The pit is taken quickly down to two and a half metres. Then four. Then eight.

It's exciting work, but also frustrating. The limited working space means we can only have two people down there at any one time. They work by hand – spade by spade – and our only mechanical support is a powered hoist that lifts buckets of waste out of the hole. As we go further down, we buttress the shaft's walls with sheets of ply nailed into a rough octagonal cross-section.

When we've excavated the shaft down to ten metres, we have a little celebration. Drinking prosecco out of white plastic cups.

Because of the increased traffic to the site, a local farmer turns a corner of one of his fields into a little car park. Charges one pound a day for parking.

I fiddle around on Amazon and buy a couple of motion-triggered security cameras. Portable things that work from batteries. I stick them in the hedge near the cars.

The ritual shaft gets down to fourteen metres.

The spoil we're taking out is increasingly rich in the clutter of ancient life and, especially, ancient warfare. Plenty of arrowheads now. An axe. A knife that, to eyes more expert than mine, looks fifth or sixth century.

It looks Arthurian.

The people who follow this stuff all share it on social media, which means that news of our finds rapidly circulates.

At night and all through the weekend, the ritual shaft is closed off with anti-climb wire fencing. That's mostly a basic safety measure: we don't want kids tumbling into our hole. But it's more than that. The site is of sufficient interest that it's potentially at risk from vandals. Looters, even. Tifford and Wisbech find the numbers for some local security firms. Make calls.

The shaft deepens.

Sixteen metres.

Most nights now, I sleep in the campsite with my fellow volunteers. I have my own sleeping bag. A tent. A camping stove and metal cooking pots. A Tupperware box with my own supply of weed and Rizla papers.

We dig.

We eat.

We sleep.

We work.

39

Midsummer day. The summer solstice.

At five in the morning, a golden sunlight gilds the nylon outers of our tents. My own berth – aqua blue with flashes of girly pink – goes from chilly to boiling in what seems like a matter of minutes.

I get up. Shower in the little shower block. There's a solar-heating thing on the roof which is meant to guarantee hot water, but definitely, definitely doesn't.

I endure the experience as long as I can, then dry off.

Make tea.

Drink, sitting on a tree stump and looking into the embers of last night's fire. For all that my tent feels like an oven the air temperature is still frigid and I sit with a thick fleece over my T-shirt.

Other people start to emerge, spiky-haired and blinking.

One of the guys, Adam, hates the cold and wriggles out in his sleeping bag, hi-tech and shiny blue. A giant maggot, in search of porridge.

The air warms.

We talk and eat and tamp ourselves into shape for the coming day.

At eight or so, we trudge up the hill.

Start work.

Slowly to begin with, then faster as we get in the swing of it.

And at nine-forty – so soon! – there's shouting from the fencing around our ritual shaft. Those of us who are employed on the more mundane trenching work drop our tools and run over.

A bone. Someone is holding a human bone. A tibia, or something like it. The soil is coming up black and sooted.

Burned.

Then more bones. Incomplete some of them, but not sheep, not cow, not goat. One of the bones is notched, as though injured in battle.

Also: arrowheads, spear-tips, buckles.

The gory clutter of ancient war.

Tifford and Wisbech are pretty much pissing themselves with excitement. You spend your whole career in archaeology, putting in the hours, writing your papers on *Patterns of Cultivation in Iron Age Kent* or whatever the hell you write about. But you came into this game for its Indiana Jones moments: the opening of King Tutankhamun's tomb, unearthing the Rosetta Stone, the stumbled discovery of the Dead Sea Scrolls.

You long held those fantasies but knew them for what they were: fantasies. Only now, here, on a windy hill, something enormous, something beyond description, looms into view.

A ritual shaft in an Iron Age fort.

An Arthurian knife.

Human bones.

Signs of battle.

All those things plus *this is Mount Badon*. Rumour has murmured that for years, but it's pretty much shouting it now. You want some slaughtered Saxons? You want to see a pile of murdered warriors? We've got warriors for you, mate. We've got bones.

Except around the shaft, no work is being done any more.

Every bone that comes up is being cleaned, photographed,

recorded. Those of us without an active role, just hang around, smoke roll-ups, watch everything.

By midday, we have a crowd of a hundred people watching. A journalist from the local paper. Tifford summons one of his security firms, and a baffled-looking guard in a hi-vis uniform parks his van up near the shaft and sits in his vehicle, door open, listening to Radio Two.

The work goes more slowly now. Each layer has to be recorded as it's uncovered. The people working the soil have to do so with gentleness, anxious not to violate what lies just beneath.

By that evening, it's clear we have a mass grave on our hands. The aftermath of battle.

The security firm arranges floodlights and a diesel generator. They plant two guys up there all night. Two guys and a van and a German shepherd.

The next morning, we start early. The whole site is a-bustle from well before eight. Our crowd of volunteers gathered here among these winds, these bones, these centuries.

I text Jones.

Say, 'We might want to have an Armed Response Unit on the scene as a precautionary measure.'

Fiona Griffiths and her ARUs.

He texts back. Says no. 'Unless circumstances alter.' His message is friendly, though. Trying hard to encourage me.

Meantime: more bones, more scorched remains.

Lots of both.

And then, glory be, at eleven-seventeen on 23 June, the word coming up from our now-sixteen metre hole is that we have a sword. A whole sword. A sword that seems to have been lying, almost triumphally, on the bones and embers and clutter below. As though the sword itself is the victor and slayer of all that slaughtered horde.

We photograph its position as we've photographed all

our significant finds, but because this is big, we film it too. Film every stage. Three phones, at least, recording the whole thing.

Down in the pit, the sword is tied with bandages of soft grey webbing to the hoist.

Is borne aloft.

Is washed off with unbearable gentleness.

Gleams in this new sun, for fifteen centuries a stranger.

The sword is a warrior's tool, all right. No ceremonial thing this, but something battle-dinged, cut about, incised. It's bent too. Bent from use. The shaft of the blade lies at a slight angle to the hilt.

And it's jewelled. Ornamented. A flash of gold on hilt and pommel.

Those things and, on the very base of the hilt, an image.

Time and the aeons have corroded what was once, presumably, a crystal sharpness. But you can still see what was there. Still read the image's encoded text.

A bear's head, crowned.

The bear and the king.

Arto-rīg-ios.

Arthur.

We are standing on Mount Badon and we've just discovered Arthur's sword.

Tifford and Wisbech are almost frozen in this moment of glory.

Frozen with the beautiful shock of what they've found.

Frozen, but not stupid.

They do what they have to do. This site isn't secure. Two unarmed security guards and a single stupid dog is not remotely protection enough for this astonishing treasure.

They wad the sword in loose grey blankets. The sort of thing that furniture movers use. They carry the sword down to Wisbech's car. She'll take it direct to the British Museum.

Their vaults. The security guys will follow every step of the way.

I call Jones this time. Say, 'I think circumstances *have* altered, sir. I'd strongly recommend we arrange that ARU.'

I say everything I can. Everything I should. But Jones thinks I'm over-reacting. He notifies the Thames Valley Police traffic guys that the movement of a valuable item is being contemplated. Passes on Wisbech's licence plate, which I've just given him. But that's it.

'No need to over-react,' he says. 'But thank you.'

We walk the sword down to Wisbech's car. Are lowering the rear seats so the damn thing can lie flat and comfortable.

Are doing those good things when a black Ford Focus sweeps into our little car park.

The car moves a little fast, a little wildly.

I get the hell away.

Up the hill. Behind a hedge. Out of sight of the new arrivals, but near enough to watch.

The Focus stops. Turns. Ends up facing the way it came, blocking the exit.

Three men get out.

Dark clothes. Balaclavas. Guns. One shotgun and two handy-looking pistols.

The men could well be the three men from the museum. I can't say for sure – one of them looks too tall, has the wrong kind of movement – but without faces, it's hard to tell.

From the shelter of my hedge, I call the Thames Valley emergency number. I tell them in a low murmur what's happening. Tell them to get their arses over here as fast as they can.

'And, please, an ARU,' I say. 'These men are armed and dangerous.'

This is Swindon, not Llanymawddwy, so the operator calmly tells me she'll do what she can. She doesn't seek to imply that my request is ludicrous. She confirms, yes, there is an ARU available in Swindon itself. I give her the number of the Ford Focus. She repeats it calmly and accurately.

And, as we talk, I watch.

The guy with the shotgun rounds up everyone in the car park. Herds them into a corner. Stands there, casually enforcing submission.

One of the two pistol guys goes round collecting phones. Dumps them into a bag. His other pistolled buddy gets the sword out of Wisbech's car. Puts it in the Focus. Then the two pistol guys go around knifing the tyres of every car in the car park, including mine.

They drive off. The whole thing takes two minutes, maybe less.

For a moment, just a moment, there is perfect stillness.

A bird, a lapwing maybe, calling aloft. The burr of the motorway.

Then Tifford, Dr Simon Tifford, Senior Archaeologist and a man now very close to tears, breaks the silence.

'They've stolen Excalibur,' he wails. 'They've stolen fucking Excalibur.'

40

There's a search, of course. A hue and cry.

The Thames Valley Police got an ARU to the scene within eight minutes. Good going, yes, but about six minutes too late.

At first, the Focus seemed to have got away scot-free, only then the damn thing was found. Two miles away. Abandoned. Burned.

We presume the thieves just swapped cars, and we have no clue at all as to that new vehicle.

Which is great. Which is just great.

And – well, failure is failure. The news is full of the whole damn affair. Not just domestically, but all over the world. One typical headline – this one from the *Times* – says simply: KING ARTHUR'S SWORD: FOUND – THEN STOLEN.

Bleddyn Jones and his counterparts in the Thames Valley put out a joint press release that begins:

THEFT OF 'EXCALIBUR' – INFORMATION WANTED
A historic sword, bearing a 'bear and crown' imprint on the hilt, was today stolen from Liddington Castle outside Swindon. The sword is believed to have a possible connection to 'King Arthur' and may well represent an antiquity of the highest possible value. If any members of the public have any information whatsoever . . .

Blah, blah.

The best way to recover the sword, I submit, would be not to have lost it in the first place. I don't like the way the press release puts inverted commas around the name King Arthur – those quote marks reek of Jonesian influence, if you ask me – but I can't have everything.

Bleddyn Jones texts, emails and calls. He wants me back immediately. He's nice about it. Apologetic even.

I tell him yes. Try to be gracious.

And in better news – in glorious, wonderful, sunshine and rose-petalled news – Bev texts me to say that Dennis Jackson has cut short his sabbatical. He's coming back to take over Major Crimes.

Praise be.

Glory be.

I breathe a silent prayer to whichever stone-faced god looks after the holiday-and-sailing habits of gruff middle-aged Welsh coppers.

I text Jackson. Invite him round to breakfast. A welcome back thing.

And of course, I've got some bits and pieces of my own to catch up on.

Computer stuff mostly. I'm not a geek, not really, but I've learned from the best and I've done a few practice runs already. Katie and I spend a pleasant day or so putting our material into order and, when we're ready, hit submit.

Katie's brought a bottle of fizz with her to celebrate. I'm feeling so celebratory myself that I have almost half a glass myself.

When, finally, I go into the office, I experience that weirdness I always get when I've been away any length of time. Weirded out by the normality. The way life without me seems to have been much the same as life with me, only presumably more peaceful and with slightly worse grammar.

And, bless the man, Bleddyn Jones has – finally, finally –

pieced the whole damn jigsaw together. He's still awkward with it. Almost deliberately clumsy, like a rugby type buying lingerie for his wife.

But still. He gets the picture. His forward-looking version of it, at least.

'It seems like this was all pre-planned,' he tells a jam-packed briefing room. 'We now suspect that the thieves have been on the trail for some time. They stole documents from Bangor Library and Saint Tydecho's church up in Llanymawddwy. They stole a bear-and-crown seal box from Dinas Powys and killed the lead archaeologist who might have known enough to put these leads together for herself.

'We don't know *how* they first came across the clues that led, eventually to Liddington Castle. Most likely, it was a chance encounter, initially, but a chance encounter that encouraged them to explore. And as well as Dinas Powys, their researches obviously took them to Llanymawddwy because our very own Sergeant Griffiths interrupted them in the process of a theft at the church there. And that's where we found the vellum – sheepskin basically – which . . . well, it was a palimpsest. Hidden text. Pointing to Swindon.'

Jones's explanation judders on a little further, before grinding to a halt.

It's hard for him, this. Partly, because subsequent events have proved me essentially right. Partly because his basic issue with me – that I don't follow orders and am not to be trusted – is spot on, no matter that I'm now the one who's looking golden. But mostly, Jones's job, all along, has been to find and prosecute the killers of Gaynor Charteris. He hasn't done that. Worse: by failing to understand the broader chain of events, he has also failed to prevent the theft of a sword which may yet prove to be the single most valuable antiquity in the world ever.

Whoops.

For a man who's only been Acting Head of Major Crime for a few months, his record thus far is looking distinctly patchy.

I don't gloat. I do help. I do what I can.

On Friday evening, George Bowen comes down to Cardiff and he, Katie and I have a little celebration. Bowen says, 'Any news yet?' And I say, 'No, not yet.'

On Saturday night, I clean my house, top to bottom. No real reason, I suppose, but it's one of those girl-things you do by way of preparation. A bride dieting ready for the big day. A mother-to-be buying booties for her unborn child.

Get everything ready.

Go to bed.

Can't sleep.

Make peppermint tea.

Drink it.

Still can't sleep.

Get up again.

Shove a chair under the handle of my bedroom door. Make a nest of pillows at the head of my bed. Swaddle myself in a soft pink pashmina shawl that my two sisters gave me as a joint Christmas present. Hold my gun in my lap, fully loaded, but with the safety on.

Feelings without names walk through a body without substance. I don't know who I am, or where, or why.

And then – I just sit there. All night. Quiet and alone here in this gunned-up darkness.

41

Eight the next morning.

A knock at the door.

A heavy, unmistakeable, masculine knock. Dennis Jackson, my once and future boss.

I open up.

'Fiona,' he says.

He looks sun-tanned. Real tanned, not the normal Welsh version, where an upper layer of skin might have taken a little colour, but the six layers beneath are still all white and scared and fragile.

I tell him to come on in.

He comes on in.

Looks around. He's never been here before. But my house is completely unremarkable and he is visibly unsure of how to find anything to say.

I say, 'It must be nice to be back.'

He agrees.

I show him our breakfast spread.

He's impressed.

I set him to work on the coffee, then do toast, and my fancy version of scrambled egg, one that has goat's cheese and chives in it. The egg doesn't come out completely right – I think I forget to stir – but I give the better bit to Jackson and the not-quite-so-good bit to me.

'The white bits are meant to be there,' I tell him. 'They're goats' cheese.'

'Very nice.'

'The green bits are chives.'

'Lovely.'

We eat and drink. Peppermint tea for me. I've never got the point of coffee.

Jackson says, 'So.'

I'm really quite sure that the word doesn't mean anything at all when it stands alone in a sentence like that, not even if you give it some good senior officer gruffness and solidity. Also, I don't see what you're meant to say in response. The word 'so' isn't a question. It doesn't indicate subject matter. As far as I'm concerned, the damn thing is no more than a vowel wearing a sun-hat and that, in my view, is no way to start a conversation.

But since two can play at the same game, I do precisely that.

Say, 'So.'

Not as deep and rumbly as Jackson's version, but a whole lot prettier.

'You've been having fun,' he says.

'Yes.'

'Leave of absence?'

'Well, Jones was going to give me another written warning, I think. I'd already had one.'

Jackson nods. Written warnings aren't really his thing. He just yells.

'So you thought you'd do a little archaeology.'

'Yes.'

I tell him about Liddington Castle and the dig.

Jackson hears me out. Eats his egg.

His face doesn't look happy. Not bad-egg unhappy, just muddled-case unhappy.

He says, 'OK. Let me get this straight. Our friend, Bleddyn Jones, thinks that someone, somewhere came across some old document, or something like that, indicating that there might really be something in all this Arthur stuff. Probably just ran across the thing by accident to begin with, but quickly realised that there might be some money to be made out of it. Loads of money. I mean, supposing you had in your hands the first proper evidence of a historical Arthur, that's got to be worth something, right?'

'Worth *something*?' I say. 'Look, an Old Master painting can go for fifty, sixty, even seventy million dollars. But there are loads of Old Masters out there. They're scarce, yes, but not that scarce. The *actual* sword of the *actual* King Arthur, on the other hand? History's most famous warrior? The man responsible for the most famous legend of the western world. I mean, what's the ceiling price for that object? It's not even a once-in-a-lifetime find. It's a once-in-a-millennium thing.'

Jackson: 'OK. I get that. So, our thieves get wind that this whole thing might be real. They follow up. They want to get there ahead of anyone else.'

'Yes.'

'They break into the library at Bangor. There are old documents there. Some of them *very* old. Whatever they have there isn't quite enough, so they go to Llanymawddwy to see if there's anything more there. Maybe take something, maybe not. We don't know if they got away with anything.'

'Correct.'

'But there *was* something there, which they failed to find. Either it was just too well hidden or you came along to interrupt. Either way, you found this bit of vellum which, when fully analysed, suggested some link between Tydecho's church and the general area of Swindon. And since the oldest bit of text on that vellum had something to do with King Arthur, there was a decent likelihood that the Tydecho–

Swindon connection also had to do with Arthur.'

I nod. 'Also, Tydecho was, theoretically, Arthur's nephew. And Llanymawddwy is only a couple of miles away from a probable location of Arthur's last battle. So yes, Arthur connections everywhere you look.'

'Right. So *we've* got something that points to Swindon. The thieves have all the rest of the Llanymawddwy material and we have to presume that *they've* got material that points to Swindon. Maybe points a whole lot more specifically than the bit we've got. Right?'

'Exactly. Yes, sir. Spot on. Would you like some jam?'

No is the answer to that. Jackson is egged and jammed to the max. But he does want some more coffee and, ever the graceful hostess, I pour him more.

'Thank you.'

'My pleasure. May I say that it's an honour having you here?'

Jackson doesn't respond to that, but his thoughts are where they should be. On the case.

'So you secure some time off work – basically by making poor old Bleddyn so pissed off with you that he's half-ready to fire you – and go tootling down to Liddington. Work there as a volunteer.'

'Yes.'

'You go there, because you're *expecting* some major find and want to be there for the action.'

'Yes.'

'Trouble is, the thieves are also expecting something and they make their own plans. They let you lot do all the hard work of recovering the thing, then they grab it.'

'Yes.'

'And at that stage, security is minimal, because no one's expecting anything, so making the snatch isn't even especially hard.'

'Correct.'

Jackson says, 'And on this story, Gaynor Charteris was killed because she came across this damn seal box and the thieves were worried that she might start shouting about a real historical Arthur. Perhaps *she'd* find something that connected him to Liddington Castle. Or maybe just interest in Arthur would reawaken to the point where that Liddington Castle dig became major news. If there was *real* security in place – police cars, cameras, armed officers, all of that – then the whole snatch would probably prove impossible.'

'Yes.'

'So she was killed and the seal box was stolen. And, as it turned out, the whole Dinas Powys dig was abandoned and that whole avenue of research was closed off, exactly as the thieves wanted. I mean, yes, there was a whole hoo-hah about her killing, but the Arthur angle basically vanished from sight.'

'Exactly.'

Jackson stares.

Says, 'That, roughly, is the story that our friend Jones is currently working with.'

I nod.

'But it's rubbish, isn't it?'

'Yes.'

'I mean, for one thing, if you want to kill Gaynor Charteris, then just kill her for heaven's sake. Don't start beheading her and sticking spears into her chest.'

'Yes.'

He stares some more. Raps his coffee mug gently with his fingers.

I think that means it's my turn and, in fairness, Jackson hasn't visited the cathedral library at Bangor, so I fill in the gap. 'Same thing with Bangor. If you wanted to steal from the library, you'd just go there during normal opening hours. The place was totally unguarded. No one thought there was anything there worth stealing. So you'd just turn up. Take what you wanted. Walk away. You wouldn't smash a lock. Why bother? Why attract the attention?'

Jackson says, 'And, OK, it *could* have been a coincidence that you got to Saint Tydecho's just as the thieves were busy there. Coincidences do happen, after all. But maybe that's not the best explanation. Maybe they waited till some bright spark in South Wales made a connection between Gaynor Charteris and the Bangor theft and went up to investigate. As soon as they heard you were investigating further in Bangor, they'd have figured out that your natural next step would take you to Llanymawddwy. So – just possibly – they *wanted* you to find them. They literally waited till they knew you were on your way.'

'Yes.'

I remember the scene outside that window by the library in Bangor. A twenty-something curate. A middle-aged woman. An electrician eating his sandwich. Any of them – most likely the 'electrician' – could have been there to monitor the movement of police investigators. An arrival I'd already communicated to the gossipy Aled Owen.

I don't say any of that, but Jackson has this line of thought firmly in his grasp now. 'And if you wanted to steal something from Llanymawddwy, why take a shotgun? Why not just break in and take what you needed. Why take a *weapon*?'

'That's a very good question, sir. Why take a weapon? Exactly.'

'So, perhaps you take a gun because you know that a detective is on her way to you. You *did* want to be found, but you *didn't* want to be caught.'

I like to vary my affirmatives, so this time I nod.

'And if that's your line of thinking, then we'd have to assume that the thing *you* found – that bit of vellum – was exactly the thing you were *meant* to find.'

'That would seem like a good conclusion to draw, sir, yes.'

'And if that's your conclusion in relation to the vellum, then you have to go back to all the Gaynor Charteris stuff and wonder about that too. Maybe that whole thing was a show put on for our benefit too.'

'Yes, maybe it was.'

'Which would explain why Charteris was killed in that rather flamboyant way. By cutting her head off and sticking Iron Age spears into her chest, the killers were kind of yelling about the importance of some sort of historical angle. Making sure that a pack of dumb provincial coppers didn't ignore that side of things. Oh, and, come to think of it, we still haven't even talked about the museum break-in. Thieves smart enough to dig that tunnel are presumably smart enough to check that the Renoir they want to steal is actually present.'

I don't answer.

Jackson stares at me. He's reading me as much as the case, I think, but that's within the rules, definitely. You use whatever clues you can.

Changing tack, he says, 'OK, I'm a thief. I've just stolen King Arthur's sword. Presumably I haven't done all this just so I can hang it on my wall. I want to sell it. But how the hell do I sell it without getting caught?'

I say, 'Would you like to wipe your hands?'

He stares.

I give him some kitchen towel.

'Just you do have a bit of butter on your fingers, sir, and I don't want it on my laptop.'

Jackson, fine man that he is, wipes his hands. We go through to my sitting room and I open up my laptop.

Navigate to Tor.

The. Onion. Router. TOR.

The entrance gate to the dark web.

'You've got this on your computer, Fiona?' Jackson asks

when he realises what we're looking at.

'It's perfectly legal, sir. I mean, if I were a Burmese democracy activist, I might use this to protect myself.'

That rouses a grunt.

For every one Burmese democracy activist that the British police encounter, we come across a thousand users of child pornography. We in the police love Tor the way Donald Trump loves overweight female Mexican Muslim peace activist hippies.

I navigate to Agora and explain, 'It's eBay for criminals, basically. Loads of sellers. Loads of buyers. Drugs and guns mostly, but you can sell anything.'

Jackson stares at me. I think he's wondering how I know all this. How come I have Tor on my computer. How come I have a user account on Agora.

But he doesn't ask, so I don't have to tell him about Steve Mason, and a horrible bedsit in Harlesden, and a bottle of cheap Algerian wine, and the way I had to lift my bra as a convicted fraudster checked for wires.

Jackson's gaze returns to the keyboard.

He finds the Agora search bar and types, 'King Arthur Sword'.

The browser thinks – slowly, because of the thousand layers of encryption – and returns its results.

The topmost result says, 'EXCALIBUR. The battle sword of King Arthur. Recovered from Liddington Castle – Mount Badon – 23 June 2016.'

Jackson raises his shaggy eyebrows and clicks through to the sales page.

Photographs.

The sword that we dug out of that hole. The one that sat atop a pile of Saxon bones. The one that glittered a muddy pale gold beneath that unfamiliar sun.

The page is long and detailed.

Little video clips taken from our stolen phones show the sword being retrieved. Pulled out of the ritual shaft. Taken off the hoist. Washed. Some close-ups. Then a little bit of footage of the actual theft. Then a ton of super close-ups of the sword itself. The bear-and-crown image at the base of the sword. The gold thread on the hilt. Some red glass and other jewelling.

Also the price.

'Bids invited. Fifty million dollars reserve. Buyers will be permitted to conduct ANY non-destructive testing of the sword and its materials prior to completion of the transaction.'

Jackson explores the listing in detail.

I'm already highly familiar with it and lean back, watching him work.

'Fifty million dollars,' he says.

'Minimum. I mean, buyers have to pay in bitcoins, but that's the dollar equivalent.'

Jackson rubs his chin.

Thinks.

Uses a thick finger to hit the back button. Navigates back to the original page of search results.

He stares with new intensity at the screen.

He's hardly Generation Laptop. But still, search results are search results. They're not that hard to read.

He says, 'No, that's not right. There are *two* swords for sale here.'

He's right.

There are.

Two swords, not one.

He clicks through to the other listing, and gets the same thing, or more or less. Another sword. Similar, but different. The same bear-and-crown stamped into the hilt. Similar use of gold. Some red glass. Jet beads. The blade similarly dinged about and damaged.

This sword has some preliminary spectrographic analysis attached. The kind of stuff you can date swords with.

Also some still and video images of the snatch itself.

Also a detailed listing of whens and wheres, weights and lengths.

Price for this one: sixty million dollars, minimum.

Jackson gets up to speed.

'Fiona, there are two swords here. But they only stole *one*. You guys only dug up the one sword, right?'

He stares at me.

I stare at him.

His eyes burn a question.

I answer it.

'Do you want to see my one, sir? It's really good.'

I go to my understairs cupboard, which is a bit of a muddle because it's quite hard fitting a sword in there along with the mop and the bucket and the vacuum hose and all the other bits you have to keep in those places.

Also, the damn thing is quite heavy – it was built for the greatest warrior of British history, not a somewhat petite Welsh detective – so in the end it's Jackson who has to haul it out.

'Excalibur,' he says. 'You've got Excalibur in your broom cupboard.'

'*Caledfwlch*,' I say, irritably. 'Arthur was British. He was Celtic. He was almost certainly Welsh. He wouldn't have used some faked-up Frenchified Latin name for the thing, let alone a name that wasn't invented until centuries after his death. The proper Welsh name is Caledfwlch. "Hard cleaving" or, if you prefer, "Hard striking". But yes: I've got Caledfwlch in my broom cupboard, or I did have until you yanked it out.'

A bit grumpily, I put back the vacuum hose and the other bits that fell out with the sword.

Jackson fingers the gold, the jet, the horn, the glass, the iron.

Then – because he is a man and a Welsh man at that, one for whom hitting things only ever lies a short half-step from consciousness – he stands in my living room, sword in hand, feeling its heft.

'It's a good sword,' he says.

'Thank you. It's my first one.'

'It handles nicely.' He says that, like he's some big expert. 'But fake.'

He looks at me, to see if I'm going to contradict him.

I contradict him.

'It's *not* fake. It's properly old. Just – well, it hasn't always been a sword.'

I explain.

Explain that we used genuine Dark Age iron. Reheated it on a fire that used the right kind of south Welsh hardwoods. Worked it using Dark Age technologies, nothing more. If we had materials we weren't sure of – we didn't like the carbon dating stats on some of our glass – we just irradiated it until we had stats we liked.

Mostly though, we proceeded just as our ancestors did.

We used Dark Age jet.

Dark Age horn.

Dark Age glass.

Dark Age gold, and Welsh gold at that.

Aside from that one spot of irradiation, we didn't use any tool or technique which wasn't used by our long-ago ancestors.

Jackson is still sceptical.

'So you're saying if I took that thing along to—'

'It's not *that thing*. It's Caledfwlch.'

'OK. If I took Caledfwlch to the British Museum—'

'Which you can't, because it's mine.'

298

'Which I can't, because it's yours. But what would they say? Assume the museum could run any test they wanted.'

'Look, iron is iron and gold is gold, and they've been that way since the beginning of time. If you treat everything just right, there's no reason why you can't make a perfect replica of anything you want.' Because Jackson is still looking at me, I answer his question directly. 'Yes. We could take our sword to the British Museum and, unless we've cocked up, they couldn't determine if it was genuinely ancient or not.'

'OK. Wow.'

'And *every* major museum, the British Museum included, will have fakes in its collections. Fakes that are indistinguishable from the real thing. It's the dirty secret of the whole antiquities business.'

'OK, good.' But Jackson's thick finger points at my broom cupboard. 'But you kept your – your Caledfwlch in there. You *didn't* dig it out of some muddy hole in Liddington Hill.'

'Liddington Castle. No.'

'But an *actual* sword did come out of the *actual* shaft at Liddington.'

'Yes.'

'And that's the sword that the thieves took.'

'Yes.'

'The one they're now selling on the internet. On the dark web.'

'Yes.'

After Bleddyn Jones, it's so nice working with Jackson, I want to hug him.

I give him all the yeses he could possibly need.

Jackson: 'OK. I'm confused here. Help me out. I want to say that the thieves have made a fake of their own. That this whole damn thing was just a way to get their fake onto the market in the best possible way. Except their sword definitely *did* come out of that hole and yours definitely *didn't*.'

I take the laptop. Show him some photos.

Show him that little construction site a few hundred metres from Liddington Castle. The digger with its Cwmbran registration.

I say, 'These are chalk downs. *Chalk*. Water drains through chalk, no problem. Yet supposedly this construction site was working on some drainage issue for a month or more. But Thames Water knew nothing about the site. Nor did anyone else I could find. And look, this digger came from a firm in Cwmbran? If you just want to sort out some drainage thing, you can find people to do that pretty much anywhere. You certainly don't need to go to south Wales for it.'

Jackson: 'Ha! But you bloody do if you want a bit of mining experience. I mean, I know the mines are pretty much all closed these days, but the expertise is still there, isn't it?'

'Yes.'

'And we're probably talking about the exact same experts who figured out a way to get into the museum.'

'You'd have to think so, yes.'

I tell Jackson about the soil bore at Liddington. The one that was conducted, and its results published, last year.

I say, 'So our thieves *knew* the shaft went down a long way. They *knew* a dig had been scheduled to explore it. So they just came in from the side. Buried some bones, some skulls, some bits of leather armour, that kind of thing. Some of those things they buried there were probably real antiquities. Others would have been modern things just doctored and irradiated to be of the right general age. And because that all looked like a lot of work and expense, they also buried a whole lot of bone-ash, because that would have been the easiest and cheapest thing to manufacture in bulk.

'Anyway, they do enough to make it look like the ritual shaft carries a mass grave for slaughtered Saxons, then they toss their sword on top. Beaten about. Decorated with the bear-and-crown logo they've already alerted us to via Dinas Powys. Then they fill in their tunnel, so it looks like the site was totally untouched. Yes, they have to do it all with extreme care, but by this stage, we know they're willing to do things right.'

I shut up now and Jackson takes over.

He says, still figuring this out, 'So anyone seeing that sword come out of that hole has to assume it's Arthur's sword. That seal box at Dinas Powys seems to confirm it. The vellum at Llanymawddwy seems to double-confirm it. The fact that Liddington Castle has long been fingered as a possible site for Mount Badon seems to treble-confirm it. Basically, this thing they've found, it *is* Arthur's sword, it *has* to be.'

'Yes.'

I think that's only half the truth, in fact.

Establishing the provenance of the sword was always going to be the tough part. Yes, you can fake a sword to *look* old, but how do you *prove* the thing is Arthur's sword?

You could hope to rely on academics, of course. The research community of which Katie is part. But how can those guys really get stuck in, if they don't have an actual sword to analyse? They can form hypotheses, of course, but more hypotheticals is the absolute last thing that our thieves needed. They needed something more definite than that. More certain. And in this case, they chose to rely on the sturdy common sense of the British police service.

Our press statements have already as good as confirmed that the sword was genuine. That it came out of that ritual shaft. That we believe, completely, in its Arthurian provenance.

I remember thinking, early on, *The single thing that disturbs me most about this enquiry so far is the idea that* we're *the intended audience: we, the police.*

I think that what the thieves wanted us to do, we've done.

'So what now?' asks Jackson.

'Well, two possibilities really, sir.'

He thinks.

Studies me.

Nods.

'OK, option one,' he says. 'We reveal the existence of this side tunnel. We go public and say that this whole Arthurian thing was just a sham. A hoax, aimed at making a ton of money on the black market.'

'Yes.'

'And that's good. That's a good, attractive option. It means those thieves will have spent loads of money doing all this and we just make their product unsaleable. If we announce this thing is a fake, no one on earth will be stupid enough to buy it.'

'Exactly.'

'So if we do that, the thieves have wasted their time and money.'

'And lots of it.'

'Except then we don't have anyone to arrest, do we?'

'Well, maybe someone at the Cwmbran end.' I say. 'We could probably find out who hired that digger. Compare faces with the people behind the museum robbery. There's an avenue there.'

'And this guy with the stupid name—'

'Alden Gheerbrant.'

'Yes, him. I daresay you'd want another crack at him?'

'Yes.'

'So that's option one.'

'Yes.'

'But,' Jackson's fingers tick off the negatives one by one, 'We won't have caught the guys trying to sell this sword. We won't have the men who killed Gaynor Charteris. We won't have the men who, presumably, paid Antony Wormold to kill John Oakeshott. And we won't necessarily have the men who broke into the museum. I mean, if the gang comprises just your

Gheerbrant fellow and maybe some Cwmbran mining types, then we get everyone, but we'd have to bet this conspiracy is broader than that.'

I think we can pretty much prove the conspiracy is larger than that, in fact, but I don't bother to say so.

Instead, I just say, 'Yes.'

Yes to Jackson's list of objections. Yes to the thinking that lies behind it.

Jackson: 'Just to be clear, I'm not ruling out option one.'

My face doesn't do much at that. It certainly doesn't say anything.

Jackson says, sharply, 'Fiona?'

'Yes, sir. I heard you. Option one – the thing about letting the criminals get away with everything – that's still under urgent consideration.'

Jackson doesn't quite smile, but his crags soften just a little. Just briefly.

Then he hefts my sword again.

Battle-scarred it may be, but it's still four feet of sharp steel in my living room.

A dangerous blade. A wicked blade. A killing blade.

'Option two,' says Jackson.

'Yes, sir. Option Two.'

'It would be more fun, wouldn't it?'

'It's not about fun, sir. It's about doing our job.'

Jackson parries a thrust from an imaginary attacker, then twists his blade so he just manages to catch the attacker in the thigh.

A flesh wound. Non-lethal.

He stands back, holding the sword out, breathing through his mouth, ready for the next assault.

He does that, grinning at my primness.

'We can do our job *and* have some fun.'

'Yes.'

The attacker returns. Leaps at Jackson, but ends up with a belly full of Caledfwlch and dies gurgling on my carpet.

Jackson stands with the point of the sword at the imaginary attacker's throat. Waits till the last gurgle is fully gurgled.

'Option two,' he says. 'How far have you got with that?'

I do a sort of half-shrug. One that takes in the sword in my living room. The Agora listing. The price tag of sixty million dollars.

I've got *that* far: that's what my shrug says.

'You've had no contact?'

'Not yet.'

'But you're thinking that the thieves will contact you?'

'I think they have to. If two people are selling Caledfwlch, then neither sword is worth anything. They *have* to get mine off the market.'

'And when they make contact?'

'Don't know. Haven't really thought about that part.'

'Well, I'd say they've got two options themselves. The thieves I mean. They could pay you to take your sword off the market. Or they could kill you.'

'Yes.'

'And you know, what with being thieves and murderers and all, they'd probably go with the whole killing-you alternative, wouldn't you say?'

'Well!' I actually raise my hands at that. Not a gesture of surrender. More of a *do-I-really-have-to-do-everything-around-here?* thing. And when my hands have finished waving around, I add some words by way of garnish, 'They *can't* just kill me. That wouldn't remove that listing on Agora. And anyway. You know. We're the police. We're allowed guns and everything.'

Jackson nods, exactly as he would have done if we were in the process of making a sensible arrangement. A good, solid, professional plan.

He checks my living room to see if any more Dark Age

304

warriors are about to leap at him, but decides we're OK. He lays Caledfwlch gently down.

'How much of this does DI Jones actually know?'

'He and I have had a communication problem, I'm afraid.'

'He's a perfectly fine officer, Fiona. Very safe pair of hands.'

'I know.'

'And look, I've had a look in your damn file. Pretty much everything he says about you is spot on. Good, accurate, honest feedback.'

'I know.'

There's a long pause.

Either the light has moved, or Jackson has, but a stray beam of light catches on one of the red glass rubies in the sword's hilt and throws a dart of red up at Jackson's eye. He doesn't blink or move away.

I say, 'That beard. DI Jones's beard.' I can't bring myself to describe it in detail, but my hands do a kind of spidery creep around my chin.

'You don't like his beard?'

'No, I don't like his beard.'

'It's not a good one.'

'No.'

I think Jackson should probably tell me that dislike of a beard is not a reason to disobey a commanding officer. If he did choose to say that, I'd be obliged to agree, but he doesn't.

And then – well, I don't know.

Nothing changes. The light still burns red in Jackson's eye.

Caledfwlch lies quiet on my floor.

The body of an imaginary attacker drips the last of its life-blood into my living-room carpet.

And Jackson laughs. A deep-bottomed, wide-chested laugh, that's born of the Welsh hills, at home on the rugby field and the parade ground.

'Bloody hell, Fiona,' he says. 'It's good to be back.'

42

The email comes later that same morning.

It's not a regular email and it doesn't come to any of my regular addresses. Instead it comes to my GuerrillaMail account, a site that scrambles an already random email address and deletes all unread messages after just one hour.

The message reads: 'You don't have Excalibur. Remove your listing. Mordred.'

Mordred: Arthur's nephew or bastard son, depending on which myth you believe. In most versions of the myth, he's a traitor too. The man responsible for Arthur's death.

His address, like mine, is untraceable.

I email back, 'Nor do you. Remove yours. Gwenhwyfar.'

Then tramp up to Jackson's office with my laptop.

My Caledfwlch lies under a tartan blanket on Jackson's sofa. The blanket is not as clean as it might be and smells more than a little of dog.

I poke at it disapprovingly.

I say, 'You should at least have washed the blanket.'

'If it's good enough for my dog, it's good enough for your sword.'

'It's *my* Caledfwlch. I might just sell it.'

'And I might just prosecute you. Fraud by false representation. I'm thinking, what, maybe five years? I'll push for the maximum anyway. The maximum maximum maximum maximum.'

An incoming email interrupts our valuable dialogue.

'Please send video of your sword cutting into the front page of today's *Times*. You have thirty minutes. Mordred.'

We don't have a *Times* to hand. We have a *Western Mail*, so we go with that.

Jackson calls down to Bleddyn Jones, gets him to come up.

Jackson has already briefed Jones. Jones doesn't particularly like the direction things have taken, but he's a pro. He doesn't sulk.

Anyway.

Jackson lays the paper out on his sofa and thrashes it with the sword. I video him do it.

The thing about cutting a newspaper to shreds is because our counterparts want to check we have a real sword, not just something Photoshopped into existence. A video of a sword thrashing around with today's newspaper should do the trick.

We check the video, then send it.

My message reads, 'Here's the video. If you want to see our spectroscopy data, our radiocarbon data, or anything else, please ask. You'll note that the jet beads on our sword are highly consistent with those recently found at Dinas Powys, thus confirming the authenticity of this exceptional piece. Your sword is a modern fake. Please remove your listing. Gwenhwyfar.'

We all stare at the laptop.

It does nothing.

Then Jones says, 'I've got news for you. It's just come in. Look at this.'

He shows us a picture of Dark Hair guy.

The picture isn't one I've seen before. It doesn't come from the museum.

Jones: 'OK, so I sent a team out to that Cwmbran plant hire place. Showed them some pictures. And we've got an identification. This man is Ivor Williams. He's a project manager at some kind of tunnelling company.'

He passes us the company brochure. They do pipe jacking, shaft sinking, auger boring, sheet piling, timber headings, anything. If you wanted to tunnel silently into a museum, Ivor Williams would be the man to do it.

One of the services offered by the company is 'No disturb excavation'. The text underneath begins, 'In sites of exceptional scientific or historical interest, it may be necessary to complete works with minimal impact on the sub-soil environment. Our group is the European leader at such excavation . . .'

I place my finger on the text.

I say, 'That side-tunnel. The one that came into the shaft at Liddington Castle.'

Jackson says, '"No Disturb Excavation". Bloody hell. The things people can do.'

Jones scowls, like he's been playing a game where no one told him the rules up front.

He says, 'Williams isn't present at his home address. Obviously we've circulated his ID. We're looking through his known contacts now. See if we can locate the two accomplices.'

That's good.

Very good.

For the first time in this case, it feels like we're ahead of the curve, not lagging some long distance behind it. And unless Williams has buggered off for good to some shady criminal paradise in South America, we'll pick him up before too long.

Still my laptop does nothing.

Jones and Jackson crawl around picking up tattered bits of the *Western Mail*. As the junior officer present, I should probably be helping, but I give them my emphatic – if silent – moral support instead.

Then – finally – the laptop talks to us.

'How much to delete your listing? Mordred.'

I stare at my commanding officers.

Jones: 'I don't know. A million? Two million?'

Jackson: 'Five?'

I type, 'Twenty million dollars. Bitcoin equivalent. Gwenhwyfar.'

Hit send.

Say, 'You think too small. That's your problem.'

43

The same day. Evening.

Lord's Wood, the Doward.

A rocky, wooded landscape. Some low cliffs, some sharp inclines.

Another hill fort, except that this one has signs of human habitation going back at least ten thousand years. There are flint tools here. Mammoth bones.

Katie sits on a rock in the golden glow of the setting sun. She's dressed in black, top to toe. Black jeans. Black boots. A long-sleeved black T-shirt. I'm in the same outfit, more or less.

I say, 'You OK?'

Katie shrugs. She's dying rapidly of an incurable illness so, no, she's not OK but she shrugs. Says, 'Fine.'

The rock here has the warmth of captured sunlight, warmer now than the air around us. Behind us, there stands a low cliff. At its base, the mouth of a cave, King Arthur's Cave. It comprises just two main chambers, the largest about twenty-five feet across. It is, supposedly, where Vortigern, a king of the Britons and contemporary of Arthur's, fought his last battle.

Above us, there's a stumble of boot on stone. A skitter of falling pebbles.

A man appears.

Vaguely military boots. Jeans. Old flannel shirt.

Shotgun.

This is Mike Atkins. A former paratrooper, now working for SO15, the Met's specialist counter-terrorism unit. We're not dealing with terrorists here, but SO15 is as fuck-off-scary as British policing ever gets, so we asked for their help and they said yes.

Atkins handles the gun like he knows how to use it.

'Our friends are here,' he tells us. 'Two of them.'

Our friends.

About two o'clock this afternoon, Mordred emailed to offer ten million for the sword, but demanded to see it first. I said no to the ten million, but yes to the inspection. Time and place of my choosing. Maximum of two people. No weapons of any kind. No phones or radios. No electronics.

Mordred accepted those terms.

I told him to go immediately to Hereford, wait there for further instructions. Then, forty minutes ago, I told him where I was. Told him to arrive within the hour or any deal would be off.

He emailed back: 'OK.'

Katie and I take ourselves into the cave. We have ski masks in thin black cotton and put them on. The damn things make us look like movie bad guys, but it's better to be safe. Atkins pulls a mask on too.

In the woods beyond the cave, Atkins has a further six colleagues. Hidden. Silent. Watching. Armed. A microphone embedded in Atkins's collar broadcasts an audio feed to each of them.

Silence. Then the sound of footsteps.

Two men come in to view.

One is dressed much as Atkins is. An old reddish shirt worn over jeans. The other wears a pale-blue shirt and chinos. The shirt looks like the sort of thing that would be more comfortable in an office than in the woods above Symonds

Yat. Either way, no man carries a weapon, or at least none that I can see.

'Stop.' Atkins's command lies as much in the movement of his shotgun as it does in the word.

The men stop.

He tosses them a couple of eye masks, the kind of thing you use to get sleep on aeroplanes.

The two men put them on.

Then – nothing.

The men just stand, blindfolded. Atkins stands a few yards away, covering them with his gun.

I scan the two men through my binoculars. Ski mask or not, I wouldn't want to be around if either of these two men saw me in the museum. But these two are unknown to me.

I pass the glasses to Katie.

She studies the men. She has a real stillness to her at times. The stillness of the hunter. The warrior.

These men are here to buy a fake antiquity, which presumably means that at least one of the two has some experience in antiquities. And, since the circle of possible experts is not that wide, that person must have a reasonable chance of knowing Katie.

But she studies the men, drops the glasses and shakes her head.

'OK?' I ask her.

'Yes.'

'Sure?'

'Yes.'

I approach the two men. Frisk them.

That word, *frisk*, somehow implies something brisk and almost light-hearted, but I'm not brisk and not light-hearted.

Check calves for hidden blades. Check thighs and groins. Remove belts. Run my fingers on the inside of waistbands. The blue-shirted guy has a glasses case in his shirt pocket.

There are reading glasses inside. Neither they nor the case itself look dodgy to me.

But I continue. Check torsos, arms and armpits. The inside of each collar. Run my hands through their hair. Check their mouths.

Have them, still blindfolded, remove their shoes, so I can inspect the soles, the inners.

It sounds ridiculous. Too much. But a razor blade, or half a blade even, can do enough damage if used fast and well, and electronics are so small these days you can conceal them almost anywhere.

Besides, I'm scared of these people. They, or their acolytes, killed Gaynor Charteris. They paid the poor fool, Wormold, to stick his knife into Oakeshott's libidinous ribs. If they realise we're serious and competent, the risk of something going horribly wrong is reduced.

'OK. You can remove your masks.'

The men do, blinking and re-orienting themselves in this glowing evening light.

The guy with the red shirt looks about mid-thirties. Six foot one or two. Fit and strong. Short sandy hair. Pale eyes. Looks wholly unbothered by this situation. The search. The mask. The shotgun.

The man reeks of alpha-male. He knows it too and that knowledge only makes him reek the more.

His buddy, the blue-shirted guy is older, maybe fifty. Podgy. Grey hair, not that tidy.

I think, *no, that blue shirt doesn't belong in an office, exactly. It belongs in a study. An academic's book-lined study, of the sort that Gheerbrant had, the sort that Oakeshott had.*

I stick out my hand. Say to the younger guy, 'Mordred.'

We shake hands.

Then the older guy.

'And you are?'

'I am – oh, I did not know we would do this – so I must say, I suppose, I am Yvain.'

Yvain's accent is pure French, which surprises me, and then quickly doesn't. When we interviewed all those academics – the archaeologists, the historians – we confined our search to British universities, British institutions. Yvain's accent tells me that we needed to roam more widely.

'Yvain, Mordred.' I wave them towards the cave.

We enter.

In the centre of the larger chamber, we've got three battery-operated lanterns. Some plastic milk crates covered over with a black felt cloth. And on the cloth, glowing like a diamond, our Caledfwlch.

Katie sits on a low camping stool at the centre of our little table. Fingertips spread lightly on the cloth.

She looks, more than ever, like a warrior queen.

Regal, fierce, dying.

And I think, no I was never a real Guinevere. Never the Frehines Gwenhwyfar I claimed to be. Katie, here, now: she is our real Guinevere, that doomed princess.

I say, 'Mordred, this is Gwenhwyfar. You can call me Gwenhwyfach.'

Gwenhwyfach: the queen's sister. The dart of Katie's grey-blue eyes beneath her mask tells me she likes her new title.

Yvain approaches the sword.

'This is it? Oh, it is good.' He gets his glasses case out. 'May I?'

Puts his glasses on and inspects up close. Katie passes him a hand-held magnifier with built-in lighting. The sort of thing that jewellers use.

'Oh, thank you.'

He inspects the sword up close. The edge on the blade. The multiple dings. The bending. The jet beads. The gold

314

wire on pommel and hilt. The stamp of the bear-and-crown image at the base. The horn. The glass. Everything.

He asks questions too. 'This iron. It looks OK. Where did you . . .'

Katie says, 'We took iron from Roman and early Celtic antiquities found in south Wales. Reworked it using a furnace fired by hardwoods native to the area. Worked the material by hand using period-accurate tools. Made some use of pattern welding techniques, but nothing inconsistent with a fifth-century sword. The damage done to the weapon was done by striking it with other period-authentic objects. We induced an accelerated rust process using more than fifty applications of household vinegar and hydrogen peroxide, both ingredients which will degrade so rapidly as to be already undetectable. The degree of bending on the blade here was calculated in accordance with recent research on the performance of these kinds of blades in battle.'

She quotes some recent research papers and Yvain nods as she does so.

He inspects the gold with particular closeness. 'It is a good colour,' he admits, 'but you know, for this sword, we would really be looking for—'

'Gold from Dolaucothi,' says Katie. 'I agree. We thought the same.'

Yvain stares at her. 'It is not so easy to get this gold. The Queen, maybe she has some—'

'Or the Museum of Wales.' Katie passes over a tiny sample of gold in a small ziplock bag. 'We took ours from the same place as you took yours. That's Dolaucothi gold, the real deal.'

Yvain darts a look sideways at Mordred. Neither man says anything, but it's pretty clear we've just answered one of their big questions. If we'd just used some easy-to-source modern gold, our sword would look pretty feeble beside theirs. As it is, we've got the right gold, have passed all the tests so far –

and we've got the jet beads 'found' at Dinas Powys, which their sword lacks.

Atkins, leaning up against the cavern wall, grins over at me. I think he's enjoying this, yes, but he's also signalling a 'You're doing well, keep going.'

And, for all his enjoyment, his professionalism is spot on. His hands never move from his gun and he keeps himself well back from the cave entrance. If anything kicks off in here, then his colleagues outside will have a clear line of fire.

Yvain returns to the sword. Asks questions about the horn, the glass, the jet, the everything.

So far at least, Katie's knowledge and our sword seem to be standing up to scrutiny. Or more than that, even. At one point, Yvain found a tiny fragment of leather lodged in a crack where the blade of the sword meets the hilt. He was about to brush it away and Katie had to stop him.

'That's scabbard leather,' she says. 'The right age, of course.'

'Scabbard leather?' says Yvain. 'Oh yes, scabbard. He makes a gesture as though drawing a sword. 'I thought they were wood, mostly, but yes, also leather, of course.'

Mordred doesn't look happy at that response and Katie too is surprised.

An actual weapons specialist, an Alden Gheerbrant, would have known exactly how Celtic scabbards were put together. Even Katie – an expert in this period, though not specifically its warfare – clearly regards that kind of knowledge as basic. All of a sudden, Yvain looks a little out of place. A historian, yes. One familiar with the period, yes. But those things don't quite add up to true expertise and Katie may just have found the guy's limits.

She doesn't comment, though. Just passes him another ziplock bag containing a fragment of leather.

'Here's our source material. You're welcome to test it. In

fact, here are samples of *all* our source materials.'

She passes over a Tupperware box containing everything Mordred and his friends could want, then reaches down by her feet to pick up a stack of paper. Spectrography results. Radiocarbon data. Ultrasonic analysis. All genuine results, all highly supportive of the sword's theoretical antiquity.

And she does. She does pick them up OK.

But she reaches down right-handed and, as she is lifting the documents, her grip flutters and fails and the papers go tumbling down. She scowls, her annoyance visible through the mask.

She tries again, fierce with concentration.

Same result.

One more time. She's looking right down at her hand, trying to force the thing to open and close through strength of willpower alone.

Alas, her body doesn't work like that any more and, a few moments later, she's forced to concede defeat and reaches across her body to pick the papers up, left-handed. She passes them across.

She says nothing about what just happened. Nor does anyone else. But Mordred's eyes are glittering and Yvain has his eyebrows raised and Katie herself is breathing fast and jerkily through an open mouth.

I break the moment. Want to move swiftly away.

I say, 'This data. It's all genuine. We've removed laboratory names and other identifiers, but when you buy the sword, you'll have full access to everything.'

I push the reports across our milk-crate table.

Yvain picks them up. Holds them. This is his chance to rip into the data, ask anything he wants to, but he doesn't take it.

He says nothing, does nothing.

Atkins looks at me.

He says, 'Guys, there's water here if you want it.'

There's bottled water standing on the cave floor, but he's not asking about our fluid intake. The interjection was pre-arranged. He's asking me if we should arrest these guys, yes or no.

And the truth is, I just don't know.

On the one hand, we could scoop these guys up now. Arrest them both. Charge them both with conspiracy to murder. With fraud.

We could make the fraud charge stick pretty easily, but we've got nothing solid to prove conspiracy to murder and I'd hate it if our big beasts got away with a relatively minor charge.

But that's not even my biggest hesitation.

Whoever put this whole scam together had plenty of cash. For the gang to get to this point, they needed to dig two tunnels, fake some documents, and construct a fake sword. That's a heck of an investment for a return that, though potentially colossal, is also seriously high risk. Putting all that together, you'd have to guess that the guy commanding this operation must be worth a good few million.

Is that guy Mordred?

I just don't think so. He doesn't have that feel. That way he handled my search earlier: that was a man who was a security guy of some sort himself. Spy. Soldier. Special forces. Counter-terrorism. Something like that. When I put my hand to his mouth, to feel inside for concealed blades, he opened his mouth, knowing what was coming. Made space for my finger.

A security expert knows to do that kind of thing. A multi-millionaire with a penchant for audacious criminal enterprise? Well, I just don't think so.

So I say, carefully, in answer to Atkins's question, 'Not for me, I'm fine.'

No.

It's not my decision whether to make the arrests or not, but Jones and Jackson, listening in, will certainly take my views into consideration.

Yvain takes some water. Katie and Mordred leave it.

Time to finish.

I say, 'OK, you've seen the sword. You've got our data and our samples. So: payment. Twenty million dollars. How soon can you get it to us?'

Mordred stares. He's too controlled to be violent here – too conscious of Atkins's shotgun – but I've almost never encountered a gaze that has so much murder in it. So much open threat.

He says, 'You're police.'

'That's right. I'm a detective inspector. You're also correct that constructing and selling a fake Arthurian sword is standard police procedure these days. Oh yes, and look at all these people who are rushing in here to arrest you.'

There are no people, of course, but it's still impressive that Mordred's gaze doesn't flicker.

He continues his slow scrutiny of me. It's like being stripped naked by some lecherous male gaze, except that here there's nothing sexual. Not unless you count the patient consideration of extreme violence.

'It would be very interesting to know,' he says, 'who told you about our plans.'

'Yes, wouldn't it just?'

'There aren't many of us and we're very, very careful with our communications.'

I say, merrily, 'Really? You think you were careful? OK.'

He's silent a moment. Brooding.

In front of us, Caledfwlch glitters. It feels like the most real thing in here. Arthur's sword in Arthur's cave.

He says, 'Twenty million.'

Since that isn't a question and couldn't really be a request for clarification, I don't answer.

He says, 'I have a counter offer.'

'OK.'

'We walk out of here with the sword. You remove the sale listing. And I don't kill you.'

That makes me laugh out loud. Mostly, it makes me laugh because each of our camping lanterns contain concealed recorders and we couldn't really ask for a better send-me-to-jail statement than the one he just made.

But I also relish the cheek of it.

'Mordred, mate, we're the one with the shotgun, remember?'

'I will find you and I will kill you. Or you can give me the sword and delete the listing.'

I pretend to think about that a bit.

'Hmm, OK, so let me just get this straight. My option is worth – what did we say? – twenty million dollars. Your way is worth exactly no money at all. And I'm meant to be scared because – help me out here – you're going to go rushing round the countryside looking for a couple of girls in ski masks called Gwenhwyfach and Gwenhwyfar.' I think about all that a little longer and conclude, 'I think we'll go with my option. Sorry.'

Mordred doesn't say anything.

Just stares at me, at Katie, at Atkins in turn.

Katie and I are mostly concealed by our masks, of course. But they still reveal mouth and eyes. And our general builds are distinctive too. I'm small and Katie is a naturally skinny woman made skinnier by illness. Mordred stares at us. Learning us. Memorising us.

He does the same with Atkins too. I don't think Mordred has any chance of placing Atkins, but his slow scrutiny is just as absorbed, just as detailed.

Then he turns back to Katie.

Says, 'Got a problem with your hand, have you?'

'Fuck you.'

Then he reaches out. Deftly, swiftly, he hooks her mask up over her face.

I say, 'Fuck you, Mordred,' and Atkins jabs the man sharply with the butt of his gun, tipping him sideways off his stool, and forcing him to lose his grip.

For a moment, just a moment, Katie sits, revealed.

A pale queen in this cave of shadows.

A queen with a nose piercing. A spray of visible tattoos at her ear. Long dark blonde braids, previously tucked up inside the mask, but now swinging free.

I drag her mask back down. Mordred rights himself. Atkins steps back. Katie and I push back from Mordred's reaching hand.

Mordred himself says nothing. Is trying, I think, to commit Katie's image to memory. Ink it in place.

I say, in order to distract him but also because it matters, 'Mordred, mate, just so you know, you can find us and kill us. You go right ahead and do that. But just so you know, we *can't* remove the listing, because we don't have access to it. The only person who knows how to delete the listing isn't even in the country. So you know what? On the whole your option versus my option thing? I've still got to say, I prefer mine.'

We glare at each other some more. And then – then we're done.

I toss the eye masks back over the table.

'Put these on, please.'

They put them on.

'Hands behind your backs.'

They do as I ask. Yvain, nervous and compliant. Mordred with a roll of his shoulders and an extra brutishness in his jaw.

I'm very careful not to get in the way of Atkins's shotgun –

I don't want to block his freedom of action – but, crouching low, I snap the two men's wrists into handcuffs. The cuffs aren't police issue. They came straight from Amazon. And, in a further departure from police practice, I interlink their arms, so the two men are locked together.

Katie takes the sword and the felt cloth. Atkins collects up our camping lamps.

I remove both men's eye masks. Dangle the handcuff keys in front of their faces. Then toss them into the deep gloom of the second chamber.

We hear the sharp tinkle of metal on stone, then nothing.

The keys are small and the floor is a mess of loose stone. Mordred and his buddy will be able to find the keys if they look long enough, though they may need to wait till the light of dawn gives them something to see by.

We leave them to it.

Atkins exits first. Then Gwenhwyfar and Gwenhwyfach.

Queenly sisters, bearing the sword of Arthur.

44

Jackson says, 'Any intentional application of force to the person of another is an assault. The use of handcuffs amounts to assault and is unlawful unless it can be justified as reasonable, necessary and proportionate.'

I say, 'It *was* reasonable, necessary and proportionate. I thought he was a fuckwit.'

Jackson laughs. We're not really meant to cuff people's hands behind their backs, but the law bends a bit in these undercover situations and, anyway, Jackson doesn't care.

We're in a pub on the outskirts of Monmouth. Me, Katie, Atkins. Jones and Jackson here to meet us. The pub is, aside from us, mostly empty. Comfortable. Smells of spilled beer and woodsmoke and chips and vinegar.

Katie has a pint of bitter, only an inch or so drunk. Atkins has the same drink, but he's halfway down already. Jones is drinking mineral water only: letting us know he's on duty, obeying rules. Jackson obeys rules too, but his version of them has a 'beer after eight' rider attached and he is currently about a pint and a half in to the exercise of those freedoms.

Atkins puts his phone away and says, 'OK, so I've just spoken with the team.'

'Yes?'

'The two men are still in the cave, still cuffed. They don't look like getting out any time soon, but we'll get a call as soon as they're free.'

'Good.'

'We obtained entry to Mordred's vehicle. We've collected prints. DNA sample capture looks OK too.'

'Electronics?'

'No. No phones. No laptop. Nothing useful. But the boys *did* find a RAKSA iDet.'

Jackson raises his eyebrows to imply that men his age should not be expected to deal with small electronic things with stupid names.

Atkins explains. 'A radio frequency detector. Top of the range. It'll pick up phones, DECT, wifi, any type of recording device, tracking beacons, any kind of radio transmitter.'

Jackson says, 'So? You're saying we can't track the vehicle?'

'Not electronically, no.'

'Fabulous. Just fabulous.'

'We can do it the old-fashioned way.'

He means with blokes in cars. SO15 has resources and experience there which we can't match.

Jackson looks at Atkins, at Katie, at me, at Jones.

'So,' he says. 'Decision time.'

Arrest the buggers or leave the buggers?

Jones says, 'Fiona, Mike, this Mordred character. How did he strike you? Is he at the head of all this?'

I glance at Atkins, letting him go first.

He says, 'OK, I don't have all the background here, but the guy spoke like a boss. He was definitely in command. But he doesn't seem like a money man. He's a fixer. An engine room guy. That means there's someone else at the head of all this. I can't be sure, but I'd certainly bet that way.'

I agree with that and say so.

All four pairs of police eyes swivel to Katie.

She says, 'What? I'm fine.'

I say, 'Yes, you're fine *now*. But let's just say we let Mordred go. We get Atkins's boys to run a good old-fashioned surveillance operation. Multiple cars. Multiple bodies. Spy movie stuff, basically. With a bit of luck, we track the guy back to his lair. Track him to wherever he has his phone and his laptop and his landline. We listen in. We watch him. When we have everything we want, we arrest him.'

Katie shrugs. 'That sounds good. So . . .?'

'He might only need to make one phone call. *One*. He calls some Antony Wormold character on an untraceable line. He says, "Find a young, female archaeologist with a dodgy hand, a nose piercing, and some tattoos. Then kill her. Oh yes, and if you can find a small Welsh friend of hers, then please kill her too." That could be all it takes. And sure, in theory, we can just barge in and arrest Mordred, but who's on the other end of that line? We might not be able to find out. It might be too late.'

A bit sulkily, Katie says, 'He only saw my face for about two seconds. What's he going to do? Put "girl with nose piercing" into Google?'

Jackson laughs.

Jones too. He strokes his beard and says, 'Well, there's Facebook. University websites. Professional associations. LinkedIn.'

I say, 'Tattoos, nose piercing, hand-related disability. Hair colour and length. Eye colour. Height and build. Face. Approximate age. Known archaeological expertise. Probable specialism in Dark Age Britain. English accent. Quite likely Oxbridge.'

Atkins says, 'Project websites. Academic conferences. Lists of Ph.D. students and graduates. Friends' and family Facebook pages. Twitter. Instagram. Pinterest.'

I say, 'Archives, don't forget them. Things like the Wayback Machine. Sites that basically photocopy the internet, so even if you take down pages, the old versions are still out there somewhere.'

Jackson says, 'Then the old-fashioned stuff. Electoral roll. Phone directories. Utility records. All those things, they still work.'

Katie doesn't say anything exactly, but her face does a kind of *oh fuck* thing.

Exactly. Oh fuck.

For now, Mordred and Yvain are still thrashing around in that cave. But, sooner or later, they'll get themselves free and, when they do, we have a decision to make.

Jones is first to declare his hand.

'Look. We can't pansy around. We arrest the two men. Hunt down this Ivor Williams character. Find his two friends. Arrest Gheerbrant. Search properties. Seize electronics. Interrogate the hell out of everybody. That guy Gheerbrant, he's not a real pro. Stick a conspiracy to murder charge under his nose. Tell him what life is like for pretty boys like him in a Category A prison. He'll wet himself and tell us everything. Same probably goes for that guy Yvain.'

I say, 'Yes. *If* they know anything.'

'They're all in on this. It's all one conspiracy.'

'Right, but if I were Mr Moneybags, I'd think, "Mordred, yes, he knows how to handle himself under hostile police interrogation. But Gheerbrant? No. Never. So I'm not going to expose myself to him. I'll operate only via guys I can trust." Same thing with Yvain. Same thing with all the second-tier guys.'

'OK, so we just hit Mordred hard. Tell him his only way to escape from some monster sentence is a whole ton of co-operation.'

'What monster sentence? OK, in that cave, he made a threat to kill. That's ten years *maximum*. But he wasn't carrying any kind of weapon and he didn't know the identity of the person he was threatening. He'll say he was just messing around. That's probably not even a jail sentence. And, yes, we can nail him on a fraud charge, but that's still only a few years. This guy has been responsible for two deaths already, but can we prove it? To courtroom standard? I don't think so.'

I'm right, and everyone knows it.

The mood, temporarily, is angry, frustrated. This whole operation, despite everything, still has a so-near-but-yet-so-far quality to it.

Jackson suddenly grins. Sinks the last of his beer.

'Katie,' he says, 'I think Fiona's got a question she wants to ask you.'

I do, yes.

I say, 'Look, Katie, we might need a bit longer here. We'd like to take our time building our case before we make any arrests.'

'OK.'

'But you're not safe. So, with your permission, we'd like to take you into protective custody. It *won't* be for long. It *is* voluntary. It *will* make you safe.'

Katie has some questions, of course, but the basic gist is *yes, OK.*

Yes to everything.

Yes to protective custody. Yes to a long process of eliminating, or much reducing, her footprint on the web. Yes, to plainclothes detectives entering her houseshare in Cardiff and removing diaries, laptops, anything that could give any theoretical attackers useful clues to her wider life.

There are a couple of minor wrinkles, but not big ones.

She has a hospital appointment tomorrow. London, not Cardiff. She wants to attend that, if possible.

Yes, no problems.

And her parents. Can she see them while she's in protective custody? They worry about her enough as it is.

Answer: no, no way, sorry.

So we dink things around.

Katie and I will go straight from here to her parents' place. We'll get an IT guy from the Bedfordshire Police to help with the whole business of scrubbing Katie from the internet. We won't be able to get it all done overnight, but we'll make a good start. Get the rest done as fast as possible tomorrow.

I'll stay with Katie right up to the hospital appointment. After that, our protective custody types can take over. Waft her away until she's safe.

It's a good arrangement. Although Katie won't be totally secure until she's in proper custody, it's hard to see that Mordred will be able to find her in the dozen or so hours that lie ahead of us. After all, he and Yvain are both still clinking around in that cave right now – and neither of them know who the hell Katie is.

Jones says, 'Mike, before we run with this, I just need to hear from you that you're confident with the surveillance.'

Atkins: 'Look, these things are never a hundred per cent. But we've got multiple vehicles at our disposal and a helicopter. And, remember, this pair must be feeling pretty secure right now. If we were police, why didn't we arrest them? I'd guess these two will just drive home and go to bed.'

He has that Metropolitan Police we-never-screw-up tone about him which is deeply comforting, until you remember that the Met screws up just as much as anyone else and maybe more.

But we have a plan, and it's a good one.

We drink up.

Pay.

Go.

45

Katie's parents' house. A biggish place. Leaded windows, herringbone brick around a timber porch. Brass downlights. The whiff and scent of money.

We're met by Katie's mother and father, forewarned of our arrival by a call from Katie. He's in jeans, old T-shirt, bare feet. She's in pyjamas and a lilac dressing gown. It's now well past one in the morning.

A little bustle of hot drinks and (for Katie) hugs and kisses and (for me) some how-do-you-dos and we've-heard-so-muches.

There's a copper there too, Danny Ingersoll. He's manfully wearing not just a suit, but a tie, and shiny black shoes, and almost manages to look like his normal hours of work are two in the morning till God knows when.

He has a laptop all wifi-ed up.

The parents, both nice enough, get shooed upstairs to bed.

Ingersoll and Katie start working on the internet stuff.

Her Facebook page comes down first. She's not on Twitter, not on Instagram. An old, little-used LinkedIn account is also vaped.

But people, especially young, sociable and busy ones, leave a lot of traces online, and Katie is no exception.

Working together, she and Ingersoll make lists, delete accounts, email webmasters, do what they have to do. Bit by bit, Katie starts to vanish from the web.

I yawn.

Over in Symonds Yat, Mordred and Yvain have got out of their handcuffs. They're in their car heading, we guess, for London. SO15 have six cars and a traffic helicopter monitoring progress.

There's no news. The surveillance is easy.

I yawn again.

Ingersoll says, 'Sarge, remind me again why you're here.'

'I'm needed for my kungfu ninja skills. Think of me as the ultimate bodyguard.'

'Kung fu is Chinese,' Ingersoll says. 'Ninjas were Japanese.'

I stare.

He says, 'And kung fu isn't a martial art. It's any practice requiring patience, energy and discipline.'

I stare.

Katie says, 'I'll show you your bedroom.'

She does. A pale-blue room that reminds me, for no reason, of a mortuary at night. The unguarded dead. That deep, impenetrable sleep.

I brought in an overnight bag from the car, so I've got toothbrush and things.

I brush my teeth. Shower. Change.

Sit on the edge of my pale-blue bed and call Jones.

'Anything on the DNA yet?' I ask.

'No.'

'Fingerprints?'

'Fiona, it's the middle of the night.'

'The imaging. The mugshots. You're going to tell me—'

'Fiona, *yes*. We captured good quality video of both men. Mordred and Yvain. That's all been downloaded and cleaned up. First thing in the morning, we're going to start running it through the databases looking for a match.'

'OK. Sorry.'

'That's all right.'

I wonder where Jones is now. Perhaps he's in bed, next

to his wife, Elaine. I've only met her once, but she was surprisingly orange and wearing a shimmery dress that was one size too small. She seemed nice.

'Did I wake you? Sorry.'

'No, I'm in the office. Wouldn't sleep tonight anyway.'

'No.'

He asks me how we're doing at my end.

I tell him we're doing fine.

Go to the window and look out.

See a beech hedge under orange street lighting. An empty drive. One of those bits of front lawn that you have to have with a house like this.

There are no black-jacketed bad guys creeping towards the house. No gleam of moonlight on gun barrel. No half-seen glimpse of night vision gear.

I say, 'Do we think we should get a squad car? To park outside?'

'No. Why? Our boy Mordred hasn't even arrived in London.'

'OK.'

We pause.

Then I say, 'Her surname's Smith.'

'Katie Smith. I know.'

'I mean, it's a hard to search name, isn't it? There aren't that many Alden Gheerbrants in the country, are there? But Katie Smiths, there must be thousands.'

'Yes.'

A pause.

Then, 'Go to sleep, Fiona. Stick around till you can hand Katie over. If anything important happens, I'll let you know.'

'Thank you.'

I don't hang up.

Nor does he.

Then we both start speaking. But I'm a girl and I don't have a terrible beard, so I win.

I say, 'Gheerbrant.'

'Yes, I was thinking the same. We've got nothing to lose, so we may as well arrest him.'

We talk it over, but the logic is sound. We arrest Gheerbrant. Charge him with conspiracy to murder.

There's a chance that simply charging the guy will make him tell us more than he has done already. But, in any event, the arrest will add to the pressure on Mordred. And the greater that pressure, the more urgent is his need to communicate with his boss or bosses. We only need to intercept one of those calls and we have, potentially, the entire gang in our nets.

Jones says, 'I'll call Durham now. Get that moving.'

I'd like to be there, of course. Outside Gheerbrant's cottage, watching.

The dawn knock. The startled face.

And then – the squad car and the cuffs and the charge and a prison future that is endless and grey and high and empty.

If it was anyone else, I'd probably say something. As it's Jones, I don't.

He tells me again to go to bed.

I go, gunlessly, to bed.

Fall asleep and dream of nothing.

46

Wake.

Pee. Do my teeth. Do all the things that regular humans do.

Go downstairs.

It's nine o'clock. No Katie. No Ingersoll.

Katie's dad, Patrick, says, 'Sleep well? Coffee? You'll need some coffee.'

That's two questions and one untrue statement. Since I don't answer any of them, he gives me a mug of coffee. Pushes milk at me.

I add milk to the coffee, much as I would do if I were going to drink it.

He tries to make me eat something. Keeps shouting the names of different types of breakfast food, as though if he only found the right one, I'd leap up and start babbling my desire for the foodstuff in question.

It doesn't happen.

I say, untruthfully, 'I'm fine with coffee.'

Katie's mother, Romilly, comes in. She chides her husband for not having got me anything to eat, then plays the name-the-foodstuff game with me all over again.

My powers of resistance remain unbroken.

She tells me, reprovingly, that breakfast is the most important meal of the day. She cites no evidence for this assertion.

I sip my coffee, or pretend to.

Patrick wears blue jeans, brown shoes and a pale-pink shirt. Romilly wears a pale-blue jumper over a nice suede skirt. They both look like Katie, in one way. She looks, as much as most people do, like her parents' child.

But also not. The braided, pierced, tattooed warrior queen who is my friend doesn't altogether belong here, in the midst of this quiet prosperity. I can understand why she wants to live independently for as long as she can. It's not about whether she loves her parents – she does – it's about being her. Being her and staying her, to the very end.

I wave my phone. 'Sorry, do you mind?'

I call Ingersoll.

He answers on the fourth ring.

I say who I am. Also: 'Ninjas. Why wouldn't they use kung fu? I mean, you're allowed to punch somebody even if some other country invented punching.'

He tells me that, yes, the original sixteenth-century ninjas probably did use versions of kung fu. Also tells me that, no, you're not actually allowed to punch people.

'Yes, I'd heard something like that,' I say.

He tells me they got on well last night. Should be fine without her this morning. 'I'll call if I need anything. Get her to keep checking messages, but apart from that, she can just have a nice morning at home.'

I sign off.

It's stupid, but I have this feeling I should be checking the perimeter. Check locks. Door frames. Window catches.

I say to her parents, 'Katie's still asleep, is she? You haven't seen her this morning?'

Answer yes and no respectively.

Stupid feeling.

Stupid jitters.

Beech hedges and kung fu ninjas.

Because I'm feeling twitchy, I do check all ground floor

doors and windows for sign of forced entry.

Nothing. Stupid.

Nothing to see here. Move on.

I check my emails.

A few things, but just two that matter. Both from Bleddyn Jones.

The first one is headed, 'Subject: FFS!!!!'

For Fuck's Sake. And a girlishly excitable use of the exclamation mark. Not his normal style.

The body of the message forwards on an email from SO15 in London.

'Subjects temporarily lost. Subjects deployed extensive and sophisticated surveillance evasion techniques on London Underground etc. Not possible to maintain contact. Descriptions issued to all Met officers. Will update soonest.'

For.

Fuck's.

Sake.

These arsey, up-themselves Met types. They're all 'leave it to us, we're the FUCKING MET,' and what you get is a bunch of phonies who screw up the one actually important thing in all of this. If we'd known that 'we'll follow these boys no matter what' actually had the invisible rider, 'unless they happen to take a Tube train,' we would have just arrested the buggers when we had them.

For.

Fuck's.

Sake.

Jones's use of exclamation marks was, if anything, restrained.

A second email too. 'Subject: Gheerbrant.'

It tells me that a small team led by Paul McGinn went to

arrest Alden Gheerbrant on a charge of conspiracy to murder. The team arrived at six in the morning. Gheerbrant's cottage was quiet, but there was a light on in the kitchen. His car was parked directly outside.

McGinn knocked. Nicely at first, then a classic police pounding. 'We're here. You're fucked. Now open up.'

No answer.

So they forced the door. Steel ram, no messing.

And found – Gheerbrant.

The man offered no comment. No resistance. Not even a mild *oh* of surprise.

Offered nothing but a slow dangle. Noose around his neck. Ankles a few inches from the floor.

And, I say 'noose', but that isn't really technically correct. A proper hangman's noose creates a fast-slipping rope and a heavy knot nestled at the base of the neck. Combine those things with enough of a drop, and the victim isn't strangled, they have their neck broken. One quick snap and it's done.

Jones's email links to the crime scene pictures themselves. Over-exposed snaps with cruel lighting. Electric glare and jagged shadows.

And the noose isn't a proper one. It's an ordinary slip-knot, crudely tied. The sort of thing which delivers slow strangulation. A fish flapping in the unbreathable air.

Gheerbrant was a weapons guy. He knew about these things. If he'd chosen to kill himself, he'd have known the right knot.

But also, probably, he wouldn't have managed to stick a sword through his belly. Entering at the front, just below the sternum. Plunged through, all the way through, to exit at his back, in a messy spew of bone and blood and spinal fluid.

The man's rectal temperature was the same as ambient, which means he's been dead a fair while, which means he was killed *before* Mordred and Yvain left that cave. Since

Mordred certainly didn't give any orders while he was with us, that meant that he either ordered the hit beforehand or the instruction came from somebody else.

There's a whole lot of blah in Jones's email, which I can't read right now.

It's bad news and I'm not thinking straight, so I just rotate through the corpse photos. View them repetitively. Click, click, click. Round in a circle.

Romilly Smith glances over my shoulder and looks away with a sharp inbreath.

I say, 'Mrs Smith, can you just show me Katie's bedroom, please? I just want to . . . just want to . . .'

Check on her.

We go upstairs.

A white Georgian-style door in this not-exactly-Georgian house.

Open it quietly. Not wanting to wake the woman inside.

But I could open it with a fanfare of trumpets and a parade of African drummers. Those things, and acrobats and dancers and elephants, and I still wouldn't wake Katie, because she isn't there.

'Oh, that's strange,' says Romilly, who really, really, really hasn't got this thing. 'I wonder where—'

We yell through the house. The garden. Open bathroom doors without knocking.

No Katie.

Romilly and Patrick start the journey that will take them from mild perplexity to outright panic. I can't advise them that things will be all right. They're not looking very fucking all right.

I call Katie.

The call goes straight through to voicemail.

Call Jones. Get his voicemail too. Ask him to ping Katie's phone. Get a read on its local area. Then Ingersoll.

Has he, by chance, got Katie with him?

He has not.

Can he get an alert out to all officers? Very high risk, threat to welfare, MisPer. Missing person.

Yes. He's on it.

Fuck.

Think.

Call Bowen.

He answers, thank heaven.

I tell him that Katie's missing. Say, 'Look, I don't think they know anything about you, but I thought Katie was pretty much safe too. I ask if he's OK hiding out somewhere for a while.

He says, 'No, I'm sorry, but I've got parishioners who need me. And I can't help remembering that Jesus Christ didn't leave the people who needed *him*, no matter what the risk.'

I want to argue with that. Jesus Christ was founding a world religion. Bowen runs a few half-arsed parishes in a remote bit of Wales. But I don't quibble. This is his territory and maybe he's right.

'George, would you be OK carrying a gun?'

In church, no. In hospitals and private homes, no. Most other places, yes.

I like that. Like *him*. Bowen is the kind of Christian who'll visit the sick, bury the dead, christen the new-born, and marry the lovers, but who will also, if the need arises and not otherwise, blow the heads off bad guys.

'Take care, George. And use both barrels.'

I can hear his chuckle following me down the phone.

As we've been talking I've been walking round the house, double-checking doors and windows. No sign of forced entry. No hint of struggle.

But if they learned where Katie was, learned *who* she was, they might also have her phone number. Called her up.

'Excuse me, Miss Smith, you're wanted for a few things at the Kempston police station. Would you mind very much if we borrowed you? Meet you out front in five?'

I think Katie never quite believed we were right to be so paranoid.

And it's my fault. Mine.

I went to bed. I should have stayed up. *Mea culpa. Mea maxima culpa.*

But my thoughts don't linger on my failures. They turn to the what nexts.

Gheerbrant, dead.

Katie, missing.

Bowen, OK or OK for now.

I call Jones.

He is as happy and peaceable and unfrightened as I am. We exchange pleasantries about the Met. We do not swear. We do not express a wish to murder everyone in SO15. We are sunnily optimistic about resolving the entire case very soon.

And, when we're done not-swearing and not-wanting-to-murder-people, Jones says, 'Fiona, what the bloody hell is going on here? We thought we were on top of this.'

Yes. We did. *I* did.

I say, 'Well, Gheerbrant first. I think that's obvious. Mordred couldn't believe we'd just figured the whole thing out for ourselves. He assumed someone must have leaked their plan. And Gheerbrant was the obvious source. The only gang member who'd come under police interrogation, police pressure. And he was an academic not a professional crook. So Mordred decided the guy was probably guilty and, even if he wasn't, he was a weak link that might as well be eliminated.'

Jones agrees and, with that, we dismiss Gheerbrant's dangling corpse from our thoughts.

So.

Katie.

Jones tells me that they've pinged Katie's phone. It's not responding. It's either switched off, or out of battery, or some bad guy has ripped the battery out of the phone, broken the SIM card and left its parts scattered in a dustbin.

Jones says he wants me to come to Cardiff and enter protective custody myself.

I say 'maybe' to that.

Jones interprets that response as 'maybe'. In reality, it means 'no chance'.

Patrick and Romilly, Katie's parents, are hovering at the door. I tell Jones I need to go. Say I'll call him back.

The two parents are white-faced and frightened. It's *me* that's frightening them. The blackness of my own foreboding.

I ask, 'Katie. Are there medicines she needs? Is there anything she takes that would cause a crisis if she went without for twenty-four, forty-eight hours?'

The answer is scattered. A bit random. But still basically a no.

Good.

'Romilly, sorry, is there a wood near here? And do you have any chocolate?'

Katie's dad tells me where to find a wood. The mother produces a bar of Lindt chocolate, apologising in case I wanted something else.

I didn't want something else. I just wanted chocolate.

I take it. Say, 'I'll be in touch. I'll keep you posted.'

Drive off.

Down this prosperously quiet street, the big houses and electric gates. Past a village shop and a golf course.

Reach some woods.

The place is no doubt full of stockbrokers and kids on bikes at the weekend, but it's empty enough for now. I walk into its green interior till I find a part I like. Smooth columns of beech rising into a green and bird-songed canopy. Threads of sunlight dandle down and pick out jewels on the forest floor.

I sit. Open up my little box of joints. Pick out the fattest.

Light up.

Breathe.

Think.

Katie didn't recognise Yvain or Mordred, and it seems highly unlikely that her path would have crossed with Mordred's at any point.

But Yvain? Katie is a striking-looking twenty-something woman. Yvain is a somewhat plump middle-aged guy who was probably never a beauty. Maybe those two *did* meet at some academic conference, and Katie just didn't remember Yvain, whereas Yvain did remember her.

That's very possible.

Smoke.

Yvain. Who is he? Gheerbrant was their weapons guy. Yvain was clearly a historian and a scholar, but he didn't even have Katie's level of expertise in the analysis of ancient artefacts. Yet he fits in here somewhere too. He wasn't a random choice.

Smoke.

Last night. Katie and I were sleeping in the same house. We'd both make good hostages, so why take Katie and leave me?

That question is easily answered. They must have known or suspected that I was a police officer. That I'd be a lot less likely to hop into an unmarked car with a Polite Young Man. Which makes sense. If they'd found out about Katie fast enough to locate her parents' house, they'd probably have found out about me too.

Detective Sergeant Fiona Griffiths, Katie's friend.

Not good.

I smoke the joint right down to the nub and, as I stub the thing out on the sole of my shoe, realise I have a very bad feeling.

Call my father.

He starts to do his welcome-blather, but I cut him short.

'Dad, we've got a thing at work. A possible security compromise. You're OK, yes? And Mam?'

'Your mam? Yes. She's fine. She's downstairs now.' I can feel his auto-blather ready to switch on. But this is him in action-mode now, and he keeps the blather nipped short.

'And Ant? And Kay?'

'Don't know, love. I'll find out.'

'Get them home. Keep them there. If you need Uncle Em or someone to help out, then fine.'

Uncle Em: not actually an uncle, but an old friend and former colleague of Dad's. A henchman, you might say, except that the term reeks of trilby hats and comic books. In any case, Uncle Em would know how to keep things tight, keep security sharp, and administer violence if necessary. By using his name, I was, in effect, telling Dad that I cared more about keeping my sisters safe than I did about whether Dad obeyed every jot and tittle of the law.

A micro-pause is enough to register that Dad has heard my message. Then 'right you are, love,' and he's gone.

I dandle my phone.

Alden Gheerbrant, weapons guy.

Ivor Willliams, tunnel man.

This case has mostly been about swords and tunnels, but not only that. Not only that.

I light another joint.

Smoke more slowly.

Dad texts: 'Ants fine. Chasing kay xx.'

I call Mike Atkins.

'Fiona, hi.' He speaks like a tired, busy man. No sleep, I'd guess. 'Hold on. I'll take you somewhere quieter.'

A door bangs. The noise level drops.

'OK, look, we fucked up. I'm sorry. That's the first thing. Sorry.'

He starts telling me about how they're going to put things right. Pictures issued to all forces. Checks on mainline rail stations and airports. Blah blah.

I interrupt. I'm not interested. If Mordred is smart enough to shake a multi-vehicle, multi-operative surveillance, he's also smart enough not to walk into the world's most obvious police traps.

'What happened? What *exactly* happened?' I ask.

Atkins tells me that Mordred just drove into London. No evasion tactics. No strange route choices. Just drove from the cave to the M4, then east to London.

'About four in the morning, they stop off at an airport hotel near Heathrow. They have coffee. Shower. Breakfast. No rush.'

'Phone calls from the hotel?'

'No, nothing.'

'Then, let me guess, it gets to about seven o'clock . . .'

'Yes. Seven thirty . . .'

'They enter the underground system.'

'Yes.'

'They head for central London. Your officers think, "Shit, last thing we want is to be following these guys in rush hour, but at least they're not playing games." So, it's a case of so far so good, as far as you folks are concerned.'

'Yes. They go right into the centre of town. Peak of the peak as far as rush hour is concerned. We've got twelve bodies on the ground at this point . . .'

'But they've got about a million commuters on their team. They start arsing around on Tube trains. Getting on, jumping off, switching trains, all that. You guys can't use your radios, because you're below ground. Yes, you've got CCTV, but there are too many people for that stuff to be useful.'

'Exactly. They're pros, or rather Mordred is.'

'Do you mean that literally? I mean, you think Mordred has some kind of surveillance background?'

'Um. Some kind of training, yes. Police, security services or military. But if he's police or military, then he was or is in some kind of special unit. No regular copper has that kind of know-how.'

I look down.

A little beastie with fifty legs and rings of brown armour-plating is crawling up my shoe and onto my bare leg. I hold a twig in its way, so he stops crawling and waves his antennae around, trying to figure out his counter-move.

I say, 'Last confirmed sighting?'

'Kings Cross.'

'Tube or railway?'

'Tube.'

'Any idea where they might have gone from there? I know you can't be sure, but best guess.'

'Um, we had guys up on the mainline station. I thought they'd probably make a break for the first train out of town, but we didn't see anything. We've been sorting through the CCTV, haven't found anything yet. So I *think* we cut that off.'

'What were his options on the underground?'

'OK, the railway station sits on top of four Tube lines. Northern, Piccadilly, Victoria, and the Circle/Hammersmith/ Metropolitan one. I don't think they were on the Circle line. Ditto Victoria and Piccadilly. It *is* possible they got onto the Northern Line. But we'll have to check. We are checking.'

He starts telling me how fantastic their automated face recognition stuff is these days. But if you do the basics right – look down at your feet, take a jacket off, or put one on, or wear a hat, or sunglasses – then the best automated yadda-yadda in the world won't do squat.

I say, 'Above ground. Could they have just walked out into the street? Did you have operatives out there?'

'We had to scramble everyone we had just to try to keep tabs on them below ground.'

I say, 'OK. Um.'

There's a pause.

The creepy crawly thing managed to evade my stick and is now heading over my knee with every intention of going up my skirt.

I say, 'I think not, buddy,' and sweep him gently to the ground. He wriggles a bit in protest, then decides he likes Leafworld better than Thighworld and crawls off to continue his brown and armour-plated life.

'Sorry?'

'Euston station. That's close, isn't it?'

'Euston? Yes. Five minutes by foot. Not even.'

'How long before you had eyes there?'

'From when we lost them? Maybe fifteen minutes. Twenty at the outside.'

'And those eyes would have been on the ticket barriers, right?'

'Yes.'

'OK. Good. Look, Mike, can you find out for me which trains were present in the station during that fifteen minute window? Anything that left the station, or anything that was sitting at a platform waiting to depart. Just text me when you know.'

A short pause. Atkins is an inspector in the elite SO15 Counter-Terrorism command and that command is housed within the Metropolitan Police, which is obviously about thirty times better than the next best force on the planet.

And I just gave him an order.

But he doesn't object. Just says, 'Fine. Will do.'

We sign off.

I dig around with my stick looking for my armour-plated friend. Can't find him.

Light another joint, though I'm not sure if I want to smoke it.

Start smoking it.

Text from Dad. 'Kay last seen by friends getting into palegreen pasat saloon on parkplace aprox 9.40 this morning driver unknown do you have tv?'

He's a bit dyslexic, my dad, and seldom texts for that reason.

I call Jones. Tell him my sister may have been taken. Get him to start pulling CCTV for Park Place.

Jones seems very disturbed. Shocked. Also, in a good way, organised and bullet-pointy and effective.

I hear myself saying, 'The CCTV. Use Jon Breakell. He looks like an idiot, but he's brilliant with that video stuff.'

Jones wants images to circulate and I send him to Kay's Instagram page.

He says, 'Do you want to go public on this? Televised appeals and all that?'

'No.'

'And what about a . . . I mean, in normal circumstances, we'd appoint an FLO.'

FLO: Family Liaison Officer.

I say, 'If you do, you'd better appoint two. Maybe even three.'

'I'm sorry? *Three?*'

'Dad will probably kill the first one. Maybe the second one too.'

'So no FLO?'

'No.'

My dad's idea of a nightmare: losing one of his daughters.

My dad's idea of a nightmare squared: losing one of his daughters and having a police officer semi-permanently stationed in his home.

Jones says some other things, but I don't really hear them. Then he says, 'You're OK, are you? This must be a shock.'

Is it? I suppose.

I say, 'I'm fine.'

'And look, Fiona, I'm not having a go at you, but where exactly are you? Mr Smith told me you drove off. You were looking for some woods, apparently?'

'Yes,' I say. 'I'm here.'

'In a wood?'

I look around. Trees, leaves, sunlight. I don't know how big a wood has to be before it's a forest. I don't think it's one of those things where you have rules.

'A wood, yes. You know, trees and things.'

Jones's preoccupations can be perplexing at times. I ring off.

Katie didn't recognise Yvain, or didn't *think* she did. And when the two of them spoke, there was nothing to suggest familiarity.

But, but, but.

I call Matteo at the Oxford lab.

Ask him if he has any French co-workers. 'About fifty. Wears glasses. Silver hair. A bit plump.'

'No, no. One or two young guys, my age, maybe, but . . .'

I ask about his 'customers'. The people who use the lab.

Matteo's answer is a bit slower there, more cautious. The lab is one of the leading facilities in Europe and its user base is highly international.

The lab had a sign-in system, though. I ask Matteo to pull the data. Everyone who entered the lab on any day that Katie was in Oxford.

'And do it right now, please, Matteo. This is urgent.'

He tells me yes.

Hangs up.

You don't always notice these things, but the bars of

sunlight entering the canopy from above are tinted a kind of bluish silver. The air is full of pollen, or dust, or the soft hang of water vapour. From a branch, about a dozen feet from me, a spider abseils on a rope spun of her own silk.

The tensile strength of cobweb silk is comparable to that of high-grade steel.

Funny the things you know and can't remember learning.

My joint has burned out. I think I forgot to smoke it.

I relight it.

Get a text from Atkins.

Various trains out of Euston, but including one to Chester. Journey time about two hours.

Text Atkins. Ask him to get CCTV images from Chester station. Any cars leaving the car park there. Also the same thing at Bangor, if possible. Chester will be large enough that it'll be fairly well covered by security cameras. Bangor – well, you never know, but you have to try everything.

Smoke a bit more.

I think maybe summer is my favourite season. I used to think it was autumn, or maybe spring, but it could actually be summer. I've got on a bluebell-coloured skirt today. Good mood wear.

I call Aled Owen, the cathedral librarian from Bangor.

He sounds instantly scared when he knows it's me, but I'm super-nice.

Ask him if he has a list of visiting scholars, or a sign-in book, anything like that. 'That's yes or no, remember, Aled.'

'Yes. Yes, we do.'

I give him the dates I care about. Ask him to get me the names of anyone who visited around those dates.

He promises speedy compliance.

I say, 'And Bangor University. Does it have a department that specialises in old manuscripts? A codicology institute or—'

Owen, bold man, interrupts me.

He says, 'Yes. They do an MA course in Arthurian literature. And various specialisms in medieval codicology, palaeography, that kind of thing. If you want, I could—'

'Aled?'

'Yes. Sorry, I went on there, didn't I? I meant yes. Yes. That's what I meant to say. Sorry.'

'Aled?'

'Yes?'

'Aled. You are a beautiful man, and a good man, and one day I will build you a halo out of crumpets and boysenberry jam.'

He doesn't quite know what to say to that, but he promises to get me the list. I ask who heads up the codicology department at Bangor Uni and he tells me.

Delyth Rowland. Gives me her phone number too.

I tell him his halo will be big and very crumpety. He sounds puzzled, but mostly pleased.

We ring off.

My joint has gone out again, but I don't relight it.

Get down on my hands and knees and see if I can find any interesting insects.

I can't, but I do find some beech nut husks that smell of leaf mould and chalk and the tiny lives of very small things.

It's still sunny.

I should spend more time outside, really. I like it when I do, but I always forget and spend too long in the office.

I get a text from Jones, but it looks boring and I don't read it.

And then – I'm surprised it took this long – a message from Mordred.

'We have your sister and Katie Smith. Please destroy your sword and remove your sale listing. We will return the girls seven days after the sale of our sword is complete.'

Girls?

Both women are in their twenties. I don't mind using the term 'girl' myself in some contexts, but somehow it seems disrespectful to use it here.

I email back. 'You can stick your broadsword up your arse, you piss-stained cockwomble.'

Hit send.

That might or might not have been a clever thing to do, but I don't seem to regret doing it, so it's probably OK.

I call Dad.

Ask if he fancies a trip. 'To go and get Kay,' I say. 'Her and my friend, Katie.'

'You know where they are?'

'Not yet.'

I tell him he might want to come prepared.

A tiny double-take, then, 'OK, love. See you soon.'

I call Jones.

He says some things. I wait until his mouth has stopped yabbering, then say, 'Kay has been abducted. I've had confirmation from Mordred.'

Jones says stuff. I don't know what.

I say, 'Ivor Williams and his tunnel buddies. You should arrest them as soon as you find them.'

Jones talks about not escalating the situation. Prioritising the safety of the two 'young women'. He said that, 'young women', not girls.

I say, 'Fuck Mordred. Just fuck him. If he wants to put pressure on us, we'll just put pressure on him.'

Jones says more things, some of which have to do with me returning to Cardiff. Something about doing my job.

I say, 'You know that thing Jackson said? Early on. The thing about giving me my head. Some freedom of action.'

'Yes.'

'Well, I think now would be a good time. The whole freedom of action thing.'

He says OK. And, timidly, 'What exactly are you planning?'

Another one of those perplexing questions. What could he possibly think I'm planning?

Patiently, as though speaking to a six-year-old, I say, 'Free Katie. Free Kay. Arrest Yvain. Arrest Mordred. Arrest Mr Moneybags. Send those three to jail for a very long time.'

I want to ask, 'What are *you* planning?'

If he's not thinking along the same lines, then we really, really, really have some issues. But I think he's OK with all that. Maybe he was just checking. Or perhaps there's a police manual somewhere which says you have to ask three stupid questions an hour and he was running short of quota.

Anyway. He says fine. Wishes me luck.

Sometimes, under that beard and behind those bullet-points, there's quite a nice man, perhaps.

I ring off. Stand up.

I feel a bit light-headed. Too much ganja maybe.

That thing about woods and forests, I remember it now. A forest is an old royal hunting ground. It doesn't even need trees necessarily: if you had a royal hunting ground without trees, it was still a forest. But because of that whole royal thing, forests were generally big, so the way it tends to work these days is big equals forest, small equals wood.

I notice that the beech trees have very smooth trunks. Leaves spread like a cathedral roof. The light is golden blue. There are no spiders, or none that I can see. My legs feel tingly, almost pins-and-needlesy.

I walk unsteadily to my car.

Open the back door. There, on its bed of felt, is my sword. *Caledfwlch.* The hard-cleaver.

It burns in this Chiltern sunshine. It is the hardest, sharpest, strongest sword in history.

I nestle it in the front passenger seat, so I can see it as I drive. Drink some water. Start the engine. Head west.

They shouldn't have taken Katie.

And they shouldn't, shouldn't, shouldn't have taken my sister.

47

Home.

Collect my gun. Collect my dad.

He does his bear-huggy 'Fi, love' thing, but not for long. He has a small black bag with him that chinks metallically.

Uncle Em stands just inside the front door. Doesn't come out. Doesn't say more than the most cursory hellos. But he's wearing a leather jacket inside a warm house on a warm day. I think the occupants of that house have as much protection as they need.

And, in truth, I think Mordred is done with the abduction game. More hostages would add to his logistical challenges without adding particularly to his bargaining position.

We go.

Dad's car, with him driving.

'Where we going?' he asks, reasonably.

'North, I think.'

He waits to see if I'm going to say more, but it turns out I'm not.

He's seen Caledfwlch, though. Transferred it carefully to the back seat of his Range Rover.

'Nice sword,' he says.

'Yes, it is, isn't it?'

Because the Excalibur theft is still all over the newspapers, he wants to ask about it. Wants to know if this sword is the one stolen from Liddington Castle.

I don't answer that directly. Just say, 'It's Caledfwlch. "Excalibur" is only a stupid made-up name anyway.'

He says, 'Caledfwlch,' a few times. Rolls it in his mouth, gets used to the sound.

My dad, it occurs to me, is not a bad model for Arthur.

Big. Welsh. Combative. A natural leader.

And that rare thing: a man who is genuinely untroubled by violence, but who doesn't need to seek it out for its own sake. Someone for whom violence exists as an option on a list of tactics, but who will make his selection unswayed by either anger or fear.

I think my Caledfwlch might be a bit small for Dad, though. Maybe we should have made it bigger.

I sort through my messages.

One from Matteo: yes, there have been some recent French users of the lab. He sends some links. Links to university sites, Université de Genève, Université de Paris, that sort of thing. Pages that show specific academics and their research interests.

Not Yvain, none of them.

I speak to Delyth Rowland, Aled Owen's contact at the university of Bangor. Ask about visiting French codicologists.

And ker-ching!

Ask for a photo.

Ker-ching!

Yvain.

Real name, Yves de Boissieu. A researcher at the Université de Nantes, doing a guest scholar thing up at Bangor. The guy is a codicologist and palaeographer. A guy who knows about ancient manuscripts and inks and handwriting. A guy more than capable of forging a vellum palimpsest.

I get an email from Aled Owen too.

Yes, de Boissieu visited the Bangor cathedral library the day that Katie and I were there. Katie and I were together almost all the time, but not quite. I went off to see a guy about CCTV stuff. She didn't come.

That allowed time enough for de Boissieu to have seen her. And perhaps she never saw him. Or saw him and forgot him. Or just had her brain too full of motor neurone disease and Gaynor Charteris to log these things in the normal way.

Anyway. De Boissieu remembered her. And his role here makes sense. He's the missing link in our list of experts.

Ivor Williams – the tunnel guy.

Gheerbrant – the weapons guy.

De Boissieu – the manuscript guy.

Mordred and Moneybags, the two people who put the whole thing together, kept it tight.

That's the whole group right there, or all the important parts of it anyway.

I get a home address for M. Yves de Boissieu. The university is pissy about giving it out, but I do my police schtick, get them to call Cathays to check on my credentials, and it's not long before they bow before the power and might of the Warrant Card.

We're up by Merthyr now. Dad glances over to see if I know where we're going yet.

I say, 'Rhyd Ddu, in the hills above Bangor. But there's someone we've got to pick up on the way.'

'Right you are, love.'

Dad drives a silver Range Rover, the car Arthur would have chosen.

It hums as it drives, transfiguring the tarmac beneath its wheels into something finer, silvered, noble.

A wash of rain. Sunlight on a hill. Our slow-paced Welsh roads.

I get an email from Mordred. Slower than I was expecting, but the guy hasn't had much sleep.

He tells me to delete the listing for my sword, 'Or we will have to start getting nasty with the girls.'

That word again.

Pisshead.

I suspend the listing. Tell him I've done so.

'Saxon fucker,' I say, out loud.

Dad looks at me sideways.

I say, 'Well, he is.'

Brecon.

Builth.

Rhayader.

I say, 'I don't like Rhayader.'

'Why not? It's all right.' Dad starts telling me about a friend of his who has a pub there.

Get a text from Mike Atkins. 'Possible sighting of Mordred/ Yvain on Chester CCTV. Chasing up. Looks good.'

I don't reply.

Llangurig.

Llanidloes.

We drove up this way once, all together. Me, Dad, Kay.

Kay had some idea she wanted to climb Cader Idris. Part of some distinctly temporary outdoorsy phase. Mam stayed at home with Ant, who must have been eight or nine at the time. And we had a nice day of it. Even the most ordinary day out with Dad always had the glitter of adventure. That sense of never quite knowing what might happen next.

We climbed the mountain. Got tired. Got lost in cloud and rain as we descended, and ended up in the wrong valley. We begged help from a local farmer, who put the three of us in the back of his pick-up together with a sick ewe and a bail of hay and drove us round to wherever we'd left the car.

Kay had been frightened by the whole thing and fell asleep against me as we drove home, her wet hair steaming itself dry on my shoulder.

I think of that now. Her hair gently steaming.

They should not have taken my sister. That's not forgivable and I don't forgive it.

I feel Gaynor Charteris's stony weight too. She is disapproving. Angry and impatient. We feel a grim unity of purpose, she and I.

Llanbrynmair.

Glantwymyn.

Aberangell.

As we pass Aberangell, I point to the hillsides ahead and to our left.

Sheep-bitten fields. Stone farmhouses. Clumps of oak and ash. Barns of corrugated iron, whitened to the colour of limestone by sun and rain and frost.

I say, 'That's Camlann.'

'Camlann, love?'

'Arthur's last battle. He died here, or at least picked the wounds that would end up killing him. The thing about him being carried to Avalon is probably just myth.'

Dad doesn't say anything for a moment.

Just studies the passing green, blues and browns of the land that is ours, the land that was Arthur's. The Range Rover hums. Carrying us forward to battle.

Dad says, 'He didn't die, love. Not really.'

Glances across at me in a but-you-know-that kind of way.

We stop at Cwm Cywarch. Pick up Bowen.

Dad gets out of the car, gives Bowen one of those big male handshakes, the sort of thing that would pretty much crush my hand if I was on the receiving end.

Bowen is wearing a tweed jacket over a black shirt and dog collar. He asks, 'Should I bring the gun?'

I nod. 'May as well.'

The gun in question, a shotgun, isn't one of those gun-porn things, all polished walnut and silver filigree. It's a farmer's

357

piece, with muck on the barrel and a faded canvas cartridge pouch that's tearing at the seams. Bowen shoves it in the car the way you'd stow a pair of dirty boots.

He's more respectful of Caledfwlch, though. Gives it its own space. A regal distance.

Bowen's dog, Tidy, is lying out in the yard, panting in the sun.

Bowen says, 'Jan's away today and I'm meant to be looking after this one,' meaning the dog. 'Are you all right if he comes along?'

Dad says yes. He loves dogs and Tidy joins the gun and cartridge bag in the back.

That is, or should be, the signal for us all to go, but Dad is busy watching sheep graze in the fields below.

'Those yours?'

Bowen says yes.

'Nice flock. Beulahs, is it?'

'Mostly Beulahs, yes. Jan's trying some Llanwenogs there. See those white faces at the back? They're good lambers and the wool's better than we've been used to.'

And then – for two, three minutes Dad and Bowen are talking about sheep as though nothing else mattered in the world.

At first, I think, *Dad, your daughter's in the hands of some fucking fuckwit who's already ordered the deaths of three people. Do you really want to be talking about some fucking sheep?*

Then I realise, I'm wrong. What I'm seeing now is leadership. The real deal. Dad's never met Bowen before. Knows nothing of him. Yet by the time these two men climb in the car, they'll feel like friends. Bowen will already have that little speck of loyalty to Dad, which, if their relationship were allowed to mature, would end up growing into some unshiftable ballast of affection. The same dense blocks which provided Dad's main protection through all his years of high-level criminality.

They get into the car now, talking of dogs not sheep. Training Tidy. The amount dogs understand.

Dolgellau.

Llyn Trawsfynydd.

Garreg.

Beddgelert.

Once Bowen tried asking about Kay.

But Dad just shakes his head and shifts the subject. I'm pleased he does. Her abduction is too big a weight to think about directly. It's there all the time, a load leaning direct against the heart.

I think that's true of Katie too, it's just that Kay sits that bit closer. It's hard separating the two of them.

I wonder again about Gaynor Charteris's funeral. Whatever happened with that? It feels strange to have missed it.

As we get close to Rhyd Ddu, Dad arrests the chatter and, swivelling, asks, 'How we doing, love?'

'Fine. We're doing fine.'

Mordred knew Yvain was a weak link. Neither brave enough nor skilled enough to evade police surveillance. So he brought him back. From Symonds Yat to Kings Cross. Shook any surveillance by messing about on the trains and in the tunnels. Then danced down the road to Euston. Train to Chester. Either change there for Bangor, or get out and do the last bit by road.

Mordred would have told Yvain to go home, speak to no one, sleep.

Perhaps, in the fullness of time, Mordred will kill Yvain too. But for now, Yvain looks like the only actual professional scholar they've got, and they've still got a sword to sell. They're not done and dusted yet.

We get to Rhyd Ddu, then navigate into the hills above.

A couple of sharp ascents. A wash of loose stone and gravel, relic of some gurgling field drain. The banks and hedges a scramble of cow parsley, foxglove and late-blooming violets.

A cattle grid. A hard left onto a farm road. Crushed grey rock with a central strip of thwarted grass.

The road takes us down to a damp hollow, dense with marsh grass and bog cotton. We see a rock, the size of a bullock, and a rowan tree, mountain ash, growing up the side.

Also a cottage. Whitewashed. Small.

A rental property. Its current tenant: a palaeographer and codicologist from Nantes University.

A red Peugeot sits outside.

No lights, or none that we can see.

Dad parks on a grassy verge a couple of hundred yards from the house.

We get out. Tidy wants to come too, but is told to stay where he is. He makes sad-eyes at us, but stays.

I take pick-locks and my handgun. Bowen carries a shotgun. Dad takes a handgun from his bag, pockets it, gives his bag to Bowen, and picks up Caledfwlch.

'You can't have a sword like this and not use it,' he announces.

He marches ahead, blade aloft.

A peregrine falcon hangs in the air and Dad turns to watch, shielding his eyes from the sun.

'Magnificent,' he says. 'Just look at that. Smashing.'

When Arthur went into battle he had the image of the Virgin Mary emblazoned on his shoulders or possibly – the words are similar in Welsh – his shield. I can't quite see Dad taking the Blessed Virgin with him into a fight, but I do find myself wondering if he doesn't have some more-than-human confidence at times like these. Some faith, however nameless, in a higher power. A light that will fall always on him.

Bowen walks with me, but something like reluctance blooms inside.

360

Before we get to the door, he says, 'Fiona, I'm happy to wait here.'

'I need you inside.'

'This isn't a police arrest, is it? And your Dad . . .'

'My Dad is – or was – involved in organised crime. He's used violence often enough in the past. And de Boissieu is part of a gang that has stolen his daughter.'

'Look, I understand why you're here, and here like this, but if anything happens in there that I think is wrong, I will have to stop it. I am a Christian and I am a vicar, Fiona. Those things first and last and always.'

I say I know that.

'That's fifty per cent of the reason I need you. If Dad goes mental, I need someone to stop him. He'd never hit or hurt a vicar. It's one of the old-fashioned things about him. He's Violence, but you're Conscience. Today, I need you both.'

Bowen grins.

'What are you, then? Brains, I suppose.'

I toss my head in a fetching manner. 'I'm Youth and Beauty. I'd have thought that was obvious.'

We walk on.

'You said fifty per cent. What's the other fifty?'

But we're at the door now and his question evaporates in this mountain air.

I have my pick-locks ready, but round these parts people don't always lock doors and when I try the latch, it opens quietly.

The door opens straight into a farmhouse kitchen. Slate floor. Two-oven range cooker. Pine table. The place mostly has the equipment and level of furnishing you'd expect from a rental place, except this one has a Krups coffee machine that looks glossily expensive and which, I expect, travelled here from Nantes.

Dad throws open a door. A living room, with broad views

down the valley. Old sofa in ochre linen. An armchair. Books.

I say, 'He'll probably be asleep. He didn't sleep last night.'

I say, sort of assuming that my words will be interpreted as, 'Let's go upstairs and seize our quarry while he is asleep and undefended.'

That's not, however, how my dad chooses to hear them.

He says, 'Oh, so we've got some time then. George, I'm gasping. Do you fancy a coffee? Imagine! A machine like that in a place like this! Things change, don't they? I remember when . . .'

He starts to tell Bowen random anecdotes from his rough Tiger Bay past.

Starts making coffee.

I doubt if he's ever used a coffee machine before. It's not that he doesn't drink it, just somehow his life works out that other people bring him drinks. But he bashes merrily around. Opening drawers, pressing buttons, figuring things out. 'What's this – a frother, eh? My goodness, the things they think of. George, there's milk in the fridge is there? Cups. What's this? Maybe I need to tamp it down. Like that, what do you think? That's better. Yes, there we go.'

He makes coffee. Three cups.

Bowen finds milk. A jug. Brings it over.

From up above: footsteps.

Bowen and I exchange glances. Check our weapons.

I say, 'Absolutely no shooting, OK? In self-defence, yes, but only if we absolutely have to.'

Bowen is singing loud from the same hymn sheet, but there's no reaction from Dad.

'Dad?'

'Oh yes, love, don't worry about all that.'

His gun is still in his pocket. Caledfwlch on the table. His hands are busy with jugs and milk foamers.

Footsteps on the stairs.

Then a door opens.

M. Yves de Boissieu. Yvain. Mordred's buddy.

Two guns point at his chest as he makes his entrance, but he isn't armed. He is wearing pyjamas, the old-fashioned sort. Blue-striped, with a collar, and buttons, and red piping. Those things and a grey dressing gown, loosely tied.

'Yves, isn't it?' yells my dad. 'I'm Tom. Tom Griffiths. I was just making coffee. Do you want some? Never worked one of these things before, but I already want one.'

De Boissieu's eyes are startled and afraid.

He's also confused. He doesn't know whether to trust the message of the guns, or the message of the coffee. He doesn't know why Caledfwlch is on the table. Doesn't know how I found my way to his house or what lies in store.

It's more than possible – probable, in fact – that he doesn't know about the abduction of Kay or Katie. If I were Mordred, I'd keep things like that need-to-know only.

'Have a seat there. No, no, there, that one. Make yourself comfortable. I mean, this is your house, isn't it? We woke you. Least we can do is look after you.'

Dad directs de Boissieu to a wooden armchair, then gestures at Bowen to pass his bag. Burrows around for some cable ties.

'Good things these are. We never used to use 'em. Used to use string and bits of rope mostly. Then they brought out those tapes, gaffer tapes and that, but probably we could have used these cable things all along. Just popped into an electrical place. Bought a few dozen. Easy. Never thought of it, though. People didn't back then.'

Dad ties de Boissieu to the chair. Wrists. Ankles. Elbows.

He doesn't worry too much about keeping de Boissieu comfortable.

Nor do I.

'There. That's a tidy job, eh? Isn't it? I should be a sparky, shouldn't I? Go and get my City and Guilds certificate.'

He froths some milk.

Gives coffee to Bowen. To me. One for him.

To de Boissieu, he says, 'Do you want some? We can hold the cup for you.'

De Boissieu's eyes say no.

The cable ties have more or less solved the guns vs. coffee dilemma. Tipped the balance in favour of the former.

It isn't true, I think, that fear has a smell, but it does, certainly, have an atmosphere. Something sour and hunkered down and coloured at the edges with sweat and piss.

'That's a proper good cup of coffee, isn't it, Fi, love?'

I say, because I know what he's thinking, 'It's Mam's birthday soon. We could go halves.'

'Yes, go halves. Done! How much is a thing like that, Yves? Expensive, I bet.'

At first de Boissieu doesn't answer. He can't believe that Dad actually wants to know. But that's an error. Dad genuinely does. Persists till he gets the answer.

Three hundred and fifty euros. Dad wants an answer in sterling. De Boissieu translates, roughly, into sterling.

'Now look, Yves, you've been really helpful, but you know who this is?'

He points at me.

'No.'

'Well, you're not really thinking there, are you? I'm Tom Griffiths, I told you that. And this here is Fiona, my daughter. You heard me calling her Fi. So Fi – Fiona, you're probably capable of working that out aren't you? Fiona Griffiths. My daughter. Also a police officer. A rising star in the South Wales force. That's right, dear, isn't it? I can say that, can't I?'

My nod tells him he can.

He looks at de Boissieu, whose fear is rising now, if possible. He is hardly the most professional of criminals, but he knows the police don't operate with cable ties and coffee machines. He doesn't know what all this is. I'm not totally sure that I do.

'So, Tom Griffiths. My daughter, Fiona. And this is – well, he's a man of the cloth, you can see that, can't you? Never go anywhere without a vicar, I say. Never know when you might need one. Now, Yves, maybe you can tell me the name of your friend Mordred. His real name, obviously.'

'I don't know. I'm sorry. He always called himself Mordred.'

'I'm not going to like that answer. You know that.'

De Boissieu, however, is obviously telling the truth. We ask the same question three different ways, but get the same answer every time.

There's a pause in the room. An empty space.

De Boissieu's anxiety is at fever pitch.

Dad keeps walking in and out of his range of vision. Sometimes fingering Caledfwlch. Sometimes drinking coffee. Sometimes standing behind de Boissieu and rocking his chair, drumming on the back, playing with it.

I say to de Boissieu, 'Your weapons specialist. What was his name, please?'

'Weapons? Our guy. Uther. We call him Uther.'

Uther, for Uther Pendragon. Arthur's father.

I say, 'That's not clever, Yves. I'd like you to give me his real name.'

While I never actually expected de Boissieu to know Mordred's true identity, de Boissieu and Gheerbrant were fellow academics, both farming different parts of the same historical field. I just don't believe they didn't know each other, didn't have some kind of connection outside this conspiracy.

De Boissieu instantly corrects his answer. 'He is Alden Gheerbrant. He works in Durham. On Dark Age weapons and this, he is very good. Best in his subject.'

He says that last word the French way, *sujet*. I like that. Like that little loss of control.

I say, 'No.'

'No?'

'*Was* very good. *Was* the best in his subject.'

I show him the crime scene photos.

Gheerbrant a-dangle in his own living room.

Gheerbrant pierced by his own sword.

Blood and stomach contents leaking at the front. Blood and spinal fluid leaking at the back.

'Do you know who did this?'

'No. No, really. This thing, is terrible.'

'You don't know who did this?'

'No, no. I tell you this. I would never . . . I don't know.'

'You *do* know, though, don't you? I mean, you can easily guess.'

De Boissieu licks his lips. He wants water. His mouth looks and sounds painfully dry.

He says, 'It is Mordred, I suppose. Him or . . .'

'He gave the order, didn't he? Someone else executed the instruction, but Mordred gave the order.'

'Yes. I think.'

'That's why you came to the cave, not Gheerbrant. You weren't the right guy. He was. But Mordred took it into his head that Gheerbrant had said too much under police interrogation and this was the result.'

De Boissieu's lips move.

This, normally, is where people would be touching their faces. Self-comforting. Little strokes of reassurance.

Bound as he is, the man can't do that.

I study him.

The trick to most confessions is flipping the suspect. At the outset, they are most worried about releasing secrets to a police officer. So knotted with worry, indeed, that they can sometimes hardly speak. Barely even ask for water.

You can bash away at those silences, but you won't get anywhere until the suspect comes to believe that co-operating is his least-worst option. That, shitty though a prison future might be, worse things are possible.

I say, 'Gheerbrant is the third one of your colleagues to die. You know that?'

He nods.

'What do you think Mordred intends for you?'

'No, no. I don't think . . . I don't think . . .'

'You think Mordred is a nice guy? That's what you think?'

His dry lips and chapped silence tell me no. That's not what he thinks.

'Mordred will wait till he's got his money, then he'll kill anyone he thinks could betray him. That will include you. Gaynor Charteris was decapitated. John Oakeshott was stabbed and thrown into a canal. Alden Gheerbrant was hanged and stabbed. What do you think he'll choose for you? What method?'

De Boissieur's answer isn't verbal, but the ammoniac smell of urine and a darkening stain at his crotch tells me our message is getting through.

'How does Mordred get in touch with you? Phone? Email? What?'

By phone is the answer. De Boissieu's language is more broken now and he has difficulty explaining the term 'pay-as-you-go'. But his answer is as I expected. I ask where I can find his phones. His regular smartphone and his cheapie pay-as-you-go one.

He tells me. The smartphone is by his bed. The other one is under a floorboard in the spare bedroom. It's not something we couldn't have found, but it *is* something we mightn't have found fast.

We poke around the house a bit. No sign of Kay or

Katie, but Mordred would have been nuts to keep them here.

I come down with the phones. Get up call logs. The smartphone log is full of calls to France, to Switzerland, to Bangor, to Oxford. To all the sorts of places you'd expect a guy like de Boissieu to be phoning.

The other one has made only one call recently and received two. The counterparty was the same in each case.

I hold the screen where de Boissieu can see it.

'This number. It's Mordred, yes?'

'Yes.'

'Good. Now this call, the one you made, what was that about?'

I get him to tell me the basic contents of each call. Where it was made and when. Not because I need to know, but because I want to be sure he's not just saying what I want to hear.

When I'm happy, I call Jones.

Give him Mordred's number and say, 'I need you to ping it, please.'

There's a short, Jonesian hesitation at that.

Yes, we can force mobile phone companies to 'ping' a specific handset and thereby obtain knowledge of the phone's approximate location. And, yes, we can do that without specific authorisation from a judge. That said, only a handful of officers in South Wales are empowered to make the request and that means there's normally a whole lot of paperworky blah involved before the Wise and the Great are satisfied. Jones knows all that but, bless the man, he's beginning to get the hang of working with me.

He says, 'This is important, is it, Fiona?'

'Yes, sir. I'm convinced it's critical to the rescue of our two abductees.'

'And, I expect, this would be a highly time-critical issue, wouldn't it?'

He's prompting my answer, in effect, telling me what I'm meant to say.

I already know, of course – I have a Black Belt and Higher Diploma in the Art and Science of Paperwork Evasion – but I respond happily. Give him all the 'highly criticals' and 'serious risk to lifes' that he needs.

Jones says, OK, he'll get on to it.

I say, 'And the whole triangulation thing, please. I don't just want the mast location.'

'Fine.'

We ring off.

Triangulation: phones will, in most locations, be able to 'talk' to more than one phone mast and the phone company can measure the strength of the signal at each mast. By comparing signal strengths and triangulating directions, we can get a pretty good sense of where the handset actually lies. The data doesn't usually yield a specific house location, but it gives us the broad area, to within two or three hundred metres.

That's not enough. In all likelihood, that's not enough.

I say to de Boissieu.

'I am a police officer. When we are finished here, I will call my colleagues and you will be arrested on a charge of conspiracy to murder. That charge carries a potential life sentence.'

He starts to babble. Says he never wanted anyone to die.

I tell him to shut up.

He doesn't hear or can't. In any case, he continues to babble.

Dad, without even appearing to move all that much, slaps the man so hard it's almost like a physical detonation. De Boissieu's head jerks so violently, I'm briefly worried that he could have dislocated something.

I have never in my life seen a harder blow.

There is, I think, a fast-dying echo. Then nothing. A moment of stillness. Bowen, de Boissieu and I try to re reorient ourselves in this altered world.

And into that little pond of silence, Dad says, at no more than conversational tone, 'Yves, if my daughter asks you to shut up, you shut up. If she asks you a yes/no question, you answer with a yes or a no. That's clear, isn't it, Yves? I mean, you've got a lot of book learning. You can understand a simple thing like that, can't you?'

He says yes, or croaks it.

I glance at Bowen, whose gaze holds steady. He won't let things go further, I think, but he's not too fussed about a single slap.

I continue, 'Now, a judge has considerable discretion over sentencing, and prosecutors have considerable discretion about what charge they choose to bring. So if you're smart, you'll do everything you can to co-operate, starting now. Do you understand?'

'Yes.'

And I start.

A debrief. If we were doing this police-style, we'd need to arrest the guy, charge him, let the bastard get a lawyer, brief the lawyer, then faddle around with the niceties of a recorded interrogation.

Ordinarily, that's the right and only way to do it. But now isn't ordinary. We need speed and we need results. If that calls for guns, cable ties and the waft of fear, then so be it.

And the fact is that, though de Boissieu thinks he knows nothing, he knows more than he realises. People always do.

Car: the first time he met Mordred he's fairly sure the guy was driving a silver Mercedes. 'The key. He have the key with the Mercedes symbol.'

Clothes: almost always smart. Suit and tie. Polished shoes.

370

That night in the cave was the first time he'd seen Mordred dressed down.

Glasses: never.

Arthur and archaeology: does Mordred actually know anything about these things, or is he just a crook setting up a scam? Answer, yes, definitely, Mordred knows plenty about the *sujet*. 'He is not a professional, I don't think. But one time, he have a letter published in a journal. He was very happy about this.'

'Which journal?'

'I don't know. So sorry.'

'What was the letter about? What subject?'

'Don't know.'

'The date?'

We have to fuss around there, but get a date in spring 2015, March or April approximately.

I look at Bowen.

'George, this is your field. Early medieval journals that will print letters from amateurs. What are we looking at?'

'Gosh, well . . .' He starts to name journals. *The Journal of Dark Age History. Medievalia. The Journal of the Royal Historical Society.* A couple of others.

I say to de Boissieu. 'You have access, yes? You can access those journals from your computer here?'

'Yes.'

He gives us the login bits that we need.

Bowen gets to work. Sits at the computer. Starts printing letters and articles.

Jones calls.

'We've tried to ping the phone, but it's dead. I'm pulling the full call history now. I'll send you everything as soon as I have it.'

'Thanks.'

There's a pause. I'm not sure who started it.

'There's no problem, is there, Fiona? Everything OK your end?'

I look at de Boissieu.

He stinks of piss and there's a bit of chafing at his wrists, but he's fine. You can't even see the slap much, though it may yet bruise, I suppose.

I say, 'No problems. Making good progress.'

Ring off.

I go on interrogating de Boissieu. Don't get much more, but do get something.

Money.

I ask if he had the impression that Mordred was wealthy.

'Oh yes. Certainly. Always a nice watch, nice wine. And when he pay for a meal, it is platinum card.'

I try to understand what level of wealthy might be involved. Twenty pound bottles of wine? Or hundred pound bottles? Answer, certainly more like twenty, but it's hard to be sure how much to read into that.

One other detail too. When de Boissieu first met Mordred, the guy had short hair – 'this military style, you know, like some American soldier.' He was extremely tanned, and fit-looking, but a couple of bad burn marks on his hand and forearm.

I don't know what all that amounts to but I don't think de Boissieu has much more to give.

We cut him free. I've only got those horrible rigid cuffs with me and the rigid ones won't let me cuff him to a radiator or anything like that. So we take him out to his car, still in his pyjamas, put his hands through the steering wheel and cuff them there.

I tell him he's under arrest. That he will be collected by uniformed officers and taken to a police station, where he will be charged.

'Also, Yves, any minor injuries you may have sustained were

received while resisting arrest. You know that, don't you?'

He says yes, but I make him repeat it, the long version, 'Yes, I resisted arrest. These injuries – but they are nothing, really – happen then.'

'And you were arrested by me only. There was no one else present in the house.'

He blinks at that, but catches my father's eye, and agrees hurriedly.

I make him say it.

He says it.

Bowen has finished his print-outs: a thick wodge of paper. Letters and article by amateur historians appearing in the relevant journals on or around the relevant dates.

I get a text from Jones: 'Home location of phone is Hathersage, Derbyshire. Full data follows by email.'

He's a good officer, damn the man.

I tell him where to pick up de Boissieu. And we leave for Hathersage.

48

The Peak District.

A place of hills, yes, but the term is a misnomer all the same. The valleys are steep and deep, but the tops themselves are high, flat moorland. It's as though an ordinarily hilly part of the world was sawn off horizontally, leaving a black, boggy plateau, a-sigh with moorgrass and red grouse, and, marking the line of the cut, a belt of dark, seeping gritstone. Low cliffs of brutal presence.

On the way here, Bowen and Dad sat up front. Talked about I don't know what.

I sat in the back.

Looked at the data coming through from Jones. A mass of it, phone data primarily.

Riffled through the pages of Bowen's print-outs. Letters from historians – professionals mostly, but some amateurs too – on the kinds of subject that interest those people. *Boom and Bust in the Early Medieval Grain Trade. Reinterpretations of Romano–Celtic Pottery. The Early Development of British Pattern Welding: Some Questions.*

The names don't mean much to me.

Carlos Herrera.

F. E. Smythe.

Dr Cornelia Rickards and Prof. Mary Bennett.

Dr Julius Kneale.

A whole list of others.

One of these names, I think, should match *something* in Jones's Hathersage data. According to de Boissieu, who was not lying, Mordred got a letter published in one of those medieval history journals. Was thrilled about it. At that stage, he hadn't committed any crime. Hadn't faked a sword, hadn't killed Gaynor Charteris.

So why conceal your name?

And yet none of the names in Bowen's print-outs match anything in Jones's data.

Homeowners.

Electoral roll.

Utility companies.

Nothing.

It makes no sense.

Even with Dad's driving, as impatient as mine, the trip across country takes two and a half hours. I have this continual sense there are four of us in the car. So strong that sense, that I keep counting. Dad, Bowen, me. No one else.

But still that other is present. Insistent.

Who is the fourth who walks always beside you? When I count, there are only we three together.

It's Kay, of course. My sister, Kay.

She who was never a part of this. Who should not have been drawn in. Who is in danger now because of me, and no one else.

I think of her in that metallic dress, dark blue and moody gold. A young woman all prepared for a night's hunting, but also a child who wanted to curl up between me and Mam.

I think of Katie too, of course, but it's like she's standing somewhere behind Kay. I can't see or feel things properly for Katie, until Kay is safe. Where my feelings for Katie should be, there's only a kind of numbness. A blanked-out horror.

I think Gaynor Charteris is there too, in that numbness. She and Oakeshott. Even the villain, Gheerbrant.

375

We get to Hathersage.

Dad stops the car on Main Road and says, 'All right, love.'

I say, 'Um.'

Say, 'He's here, somewhere, but . . . um . . .'

Luckily, Dad knows me well enough. He pops out. Buys a couple of pasties, one for him, one for Bowen. For me, an orange and a bar of chocolate.

I say, 'Oh, chocolate.'

I look at it.

'Can we go somewhere . . . um . . .'

Dad drives out of town. Finds a bit of moorland. A line of cliffs.

Dad stares at me.

He's been super-calm, right from the very first here. Anything that's needed doing, he's done it fast and well, but he's had this glassily unconcerned calm, even with his daughter missing.

And I realise: *he's doing this for me.* Throwing a canopy of parental calm over me, so I can figure out how to do this thing. I realise that Dad is as intensely worried as I am. But he knows that I'm his best route to getting Kay back, so he's just giving me what I need.

He trusts me. Trusts me to do this thing.

I say, 'Dad, maybe you and George could go for a walk. I need . . .'

Dad checks my face another moment, then 'Right you are, love. Good idea. We'll get some air.'

Bowen opens the back door. Tidy bounds out with a yelp of delight.

Two anxious men and one happy dog walk off and away.

I watch them go. Rearrange things. Make a papery nest for myself across the rear seats. Print-outs. Data. iPad. Sit cross-legged in the middle of it all.

Light a joint. Eat chocolate. Smoke.

What do I know about Mordred? What do I know or reasonably believe?

Ex-military, or something like that. It's not just the buzz-cut hair, that look of physical fitness. It's things like that iDet scanner. The extreme care with communications. Those things are too specialist for a regular soldier, but a soldier-turned-security-pro? If I had to guess, I'd say he was an Iraq veteran who shifted over, like so many of those guys did, into private security work. Blackwater. DynCorp. Control Risks. Modern mercenaries.

I think, *Maybe our guy is a former employee of one of those firms.*

Then think, *Why former? Maybe he's working for them right now. Perhaps this whole Caledfwlch thing is just a little personal project on the side.*

That feels more like it. Mordred is a young guy. Not retirement age or anything like it. And this whole Caledfwlch adventure has been, to put it mildly, a high-risk game. It's a side gamble. Something you do while drawing a regular salary.

Holborn.

Alden Gheerbrant made those calls to Holborn. I couldn't find any archaeologists there, but perhaps I was looking for the wrong thing.

My stupid joint has gone out.

No.

Correction.

Someone seems to have smoked it.

I eat the orange.

The money thing. The Mercedes, the platinum card, the twenty pound bottles of wine. Those things sound like the lifestyle of some successful private security type. The kind who earns, what?, a hundred, a hundred and fifty thousand pounds? Nice money, but not bankroll-this-operation money.

Burn marks.

De Boissieu mentioned burn marks.

Stupid.

Me, stupid.

I call Jones.

Is De Boissieu now in custody?

Answer: yes, he's been taken down to Cardiff. Is currently being processed. Charged with conspiracy to murder.

Can I speak with him?

Yes.

Some messing around. Finding the right person in the custody suite. Getting de Boissieu brought to the phone.

He starts talking, fast. Tells me that he said what I told him to say. Says that he will co-operate 'to the maximum, don't worry'.

I tell him that I'm not fucking worried. I tell him to shut the fuck up. And I ask about those burn marks.

'Ah yes, burning, definitely.'

'Burn or scald? Was it an actual burn, or maybe just boiling liquid?'

'Oh, like coffee, maybe? No, not this.'

'And the marks. Were they defined? Did they have a clear shape or were the edges messy?'

'Yes, quite clear, I think.'

I ask to speak to his custody officer. Tell that person, a Hywel Someoneorother, to get some make-up.

'Make-up?' he says, 'Like, what, lipstick?'

'Yes, like lipstick. Eyeliner. That kind of stuff. Get the prisoner to draw out on your arm, what exactly those burns looked like. Yes? This is really urgent. Do it now. Yes? Like right now. When you're done, I want a picture, OK?'

Ring off.

Are Kay and Katie being kept together?

Yes, I'd guess so. Simpler that way. And that's good. Katie's courage will be good for Kay, and vice versa. These things, anyway, are always easier in company.

I wonder about violence. Possible rape.

I don't doubt that Mordred has violence in him. A dark lava, a buried crimson. But he's also professional. A man looking to make his fortune.

I think Kay and Katie are more useful whole and unharmed.

I *think*.

I'm not always right.

I check Agora.

I've already suspended the listing for my sword, but Mordred's listing is still there.

The 'bids received' icon has always read '0' before, but I notice with a shock that it reports three bids now.

Fuck.

If real bidders are putting in real bids, then the clock is ticking for Katie and Kay. There's no chance, I think, that Mordred will simply release them when he's done.

The listing shows 'reserve price not met', which is good. The auction is still marked as open-ended, which means no firm end-date has been set.

There's still time. The wheel's still in spin.

Think.

Get nothing.

Then: a text from Cardiff. A picture of some custody officer's hairy arm, adorned with lipstick and eyeshadow.

Burn marks.

Not the flared and bubbling red of a scald.

Not the patchy, ragged-edged burn of fire or flame.

But distinct marks. Almost linear. Marks as if something very hot had touched the arm.

A metal plate. A metal edge.

Stupid, stupid, stupid.

How many times, how often can I be blind to the same thing?

F.E. Smythe. The guy who wrote a letter to *Medievalia* on the topic of early Celtic pattern welding.

Smythe equals smith.

FE: the atomic code for iron.

An ironsmith who knows about pattern welding. The Dark Age technology that produced the first high-quality swords.

Stupid.

I call the editor of *Medievalia*. Do my police officer thing. Ask if he has an address for Smythe. Answer, after a bit of farting around, yes.

Brocéliande, Hathersage.

'That's a house name, is it?'

'I suppose so. It's all we've got.'

There is no house called Brocéliande in Hathersage.

But progress sometimes comes in baffling forms and here, I think, things are beginning to fall into shape.

Mordred was covering his tracks from the very outset. Before the death of Gaynor Charteris and even when in communication with the editor of an obscure history journal. It's details like that which make me increasingly confident the guy is some kind of security professional. A man whose habit of life is concealment.

I call Jones.

'Sir, I'd like the names of top-end security firms in Holborn. And I do mean top end. The kind of outfits who can provide bodyguards in Baghdad or hostage negotiators in Caracas. Our guy works for one of them.'

Jones says he'll get onto it.

Brocéliande.

A broad path curves down from the low hills above. Dad and Bowen descending. Dad swinging his arms, telling a story. Bowen laughing, responding.

Laughter over darkness.

And Kay and Katie gone.

Tidy still bounds, as though he's not had so much as a minute's exercise.

The men and the dog reach the car.

Dad opens the door. A clean, damp air blows through my smoked-and-orange-peeled fug.

I say, 'George, Brocéliande. What's that?'

His eyes take a moment to catch up with the unexpected question. Then, 'It's an enchanted forest. In Brittany, France. It has various Arthurian connotations, but the main one has to do with Merlin.'

'Go on.'

'The story goes that Merlin was trapped there, inside an oak tree. Some sources say he died there. But one version of the myth has it that he's still alive. Trapped in the tree. Unable ever to leave.'

Brocéliande.

A forest, an oak tree, a grave, a trap.

Here's the other fifty per cent now. Yes, I wanted Bowen as a restraint on my father. But I wanted him also for his knowledge of all things Arthur. I didn't know *how* it would help, or *if* it would help – but I knew I couldn't be without it.

F. E. Smythe.

An ironsmith. A maker of swords. A man with burn marks on his forearm.

I call Jones.

Say, 'A timber merchant in south Wales delivered a large quantity of hardwood to an address in Hathersage. Not building timber, nothing like that. Just firewood. All native species. All locally grown.'

Jones says, 'You want the delivery address, right?'

Yes.

He says he'll get on to it. Also: 'Leaman Brown. That's the security company. Works all over the world, but it mostly

381

operates in high-risk environments. Based in Holborn.'

'Thank you.'

'Do you want me to go and kick the door down?'

I'm not sure. I don't know.

Jones, however, is decisive. 'Too risky, I'd say. You don't know whether the place is clean and your boy Mordred is dirty, or whether the whole place stinks. Either way, we can't risk alerting the target.'

He's right and I say so.

Ring off.

Look at a map of Hathersage on Google Earth. The village isn't in a particularly wooded spot, but out towards the northeast, there are some patches of more significant woodland. Some larger houses, the type that have outbuildings.

Everyone is looking at me, I notice. Dad, George . . . and Kay. I feel her too. Feel her especially. My tall, beautiful, impatient sister. She and Katie, that warrior queen.

And my corpses, of course. The bruised stump of Charteris's bloody neck. Oakeshott's face-down gurgle, his leaking ribs. Gheerbrant's slow swing.

In that jostle of gazes, I find it hard to pick out the two men, the living ones. They seem dimmer, somehow.

'You all right, love?'

Dad's voice.

I say, 'Is George there?'

Bowen says, 'Here, Fiona. I'm right here.'

I point at the map. Say, 'This area around here. By the river.'

'Yes?'

'They need leaflets. Church things. They need some high quality vicaring.'

I explain what I want.

Bowen says something. His lips move, anyway.

Dad says, 'Okie-doke,' and climbs into the car. Someone says something. We drive down the hill.

Brocéliande.

A forest, an oak tree, a grave, a trap.

49

A text. From Jones.

'Supplier traced. No delivery address given, just "meet customer at the church". We're locating the driver now.'

Multiple precautions, layer upon layer.

But his defences are crumbling faster that Mordred can build them. Like those eroding coasts, those streets and houses that tumble, slowly but unstoppably, into the sea.

Dad and I sit in the car.

Bowen, with a bunch of random leaflets nicked from the church, is working his way door to door. Ringing bells. Telling people about some village something-or-other. Tidy trots by his side, his training immaculate.

The houses we're interested in are larger, set back from the road, with outbuildings. Preferably with a fringe of woodland at the back. But Bowen can't be seen to pick and choose, so he goes to every door. Rings every bell.

We watch.

I have binoculars with me, but don't use them.

Have a joint, but leave it unsmoked.

Dad says, 'What are you going to do when we find the place? Bring in the stormtroopers?'

Stormtroopers: he means SO15.

Men in body armour. Sniper rifles. Stun grenades.

Training, practice, readiness. More firepower, more experience, more everything than our little team could supply.

But also, exactly, exactly, exactly, the thing that Mordred would anticipate. If he's planned for this – and if I'm right about Mordred, then he's planned for everything – he'll have figured out how to handle that final, black-jacketed assault.

Maybe he'll just shoot himself. That's one type of ending. A good, clear, military one. But it's not the only option and I'm not sure Mordred is just the kill-himself-and-be-done type.

I ask my corpses, those chattering bones.

They agree. Shake their bones, their stumps, their tattered bodies, and agree.

Dad and I watch Bowen at a farm gate. The gate is locked, but a track runs up beyond it. There's some kind of signage, a brass plate or something like it, on the gatepost, but I can't see more. Bowen tucks a leaflet into a letterbox, moves on to the other side of the street. Does a couple more houses, coming back towards the village proper.

Lifts his phone. It looks like he's answering a call, but he's not. He's calling me.

'It's that farm there.'

I ask how he knows, how he can be sure.

Bowen says, 'Oh, the gate looks ordinary enough. Ordinary name, Derwent Farm. But the nameplate has a little illustration. Trees by a river or lake. Perfectly appropriate for a farm with a bit of water frontage. Thing is, though, it's taken from Aubrey Beardsley.'

'What?'

Bowen explains. 'Aubrey Beardsley. A late-nineteenth-century illustrator. Died young, but his first big commission was a series of illustrations for *Le Morte d'Arthur*. The death of Arthur. This farm has an Arthur reference right there on its gatepost. I think we've found our man.'

I say good. Tell Bowen to keep it up with the leaflets.

Make some arrangements with Jones. With Dad.

He says, 'Are you sure, love?'

I'm not sure, no. How could I be? All you can do with a thing like this is bet on the probabilities. Hope the wheel spins your way.

Kay taken.

Katie taken.

Dad opens the door for me.

I get out.

Tuck a gun into my waistband, which isn't particularly comfortable but makes me feel all gunned-up and cowboyish.

Take Caledfwlch. In this evening light, it shines gold and red and a fiery silver.

Dad kisses me.

Hugs me. One of those crushing hugs, that will, one day, break all my ribs, collapse my lungs and send me, bubbling feebly, to the nearest Accident and Emergency unit.

I give him an 'it's going to be fine' grin, though we both know that I can't know and that it might not turn out fine at all.

I go to the gate.

Climb carefully over and head down the track towards the farm.

Brocéliande.

A forest, an oak tree, a grave, a trap.

50

The farm track, dry and dusty in this evening sun.

Meadow saxifrage and some kind of trefoil. A few random poppies. A thick hedge to my left. On the right, a field, mown for hay. Beyond that, fields. A fair-sized wood. A scramble of wild plants marking, I guess, the line of the River Derwent.

Saxifrage has little white flowers, like a child's drawing, but threaded with green. I pick some. Tuck them behind my ears.

Put the sword down as I do all that. It's quite heavy and I think maybe I'm a bit tired.

Walk on.

The farm comes into view.

A handsome stone farmhouse. As many farm buildings as you'd expect. Barns for hay, for overwintering sheep. Stores. Tractor sheds. Whatever a medium-sized farm in Derbyshire needs.

A forge too, I'll bet. A home-made amateur thing. The place where Mordred acquired those burns. Iron hot from the forge. Straight-edged marks. Fiercely red.

Did he make his damn sword himself? Maybe. Probably. I'm guessing yes.

I walk up to the door.

The knocker is a woman's brass head in a tangle of leaves. I slam it down. Hard. Two or three times.

First, nothing. Then a little loudspeaker by the door says,

'Lay the sword down. Put your gun on the ground. Raise your hands. Do not move.'

I say, 'Oh, for fuck's sake.'

I don't put the sword down. Don't drop the gun. Don't raise my hands.

The loudspeaker wonders whether to get into an argument with me, but I've got a gun and I've got Caledfwlch, so the stupid bit of tin can fuck right off.

Across the yard behind me, footsteps.

I turn.

It's Mordred, of course, with a very business-like machine pistol pointed straight at me. The gun is a nasty piece of kit. A pocket-sized machine gun, in effect.

I say, 'You don't make yourself easy to find, Mordred, old son. You are not at all easy to do business with.'

He says that thing again. About putting guns down and stuff.

He's wearing a mike that's connected to the loudspeaker, so I hear the same thing from two different sources.

I put my sword down. The gun too.

Hold my hands up and apart.

Mordred moves my weapons, then frisks me.

I'm still wearing my very nice bluebell-coloured skirt. A blue and white striped top. A perfectly good fashion choice when I woke up this morning, but less good now that I've got Mordred's hand between my legs.

Oh well.

It moves away. The search is business-like not pervy.

I say, Happy now?'

'Yes.'

'So this is where you say, "Do you want a cup of tea?"'

Mordred says, 'Do you want a cup of tea?'

'Yes, please. That would be lovely.'

Mordred opens the front door. He has a gun in each

388

hand, and we can't exactly leave Caledfwlch lying on the ground, so I say, 'I'm going to pick up Caledfwlch now,' and do so.

Walk through the door, under the stare of those gun barrels.

Stone-flagged hall. Handsome staircase in dark wood. On the left, a door into a kitchen. More stone flags. An off-white, vaguely classical kitchen. Dim brass fittings. A range cooker. No sign of kids. No wife.

'Family place this, is it?' I say.

He stares at me. Something evil glitters in the stare. Then, 'Yes. It was my father's. I rent the land out now. The barns and everything. But I kept the house. I couldn't part with that.'

This doesn't look like a Derbyshire farmer's kitchen, though. Its ancestry is more Kensington and Chelsea, than Peak District. More *World of Interiors* than *Farming Monthly*.

I put the sword on the table. Take the saxifrage from behind my ear.

'Do you have a vase for these? They look nice, but they keep falling out.'

He finds me a vase.

I arrange the flowers. He makes me peppermint tea, using a tea bag from my bag. I think he wants something stronger, something alcoholic, but he fights the impulse and restricts himself to ordinary tea.

We sit at a table that probably wants to be thought of as a rustic oak table, but just looks like the kind of very expensive designer piece that no actual countryman would ever have.

We look at the saxifrage.

I say, 'Those flowers are bisexual, did you know that? They've got male parts and female parts. Look.' I show him.

He looks, but doesn't comment.

Caledfwlch lies between us, but he tweaks it over towards his side. Possessively.

I tweak it back again. Say, 'Twenty million dollars. That was the deal.'

Mordred laughs.

He says, 'You're police.'

'Oh, for fuck's sake. *Yes.* I'm Detective Sergeant Fiona Griffiths. As you know because you abducted my sister and my friend, Katie Smith. If you knew enough to take them, you certainly know what I do for a living.'

The kitchen has broad Georgian windows looking out over a small garden, a field, and a curve of silver water.

'Look, Mordred, you work in the international security field, if that's the right term for it. Leaman Brown, anyway. So presumably you know quite a lot about police forces. Things like, "Do police raids usually commence with lone saxifrage-wearing females arriving at your front door, or do they usually commence with a few truckloads of armed officers waving assault rifles?" I'm going to go out on a limb here and say that the saxifrage option is relatively unusual.'

He laughs again.

A laugh of release, even. He asks me to stand and face the wall, hands up and out.

I do as he asks and allow him to search me properly. He was working one-handed the first time and still worrying that I might attempt some judo move against him, or some stunt like that.

He's feeling more secure now, and searches me two-handed this time, looking for concealed microphones as much as weapons. My skirt comes with a matching fabric tie that joins in a bow at the front. The belt itself is thin enough and flexible enough that it can be easily searched, but Mordred's fingers keep returning to the knot of the bow, trying to figure out if there's some complicated bit of electronics in there.

I undo the bow. Pull the belt off. Let him feel it, every inch. His fingers decide that the fabric thing is just a belt. He scans me with his RF scanner, the same raksa iDet that he had in the car.

The iDet agrees with me that my belt is just a belt. That my bra is just a bra.

He tells me I can sit again, and I do. He gets himself a can of beer.

'How did you find me?'

'I went to see de Boissieu in Rhyd ddu, and put electrodes on his balls until he told us where you live.'

'He doesn't know where I live.'

'I used really big electrodes.'

Mordred laughs. Waits to see if I'm going to tell him more. Isn't fussed when I don't.

He does note, however, that I have the name and address of 'Yvain'. And Mordred's own address and place of work. I'm already far further ahead than he had imagined possible.

He says, 'And you have or you have not passed your information on to your colleagues in the police?'

'What do you think? I mean, what the fuck do you think?'

I gesture out at his empty courtyard.

I let him gaze at the non-hordes of non-police officers, and say, 'The police service pays me thirty grand a year and I hate my job. This whole Gaynor Charteris thing – well, I figured out that if *you* could play this game, then I could play it too. And maybe not have to work in the police service any more.'

'OK.'

'And I met Katie. She had the expertise I needed. And, I don't know if you know this yet, but she has motor neurone disease. She's dying. She doesn't really have much to lose and when I put the idea to her, she just said, fuck it, let's do it.'

'OK.'

'And my Dad.'

Mordred nods. 'Tom Griffiths. Yes. I looked him up. He has previous.'

I say, because I know Dad would want me to, 'Allegedly. He was never convicted.'

'So that's your team? You. Katie Smith. Your Dad.'

'And one of Dad's IT guys offshore. I don't understand any of that stuff.'

I need to give Mordred the idea that there's someone else, someone unreachable, because otherwise Mordred would probably figure he just needs to kill me, kill Katie, kill Kay, kill my dad, and he's golden.

Mordred drinks his beer. Stones. That's the brand.

He says, 'You've presumably got some idea about how you see all this working.'

'The way it works is this. I give you my sword. You give me twenty million dollars *and* Kay *and* Katie. Then we all fuck off out of here. You sell your crappy fake Excalibur to some Chinese zillionaire. And we all live happily ever after.'

'Or I kill you *and* the hostages *and* keep the sword *and* not pay you twenty million dollars. Remind me what's wrong with that option.'

I nod.

Say, 'Do you have a phone I can use?'

He's watchful, but nods. Pushes a phone over the table to me.

I say, 'I'm calling my dad.' Show him the number as I dial. Say, 'OK?' before I connect the call, then do so on his nod.

He's OK with me using the phone, but his hand is on his machine pistol now. He shifts position a little so he can keep an eye both on me and the courtyard outside.

I move slowly. No sudden moves. Put the phone on speaker.

One ring. Two rings. The ringtone too false and bright for the moment.

Dad answers in his normal yelling way.

'Hello. Tom Griffiths here. That's you love, is it? You must be with Alexander, then. Or, help me out here, Alex. I don't know if you use Alex or Alexander. Mr Devine, even.'

Mordred's face moves. Says Alex is fine.

As soon as we knew Mordred's location, it wouldn't have taken Jones too long to get a name to go with it. Dad's welcome blather is just a way to make sure that Mordred – Devine – knows that we know every last thing about him now.

Name. Address. Place of work. Occupation. Everything.

Dad continues, 'Now, look here, Alex. Fi told me you'd be calling. I expect you want to know what we've got planned.'

Devine nods. His eyes are very watchful. Adds, quietly, 'Yes, go on.'

'OK, Alex, so you've got until six o'clock in the morning. At that point, I need the girls safe and the money. I don't understand all this bitcoin business, we didn't have that in my day, but if Fi tells me things are OK, then I'll be happy. But if I don't have everything by six o'clock, then I tell the police who you are, where you are, who you work for, everything like that. Fiona's already asked – what's the name of that outfit, Fiona?'

'SO15.'

'SO15, that's right. She's told that lot to assemble in Sheffield and await instructions. So they're – what? – about twenty minutes away, I suppose. And obviously, I'll have to tell them why you're the one they want. So I'll need to tell them about how you are responsible for the deaths of that archaeologist lady and those others too. We'll also explain how your Excalibur is a total and utter fraud. And we won't just tell the police, we'll put it out there on the internet and pass the information on to every Tom, Dick and Harry out there. And before you say, "Tom Griffiths, you bugger, you don't know the first thing about the internet," I should tell you that we're working with a fellow who knows all about that type of thing. I'm sorry, I'm rambling now, but you get the picture. I'm sure you do.'

Devine does. Asks one or two questions, then rings off.

He's perplexed. Troubled by all this.

Give the man a standard assault to deal with, and he'd know exactly where he stood. How to combat it. But the problem we've given him is wholly unexpected. Difficult to solve. Truth is, I think his easiest solution will be to give us some version of what we want. A version, I'd guess, that involves a lot less money than the twenty million I've demanded.

He finishes his beer and I get him another. Go wandering round his kitchen, opening cupboards, looking for chocolate.

Don't find chocolate. Do find biscuits.

I take the biscuits and start eating.

Devine, curtly, 'We aren't paying you twenty million.'

'Then you have a problem, Mordred, old son. Do you really not have chocolate in the house, or do you just have to hide it to stop yourself eating it?'

Curtly: 'I don't have chocolate. Look, stay here, I need to make a call.'

He goes outside.

I take a biscuit and start exploring the house.

I'm not looking for Kay or Katie.

Devine is far too careful to have hostages in his own home. If I had arrived here as part of a police raid, he'd have opened the door in bewilderment, welcomed us in, and swept his arm around inviting inspection. That's why the SO15 kick-the-door-down route wouldn't work here. He'd just deny all knowledge of the hostages. Challenge us to find them. On the other things – the conspiracy to murder charge, the fraud – he'd just take his chances in court. At the moment, our case is still more circumstantial than solid.

I go into the living room.

Wide oak floorboards. A large and handsome fireplace. Two wide, luxurious sofas facing off over a coffee table. It's all nice, but hotelly.

And no dog. A place like this should have a dog.

A long side-table carries a line of photos. Parents, mostly. Getting married. Here on the farm. On a beach somewhere, a British one. Devine and his father at a clay pigeon shoot. Devine in uniform. Grinning at the camera in a sandy sunshine. Iraq, I presume.

No brothers and sisters, to judge from these pics. And, I notice, the mother seems to have disappeared by the time Devine is twelve or thirteen. Divorced, possibly, but something in the line of these photos, the way Devine referred to the farm as 'my father's', makes me think that an early death is more likely.

An orphan.

A boy who fired shotguns, shoulder to shoulder with his father.

A serviceman, who saw violent action in Iraq.

Who tumbled into the lucrative and only dimly legal world of high-end security work thereafter.

And who – somewhere, for some reason – developed an interest in Arthur. An interest, an obsession, I don't know. But along with the photos, there's a book open on a stand. I was slow to notice the thing – more interested in the photos – but it's Malory's *Le Morte d'Arthur*, illustrations by Aubrey Beardsley, a first edition, dating to 1893. I've no idea if the thing is valuable or not, but it's arranged there along with the family photos.

Mum. Dad. Me. Arthur.

I hear Devine coming through the front door. He finds me in the living room.

I say, Well?'

'We can pay you one million.'

'The price is twenty.'

'That's too much.'

He moves towards me. A muscle in his jaw tightens and

loosens repetitively. There is something darkly savage in his eyes.

I am suddenly very frightened. My whole strategy tonight relies on Devine making coolly rational decisions in a highly-charged situation.

I move so there's a sofa between me and him. He sees the move. Sees my anxiety. And he changes posture a little.

The savagery is still there but the rationality returns.

'Five million. We can give you five million tonight. And the girls. But that's it. You either accept that offer, or I kill you. That's what's . . . that's what's been agreed.'

He makes a kind of half gesture out to the yard. To the phone call he made there.

I don't say yes straightaway.

Just watch Devine's face.

Lying is hard work. Literally. It uses more mental resources than simply telling the truth and my whole strange saxifrage-wearing and biscuit-eating strategy is, in part, designed to mop up those spare resources. Make it harder for him to deceive me.

And I think he's probably telling the truth here, or near enough. You never absolutely know, though, and Devine's whole experience and training has equipped him for high-intensity situations.

But in the end, I have only one option.

I put my hand out.

'It's a deal.'

We shake.

We agree how this is going to work. He'll take me to the hostages. Transfer the requisite number of bitcoins to my account. Release us all.

The way he's looking at this, we can't betray each other. He can't come and kill me afterwards, because I'll release an 'in the event of my death' statement to the police, to the media, to everyone.

And I can't betray Devine, because (a) why would I? I've got my hostages and my cash. And (b) he can always demonstrate that I accepted five million dollars from him in illicit cash, which would put me into prison right alongside him.

A thieves' compact.

It's late now. Gone ten o'clock. The day's been warm, even close. A damp heaviness in the air.

Mordred gestures out beyond the window.

'OK. Let's get them. They're not far.'

I ask to borrow a jacket. Any actual jacket he's got is way too big, but he finds me a fleece. It's still far too big, but I roll up the sleeves and wear it like a mini-dress, with my skirt poking out at the bottom.

It looks nice, actually. Almost cool.

Devine is in cargo pants and T-shirt. He reads a text on his phone and laughs quietly to himself. He slings his gun from a belt-loop and, ever cautious, takes Caledfwlch too. If any police do burst in here, he doesn't want them to find a Dark Age sword on his kitchen table.

We go outside.

It's dark now. Still not absolutely dark, though, because we're only a few days past the solstice. A paling lingers in the west, where the sun mourns its own departure.

Devine's four-by-four. A farm vehicle. Dirty, not glossy.

As we walk over to it, I point upwards. Say, 'Arthur saw that. The sky at solstice. Looked up and felt the same way we do.'

Devine doesn't answer. Tells me to get in the car.

I do so. Watch him stride the yard under this dying, yellow light. He makes one last call, glancing at me.

I leave my door open.

Why is Devine on his phone now, of all times? And why does he look at me like that?

Those questions might have any number of answers, but it occurs to me that one of them is very ugly indeed.

I've no idea what is happening out there on the phone, but without moving my hands too much, I slip off my belt. That same fabric tie whose bow so bothered Devine earlier.

Slip it off. Run one end through my hand. Through the sweat on the inside of my elbow. The dirt on my sandaled feet.

Devine finishes with his call. Comes over to the car. He gets in. Closes his door.

As he does so, I drop my belt into the footwell, with its now sweaty, dirty trailing end hanging out on the ground. I close my door over the belt. Grin an 'OK' at Devine.

He lets in the clutch and we set off.

Mordred and Gwenhwfach journeying to Brocéliande.

51

Farm track and field. Pothole and stone.

We drive around for maybe twenty minutes. Sometimes on proper public roads. Mostly on farm tracks or just bumping along the edge of some field. Except on the roads, we have our lights off completely.

I seriously doubt if the place we're going to is as far as he's making it seem. I think he just wants to make sure I'm disoriented. Also to verify that no one's following.

They're not.

In the back of the car, Caledfwlch jolts and bounces. It feels like the only real thing right now. The only dependable thing.

The car stops.

We open our doors.

Air blows through trees.

Something feels wrong. Askew.

The air, I think. There's going to be a storm. It's been building the whole day. There was something in that dying, yellowy light that spoke of something seeking release.

Devine comes round to my side and puts his hand on my arm.

Get your fucking hand off me, you bastard.

I don't say that, but I do think it. Or not think, even. Just an instinctive flick of rage.

I get out.

Devine has left Caledfwlch in the car, but his machine

pistol is in his weapon hand now. A nasty piece of kit, that. An assassin's piece.

My belt has fallen to the ground below my feet. Devine doesn't notice it. I hardly do.

The night is close to fully dark now. There's a whisper of light from the car dashboard, a little glow from the eastern sky, where the lights of Sheffield burn.

Trees.

We're on a field margin running alongside an area of woodland. How far it extends, I don't know, but the whisper of air through leaves is all around. A smell of green. Of exhaling earth.

Somewhere still distant, I hear the first growl of thunder. Lightning flickers over gritstone. Sparks on a giant anvil.

I feel a little lurch of panic. The bite of a fear-rat at my stomach wall.

Devine is busy with some night vision gear. Not just binoculars, but a headset. The sort that leaves you with your hands free.

He never releases his grip on his gun, but adjusts his headset one-and-a-half handed.

For a short while, he scans the forest in front of us, the field behind. He's watching for anyone following. Anyone at all.

There's no one.

No threat. No SO15. No highly armed guys with hi-tech weaponry and nightscopes.

I was utterly explicit with Jones about that. I said, 'The hostages will be hidden from view. This guy has top-level skills in concealment and evasion, acquired in the military and honed in the private sector. If you bring in an assault team too early, you will lose the hostages. Do you understand that? You will lose them and you will lose me.'

That theory was sound, but I'm getting uneasy about the possible implications.

Why does Devine even need a gun? If we're here to release hostages, he doesn't need a gun.

He finishes his surveillance, then just says, 'Let's go.'

We walk along the field margin to a place where the hedge thins to almost nothing.

'In here.'

He flicks his gun at me. A gesture of command. That snub little barrel narrowing to a single black O.

I say, 'Brocéliande? It's in there?'

'Yes.'

'The hostages are there?'

'Of course.'

Very quietly I say, 'You're not letting us go, are you?'

'No.'

That doesn't make any sense. If – when – Dad releases his information to the world, then Devine's world collapses in an instant.

It doesn't make any sense, unless . . .

'You've sold the sword?'

'Yes.'

'That text. The one you read just before we left your house.'

'Correct. That was the confirmation coming through.'

'How much?'

He hesitates briefly, but shrugs away the doubt. 'Seventy-eight million dollars. It's an exceptional piece.'

I'm shocked. It just hadn't occurred to me that things could move that fast. Perhaps they had pre-identified buyers. I guess they must have done.

'Tests on the sword. Wouldn't all that take longer?'

He grins, teeth fierce in the darkness. 'The buyer has conducted *some* tests, yes. But your friends and colleagues in the police pretty much did the authentication for us.'

As they always planned. As they always intended.

I even helped them, that's the truth. By whipping up

enthusiasm online, by spreading the word inside the police force, I helped bring about Jones's 'THEFT OF EXCALIBUR' press release. It wasn't even an error on my part, whipping up that enthusiasm. Their version of laying a trail involved multiple murder. I had to let them know that their clues were being correctly read and interpreted or other people might have died along the way.

I want to understand more, but Devine's pistol flicks again, more impatiently this time.

I do as I'm told.

We enter the wood, ducking under and through some low branches. Hedge maple, I think.

I can't see any path. I don't think there is one. But Devine – whose night vision stuff enables him to see where I can't – just grabs my top and steers me.

I stumble forwards. Invisible sticks and briars tangle with me as I move, and my bare calves feel their snatch. Devine isn't particularly rough with me, but he's not gentle either.

He's about a million times stronger than I am.

He can see where I can't.

He has a ton of combat experience.

And he's armed.

I count through my various options for escape. I come up with nothing at all – but I also keep bumping up against the whole damn reason I'm here alone in the first place. Devine has his hostages somewhere where we can't find them. Even if I somehow managed to escape right now, we mightn't be much closer to rescuing the two people we most need to find.

I think I'm walking to my death.

The thunder is closer now. The lightning. Blue fire between trees.

As we get further into the wood, the undergrowth thickens. Devine is wearing boots and tough utility trousers. He just marches through whatever there is without caring. Me, I have bare legs, and Devine just shoves me through whatever obstruction lies in front of me. Once or twice I fall, hoping that Devine will lean down to pick me up. Will allow his attention to flicker away from his pistol.

No such luck. When I fall, he steps backwards not forwards. Tells me, curtly, to get up.

His tone says – and I believe it – that if I fool around too much, he'll just put a bullet in my head and carry my corpse to Brocéliande, wherever and whatever it is.

I stop fooling around.

After maybe five minutes, we reach a huge oak tree. Massive. The sort of thing that three or four of me standing in a circle couldn't link arms around.

I stand at its base, looking up. Crooked arms outlined against this flickering sky.

Devine has the pistol trained on me, but he doesn't say anything. Doesn't move.

I say, 'Brocéliande. We're here.'

He nods.

I stare at the trunk of the oak, but it looks solid, impenetrable. Devine laughs.

Moves away from the trunk. Pulls out a torch. Searches the ground till he finds what he wants. Then takes something like a long metal key from a pocket.

Torchlight. This oak tree. The flicker of lightning.

Somewhere, far off, a dog barks once and is swiftly silent. We both stare out at the night, but any invisible policemen remain strictly invisible, more's the pity.

And then – he pulls up a drain cover. It's one of those covers that gives you space to lay your own chosen insert on top. Paving slabs, or whatever else. Devine has packed his cover with earth from the forest floor. Laid twigs and leaves and whatever else over it, so even though I was at one point almost standing on the thing, I didn't see it. Wouldn't have seen it, even in broad daylight.

I don't honestly know if a shoulder-to-shoulder police search of this woodland would have found this place. I'm guessing not.

Devine lays the cover aside, leaving me to stare down the hole in this dark earth.

The gun flicks at me and at the hole.

When I peer in, Devine's torch reveals a metal ladder stretching down.

'There used to be a quarry here,' Devine says. 'Just stone for the farm, nothing commercial. Then Dad decided to cover it over. No reason, really, just we weren't using it any more. We thought it would be fun to make a cave though. We had an old Dutch barn that wanted demolishing so we broke it up. Used the steels to make joists. A bit of sheeting over the top. Filled everything in. That was years back now. No one even knows the place is here. These days, I'm the only person in the whole world who knows about it.'

I set my foot on the ladder. Top rung only. Bum on the earth. Lightning slowly fading from the sky. The first fat plop of rain that I note vaguely, but don't really feel.

I feel limp and failed and useless.

I say, 'Mordred? Your sword. Can I see it, please? See it properly, before you . . . before . . .'

Before you kill me and Kay and Katie and fuck off to Costa Del Somewhere with your money.

Devine says, 'Yes,' but his tone is impatient.

The hole. The darkness. This summer storm.

I put my hands to the ladder and climb slowly down.

52

An iron ladder. A rocky floor.

But a tiny space only. A rough wooden wall blocks my way. A heavily padlocked door, low enough that even I'll have to crouch to go through it.

Devine follows me down.

This is a krav maga moment, of course.

A narrow space. Hard walls. The opportunity for a surprise attack.

But—

Devine.

The gun.

My own limp state.

I've no more got the spring and force needed to attack my captor, than I have the ability to jump to the moon or overfly the stars.

I sit.

Devine unlocks the door, eyes on me more than the padlock. Gun steady in his right hand, even as his left fumbles with the key.

Padlock off.

The door isn't properly hung and needs a kick.

Devine moves to do so, but first I ask, 'Do you ever feel sorry for people? In combat or, I don't know, things like this.'

'Combat? No.'

That's a half answer if ever I heard one.

'And now?'

Devine says, 'I'll make it gentle. This isn't personal. None of this is personal.'

I think, it probably felt quite personal to Gaynor Charteris. Personal enough to Oakeshott and Gheerbrant too.

And all of a sudden, their presences blossom here in this little rocky chamber. Gheerbrant and Oakeshott certainly, but mostly Gaynor Charteris.

The tattered stump of her neck. The bloodily tutting head that she carries in her lap, squidging red into her sensible tweed skirt.

I feel a rush of affection. Love, even. Companionship. A happy-sad, sweet-sour moment that I could live in for ever.

'Thank you,' I say. 'Thank you.'

I don't know if I'm thanking Devine for his promise or Charteris for her comfortable, tweedy presence.

Both probably. I think both.

I stand up – too fast – bumping my head stupidly on the low ceiling, but not minding. Devine boots the door hard. It staggers open. Devine's gun pushes me through.

A quarry. Rough stone. Damp earth.

Water pooling in the uneven bottom.

Dead grass and sticks and other reminders that this place was once open to the air.

A darkly seeping ledge with food, water and other supplies. In several places, the dark shine of oak roots, sinuous and dark. This is Brocéliande after all. A prison hidden in the bowels of an oak tree.

There's light too. Enough to see by. The blue glow of an LED camping lamp sitting on a ledge of stone.

And Kay.

And Katie.

Both in one piece. Not hurt, not bruised. Frightened women with frightened eyes.

They're both wearing jeans, with blankets in a military grey pulled over their shoulders.

They're chained. Kay's left wrist secured to Katie's right via a chain that passes through a heavy iron ring bolted to the rock.

That puzzles me briefly – why chain them when they're already captive? Then realise he didn't want them jumping him as he came through the door.

Their immobility is unhelpful, but hey-diddle-diddle. We can't have everything we want.

I say, 'Hi, Kay. Hi, Katie.'

Then bite Devine as hard as I can in his gun-carrying arm.

53

Biting.

That sounds a bit girly, of course. Scratching, biting, pulling hair. Playground stunts that only girls ever pull. Girls with tears and bunches and grubby knees.

But there's playground biting and real biting.

My fighting instructor, Lev, once told me that the human jaw can exert as much as a hundred kilos of force. I slightly doubt that my own pearly whites can inflict that much pressure, but they're still handy. The trick – another of Lev's much-reiterated nuggets – is to bite with the molars not the incisors. You get double or quadruple the amount of force, and the victim's area of muscle damage is that much greater.

'Take the biggest bite you can. Bite hard. And don't stop. The more your man struggles, the more hurt you do.'

Wise advice.

I bite into Devine's bicep. Feel the gush and taste of blood. He yanks the arm away, or tries to, but Lev is right. The movement actually helps me get a better grip. Provokes more tearing, more injury.

But it's not about the bicep. It's about the gun. The battle for the weapon.

When I launched into my bite, I grabbed for his gun-holding hand.

In that first, sweet second of shock, I felt his hand loosen. I thought, for one lovely moment, that I could wrestle the gun off him.

But no such luck. The guy is easily twice as strong as me, maybe more. Even with my two hands grappling with one of his, I can't pull the thing away.

But, in the fight, the trigger gets squeezed. I'm not sure who did it or quite how it happened, but there was a short burst of fire.

A burst, not a shot.

So I yank hard on Devine's own trigger finger and the gun fires again. A burst of bullets.

A spray.

A scatter.

A steel rain.

Then nothing. An empty gun. A hammer closing on emptiness. The sound of uselessness.

We're left with a smell of cordite, or whatever cartridges use these days. The smell of explosive and an echo that lasts forever.

We were pointing away from Kay and Katie through the tussle, but the chamber here is small enough and rocky. I don't know what damage could be done by ricochets alone.

I want to look, but don't get the chance. With his free hand, Devine hits me.

He hits me in the head, so hard that the world goes black for a moment. I see stars. Stagger back.

Devine, panting hard, drops his pistol and looks black violence at me. Dabs at his damaged arm, inspecting the damage.

'That thing I told you?' he says. 'About making it gentle? Well fuck that.'

Still watching me, Devine finds a handkerchief, or something of that sort, in his pocket. Ties a crude bandage over his bicep, wanting to stop the bleeding, I guess.

He's wondering quite how to play this next bit. He'd quite like to kill me right now this minute, but the maths doesn't look quite as simple as it did.

Instead of a few simple bullets, he'll have to batter me to death. Kay and Katie too. That's harder than shooting, and messy.

And, just for now, we have a pause.

Devine is about four or five yards from me. About the same distance from Kay and Katie. We sit in a kind of loose triangle in this place of rock and earth and dampness.

To Kay, I say, 'You OK, sweetie?'

She says yes.

I ask the same of Katie.

She succeeds in implying, with relatively few words, that she has seen better days, admittedly, but overall she's bearing up reasonably well, given the circs.

I jerk my thumb at Devine.

'This is Alex Devine. If he gets close to you at all, grab for anything soft. Eyes. Windpipe. Balls. Mouth. Just hold on as hard as you can and do as much damage as you can. An arm over his windpipe would be a particularly excellent outcome.'

Neither Kay nor Katie are going to be the world's greatest ever fighters, but in a three-way contest between Devine and the three of us, I'd probably lay my money on us. Two to impede his movement, one to choke him, bite him, gouge him, hurt him.

They tell me OK. Look fierce.

The shelf of stores is over to my left. I give it my attention for the first time, hoping to find a weapon. A gun, a knife, anything.

Nothing.

Tinned food, lots of it. Spare batteries. Two large plastic jerrycans of water. A bundle of clothes. Some cooking equipment, but nothing that looks useful.

Also – of course – peeping from a roll of blanket – Excalibur.
Devine's version.

'May I?'

He doesn't say anything. Goes on scowling at me. Dabbing at his bloodied arm.

I realise that he'd actually like me to occupy my hands with the sword. The thing makes me less dangerous, not more.

In here, a sword is a clumsy old weapon. The roof is mostly too low, the walls too close, to permit much slashing action, and I'm just not strong enough to use it effectively as a thrusting blade.

To top it all, the floor is far too uneven for that kind of fighting. When this place was quarried, I presume they just lifted stone from wherever it was easiest to extract it. What they left was a cavity, like a downward pointing funnel, only much more ragged.

The lowest point of the chamber – one with probably permanent standing water – is perhaps twelve or fifteen feet below the crudely-made roof. Around that low point, the floor rises in a series of uneven, rising ledges. There's almost nowhere you can walk, one foot in front of another, without stepping down, or stepping up, or in some other way having to watch your footwork.

Kay and Katie are chained up on the back wall of the chamber. Devine occupies a place just right of the door. I'm with the stores, crouched up under the left-hand wall.

I look at the sword.

All this, everything we've done, centring on this one damn object.

The sword blade looks much like my own. They've done a slightly better job of ageing it, maybe, but they had longer to do it.

The hilt and decoration is less nice than ours. A tad clumsier. Less refined.

I lift it.

It's a nice sword, but cold. It has no life. I don't like it.

I say, 'This isn't Caledfwlch.'

Devine says, 'What?'

'It's not Caledfwlch. It's not Excalibur.'

'Of course it's not fucking Excalibur—'

'No, but . . . it's not . . . don't you see?'

I don't quite know how to say the thing I'm trying to express. Just – this fakery. This business of forging something for sale. Yes, there's the whole technical correctness aspect. Getting the blade right, the hilt right, the decoration, all that. But this sword, of all things, is meant to embody something more. Fifteen centuries of British liberty. British valour.

In the doorway, a shadow moves, black on black.

Devine is finished repairing his arm. He's searching around now in the litter of loose rock next to him for a good-sized stone.

The one he chooses is about the size of his two balled fists together. A smooth lump of rock that could knock me unconscious if he gets the blow half-right. That could empty my brains in a splatter of grey, if he times things exactly so.

I clamber down into the low point of the chamber. Up to my ankles in water. My stupid bluebell-coloured skirt and stupid-stupid strappy sandals are really not made for this kind of treatment. The water is cold and that fine mud of pond bottoms – so fine, it's almost silky – begins to ooze between my toes.

I wield the sword.

Face Devine.

I say, '*Rex quondam, rexque futurus.* The once and future king. This was meant to be *his* sword. It was never just about making something that looked old.'

Devine stands. Stone in his right hand. A let's-finish-this-thing look on his face.

He's taller than me. He's higher than me. He's stronger than me. He's more effectively armed than me.

But he is standing right where I want him, with his back to the door.

And just as he's poised to attack, an attack which will kill me, the doorway is no longer empty.

My father is there. Eyes flaming. Face angrier than I've ever seen it.

And Caledfwlch. The proper sword, *my* sword, rescued from the back of Devine's car.

Dad says, 'You stupid English fucker,' adding in Welsh, '*Twll din pob Sais.*'

Every Englishman an arsehole.

Devine whirls.

Dad thrusts.

He gashes Devine in the belly. A two-handed blow that has all of Dad's, now considerable, weight behind it.

When we made Caledfwlch, we made it the way Gheerbrant suggested. The hardness of steel over a springy iron core. We got a very sharp edge on it. A very sharp point.

But then we had to age the thing. Make it look like it had been dinged about in combat. Like it had spent fifteen long centuries buried under the earth at Liddington.

By the time we did all that, the edge was gone. The point blunted, dull.

All the same, my Dad is two or three inches over six foot. He must now weigh well over two hundred pounds. And if he's hardly a servant of the Body Beautiful, he's still a strong and powerful man who does not shrink from violence. Whose two daughters have been carried at gunpoint to this place.

Whose daughters were brought here to die.

Devine's belly rips open.

A jagged, long, uneven tear. Blood red and peeping with the first spillage of guts, grey-white and slippery with fluid.

The blow, the sheer force of it, knocks Devine off-balance.

He lurches backwards and, on this uneven surface, an unguarded lurch turns quickly into a sprawling fall.

He ends up, head lower than his feet, by me in the little pool. He's torn about, but perfectly alive.

I clamber back. Away from his arms. Away from that rock. Go to Kay and Katie. Put my arms around them. And we shelter there, cramped up against these damp walls, the three frightened naiads of this place.

The fight is not yet done.

Devine, professional soldier that he was, professional mercenary that he still is, assesses his belly wound with a calculating eye.

Is it bad? Yes. Is it disabling? No.

Devine, checking his balance, stands again. Reaches for his sword, the one that has just sold for seventy-eight million dollars.

'Fuck you,' he says. 'And fuck your family.'

For a moment, just a moment, there is silence and standoff.

Two adult men, holding swords.

Dad is on higher ground. Devine stands where I was, feet in water and that silken mud. The swords are big – two-handed affairs – but Devine, I notice, is still a bit distracted by that slash to his belly. He doesn't remove his hand from the sword exactly but, still gripping the hilt, he uses the heel of his hand to explore the tear.

Dad is utterly still. Entirely watchful. And somehow massive. Castled against the light.

Then Devine strikes upwards.

He's realised he's too low to strike effectively at Dad's head or chest, so instead he seeks a slashing blow to Dad's thigh. A disabling blow to even the odds. Indeed, if this battle lasts for any length of time, then the younger, stronger, fitter man will likely win it.

414

But Dad is equal to the attack. Fends it with his sword pointing down into the rock, immobile and grave as a statued king.

Three times, Devine attacks. Each time the same result.

Dad parries, deftly but with an immensity of stillness. As calm as though protected by a stone wall.

After those three assaults, Dad murmurs, 'Is that all you've got, Saxon?'

Twitches his blade one way, but not fast enough to secure a hit.

Too slow, I think, *Dad, that's too slow.*

Devine thinks so too. Moves his sword for the parry. Is already, I think, considering his instant counter.

But Dad was feinting, not striking. With Devine's sword tempted out to his left, Dad's Caledfwlch flashes up in a sweeping curve to Devine's right armpit. Devine sees the move and tries to counter, but there's something wrong, he's too slow. He misses the parry, by an inch or two only, perhaps, but a miss is as good as a mile.

There's an audible impact. A spurt of blood. And, as Devine is still trying to understand the damage – trying to refigure his odds, his strategy – Caledfwlch returns. An arcing descent. Dad's weight, two-handed, piled behind the blow.

Caledfwlch bites deep into Devine's arm. Is stopped only by a shudder of bone. A whole tearing flap of muscle flops loose, like something seen in the backroom of a butcher's shop.

Devine drops his sword.

Drops it from shock. From the physical impact.

But also and anyway – the thing is useless now. A sword like that carried one-handed is an encumbrance not an asset, and Devine has only one working arm now.

There's shock on his face, certainly. A taut, shining emptiness. But also fear.

Recognition that this is where it ends. Everything.

His job. His criminal activity. His passions. His freedom. Perhaps his life.

Dad, implacable, places his sword tip on Devine's chest and pushes hard.

Our Caledfwlch didn't have much of a point left after all the work we'd done to age it. Its tip, so sharp and bright when it first left the blacksmith's fire, became dulled. Softly rounded even.

But Devine was already tottering when the shove came and that cave bottom remains treacherous. In any event, Dad pushes. Devine falls. He strikes his head hard enough on the stone floor, that there's an audible lift to his head as it bounces.

There's more blood, but not much and, anyway, in this dim light it's hard to tell.

Devine is useless now.

Disarmed. Disabled. Defunct.

On my right, Kay, realising for the first time that she is completely safe, that no more bad things can happen, starts to cry. Sobs, bundled into my shoulder.

She won't watch what happens next, but Dad, I know, is not about to leave this man alone. I remember that line about Gwawrddur feeding black ravens on the rampart of a fortress. Dad shifts his grip on Caledfwlch. Checks the rocky slope in front of him. And steps forward.

Here, in the dimness of Brocéliande, we are watching a man being turned into raven meat. I don't want to watch, but can't help myself. Katie too. I feel her beside me, watching with a shared intensity.

And because we're watching the last sickening round of this battle to the death, no one sees that George Bowen has arrived here too. Gunned up, but also wearing his dog collar, that curve of Christian white.

'Tom,' he shouts.

My dad's attention barely flickers. He has a man to turn into raven meat. That first, everything else second.

Devine is trying to crawl away. But the slope is against him and there's nowhere to go.

Dad considers his next blow. It will be a final one, I'm certain. Head or chest? Or neck?

I think it's going to be the head.

Bowen again: 'Tom Griffiths, you bugger.'

At that, Dad does pause.

A pause only, mind you. He still doesn't turn to Bowen. Still doesn't shift his eyes from his prey. This about-to-be carcass.

Into that pause, Bowen says, 'You will drop that sword or I will shoot you in the arm. And I swear to do it, so help me God.'

He would too.

He has the gun raised and levelled. And if you're a farmer capable of shooting a fox galloping across your sheep field, you've got the calmness and accuracy to do what's needed here.

I say, 'Dad, drop the sword. We're all safe. Please drop the sword.'

Kay too. 'Dad. Dad.'

And – slowly – Dad returns from whatever dark place he was to this world of ours, his happy, living daughters.

He shakes his head.

In front of him, Devine's leg lies at an angle over a shelf of stone. Dad uses his foot to shift the leg. He's gentle enough about it. Almost looks as though he's making the man more comfortable. When he doesn't get exactly the effect he wants first time, he nudges again until everything is exactly so.

He lays the sword down.

Looks at Bowen with a kind of 'satisfied now?' move of his eyebrows.

Then stamps hard, brutally hard, on Devine's exposed knee joint. The injured man gasps in pain. He hasn't gasped this way before. When Dad moves his foot, Devine's leg lies at the wrong angle. Blood darkening at the bend.

Bowen's face is fierce and he hasn't shifted his gun.

But Dad moves. Up and away from Devine, his mood rising and lightening as he does so. Bowen softens his hold on the gun, pointing it loosely at Devine in a 'no false moves' sort of way.

Dad, approaching us, says, 'Kay. Kay, love, are you all right? And Katie, is it? Lovely to meet you. That silly bugger won't cause any more problems.'

Dad's huge paws embrace the three of us in a giant squeeze, Katie hugged in as chest-crushingly close as all the rest of us. Kay's crying, but she's OK. These are tears of relief, not hurt. She's OK. We're all OK.

And by the time I manage to pull away, in search of those little things – air, light, the ability to breathe – I find Katie, staring intently at Devine's fallen sword.

'Look,' she says.

I look.

Devine is lying back. Holding his tattered arm, shadowed and watched by Bowen's implacable gun.

On the floor of the cave, Devine's sword. Seventy-eight million dollars' worth of fakery.

And first I don't see it, but then I do. The blade bent too far. It's twenty degrees off true, maybe more.

That's why Devine was too slow to counter Dad's thrust to the armpit. That's why his parry missed Caledfwlch by that crucial inch.

Katie says, 'They overworked their metal. That sword has too much steel. They needed some spring in the centre of the blade, that soft iron core, and they just beat it out.'

That makes me laugh.

I call over to Devine. 'Alex, mate, did you hear that? Your sword is shit. All that – all that – and you couldn't even make a good sword.'

Devine doesn't answer. But the dull lamps in his eyes swerve to his sword. Then to Caledfwlch. His lips move, but say nothing.

I say, 'George, it's nice seeing you and everything, but do you think someone should call the police?'

He tells me that SO15 are on their way. That's why Bowen entered the cave after Dad. He was on the phone above ground, giving directions and making arrangements.

Fifteen minutes pass.

Bowen, peaceably, pointing his gun in Devine's general direction. But Devine's eyes are closed now. He's not dead or anything like it, but he's sunk into contemplation of his own injury. His general fuckedness.

Dad uses the bad sword, not Caledfwlch, to smash Kay and Katie out of their chains.

'That's better now,' he says. Then, 'Oops, look at that. Clumsy.'

Says that, as he leans his weight on Devine's blade and actually bends it back on itself, the weapon as vanquished as its owner.

And then—

Finally, SO15. Four men in black Kevlar. Sub-machine guns. The whole deal.

A bit over-gunned for this particular situation and all a bit better-late-than-never, but what the hell. We greet them anyway.

The men drag Devine ungently from his fallen position. Frisk him.

One of the men pokes at Devine's gaping arm wound.

'Ouch, that must hurt, right?'

And pokes again.

419

Another man plays with Devine's injured leg. Moving it this way and that. Saying, 'Nasty. Oh, that looks really bad.'

Moves it more.

Devine's injuries are nasty but, unless there's a lot more damage than we can see, nothing there strikes me as lethal. The SO15 guys have some type of compression bandages with them and they strap Devine up. One bandage over the arm. The other one over his torn belly, so he won't just spill his guts as they drag him away. Devine's other injuries aren't bad enough to need treatment, or not down here, not in this rocky little operating theatre.

When they're done bandaging him, they start to move him, and every single movement they make is designed to hurt. When they shift him around, they grab his torn arm and just jerk. When they carry him towards the door, they keep 'accidentally' slamming shins and belly against the hard gritstone edges.

I'm not mostly a fan of police violence, but I don't count this. I watch them deliberately hurt the man. Watch the set of his face as he takes the blows.

He's combat-experienced. He knows what happens to the losers. He knows too that this is still the good part. That some breath of open air, of freedom, of young leaves and rain-freshened earth can still reach him here.

In a few minutes time, the guy will be in a police van. Then custody. Then prison.

For ever.

No remission.

No exit.

A well-deserved end.

Katie watches him go. She leans into my neck. Her hair – the braided hair of that Anglo–Saxon warrior princess – still smells of the shampoo she used last night, lemony and herbal.

And beneath that smell, better than it, *her* smell. Warm and intimate.

'Thank you,' she says to my neck. 'Thank you.'

I don't answer. Just embrace her and Kay and Dad, and watch as Devine is led through the chamber's little doorway. The officers guiding him 'miscalculate' how low he has to stoop to get through and just ram his forehead into the heavy wooden lintel.

They say sorry. Then do it again, harder.

One of the SO15 guys lingers behind. He'd quite like to be playing the hurt-Alex-Devine game too, but duty pulls him back.

He's waiting to speak to me, but not wanting to interrupt.

Still with Katie's head in my back, and still in a warm and loving tangle with Dad and Kay, I say, 'Did you get it?'

'Yes.'

'The phone call?'

'Yes.'

'And that number he called? You were able to triangulate?'

'Yes.'

I push the final question at the officer with my eyes only.

He grins. 'It's one of those good news, bad news things,' he says. 'The call went through to a residential district. You know, these things are never that precise, so we were probably looking at thirty or forty homes in total. Houses where that call could have been received.'

That's not good. Thirty or forty homes. You can't kick down the doors to thirty or forty houses, just because you think that one of them shelters a seriously nasty villain.

But my man isn't done. He has more to tell me.

'Thing is, though, we've got previous with one of those homes.'

'Previous,' I say.

Not a question. Not a request for clarification. A prayer, more like. A supplication.

'Yes. Good previous too. Very good.'

He tells me that one of the residents in the relevant area was the target of a recent major police investigation. No prosecution was ever brought, but the man was found to have had eight boxed mobile phones. Cheapies. Pay-as-you-go things. Unregistered.

A criminal's toolkit.

'Eight phones?' I say. 'Literally that? *Eight*?'

He nods.

'And the triangulation? The area you located?'

He says, 'Was in an area you probably know better than me.'

I say – breathe, whisper, pray – 'Penarth. Outside Cardiff. Marine Parade.'

He nods.

I start to ask, 'And are you—?'

But he interrupts. Doesn't need the question.

'And what are we doing about it? Now you're safe, you mean?' He shrugs. Sometimes policing is as simple as pie. 'We're going in right now, this minute. Your man Idris Prothero? He's already fucking fucked.'

I like that answer so much, I'd like to kiss the entire world.

54

Home, or near enough.

Cwm George, outside Dinas Powys.

Same hill. Same fort. Same dim beeches and the cantering of invisible knights.

I'm lying back in long grass.

Blue sky above.

Real blue. Clear blue. Summer blue.

An unWelsh version of summer, admittedly, because today is cloudless, and warm, and will probably last for ever.

Somewhere beyond my view, Katie is showing Dad the hill fort.

The ditches. The ramparts.

The fires, the middens, the vanished halls.

Dad will come back vastly overexcited. He'll start telling everyone about it, in a narrative that will bear only scant resemblance to what Katie is now telling him.

He'll start buying things too. A handful of Roman coins. Some Celtic pottery. Something for Mam, a necklace probably. A modern reproduction thing that she'll wear once with a faint and unconvincing smile, then silently discard. The whole enthusiasm will last maybe a week or, if nothing else comes along, two at the outside. Then he'll be off again, chasing some other hare, racing off down some other track.

The one thing he won't acquire will be any kind of weapon.

Partly, that's because Dad has none of that icky male

thrill around weaponry. But mostly it's because he's already acquired a sword.

Mine. My Caledfwlch.

He didn't ask for it and I definitely didn't give it to him. Just, since that night in Brocéliande, the sword has never been in my possession, has always remained in his.

He's commissioning a presentation mount. Got it sharpened. Brought in someone with a grinder who brought a wholly new, modern sharpness to the blade. ('Don't get me wrong, love, you did a fabulous job and all, but if you're going to have a sword, you've got to give it a proper edge.') As a fake antiquity the thing is ruined, but as an actual weapon – well, it's never been better.

I don't care, or don't think I do.

Things move on. People die. Cases get solved. Swords leave one owner and find a new one.

Hic iacet Arthurus, rex quondam, rexque futurus. Here lies Arthur, the once and future king.

Even in death, Arthur didn't plan on staying still. There's no reason why his sword should be so different.

On the stony path that leads up to the fort I hear the tramp of footsteps.

Heavy. Male. Jackson's.

He makes the ascent, finds me, plonks himself down.

'Fiona. Morning.'

I give him my best good morning smile, which is so good it needs no words.

I've part-made a daisy chain and start to pick more daisies. Jackson gets out a Tupperware container. Presents some chocolate brownies.

'My wife made them,' he announces, with a curious sweet pride.

I nibble a brownie, build my daisy chain and tell Jackson about the hill fort. He's sort of interested, but only sort of.

After a bit, he says, 'Fiona, help me out. I understand most of this thing. Some bad guys want to build a fake sword that they think they can sell – almost *did* sell – for some crazy amount of money. Fine. And to do that, they need some proper academic expertise. They needed people like Gheerbrant to help with the construction. Getting all the details right, that kind of thing. Same thing with de Boissieu. They needed him to help create their – what d'you call it—?'

'Palimpsest. It comes from the Greek, and basically means *rubbed smooth, again*. Rubbing was how you prepared your animal skin.'

'Thank you. I needed to know that.'

I agree happily. 'Everyone does.'

'So Gheerbrant does his stuff. De Boissieu does his. Both of those two were bad guys. Not lead bad guys, but part of the conspiracy. I get all that.'

'But what about Charteris?' I say. 'What about John Oakeshott?'

'Yes. What about them? How did they get mixed up in this?'

'I don't know.'

'OK, but if you had to guess . . .?'

I continue work on my daisy chain. Open a hole in the final stem with my fingernail, then pull a fresh stalk through the gap until the flowerhead is pulled snug.

'I'm running out of daisies.'

'You're not going to say?'

'I *am* going to say, but I can tell you *and* make daisy chains. The good daisies are all there by your foot.'

Nodding gravely, Jackson picks some flowers. He does a good job of it too, pinching them off close to the root, to yield the maximum length of green.

I say again, 'I don't know . . .'

'But?'

'Look, I don't think Charteris was up to anything so awful, but she was an Arthur nut. An academic historian, yes, but with a personal passion that went far beyond anything narrowly professional. And – we've seen her emails – she was worried about the future of her subject. She cared about declines in funding, a loss of interest. It was almost, to her, like twenty-first-century Britain had lost its connection to its one-time saviour. *She* thought that. I suspect Oakeshott thought so too, or something like it anyway.'

Jackson has now gathered a couple of dozen daisies, maybe more. I need to discard two or three, because the stems are too short or too weedy, but it's a good pile.

He says, 'So Charteris and Oakeshott, maybe some others like them, decide to get a little bit naughty. Build some fake antiquity and release it as a PR stunt, something like that.'

'Yes. Maybe they wanted to show how easily this could be done. Unveiling some potentially Arthurian artefact, before revealing the truth. Or use some kind of "is it real or is it fake" stunt to grab some TV airtime and get attention to their subject. Or something else. My guess is that they hadn't even decided. And I seriously doubt that they were ever intending to do anything as bold as build a fake Excalibur. I'd have thought a modest little seal box or something was more what they had in mind.

'Anyway, as the whole idea got more real, Charteris got cold feet. She felt relieved when – as she imagined – the idea was binned. And of course, the idea of faking some minor little piece for basically publicity-type reasons doesn't sound particularly awful to us. We're Major Crime types and what they were talking about probably wouldn't even have qualified as fraud. But they were academics. They risked losing their jobs, their reputations, their own little everythings. So all these not-very-scary academic types played at spies. All their secret emails and phones that no one else could use. They weren't hiding from us, they were hiding from their fellow-academics.'

Jackson says, 'And then somewhere along the way, this little group stumbles across the path of some genuine badass criminals. Those criminal types realise that faking antiquities is a massive global market and all this Arthurian stuff gives them a massive opportunity to get in on it.'

'Right. The art and science of forgery is now way ahead of the art and science of detection. Fakery is *already* a multi-billion-pound industry – mostly in China and the Middle East – but the same techniques would work just as well here.'

'And they killed Charteris because . . .?'

'I don't know. Because they thought she'd spill the beans, I guess. Her ethics wouldn't allow her to stay silent as Devine and gang pulled a fake Excalibur from the ground at Liddington. Plus she was working right here, at Dinas Powys. A perfect fort. Perfectly located. Lots of evidence of metalwork. The perfect setting for a fifth-century Arthur.

'So they planted that seal-box, using an image that they'd use again on the sword. Then killed her spectacularly enough that they could be sure of attracting attention. Their stage-management was intended to reference the Kirkburn Sword, the one the British Museum describes as the finest Iron Age sword in Europe. By killing Charteris like that, they were disposing of a potential blabbermouth *and* trying to broadcast the idea that some new, amazing sword might be at the heart of this.

'Same thing with the stone from Llanymawddwy. They *wanted* us to make the connection to Bangor, to Saint Tydecho, to Camlan. I suspect they were surprised we got there as fast as we did, but I'm sure they were ready to give us another nudge if need be. I took care to let them know that yes, thank you, we'd got the message. Their nudges tended to involve shotguns and/or corpses.'

Jackson says, 'And Oakeshott?'

'Oakeshott's easy. We went in there – *I* went in there – all hot and heavy. Threatening exposure to the police. Pressurising him. He was scared that he was going to get tagged into a police investigation. That investigation might well reveal that he had dabbled with the idea of deliberately faking an antiquity. That wouldn't bother *us*, but as he saw it, he stood to lose his job, his reputation, everything.'

'Right, OK. So Oakeshott doesn't just come clean with you. Instead, he gets on the phone to all his mates, trying to figure out a strategy. Trouble is, one of his mates was in league with the bad guys and passes the news on. The bad guys don't think they can take the risk of letting Oakeshott talk to the police, so they find a bit of local talent, this Wormold guy, and arrange the killing. All a bit messy and last minute, but anything to get the job done.'

'Yes, exactly. If we work hard enough, I expect we'll find a link between Devine and Wormold. At any rate, I'm pretty sure that Devine gave the order.'

Jackson thinks about that. Gathers more daisies.

We're motoring now. Him gathering, me stitching them.

He says, 'So we've got two groups. The first group is a bunch of mildly obsessive academic types. They were basically harmless and their little conspiracy was in the process of disintegrating anyway. The second group – Devine, Ivor Williams, those people – were genuinely dangerous and ambitious men. But somewhere along the way something or someone connected the two.'

I nod. 'I think the connection ran from Gheerbrant to Devine. Devine was a skilled amateur blacksmith with an interest in the period and plenty of experience in combat and weapons generally. Gheerbrant was the leading researcher in Europe when it came to Dark Age warfare. It's more than likely the two men knew each other innocently in the first instance. Then got talking. And that's when things started to turn serious.'

Jackson agrees.

In this blue and bee-buzzed air, it's hard to get too exercised by what are now no more than details.

Jackson tries opening up a daisy stalk with his thumbnail, but his nails are too short to be of use.

I say, 'I'll do the stalks, if you do the threading.'

'OK.'

I watch him set to. He's not very good, if I'm honest, but I'm not honest. I tell him he's doing a wonderful job.

'Are we doing this for a reason, Fiona?'

'I always have a reason, sir.'

'And on this occasion, the reason would be . . .?'

'To build a super-massive daisy chain. Obviously.'

He shrugs.

We thread daisies.

On a rampart to our left, Katie and Dad are looking out at the view.

She uses a crutch always now. Her legs are OK, but that right foot drags almost permanently.

Jackson studies the two figures. We're not here on a jolly. Jackson needs to talk to Dad and I chose this spot to arrange the meeting, because Dad is always more communicative when he's relaxed and a bit excited. If we met up in Jackson's office, Dad would freeze completely. We'd get nothing.

Jackson drops his eyes from that blue-green horizon and says, 'You took a hell of a risk that night.'

Did I? I still don't think I had any alternatives. Unless I'd coaxed Devine into taking me to Brocéliande, I think we'd never have found the place. I think Katie and Kay would have died there.

But yes, I took a risk.

I never thought Devine would actually hand over five million bucks, but I did think that he'd let me and the hostages go in exchange for my Caledfwlch and my silence. Turns out I was half-right, half-wrong. Right about the money, wrong about the whole letting us go free thing.

'Good old Tidy, then,' says Jackson.

Yes. Good old Tidy. Good old Bowen.

My dad and Bowen didn't just watch me go and leave it at that. They worked their way down the edge of a neighbouring property until they could see into Devine's farmyard.

They saw him striding about his yard. Saw me moving about in his living room. Saw us climb into his four-by-four, my belt-end trailing on the ground.

'That's not right,' my dad said. 'She wants help.'

Bowen too. 'Tidy knows her,' he said. 'Let's see what he can do.'

Tidy.

Not a sniffer dog, but something at least as good or, truth be told, a good bit better. He was – is – a Welsh sheepdog, the single most intelligent, most capable dog breed on the planet.

Bowen let Tidy out of Dad's car. Gave him some bits and pieces with my scent on. Took him to the scent of that fallen belt.

Dogs can't shrug, but if they could, I think Tidy would have shrugged, muttered, 'Jeez, humans, honestly.' Then gone off to do his stuff.

A dog handler once told me that sniffer dogs aren't recruited for their powers of smell. 'They can all smell well enough. Asking them to follow a trail is like asking you to pick a red ball from a basket full of green ones. The only issue is whether the dog understands what you're asking and feels like helping.'

Well, Tidy understood and Tidy was happy to help.

He trotted diligently through the night, nose to the ground, nose to the trail I'd left for him. According to Bowen, he only ever paused to check that his doltish human companions were approximately keeping up. 'He never even came close to losing the scent.'

Tidy led the two men straight to Devine's four-by-four. The men checked inside, in case I was there, dead, bound or bleeding. They didn't find me, but did find Caledfwlch.

Dad took it. Let Tidy pursue the, now much stronger, trail into the wood itself.

Tidy bounded through the undergrowth. Found the drain cover. The hole that led down to Brocéliande.

And as for the rest? Well, I was there for the rest.

I did ask, later, why Dad chose to enter with the sword, not the gun. It wasn't, I gently suggested, the most obvious of tactics.

'Oh love, I had the gun too. I mean, it was there if I needed it. But the sword just felt better, really. There was no way I was going to mess things up with you and Kay down there.'

That makes no sense. No sense at all. But the way he tells it, the choice was natural.

'Tell you what, though. That man of yours, Bowen, he's quite something, isn't he?'

I agreed, and agreed heartily, but asked Dad what he meant.

'Before I went down there, down that little hole, Bowen made me stop. He put the sign of the cross on both my shoulders. I mean, that's not normal, is it? It should be on the chest or something.'

I do a little double-take at that. Remember my Nennius.

The eighth battle was at the fortress of Guinnion, in which Arthur carried the image of holy Mary ever virgin on his shoulders; and the pagans were put to flight on that day. And through the power of our Lord Jesus Christ and through the power of the blessed Virgin Mary his mother there was great slaughter among them.

*

I said, 'George is a vicar, Dad. Of course he likes the sign of the cross.'

We left it there.

Jackson studies me in the sunlight.

My daisy chain is yards long now.

Long enough.

I thread the leading flowerhead through a slot in the trailing stem. Turn the chain into a loop. Double it over, and again. Tease the thing into shape until I have a many-braided crown.

Jackson makes as if to help me put it on, but I tell him it's not for me.

We leave it.

He says, 'Bleddyn Jones. You and he have had your ups and downs.'

I can't remember so many ups, but I say yes anyway.

'He says you're a total pain in the arse.'

'I know. I mean, I know that he says it, but I also know that I am it.'

'And one of the best officers he's ever worked with.'

'He said that? Really?'

'Yes. He was very complimentary. I mean, in some respects. Some very narrow respects.'

'Oh.' Pause. 'That's nice of him.'

'Yes.'

'He's a good officer too. I mean . . .'

'Yes?'

'That beard.'

'Fiona—'

'I *know*. I know. Terrible beards aren't a valid reason for dislike. And he *is* a good officer. And I *am* a pain to work with. And on that final night. When I was at Brocéliande . . .'

'Yes?'

'Well, he was outstanding. I know that. Then, and when I

was with de Boissieu. He did as much as anyone to save those hostages. To save me.'

Jackson nods. He has this fatherly pleasure when, temporarily, I behave like an almost acceptable human being.

He says, 'There's a vacancy at Bridgend. Now the Chief's in Cardiff, they need someone to run things there. They've offered it to Jones and he's accepted.'

I let out a breath. A deep wash of relief. The loss of a tension I hadn't even known was there.

I can't speak for a moment, but my face probably says enough.

Jackson: 'And do you know what he told me?'

That's a stupid question. Of course I don't know what he told Jackson. I do my stupid-question face.

'He wanted the job. He wanted *my* job. And I was more than half-inclined to give it to him. I did wonder whether a younger, more active type might not be better. I wondered whether early retirement or some part-time role might not suit me better.'

'What changed his mind?' I whisper, worried that I already know the answer.

'You. He said he'd never have been able to work with you. One of you would have killed the other, most likely, and he thought that your contribution to the team was, on balance, going to be the more important one. So he stood aside. Took a job that wasn't really the one he wanted.'

'He did that?'

'Yes.'

'He said that?'

Jackson does his version of a stupid-question face which – like most of his faces – looks a lot like craggy immobility.

I say, 'I am a terrible human being, I know that.'

'You should thank him. Actually go and see him. Say thank you.'

433

I nod. I will. I make a promise, the sort I will actually keep.

'Good.'

Jackson turns his face to the sun.

Gulls swoop.

Bees bumble over clover flowers.

Dad and Katie come towards us.

Katie's limping badly: she gets tired more quickly now and Dad isn't very sensitive to that kind of thing.

When they arrive, Katie flops exhausted on the grass. Gives me a tired-looking smile.

I say, 'I made you a crown.'

I give her her crown.

I have to re-pin one of her braids to make it look right, but my honoured mistress is worth the labour.

When I'm done, she gives me a nice smile and says, 'Thank you, slave.'

I bow my gratitude.

The older guys look awkward, not knowing if they're meant to say something or just ignore our Embarrassing Girly Moments.

They look out towards the south, where a blue sea lies, and choose the latter option. Always safer.

So.

The Thing.

The thing that brought us here.

The thing on which everything depends. Or not everything. Not really. Just – just, it feels like that sometimes. With Kay safe, and Katie safe, and me safe, and Devine in jail, and Charteris neither deader not aliver than she was before – with all that sorted, then this last thing is the pole about which an entire planet of crime revolves.

Jackson says, 'Lovely spot this, isn't it, Tom?'

Tactical use of first name, there. A good, careful opening gambit.

The fact is, my dad regards police officers the way most people would regard a nest of tarantulas intermixed with a boxful of puff adders and Indian cobras. When I joined the force and, worse, when I moved into CID, my dad and I suffered the only real relationship breakdown of our lives. We got over it, yes, but it took time and patience on both sides. Also: Dennis Jackson isn't my father's daughter.

'Oh, it's wonderful, isn't it? Never been here before, would you credit it? Born only over there—' he points to an unseen Cardiff, the lost world of Tiger Bay, 'but never once set foot here.'

He witters on.

Jackson reciprocates. They exchange stories, humour. Some shared memories.

And slowly, slowly, they edge closer to The Thing.

Edge closer, then arrive at its lip.

Jackson says, 'When your girl here barged in on Devine, he went out into the yard to make a call. You probably know that. She probably told you.'

Dad wrinkles his face in a way that might mean yes, might mean no, or might just mean the sun is in his eyes.

But he does know. I did tell him. And told Jackson that I had.

'We think Devine was calling his boss. The money man. We think he spoke about how to proceed. What to do next.'

'Well, that would be logical, I suppose,' Dad murmurs, as though the ways of crooks were entirely unknown to him.

'We tracked the call. He was calling a mobile, of course. An unregistered one.'

Dad sighs – scratches – looks upwards at the blue.

Jackson: 'I don't know how much you know about these things, but we can get an approximate location for the telephone receiving the call.'

He explains about triangulation. The limitations of the technique. But explains too that the technique on this occasion did enough.

'We arrested a man named Idris Prothero. Your daughter here, Fiona, almost had the bugger on another investigation a few years back. Weapons smuggling. We didn't get him then, but we've got him now. We've got his actual prints on the actual phone that took the actual call. Not just that, but we got his computer too. He had a webpage open on – what's it called, Fiona? – Tor. Part of the dark web. I don't understand that stuff, not properly, but basically he was negotiating the sale of King Arthur's sword. Seventy-eight million dollars. Sixty million quid. The deal was almost done when we broke his bloody door down.'

Jackson stops.

Prothero is in custody now. He won't get bail. When we bring him to trial for conspiracy to murder, along with multiple other serious charges, he'll be found guilty. He'll go to prison. Maximum security. The kind of place that's full of tattooed fuckers with shaven heads and one-stud earrings and some serious anger management issues.

He'll never leave it.

But Jackson isn't done. 'So obviously, once we have the bugger, we start pulling his life apart. We search his property.' Proper*ies*, actually. In the plural. His place in Penarth. His apartment in Chelsea. Ask the Italian Carabinieri to do the same to his villa in Umbria. 'Look at his phones. Landline and mobile. Give his electronic stuff to our tech people, so they can take a look at what he's been up to. Bank accounts, of course. Onshore and offshore. It's not like these people pay taxes like the rest of us, is it?'

Dad mutters something. Barely audible, but to the effect that no, these bastards never pay their taxes.

Jackson says, 'I mean, I earn decent money. I get about

fifty-five grand, and I pay tax at forty per cent, on the last chunk of that amount, anyway.'

Dad sharpens his gaze. Focuses more closely on Jackson. This isn't like any police interrogation my dad has encountered in the past. But then again he's never had the pleasure of being interrogated by Detective Chief Inspector Dennis Jackson.

Dad says, 'Well, they've got to pay for schools and hospitals, I suppose. Them and the bloody police force.'

Jackson says, 'Oh, I don't complain. It all seems fair enough. Except our boy Prothero was paying maybe six or seven per cent on his income. *Legally* paying that. Just filtered all his profits offshore. Totally, utterly, completely legal.'

Dad says, 'You have access to his bank accounts?'

'Yes.'

'All of them?'

'Yes.'

Dad's eyes push a question, but his lips say nothing.

Once, just once, I feel his eyes dart over to me. Trying to read me. Trying to learn whether this is all a trap, whether I would trap my own father.

Jackson says, 'This isn't a regular interview, you know that, right?'

Dad nods, but Jackson continues: 'We're not taping anything. We haven't charged you. We haven't read you your rights. We haven't offered you a lawyer. And your daughter, a police officer, is sitting right here next to you, which means that any investigation on our part is so totally and utterly compromised, we could never even think of bringing anything to court. Plus, of course, we regard you as a victim in all this. You had one daughter abducted. This one here risked her life trying to rescue her. And you? You *did* rescue them. Rescue them both. You were the hero of the hour.' Jackson pauses and his gaze floats on the mild air. To a far distant horizon, he murmurs, 'We're not about to charge you, Tom. We're not charging you with anything at all.'

Dad remains silent, but silences are never only one colour. And this one?

Well, it's turning an almost pinky silver. Like cherry blossom viewed from below, against blue sky and sun.

Dad's lips move, but nothing comes out.

Jackson stuffs brownie into his mouth. Turns his face to the sun and says, 'You've been paying money to Idris Prothero for six years. Six years, *at least*. We're still gathering the data that will let us look back further. The sums aren't small. Ten grand one month. Twenty grand another month. Over the average year, you're looking at just about two hundred grand. Paid offshore. To Idris Prothero. We thought that was interesting. I'm just saying.'

Dad looks direct at me. Trying to get a read from my face. I try to give him nothing at all.

Katie looks ill at ease. She didn't know this thing was going to be happening and she feels like she shouldn't be part of it. But she should, she really should. She's like a heat diffuser for the rest of us. Someone whose mere presence can prevent things hitting combustion point.

Jackson pushes his brownies at Dad.

'Homemade, these are.'

Dad takes a brownie. Mutters something vaguely wife- and bakery-related.

Jackson says, 'Plus *you* made a phone call. To Prothero, I mean. A mobile located at or close to *your* home address went straight through to Prothero's office landline. The call was made about twenty minutes after you learned of Kay's abduction.'

Dad laughs softly.

'Amazing what you people can do these days,' he says, in a way that does not suggest he is delighted about it.

Jackson passes a brownie to Katie.

'They're made with nut flour,' he says. 'I never knew that.'

She takes one. Nibbles.

This is, I realise, the first time I've ever seen Jackson interrogating anyone. Such things are way below his paygrade these days, but the man is a pleasure to watch. I relish the experience.

Dad says, 'I don't suppose there *is* any charge you could bring in any event.'

'No, no. There's nothing illegal about paying people money. Nothing illegal about making phone calls. And you were anxious about Kay. You wanted to help her. So you made a call. You called someone you thought might be able to help.'

'He *didn't* help.'

'No. No, he certainly didn't. But then greedy murdering criminal bastards aren't known for their general niceness, are they?'

'No.'

Jackson and my father.

Two men. Similar age, similar build, similar backgrounds, similar everything. Except Jackson has spent his life in the police service and my father spent his career, the first part of it anyway, involved in large-scale crime.

Prosecuted five times, convicted never.

Their gazes duel in this unreasonable sunshine.

Katie shifts position. Adjusts her crown of daisies.

She is withering, Katie. Her last set of hospital tests was all bad. She is withering and shrinking and losing her symmetry.

The warrior queen is dying and her favourite slave is troubled.

Dad says, 'Who knows about this? This conversation, I mean?'

Jackson points. Himself, me, Katie, Dad. We four and no one else.

Dad checks and double-checks, but I tell him it's true.

Dad: 'Thing is, I know you people. You've got to write things down and put them in a file somewhere and then who knows who sees that file.'

I say, 'Dad, there'll be no writing. No file. No record. No nothing. And—' pointing at Jackson, 'you can trust this man. I do.'

'No file?'

'Nothing.'

'You don't have to report anything to anyone else?'

'Dad, Dennis here is a Detective Chief Inspector. He's like the Archangel Michael. When he farts, he farts thunderbolts. He doesn't have to say anything to anyone, except maybe to God, and God won't ask.'

Dad nods.

Breathes out.

He's never done this before. Me apart, he'd never spoken to a police officer with the intention of disclosing an actual self-revealing truth.

But he trusts Jackson. He trusts me. And he says, 'So. Me and Idris Prothero. Everything you need to know.'

55

July.

The churchyard at Llanymawddwy.

The strangely hot, strangely cloudless weather of a few days back has scurried away, back to France and Spain and other places cursed by a lack of wind and foul weather.

No such curse for us.

Low cloud skims the surrounding mountains. Cloud that, from time to time, lets fall a handful of rain, a shower of silver.

The views here are wide enough that you see the rain coming, long grey curtains that are, nevertheless, full of light. A darker light enclosed in something brighter. Somewhere far beyond, over Camlan, a patch of hillside is caught in a flash of temporary sun.

Bowen, seeing my gaze, murmurs, 'I have seen the sun break through to illuminate a small field for a while, and gone my way and forgotten it. But that was the pearl of great price, the one field that had treasure in it.'

I stare at him, but he doesn't explain, and perhaps now is not the time, here is not the place.

In his hands: a casket.

In the casket: ash.

And in the ash: all that is left of Dr Gaynor Charteris, her head and her stump, her tweed and her tutting, her piercing gaze and her outdoors hands.

Her two children didn't desert her in death. They flew over from Australia to grieve, to tidy her affairs, to host little tea parties of remembrance, to participate in a sung mass with the choir she'd been part of.

Also: they arranged and hosted a cremation, at a service that included all Charteris's known friends and family. But the children weren't themselves religious and didn't much mind what finally happened to Charteris's ashes. The default option was to have the ashes interred at the crematorium itself, which is a perfectly fine place, but also the blandest, safest, dullest, most rose-spiked and lawn-clipped place in the universe.

And it was Katie – also not religious, but better knowing Charteris's tastes – who insisted that Gaynor would prefer an interment in an ancient country churchyard. Wind blowing in the grass and lichens creeping over tombstones.

The kids – with plane tickets back to Oz, with lives and jobs and duties that summoned them home – said fine. Left Katie with the ash.

And we have it now.

The ash.

A hole.

A tombstone.

Welsh sandstone. Hand carved. A clean and sober grey. A little fretful at entering on this first day of its new life. The first day at school in Tombstone World.

We're at the shaggy fringe of the churchyard. A fringe not usually reached by whatever goodly soul walks round this place with a lawnmower in summer. The grass here is thick with cow parsley and buttercup and vetch and, by the wall, the first tall stands of willowherb.

Me, I like the spot precisely because it *is* marginal. I'd like a death here amongst the vetch and willowherb, hearing the thrum of that summer mower passing quietly over other people's graves.

But Bowen didn't choose the spot for that reason. He chose it because this as close as he can reasonably get to the last resting place of Saint Tydecho himself.

Holy man and warrior.

Saint and madman.

Arthur's nephew and comrade.

Worms fed to bursting on that holy corpse can wriggle across and wash themselves in Charteris's salty ash.

I like that thought. Charteris would have done too.

The saint and the scholar, commingled in death.

Bowen reads a funeral service. Katie and I give the responses. Bowen has a prayer book in his hand, but he knows the service well. Delivers it, mostly, by heart.

No oration.

No eulogy or tribute.

Those things happened already in that bland crematorium in the south. These hills, these grasses need no oratory.

We inter the ash. Scatter earth.

One solemn handful each but, at the end, Bowen just says, 'May as well,' and sets to with a spade. The earth thumps down in solid chunks. A good weight. A solid pressure.

A rain shower comes and goes, but doesn't trouble us.

When we're ready to leave, we share a pub lunch. Exchange thoughts. Reminiscences.

Katie is blitzing into a new Ph.D. thesis now. Her topic: the most sophisticated antiquities fraud ever to have been studied almost, in effect, from the inside.

She's aiming to have a first draft completed as soon as possible. She can't type two-handed, but she's got a voice recognition thing that works well, and her left hand is still fine for when she needs it.

She thinks she'll claim her doctorate before her illness claims her life. If anyone can do it, she can.

We have a nice day. Drive home. My house, not Katie's.

I take her up to my spare room.

She says, 'What's this?'

I tell her.

Say that she can't go on living in a shared student house, especially not when her room is on the first floor and there's no disability support at all. I tell her she should live here. Say we'll go and collect her stuff tomorrow.

She sits on the bed, blinking.

'But Fi, this is your home. I couldn't—'

'You can. I'm inviting you.'

'And anyway—'

Those anyways. Those tedious anyways.

My house isn't much better arranged than her house-share for disability. Bedroom and bathroom upstairs. Too complicated. Too difficult. Blah blah.

'Katie, who cares? We just put in a stairlift. Or a downstairs shower. Or whatever.'

I shrug. Her parents want the best for Katie and Katie still wants to live and work independently. Disability and an oncoming death will, one day, drive her back to her parents' Chiltern paradise, but Katie should herself choose the timing of that return. In the meantime, if Katie wants to live with me, then her parents can fork out a few grand for a stairlift. Or a shower. Or whateverthehell. I don't care. When Katie is no longer living here, I'll put everything back the way it was, and her parents can pay for that too.

Katie says, 'I'll be in your way.'

'No you won't.'

'There's no reason you should give up your life to look after me.'

'I'm not going to give up my life and I'm not going to look after you. If you want nurses, get nurses.'

I sound snappish. I know I do. So I add more gently, 'And

444

Katie, you should be with friends. I'm your friend. You should be here.'

She should. And she knows it. And she says yes. And she cries.

I can't cry – it's just something my eyes have chosen never to do – but we hold each other, and that feels nice. Being dead, I think, is easy, but the whole journey there can be mighty taxing. We each find our own dark path into that land of stone and shadow.

When we're done, Katie punches my arm quite hard, and says, 'Best slave *ever*. Best slave *ever*.'

I punch her back, but softly. My warrior princess. My dying queen.

She's tired and goes to bed.

I feel pleased. I like Katie and it feels right having her here. Right for her and right for me.

But also scared.

Living with a woman who is dying, slo-mo, in front of me? Sharing a house with someone whose mere presence has already, twice, sent me shivering back to that place of dissociation and emptiness? That place of living death.

I'm scared enough that I actually go to the kitchen. Run the tap. First hot, then cold, then again hot.

Put my hands beneath the silver water and check. *Yes, that's hot. That's cold.*

I feel the difference. Feel myself.

I think, *Living with Katie will, at times, drive me out of my mind. I will lose myself. Vanish into the void. But that's OK. I can endure that. I can survive that. And if I do, then I can survive anything. I will, almost literally, have nothing more to fear.*

That's a pep talk more than a set of beliefs, but for now the pep talk will have to do. And, I notice, I don't actually have any doubts about inviting Katie to live here. That part, certainly, feels right.

I make peppermint tea.

Turn the lights off, almost completely. The ground floor is now lit only by a street lamp burning outside and the *electronica miscellanea* of any modern house: an oven clock, stand-by lamps, the router's green wink.

It is 9 July 2016.

I take a blank sheet of paper and take it over to the kitchen table.

Write the number eleven. A large outline that fills the page.

Colour the outline in. Not particularly neatly. But not too messily either.

Big. Black. Obvious.

Add the page to a pile of ten similar pages, that count down from ten to one.

On the bottom page of the pile, a simple message:

28 June 2016
Alden Gheerbrant
RIP

Eleven days since my most recent corpse. I hope I don't have to wait another 453 days for the next one.

To the topmost page, I add a little doodle. A flower. Red head, red petals.

No reason for the doodle. Just feeling doodly.

I drink my tea. Go upstairs. Listen briefly at Katie's door. I can't hear anything, which means, I presume, the princess is sleeping. I go to my bedroom and do the same.

THE END

Author's Note

So. You've finished the book and, I'd guess, you're likely to have two thoughts, or questions, uppermost in your mind.

The first is: Arthur – *really*? Do we have to take him seriously as a historical figure, or does the whole Arthur myth have as little historical reality as Alex Devine's faked-up sword?

The second question is simply: this book – *really*? Fiction is fiction, OK, but doesn't an author have some kind of duty not to strain the bounds of credibility? And if so, then doesn't a police procedural about Excalibur feel like a step too far?

Good questions both, but we'll deal with Arthur first.

And I suppose I need to admit, straight out, that if what's being demanded is courtroom-standard evidence then, no, we can't be confident of Arthur's existence. There's not a single solid, undisputable fact to demonstrate he existed. Even the circumstantial evidence has a mistily uncertain quality. Dates are scarce, sources dubious, archaeological confirmation wholly absent.

But, to be clear, there's nothing particularly suspect about that. When you are dealing with the history of fifteen centuries back, there are few fixed facts of any sort. So, for example, we do know that a once-Celtic country became dominated by an Anglo-Saxon culture and language. But was that because the invading hordes simply slaughtered and displaced the Celts? Or was it that the Celts gradually came to adopt the culture and tongue of these newcomers? Up until fairly recently, the slaughter-and-displace theory was in the ascendant. These days, the peaceful assimilation hypothesis probably has more adherents. But we don't actually *know* either way. Even modern genetic testing hasn't really settled the matter.

If we can't be certain about the answers to such huge questions, it makes sense to drop any demand for courtroom standard of proof in relation to Arthur. Forget 'beyond reasonable doubt', and ask instead where the balance of probabilities lies. And that question, I reckon, has a rather simpler answer.

The earliest British (Celtic) histories talk about a Battle of Mount Badon. The earliest Anglo-Saxon (English) history does too. The only man ever named as the leader of the British at that battle was Arthur. There does seem to be – modest, arguable, not decisive – evidence that there was a temporary pause in the line of Anglo-Saxon incursion, a pause that could well have been brought about by a major battle of the sort described.

So it seems a little contrary to argue that there *wasn't* a battle or that the British leader *wasn't* called Arthur. What's more, the torrent of myth (largely Welsh in its earliest origins) doesn't discredit the Arthur-as-real-human theory simply because, in that day and age, legend was always likely to accrue around warriors of such stature.

Finally, there's that telling nugget which I quote in the text. The poem, *Υ Gododdin*, which Fiona and friends translate in the restaurant, is genuine, all right: you can look it up on Wikipedia. The verse seems to give a broadly historical account of a real historical battle. The battle itself is of no great importance, but the poem contains that crucial throwaway line – the one about how Gwawrddur was a terrific warrior but, no, he wasn't as good as Arthur. That's a little like saying David Beckham was a terrific footballer, he was just never as good as Lionel Messi. And why would you even say that, if you knew that your point of comparison – Arthur/Messi – was simply a work of fiction? An invented superhero?

That one line hardly gives us our smoking gun. It's still a long old way from courtroom proof. But me personally, if I had to place a £100 bet on Arthur's existence, I'd bet yes. I'd say he was probably real. Probably Welsh. And probably fought a major battle against the Anglo-Saxons. As for the *place* of that battle – well, I've no idea, but Liddington Castle is as plausible a spot as any.

We turn now to this book and this series.

And yes: there's no question that my storylines can be somewhat exotic and some readers are, I know, in two minds about whether to accept them. The case for the prosecution runs roughly like this. The crime genre is a realist genre. It is there to explore the darker facets of our society. Yes, for sure, it is also there to entertain, so there'll always be room for a little storyteller's embroidery. But there are limits. And a hunt for a fake Excalibur simply breaches those limits. No police officer alive has ever encountered a case comparable to the one recounted in this book and that fact simply disqualifies this book from serious consideration as a crime thriller.

And, well, I know what you mean. I really do. And when actual readers have said something similar to me, at festivals and the like, I find myself offering three lines of defence.

The first defence is simple. Crimes like the ones I describe *do* exist. I didn't invent the fact that the trade in fake and looted antiquities is huge. It's a global, multi-billion dollar business and it flourishes everywhere. If you walk the streets of Hong Kong looking for a nice little Ming vase for the mantelpiece, you need to know that at least nine out of ten of the 'Ming vases' for sale there are fake – but nobody knows how to tell the fake from the real.

The same is true in Europe too. There are fake artworks, fake statues, fake books, fake everything. I haven't, as it happened, come across a case involving a fake sword, but the vast majority of quality fakes are never exposed anyway. So in the end, all I've done is taken a real-life criminal industry and asked the question: what if fakers turned their hands to ancient Welsh antiquities? And what kind of antiquities might be involved . . .?

My second line of defence turns into attack. I want to ask whether all those other police procedurals are really as realistic as they purport to be. So, for example, there's a Jo Nesbø novel in which a woman is found murdered, with one finger severed and a diamond, shaped like the devil's pentagram, secreted beneath her eyelid. Now I'm not having a go at Nesbø – there are any number of novels with similar starting points – but I do want to ask: do crimes like that *ever* actually happen? Have you ever read of one? Has any living police officer actually encountered such a thing?

I want to say no, never. And are such novels really exploring the dark side of our society? Or are they just having some good old-fashioned fun? Where you stand on such issues is, I'm aware, a matter of personal taste as much as anything – but, for my part, I find it hard to see that my tale of fake antiquities is any less realistic than Nesbø's tale of diamond pentagrams. On the contrary: my story simply adds some Arthurian juice to what is already a very well-established criminal enterprise. There just *isn't* a criminal enterprise involving eyelids and devil's pentagrams.

And all that sounds good, I hope. Convincing.

But in the end, I know that I'm not being completely honest. Yes, my plots aren't as wacky as they look. And yes, there are plenty of more standard crime novels with plots that don't really pass any strict reality check either. But my third line of defence, and the real heart of it, is this.

There are, to my mind, two great poles in crime fiction. The first of those – of course! – is Conan Doyle's Sherlock

Holmes, a more-than-human mastermind, solving crimes that were darkly, gothically bizarre. No reader of Conan Doyle's ever mistook Holmes's casebook for a careful analysis of late Victorian criminality; they were just wonderfully intoxicating, stimulating fun.

And because Holmes was so European, so gothic, so bizarre, so unworldly, it was perhaps inevitable that the reaction, when it came, would be centred in the New World – and not just anywhere, but in its sunniest, brashest, Westernmost city, Los Angeles. Raymond Chandler got his private eye to walk the same mean streets that his readers encountered for themselves. Not for him any mysterious hounds, or exotic poisons, or bizarrely well-trained serpents. Chandler wrote about crimes that felt real, populated by criminals who felt alive.

Chandler's revolution pretty much demolished that older tradition. The great, recent American crime writers (Elmore Leonard, Patricia Cornwell, Michael Connelly and the like) all write, or wrote, in a broadly Chandlerian tradition, not a Holmesian one. The same is largely true of most European crime writing too (think of Ian Rankin, or Henning Mankell, or Tana French, and most others you care to mention.)

And that's fine. I love Chandler and I love the tradition he created . . . but I love Sherlock Holmes too.

So the real, naked truth about my stories is this. I *know* they're exotic. I *know* Fiona is almost too good to be true. But I love that! I relish the fun and the freedom and that sense that you never quite know where the story will end up.

Now, to be sure, because the Chandlerian tradition is so very strong, I use it as a cloak. So I've made sure Fiona is a police officer, because in peaceable Britain private eyes don't have much to do. The police force she works in looks roughly like a real police force does (and I've had a fair number of serving and retired officers telling me that, yes, I've got the flavour about right.) My crimes, though exotic, do indeed have a firm basis in reality. I make no use of magic. Nothing superhuman. The various technologies and techniques do all exist and are in widespread use.

But . . .

It's a cloak. A Chandlerian cloak. My books, at their heart, look more towards Sherlock Holmes than Philip Marlowe. And that's why Fiona feels that bit other-worldly. Why the crimes have an extravagance that even Nesbø's lack. It's why the story-architecture for the whole series has more than a whiff of the Holmes-Moriarty battle.

You may like that or you may not like that. It's entirely your choice. But if you like my stories but find yourself feeling a little uncomfortable with some of the storylines, I think I know the reason why. You've been trained to like Raymond Chandleresque realism and to believe that that's what crime fiction is all about. What it *has to be* all about. And then along comes Fiona Griffiths, who messes about with those ideas. However much she pretends to play along with the disciplines of the modern police procedural, she's really got her feet firmly planted in the fogs of a certain house in Victorian-era Baker Street and, somewhere on a far-distant moor, we sense the footprints of a gigantic hound . . .

We started with two questions and I've given you two (over-lengthy) answers. But that's it from me. I do hope you enjoyed the book. If you did, then I'd love you to review it on Amazon, or anywhere else. I read all those reviews and I know that other readers really benefit from them too. It's a great thing you do for other readers – even a line or two helps.

I hope too that you'll feel motivated to explore the series more fully. The listing in the back of this book gives you a chance to check you've got everything. Do take a look and grab anything that takes your fancy.

And finally – are you a member of the Fiona Griffiths

Readers Club? And if not, don't you think you should be? You get some free stories to download (ones that are available nowhere else) and every now and then you'll get an email from me telling you when I have a new book ready for release. You can sign up via my harrybingham.com website. It's as easy as pie and I look forward to welcoming you.

I have the best readers in the world. I'm a lucky author.

HB
Oxfordshire, England

Stay in touch

Very occasionally, I email readers when I'm about to launch a book or have anything else significant to tell you. If you would like to get those email alerts – and also, by the way, get free access to a Fiona Griffiths story that is available nowhere else – you can do so by just trotting over to HarryBingham. com and clicking on the 'Free Download' link.

I promise not to clog your inbox with rubbish. I won't sell your details to the good folk who sell Viagra. And if you ever want to unsubscribe from my mailings, it'll be incredibly easy to do so.

I'd be thrilled if you did want to stay informed. Books need readers, and Fiona and I are blessed with an unusually committed and intelligent bunch. We're both mightily grateful.

About the Author

Harry Bingham is an author of fiction and non-fiction. He also runs The Writers' Workshop, an editorial consultancy, and Agent Hunter, a service which helps connect writers with literary agents. When he isn't working, he's probably looking after not one but two sets of twins, but can still just about remember a time when he found time for rock-climbing and wild-swimming. He is married and lives in Oxfordshire.

Make sure you've read the other books in the series

TALKING TO THE DEAD #1

Fiona Griffiths is the youngest, most junior detective on the South Wales Major Crimes Unit. And when a young mother and her six-year-old daughter are found dead in a squalid Cardiff squat, Fiona is given a minor-seeming task to perform. She performs that task — sometimes following the rules, sometimes not so much — and starts to uncover a much wider and more brutal crime.

That crime is finally solved, in blood, on a remote Pembrokeshire coast. And the reader learns just who this detective is . . . and quite why she's so interested in corpses.

LOVE STORY, WITH MURDERS #2

It's end-of-shift. Fiona and a uniformed colleague get called on their way home — illegal rubbish in Cyncoed; how hard can it be? But when they arrive they find, in the stinky bottom of a dead woman's freezer, a woman's leg, complete with high-heeled shoe. The victim is Mary Langton, a pole-dancer who vanished some five years earlier . . . but then new body parts start appearing, and these are dark-skinned, and male, and totally fresh.

Fiona's investigation takes her to some dark places — and some very cold ones — and as she seeks final justice, she realises she's lucky to be still alive.

THE STRANGE DEATH OF FIONA GRIFFITHS #3

A Cardiff superstore has suffered a payroll fraud: phantom employees siphoning cash. It's an assignment that Fiona hates — no corpses — but she's lumbered with it anyway. Then she finds the body of a woman who has starved to death. And it becomes clear that within the first, smaller crime, a vast one looms: the most audacious theft in history. The Serious Organised Crime Agency need a copper who can go undercover, and they ask Fiona to take on the role.

She'll be alone, she'll be lethally vulnerable — and her new 'colleagues' will stop at nothing to get what they want.

THIS THING OF DARKNESS #4

Artwork stolen then mysteriously returned. A security guard dead in a cliff fall. A marine engineer who committed suicide in a locked and inaccessible apartment. These things couldn't be connected, could they? Everyone thinks not, but Fiona — jammed into an Exhibits Officer role she hates — thinks otherwise. As Fiona continues to pursue her enquiries, she comes to realise that she's looking at a crime of breathtaking ambition.

Trouble is, as Fiona closes in, the gang realise they need information and with the police operation in data lockdown, they realise they've got only one place to get it: Fiona herself.

THE DEAD HOUSE #5

t's a howling October night. Midnight in a country churchyard. And lying in an outbuilding is the body of a young woman. There are no signs of violence — but why is she wearing only a in white summer dress? Why are her legs unshaved? And why is she surrounded by a hundred guttering candles?

Those are the questions that provoke the strangest — and perhaps the darkest — case of Fiona's career. And, in an nforgettable climax, her investigations come to close in on her so very literally that she wonders whether she'll ever see the light of day again.

FIONA WILL RETURN

If you want Harry to let you know when the next Fiona book is due to launch, just sign up to the Fiona Griffiths Readers Club now. You'll get a free, exclusive Fiona story to read, and you'll be the first to know when the next Fiona title is published.

WWW.HARRYBINGHAM.COM/LEV-IN-GLASGOW/